Under Blood Moons

By J. J. Partridge

ISBN 978-1-64663-251-0

Published by

◤ köehlerbooks™

3705 Shore Drive
Virginia Beach, VA 23455
800–435–4811
www.koehlerbooks.com

UNDER BLOOD MOONS

J.J. PARTRIDGE

VIRGINIA BEACH
CAPE CHARLES

"My offenses, truly I know them,
My sin is always before me."

"Be without reproach when you judge."
—*Psalm 51*

AUTHOR'S NOTE

ANYONE FAMILIAR WITH RHODE ISLAND, particularly its East Side, Fox Point, India Point and Seekonk River areas, will realize that I have, as I did in *Carom Shot, Straight Pool,* and *Scratched,* taken liberty with the geography and the institutions portrayed. This is wholly intentional according to the demands of the story. Any resemblance of the characters or events or places or parole board cases with real persons, living and dead, historical events, and places are entirely coincidental. However, some of the buildings at the state prison complex are described in their bleak reality.

Rhode Island was chosen for dramatic purposes only. Procedures and state law may or may not be consistent with those described in the book. Importantly, and consistent with my promise to Dr. Kenneth Walker, former chairman of the Rhode Island parole board who was helpful and supportive of my effort, I want to make it clear that this work does not necessarily reflect any thoughts or ideas of Dr. Walker or other members of the parole board past and present. As this is a work of fiction, the portrayals of parole board members and corrections administrators or inmates are imagined.

GREENWICK, RHODE ISLAND
Thirty Years Earlier

GIDDY WITH EXCITEMENT, Aaron Underwood jumped from the school bus and ran down Slocum Road toward his family's farm.

In the late October briskness, he was sweaty under a hand-me-down lumber jacket of red and black checks and itchy wool trousers as he relived his encounter that day with Bainsy and Tingle, his tormentors at school. Beaten down by their frequent bullying, Aaron had prepared to submit to jabs to his chest, bruising Indian twists to his forearms, and their verbal abuse when they had shoved him out of the lunch line at Greenwick Junior High and into the janitor's closet.

Aaron had shuddered when Bainsy draped his arm around his shoulders, like the pal he was not. Instead of being abusive, Bainsy laid out a scheme and reward for Aaron's participation in a Halloween prank. Tingle finished with a promise, "She'll let you do *it and* you'll be part of the gang!" He gave Aaron a handful of Skittles to seal the deal. With smirks, the two bullies had given each other slaps on the backs, and left Aaron dumbfounded.

In that confounding moment, Aaron unexpectedly envisioned school life without being called out for being stupid or awkward, or shabbily dressed, or for his looks. *"Part of the gang."* All he had to do was to devise and execute a prank at Gist Castle on Halloween. *How about that!*

He entered the farmhouse through the kitchen door. Deafening, high pitched voices came from the television in the parlor where Grandma Underwood was in her recliner, engrossed in an afternoon soap opera. His parents' strict instructions for his return from school were to first check in with Grandma and do whatever she asked, then apply himself to his chores.

He dreaded even a few moments alone with Grandma. After her stroke the previous fall, she had become demanding, impatient, and demeaning, treating Aaron as a clumsy nuisance, pinching his ears, poking him with her cane if he didn't understand her often unintelligible speech. He suffered her mistreatment in silence under threat of parental punishment, and with a deepening resentment. Then, he remembered that at breakfast his father said he planned to spend the day working on a tractor's balky engine, then turning over their late harvest potato fields; his mother responded that she would take Baby Sister with her to shop at the Almacs grocery in Kingston. Their absence allowed Aaron the rare opportunity to dawdle in the kitchen with a peanut-butter-on-Ritz-crackers snack and a glass of milk. For a quarter hour, he considered various pranks, his prize for being successful, and the prospect of a better life at school. Only then, and with great reluctance, did he brace his shoulders, and with his eyes focused on his shoes, enter the parlor.

"Grandma, I'm home," he shouted.

The television voices no longer masked Grandma's gasps for breath. Aaron looked up to see her open-mouthed, dentureless, her eyes bulging in a flushed face, drool and vomit dripping from her chin, her torso in contortions, her fingers clawing at the arms of the recliner.

Aaron's heart pounded like a parade drum, his throat constricted, he put his hands over his ears, and he fled to the kitchen where he flung his chest on the table, sobbing in panicked indecision. It took more minutes for him to recall his parents' instructions if Grandma "took a fit." He straightened, ran to Grandma's bedroom at the rear of the house and saw a clutter of pill bottles—some on her dresser, others on her night table. At a loss as to which medication he was to give her, he swept up the bottles and raced back to the parlor so she could point to the appropriate remedy.

"Grandma, I got your pills!" he shouted as he reentered.

Her chin was on her chest, her pupils had disappeared under her eyelids, her hoarse breathing had stilled. The acrid smell of vomit filled the parlor. Vaguely aware of the presence of death, Aaron was rooted in place, his mind mush, his stomach in turmoil, when another parental instruction came to mind: *In an emergency, call the sheriff, or the Greenwick volunteer fire department, or Doc Smith.* Their phone numbers were taped above the wall phone in the kitchen. He returned to the kitchen, dropped the pill bottles on the counter, fingered the rotary dial and told the woman who answered Doc Smith's phone that his grandmother had taken a fit. He remained at the kitchen table waiting for someone—anyone—to come to his relief.

As his anxiety diminished, he realized that he was suddenly free from Grandma's belittlements, *and* on the same day he had been given the opportunity to be delivered from bullying at school. He saw his future, no longer as Grandma's flunky nor the scorned class clodhopper. Then, he considered his parents' reaction if he admitted to his delay in discovering Grandma's plight while he snacked. In a moment of intuition, he returned the pill bottles to her bedroom so he wouldn't have to explain how they got to the kitchen.

When an ambulance with its siren blaring arrived a half hour later from Tri-Town Hospital, he led two uniformed men to the parlor door, not allowing himself to enter and chance another view of Grandma's corpse. His mother arrived moments later. When she recovered from her shock, she ordered Aaron to fetch his father from the fields. Later, his parents praised him for following their directive and quickly phoning Doc Smith's. But he didn't disclose his lingering in the kitchen while Grandma was gasping in need of her pills. His easy acceptance of their praise, he knew, was as deceitful as was his tearful display of grief.

On the night of her burial, Grandma Underwood began her beyond-the-grave visits to Aaron. In his nightmares, he felt the poke of her cane, heard her snarls of accusation as to his stupidity, his paralysis when he found her. "You coulda saved me!" she croaked, her face as contorted as when last seen in the parlor. "You let me die, you murdered me. You are happy that I died. I'll never let you forget what you did, you stupid boy. Never."

Aaron wet himself that night, and again on following nights when Grandma Underwood broke into his sleep. His mother was sympathetic because of what he had witnessed, his father less so. Aaron didn't tell them of Grandma's hauntings. They might suspect that he had killed her through his inaction and stupidity. He began to accept his guilt—he was a coward, and a liar, and through his failure, a murderer.

|||||||||||||||||||||||||||||||||||||||||||||||||||||

The Underwood family was in its usual pew at the Four Square Gospel Church before the ten o'clock Sunday service in the unadorned country church off Route 102. Aaron's father was tie-less in a denim shirt and his only suit. His mother, with Baby Sister cradled in her arms, wore a prim, dark blue dress with white buttons at the back, and Aaron had on his go-to-service trousers and white shirt. Those congregants, potato and vegetable and dairy farm families for the most part, who had not attended Grandma's burial, stopped at the pew to express condolences. Their pats on Aaron's shoulder made his stomach roil with guilt.

Precisely at ten, Pastor Ellsbridge, a black robe covering his bony figure, mounted the two stairs within the pulpit to begin the worship. Behind him, a huge wooden cross hung on the wall; two flickering candles framed the pulpit. After leading *Over Jordan* to the accompaniment of a tinny electric organ, the preacher quickly ramped up from a low-key Scripture commentary to his anticipated handwringing harangue against the evils of modern lifestyles, divorce, harlotry, alcohol and drugs. Sweat soon beaded his brow. His longish silver hair, stiff with pomade, glistened in the candlelight as his voice reached a feverish pitch of earnest righteousness.

"Tonight, on Satan's night, on Halloween, God's omen, a blood moon, a moon painted with hell's eternal flames, is upon us!"

Aaron raised his eyes from his lap as Pastor Ellsbridge surveyed reactions in the rows of sinners facing him. To Aaron, his withering stare was a slash of accusation directed at his guilty soul.

"Foretold, brothers and sisters, yes, foretold in holy Scripture!" Pastor Ellsbridge thrust a leather-covered Bible toward the church's rough-hewn rafters. His black robe, buttoned at the neck and draped over his shoulders, became a shroud of forbidding darkness. "Joel, Chapter 2, verse 31." He lowered the Bible to the pulpit's lectern, opened it, and enunciated each word with unnerving clarity and vehemence: "'The-moon-will-turn-into-blood-before-the-terrible-day-of-the-Lord.'"

Aaron's father murmured, "Amen."

"Again! In Acts, Chapter 2, verse 30! The Apostles predict a blood red moon!"

Aaron heard "amens" from scattered voices.

"And, in Revelations, Chapter 6, verse 12, brothers and sisters . . ." The preacher sucked in a deep breath as a ribbon opened the Bible to the verse, "'When the Sixth Seal is opened, lo, there was a great earthquake . . . the sun became black as a sackcloth of hair, and the moon became as blood!'"

The Bible was slapped shut, its words incontestable, and laid on the lectern.

"God's omen tonight warns us that the end of days is near," the preacher continued, his index finger wagging in admonition, his voice pitched lower for effect. "The blood red moon will hover over your homes tonight, a warning that *He* gives because *He* loves you. What does *He* want you to do in return?" Pastor Ellsbridge leaned forward, his fingers grasping the lectern tightly, his resonant voice probing the inner turmoil of those cowering before him in examinations of conscience. "Repent!" Spittle sprayed with his shouts. "You must repent! You must be born again, come to God and repent! Remember the sinful people of Nineveh recorded in Jonah? God would have struck them down, but they repented in sackcloth and ashes and saved themselves." The lectern shook from his pounding fists as he reached for the evangelical peak that he knew would spark audible cries of pent-up guilt.

A thin, male voice from the rear of the church was the first response: "I do! I do! I repent! Lord, take my sins and wash them away with your blood!"

"Yes, Lord, yes," a woman echoed in the front pew. "Amen, Lord," shouted others in the congregation as they got to their feet, some with arms raised heavenward becoming supplicants, others swaying in a wave of expiation like a field of hay before the autumn wind. Aaron's parents joined in. His father's work-hardened hands began to clap in unison with others; his mother held Baby Sister at her breasts. Only Aaron remained seated, his head at his knees, his cowlicked hair covered by trembling fingers, his body cringing in a guilt swelled to near-bursting by Pastor Ellsbridge. That moon dripping blood foretold his fate.

Aaron's stomach churned; his tongue probed the space between his front teeth; his pimpled face drained of color. He pushed past his parents to the end of the pew, his fingers at his mouth signaling distress, and rushed to the rear of the church, barely making it outside before he threw up, his vomit soiling his shirt, the cuffs of his trousers, his shoes.

When he recovered from retching, he ran to the well behind the church and cranked its pump until water gushed from its spout. With a wet handkerchief, he wiped his chin and clothing, then washed his fingers in the cold water to rid himself of the dreadful stink that starkly reminded him of his last moments with Grandma. And of his sin.

He wrung out the handkerchief and stuffed it in a trousers pocket, then wiped his hands in the grass near the well. *If only my soul could be cleansed like this,* he thought. But it wouldn't be. Never. He had murdered his Grandma.

<hr/>

The entire town had knowledge of Gist Castle and of its peculiar sole occupant. The Gist family had built their oversized, hip-roofed bungalow with more than its share of 1890s architectural oddities, add-ons, and embellishments, including gaudy gingerbread moldings above doors. A window centered in the bungalow's overhang reflected sunsets as a brilliant, unblinking eye flashing down at Slocum Road, and at the folly that gave Gist Castle its name, a castle-like turret attached to a wraparound porch.

Back then, the farm's Rhode Island potatoes, sweet corn, and silage, its piggery, its cheese-making operations, and its dairy were moneymakers. The Gist family was South County royalty, and Gist Castle was where the local gentry arranged town affairs. Nowadays, the bungalow was a weathered shambles, its multiple chimneys garnished with lightning rods seemed poised to totter down in any wind. Its clapboards had popped, its porch sagged, its rotted gutters were stuffed with blackened leaves. A skeletal, crooked television antenna sprouted over the ell at its rear. The bungalow's interior reflected the dilapidated condition of its exterior. The rooms were musty and crammed with shabby furniture, its carpets were threadbare, and dust kitties curled in corners.

Lucretia Gist, the only child of Elmer and Ernestine Gist, lived within the ruins of Gist Castle in self-imposed isolation, surrounded by acres of abandoned fields fenced by barbed wire with faded postings forbidding hunting or trespassing. For decades, she rebuffed neighborly attempts at social contact. She didn't attend church, she drove her beat-up car to the village only to shop at the IGA, the local grocery store, or bank at South County Trust Company. No neighbors called on her; the town's social worker stopped offering services after angry shouts from behind closed doors became threats of bodily harm; the frustrated rural delivery carrier left her mail in a strictly illegal, rickety box out on Slocum Road; the heating oil delivery man made sure he filled her tank only when absolutely required.

On that Halloween, she was thought of as a mean, miserly, and miserable old crone, a "piece of work" in local jargon, who folks said was likely to die alone and would be stone cold for weeks before a chance discovery.

After a skimpy supper of canned soup and a Spam sandwich, Lucretia Gist settled into a wingback chair in the ell off the kitchen, her shawl wrapped around her shoulders, facing a black-and-white Motorola television console with its volume turned on high. Her withered face was set with stubborn grimness at the mouth. She knew what night it was, and what to expect.

No costumed children holding open pillowcases for treats would ring her doorbell; Gist Castle was a good three miles from the village and off-limits to children from neighboring farms. But tricks? There were always tricksters targeting her home with stupid, malicious pranks. One Halloween, a truck had smashed into the barn, knocking a corner off its stone foundation, the woebegone chicken coop was torched three years prior, and last year a reeking pile of manure was dumped on the track halfway up the knoll. But tonight when the hooligans came, she would suffer no tricks. This year, she was determined to be ready, to give them "what for."

A thermos of coffee would keep her alert as she waited at a window in the darkness of the parlor where she could spot a telltale flashlight, or headlights on the track; in her deafness, she'd have to rely on her eyes. The front door was unlocked so she could quickly get out to the porch and confront the hooligans. Until pitch darkness when the hooligans would come, she would watch her television programs with her father's double-trigger, over-and-under scattergun at the ready.

The scattergun, loaded with birdshot, dependably scared away rabbits from her vegetable garden and crows from the roof of the barn. She was certain its muzzle flash and noise would frighten off intruders. Not that she wouldn't mind if a few tiny pellets found their way home.

Teach them a good lesson.

_____

Shhhhk! Shhhhk!

Barn owls, Aaron said to himself, *only barn owls,* as he gingerly climbed over a crumbling fieldstone wall, stomped his boots on loose strands of barbed wire, and set off across long abandoned potato fields. Behind him was darkness,; to his front, he barely discerned Gist Castle against a fading amber horizon, a smudge of gray taking on the shape of a turtle. Coming up from Slocum Road, making his way through thickets of scrub oak, knee-high grasses and scattered bushes, would have been an easier approach but might have exposed him to the headlights of a car taking the shortcut from the village to Route 2. Couldn't risk that.

Several times, and now once again, he stopped to look over his shoulder, relieved that the moon that he expected to soon be a fearsome red was encased in clouds. Even so, the clouds held an unnatural orangey light.

Aaron thought of himself as daring to have escaped from home unnoticed, and brave to attempt the prank, despite the threat of an ominous blood red moon. In the back of his mind, he harbored a smidgen of hope that there might be some truth to his science teacher's depiction of a red moon as a natural phenomenon not to be feared, the color no different than the red of a sunset. Aaron's father had instructed him more than once to ignore the science teacher's notions about nature that conflicted with Pastor Ellsbridge's preaching or the scripture passages read aloud before every dinner. And he did, *but just maybe—*

He pulled up the zipper of his jacket, bent into the scrappy gusts of wind—a falling temperature promised a second night of frost—and picked his way through straw and thistle, feeling neglected furrows under his boots, aware of night scavengers scurrying to nests and burrows. *Will this prank,* he asked himself, *really make me pals with Bainsy and Tingle?* He had been so focused on the prank that not even Grandma's nightly visits, nor his fear of the strapping he'd get from his father if he was found out, eroded his determination. Only Bainsy and Tingle knew what he planned to do; they had promised not to tell.

At a line of spindly ash and birch close by the barn, the gathering darkness hid its sagging roof, barred and rotted doors, and cracked glass in the windows. A rustling in the high weeds froze his steps; everyone knew Gist's barn harbored a colony of caterwauling, scabrous, feral cats. Aaron shivered as he imagined the vicious creatures lying in wait, ready to claw at his legs or bite an exposed ankle.

A light shone through an unshaded window at the rear of the bungalow. Keeping low to the ground, Aaron crept forward until a piercing cat screech caused him to duck behind the old lady's rust-spotted Chevy Nova parked between the barn and the house. Not until the cat settled back into its nasty business did Aaron continue across the track to press himself against the ell's clapboards so he could risk a quick look through a grimy window. He saw and heard a television with the volume up and a gray head cushioned in a corner of a wingback chair set at an angle to the window. Skinny legs protruded from a green dress; ankle-length socks came up from nondescript black shoes; an arm hung limply from the chair, its fingers almost touching the bare floor.

She's asleep, he thought. *Phew*! Aaron exhaled and unzipped his jacket and pulled out the pry bar tucked into his belt. At that moment, the cloud cover gave way to a blood red moon.

CHAPTER ONE

"FUCK! FUCK! FUCK!" echoed within the three tiers of Cell Block 3, Medium Security, followed by the smash of metal on steel bars and shrill whistles from COs.

Before the dinner count, prison trustees distributed brown envelopes containing recent parole board decisions pertaining to Medium Security inmates. Those rejected for parole immediately vented their anger and disappointment; those whose petitions had been granted usually waited for their meals before quietly spreading the news, to avoid the vitriolic reactions of those denied.

"Gioli, you prick. In or out?" A deep-throated shout came across from the second tier of cells. "Fuck, I wanna know."

A CO's whistle quieted the complainant.

Aaron Underwood, with his undamaged ear pressed at the bars of his cell, heard the scattered bawls and whines that would be replicated in Medium Security's three other cell blocks. Tonight, after lights out, the howls would become louder, more violent, despite CO warnings, until exhaustion claimed the embittered.

Aaron's cellmate, a tattooed, corn-rowed, musclebound hulk, lay on the cell's upper bunk. Yesterday, the new arrival had been rousted out of the food line and delivered to Aaron's handicapped cell at the far corner of the second tier, a punishment for mouthing off at a cook who had slopped a mound of mashed potatoes on the hamburger and green beans on his tray. That outburst got the attention of a guard with whom he had prior run-ins.

"For how long?" the miscreant complained loudly as the guards pushed him into Aaron's cell, although he knew as did all the other transients the answer depended on when somebody else ran afoul of a CO.

"Is Mason out?" the cellmate asked. Like other bored-to-distraction inmates, he had wagered canteen chits on paroles just as he gambled on NFL games, or on how far somebody could spit in the exercise yard, or whether a fly would land on a piece of sugar.

Aaron ignored the question and continued to smear his scarred lips with a peppermint Chap Stick, one of sixteen different flavors especially ordered for him by the canteen. This jerk was as forgettable as all his predecessors, short-timers and nuisances to be put up with, which he would do as long as it was recognized that this was *his* cell, crammed as it was by upper and lower bunks, the desk and lamp were *his*, *his* chair, *his* footlocker, and *his* one-piece aluminum sink-toilet that *he* could sit on as though he owned it. He heard his cellmate drop from the upper bunk and urinate. Aaron, always sensitive to others' bodily functions, smelled piss and heard the splash in the bowl.

"Flush it this time," he snapped.

"Fuck you!"

Aaron heard two quick steps before he was grabbed at a shoulder and turned around. His shirt was yanked up to his throat. With his good eye, he saw a fist curled within inches of his face, and turned his half face of knobby scars, with the scabby pouch that once held an eye, and what was left of a mouth in a gaping, crooked jaw, and his misshapen ear toward the attacker.

"Go on, go on, let me have it," Aaron taunted, the stench of his breath wilting his cellmate's rage, "and you're gonna be in here with me forever."

Aaron's shirt was released. As his cellmate backed off, Aaron turned to the bars. In victory, he farted loudly.

"Watch it, fuckface."

An inmate knocked into Aaron Underwood's shoulder at the door that led to the outside, the concourse, and the mess hall. Likely on purpose. Aaron ignored both the knock and the insult. He'd experienced both a thousand times in the past thirty years, and they no longer had significance to him.

Wrapped inside a quilted work jacket, he continued his shuffle, his bowlegs bent into the chill of a northeast wind that swooped into the open space on the slope between the cell blocks and the mess hall. In the light of a full moon, the hulk of Maximum Security, *the Max,* was starkly visible over the roofs of Medium Security's administration buildings. Beyond were pinpricks of light from the outside world. The Max, a fortress of rusticated granite blocks darkened by decades of soot and weather, was circled by crenelated forty-foot walls edged with wire and observation towers, continued on a hexagonal stone tower capped by a greasy-green cupola—a graphic reminder to those in Medium Security that any egregious breach of discipline could lead to a detention bout of segregation within the darkened bowels. Twenty-three hours a day, alone.

Aaron still had nightmares from his early experiences in the Max that kept his memories fresh.

He ate a solitary meal in the room in the mess hall reserved for wheelchair or otherwise handicapped inmates, facing a wall with a poster listing *Do's and Don'ts for Inmates,* all the things you do if you want to keep your record clean for "good time" credits or parole: *Obey orders from Correction Officers. Be respectful. Live by the rules. Avoid confrontations,* and one that always made Aaron wonder what idiot had placed it at the bottom of the list, *Take your prescribed medications.*

Aaron didn't need admonitions. He had become *routinized*—a word he heard used by a staff psychologist. He had survived three decades of incarceration, having stood through forty thousand outside-the-cell counts, lived with maybe a hundred short-term cell mates, with every day as numbing as the last. He was resigned to an existence without any real chance for parole after three prior denials, each opposed by the determined hypocrites in the Town of Greenwick. To prevent his hideous face from being seen in their community, they'd do or say anything to dredge up fears that he'd kill again. *If* he did get out, in his dream of vengeance on them, he'd put his face in theirs as often as he could, be their boogeyman. Baby Sister—his sister Millie—had been nagging him to petition for parole again, but he was determined not to let himself be humiliated by the town trotting out lies about him. *No fuckin' way!*

CHAPTER TWO

IN THE ADJOINING MESS HALL, Francisco "Fat Frankie" Gilletto looked down his table at thirteen inmates garbed like himself in buttoned-at-the-neck khaki shirts and pants, all shoveling down their meals without tasting. His plastic fork fiddled with a plate of meatloaf smothered in brown gravy, green beans and mashed potatoes. He thought of the upcoming St. Joseph's Day, when his *goombahs* on Providence's Federal Hill would devour mouthwatering cream-filled *zeppole*, dusted with powdered sugar and topped with whipped cream and a cherry, at Gucci's and Il Capri. *Lucky to get a glazed donut in the fuckin' ACI.*

Fat Frankie hungered for—dreamt of—a homecooked real Italian meal to fill his belly like he did when he lived his persona as the Hill's go-to pawn shop operator. What he wouldn't give for a stuffed veal chop, pasta with *cipollini* and *porcini* mushrooms, a fennel *fociacia*, his Mama's fig ring, and a glass of *nero d'alva*, maybe with a *grappa* to finish. After two and a half years inside, he was down forty pounds to one-eighty, skinny by his standards, although his flaccid belly still lumped over his waistband. He longed to be fat again, fleshy, and on the street.

Could he rely on assurances from his cousin, Chris Gilletto, that he would be an exception to the norm that nobody got paroled the first time up? Chris, with union, street, and political contacts, boasted he had the juice. Fat Frankie had done his part; he had paid his cousin twenty g's for the parole on top of another twenty upfront to "the Brow" for goodwill and protection against abusers while inside, which got him an administrative job in the license plate shop and a cell without a cellmate. He had kept his prison record thin and clean, except for a single, early blotch, and that was a not-his-fault-incident with "Fuck Face" Underwood.

Second week inside, while coming down with a flu, feverish and headachy, he wolfed down greenish Salisbury steak that soon had him rushing across the mess hall to the can. With his hands pressing his belly and his head down, Fat Frankie body-slammed Aaron Underwood coming off the food line. Fat Frankie looked up into that God-awful face and upchucked, spewing undigested lumps all over himself, on Underwood's shirt and dinner tray, and the tile floor. Nearby inmates roared with laughter, causing on-duty COs to quickly congregate and order Fat Frankie to clean up the mess.

Still new to the prison's pecking order, he argued and pointed to Underwood as the cause of the incident, just as whatever was left in his gut coughed up on a CO. That earned him a ten-day detention and a record note for causing a disturbance.

The incident had long been forgotten by all except Fat Frankie and Aaron. Fat Frankie made a point to avoid Fuck Face. They were in cell blocks located at opposite ends of the Medium Security complex, and had meals at different times. Whenever Fat Frankie caught Underwood's eye— his only eye—he saw an unnerving glare of hatred in that shattered face. When Fat Frankie let his concern be known to his paid protectors that Fuck Face gave him the evil eye, they replied, "Too fuckin' bad," and "Lay off." To avoid Underwood, he visited the prison library where Underwood worked only after evening meals, long after Fuck Face was off duty.

Giving up on the unappetizing meatloaf, Fat Frankie lugged up his girth, picked up his tray and walked it over to the conveyor belt and the dish washers.

"I gotta get out of here!" he muttered.

CHAPTER THREE

RICKY SQUILLANTE CHECKED HIS WATCH, a garish, glow-in-the-dark, multi-dial Citizens he got off the shelf at Fat Frankie Gilletto's pawnshop. The watch was a bonus for taking down a deadbeat and collecting two grand more than what Frankie had demanded. Ricky had hoped the wiseguy chatter about his success would have gotten him more action from the fat man's associates. But Fat Frankie got pulled in for having guns in pawn, and a judge sent him away.

"Fuckin' two-thirty," Ricky said aloud. "Shit! Why don't cranes have heaters?"

Middle of the night, he was freezing, and he suffered another sting of acid reflux. "Must've been some goddamn fuckin' green peppers in the free meatballs I had eaten at the Action Club!"

He burped loudly as he pushed a hand control forward. The crane's huge mechanical pincers pulverized a rusted Pontiac's windshield and side windows, buckled its roof panel and grasped its innards. In response to his pull on a separate control, the crane's arm twisted to raise its catch and swing it toward the gaping maw of a vehicle compactor. Ricky always felt a rush from the crunches and screams of distressed metal, the splintering glass, the throbbing power of the engine vibrating through the cab to the controls. Sometimes he'd even get hard.

With the Pontiac centered for a drop, he set the controls to neutral, shook his head, felt the rub of his ponytail inside his hoodie, and pulled at his chin's pointed beard. Earlier that evening, he had closed the Action Club on Allens Avenue by the harbor, and after a twenty-five dollar parking lot blow job from a strung-out hooker, Ricky had downed a half pint of Jack D, draining half of it on his way to the yard. Booze always steadied him, but since the delivery was late, the effect had dissipated.

Ricky wiped the cab's fogged up window with his fingers, then found his Marlboros in his jacket's pocket. He lit one, took a deep drag and watched smoke curl and vanish through the tiny opening in the cab's window. After so many of these specials, he no longer gave a rat's ass whose body the Drago family had delivered to Rhode Island Scrap. His uncle, Sal Gianmalvo, "Sallie G" to intimates on Federal Hill, had to be coining it for his role in the disappearance of deadbeats, rats, wiseguys on the outs, taken down by the Drago family, the Mob's dreaded enforcers, from up in Revere. *Fuckin' badass sons of bitches! Geezus.* Ricky wanted to connect with them. His thoughts echoed the complaint he had been nursing earlier at strip joints around town. "Some fuckin' respect be nice, Uncle Sal, a little fuckin' respect wouldn't hurt. Cost ya nuthin'," he said aloud. "So, how about it? Huh, Sallie?"

He didn't have the balls to say anything remotely like that to his uncle, who was very close to the Brow, the Hill's *capo di capos.*

Ricky took another drag, ruminating on his hated chicken-shit day job—driving the yard's flatbed tow truck to a junker stripped of anything salvageable, checking to make sure its gas tank had been drained, attaching the tow's cable to the junker's front axle, winching it on its rear wheels on to the flatbed, driving the thirty yards to the compactor at the rear of the yard, removing the cable, waiting until the crane's claws grabbed the junker for delivery to the compactor, and back again. *Dirty fuckin' work, fit for a stunard.*

Ricky hacked a cough, took in a last drag, lowered the window, and flipped the butt out of the cab. *Nemesis!* Ricky liked the word the first time he'd heard it, something from a movie or computer game, a robotic phenom—unforgiving, unstoppable, lethal. Had the word tattooed on his right shoulder and on his knuckles, lettered on the rear of the cab of his Dodge Ram pickup. *Nemesis.* That's how Ricky saw himself when he had some action. *Nemesis* crimped stoolies, extorted payments from club owners, worked labor disputes, squeezed juice from deadbeats, would clip a guy, no problem if that was the job. But nobody gave him the nod because he was tagged as belonging to Uncle Sal.

"Fuck it!" He hit the release bar and dropped the Pontiac dead center into the compactor. After he swung the crane's arm out of the way, he set the controls at neutral, left the cab, climbed three rungs to the compactor's hutch, snapped on the main power switch that illuminated green and red dials on its panel, and activated the compressors for its hydraulic systems. The familiar whine grew in intensity as the dials indicated a build-up of pressure; at six thousand pounds per square inch, he pressed a hand grip lever forward.

Groaning, the compactor's left wall slowly closed a fifteen-foot gap to the right. It didn't hesitate when it struck the junker, twisting it away, animal-like, until it crushed the car against the stationary wall. The Pontiac's frame buckled, joints and welds cracked and caved in, its hood popped, the engine block resisted until it was wrenched from its bolts. Ricky backed off the control to a designated mark and the wall retreated. Gravity did its part and the crumpled junker toppled. He then sent the compactor's rear wall forward, upending the heap into the facing wall. *Pretty good,* Ricky thought. *Maybe ten by six by four now.*

For Ricky, the next stage was the most satisfying. He threw a third control forward that activated the pancaker, a massive steel plate that arched from the shadows on the far side of the compactor, and sent it crashing down with a resounding *thump.* Up, down again, then a third time, then he returned the pancaker to the dark. After two additional side crunches, the jagged, flattened metal was in shape for removal.

With the compactor's walls reset to their original configuration, Ricky turned off the hydraulics, left the control hutch, and returned to the crane. Its pincers clamped around the ton and a half of metal, picked it out of the compactor, and deposited it neatly on top of the stack of junkers processed during the day shift. A "special" always had to be on top. First in, it would be at the bottom of the trailer when it left the yard for the Port of Providence and a waiting Chinese freighter. A lesson learned the hard way was that specials could be shitty smelling and messy; get it out of the yard the next morning, and better not let a yard grunt get too close.

Tonight's special had taken Ricky less than ten minutes to work into shape after the Dragos' delivery crew left the yard. He worked the crane and compactor faster than any of the dolts working days, the fuck-offs who gave him no respect, dissed his cockeye behind his back. Uncle Sal warned him to not retaliate; if not for that, Ricky would have iced a couple of the pricks.

He lit another cigarette, sat back and remembered the second or third special when Uncle Sal was still supervising, and the dead guy in the trunk of the junker turned out not to be so dead. Christ, did he scream and bang the trunk lid! Uncle Sal went back to the yard's trailer, returned with a Glock with a screwed-on silencer, and popped three into the trunk. *Pfft, pfft, pfft.* That shut the fucker up. And reminded Ricky not to fuck around with Uncle Sal.

Ricky switched off the crane's engine, leaving the key in its ignition, left the cab, and push-broomed metal bits and glass shards inside the compactor into a heap, which he collected and hand carried to a dumpster. Then he unwound a thick hose hung on a hook on the side of the compactor, pressure flushed oil, grease—no blood or guts visible tonight—and crap into a waste pit, turned off the water, rewound the hose, and clicked off the lights.

Ricky needed coffee. Badly. The Dunkin' Donuts on Plainfield Street would be open by now. Then, he'd go to his apartment off Manton Avenue, feed Bitch, his pit bull, and sleep. He had the day off after a special and he'd hang out around the Hill, or at the Foxy Doll off Eddy Street. Uncle Sal would pay him two grand after the yard shut down.

Not bad for an hour's work, but not enough for Nemesis.

CHAPTER FOUR

JAKE FOURNIER'S EYES OPENED to a stab of teeth-clamping pain from below the stump that ended his right arm.

Army shrinks called it *nociception*, distress constructed in the brain where location and duration and intensity of pain were determined. They said his hurt didn't need a body part, calling it a "corporeal presence."

As his brain organized to ease the pain, Jake's thoughts, as they sometimes did during nociception, went to his right arm's missing elbow, hand and fingers. His "corporeal" arm must have been warm when it was plucked from the Iraqi sand. He wondered where and how the Army disposed of the limb when it wasn't reattached. Early on, he asked an Army male nurse working in his ward at Walter Reed Army Medical Center, a know-it-all who had something to say about every injury. "It was never completely severed," was the reply, "it had to be hangin' by cartilage or muscle or bone or even skin. What saved you from bleeding out was morphine and some medic with his knee pressed on what remained of your arm while he clamped on a tourniquet, cleared out your throat and gave you a trach. Your arm went into an incinerator. Medical SOP. You are one lucky fuck to be here."

Jake checked the digital clock on the night table. Five-ten, close to his normal wake-up time during his years working construction. He lay back on the king-size bed, stretched his sinewy body, and went through forty bridges with his knees raised and bent, and his torso lifted into an arch with his shoulders. A set of kick thrusts and one-arm push-ups followed, and he finished with crunches that rippled stomach muscles and contracted hamstrings. Keeping his body rock hard—his abs the envy of the bodybuilders at the Pawtucket Y, his one-arm push-ups the subject of whispered admiration—was how he dealt with the reality of his missing part.

He stood and picked up his parole board laptop from the night table to complete his review of the twenty-two parole petitions for the day's session in Medium Security. Each petition—and they tended to be repetitious—included a conviction record, behavioral status reports, records of education courses, remedial treatment, and a parole counselor's recommendation, along with correspondence from victims, prospective employers, family, friends or the clergy.

Jake, an instinctive scheduler of time, allocated ten minutes for each, meaning the balance of the petitions would take him a little over an hour. The meeting, at the Adult Correctional Institution (the ACI) in Cranston, would start at noon. That left him forty-five minutes for a mug of herbal tea and a buttered slice of egg-crusted Portuguese bread at the kitchen's island counter while finishing a crossword from the *New York Times Sunday Magazine*, and then ninety minutes to shower, dress, and walk to Operation Safe Return, a center for vets returning from Iraq and Afghanistan, for an hour's session in downtown Pawtucket where he volunteered, before he drove to the ACI in Cranston for the parole board hearing.

He was awkwardly toweling off after his shower when his glance went to his reflection in the mirror over the sink. He let his left hand's fingers rake his thick brown hair behind his ears to curl at his neck, and took a step forward. His black eyes, angular unshaven face, and the set of a jaw that narrowed to a dimpled chin, gave off an impression of calm confidence and no bullshit that harkened back to a younger version of Jake

Fournier—composed, self-contained, determined, easy within his skin—Jake Fournier before suffering his wound in Iraq and before his pregnant wife, Hope's, hit-and-run murder three years later. His creased forehead and the yellowish bands beneath his eyes evidenced their aftermaths. But his face still reflected his intelligence and his take-charge attitude.

By seven-thirty, he had dressed in pressed jeans and black polo shirt with one sleeve hemmed at where his right elbow would have been, and a pair of Nikes, and entered the mahogany paneled library of graceful proportions like the other formal rooms in his spacious first floor condo in the historic Governor Foley Mansion on Pawtucket's Park Place. A refurbished chandelier dripping with crystals—an antique that came with his purchase of the mansion—was centered in a thirteen-foot-high ceiling over a bare yellow oak plank floor. He snapped a light switch and sparkles danced off the crystals to unadorned walls, empty bookcases, a beige sofa in front of a large screen television, a fireplace with white birch logs for show, and a desk with a laptop computer and chair. Tucked in a corner was a whiteboard with smudged highlighter printing, arrows and lines and boxes untouched in over a year—a legacy of his fruitless search for his wife's killer. He sat at the desk, removed a few index cards from a drawer, and prepared for his session as a discussion leader at the vet center.

An hour later, Jake opened the glass front door of Operation Safe Return at Main and Union Streets. In addition to social and educational services, it operated a twenty-two unit temporary housing building off Union Street, and a food pantry for needy vets. Above the front door, welcoming lettering read, *You served, we serve you,* and *Let's finish the mission together.*

Jake, an anonymous contributor to various veterans groups, had within the past year focused on Operation Safe Return after it opened its offices and apartments within walking distance to his condo. Jake's relationship might have remained financial and impersonal but, as a parole board member, he had been faced with veterans who experienced addiction and PTSD that led to their criminal behavior. He began dropping by the center to lend an attentive ear to a vet who needed companionship, or to play gin rummy or to accompany a vet on a short cigarette walk down to the park by the Blackstone River at Slater Mill. Two weeks earlier, the center's director, a balding vet of two tours in Afghanistan with a quiet manner that suggested patience and understanding, asked Jake to lead a group discussion with some down-and-out vets who needed to hear a new voice.

Jake was hesitant about his ability to lead a session. "What can I add to what the vets have already heard?"

The director had replied, "All you have to do is talk about what happened when you came back. Just be yourself and don't worry about responses. There will be some hard cases, been through addiction, family issues, assaults, petty crime. All are on meds of some sort or another. The idea is to reinforce what we do here, that you can come back, fight off the demons, and make it."

Ushered into a conference room at the rear of the center, Jake sat at a round table with a dozen or so vets sitting behind coffee mugs and bottles of Poland Spring water, unshaven for the most part, some in jeans and tees, others in pieces of khaki military uniforms, several with bloodshot eyes or disguising theirs with sunglasses, and mostly rake-thin, the physique of the addicted. One with a particularly vacant stare was wearing a bandana that might have been a piece of flag, like Willie Nelson, another wore a biker's cap, brim up, a scar across a cheek, and had chipped front teeth. In his left hand Jake held index cards with notes for his practiced points, along with a couple of throwaway lines on one-arm bandits, one-arm jokes, and a list of one-arm heroes. He was introduced only as Jake, an Iraqi war vet.

"So where did ya lose it?" was the immediate question from a vet with a two-day stubble.

"Anbar Province, May 5, 2009. My 'I'm alive' day." It seemed a lifetime ago.

"There in 2008. Second tour," was the response.

"I was in the 525th National Guard MP's based at the Pawtucket Armory," Jake added. "Any other Guardsman here?" Nobody moved.

"When did you join?" the same vet asked. "Bet you never thought you'd get called up, see action, right? Or lose an arm." That came with the sneer of a dog-face regular.

Jake hadn't expected snideness but wanted to get his answer right. "I was single, working construction for myself, and had some wrestling from high school and kickboxing at the Y. A couple of buddies from my high school, St. Ray's, joined up and somehow it fit me," meaning his energy was translated into leadership abilities as he became a sergeant. "Anybody else like that?"

One vet stood. Jake expected a connective moment from a vet who moved in his chair and stood, but the vet mumbled, "I gotta take a piss," and left the room.

So much for connections. Jake tried one of the one-arm jokes he had found online. "I hear this one all the time. Why did the one-arm man cross the street?"

A sleepy-eyed vet mumbled, "To get to the secondhand store."

The others vets shuffled in their seats.

Okay, Jake thought, *I've lost them already. Forget the one-arm heroes like Admiral Nelson and John Muir. Just get the spiel out and leave.*

"My company was assigned to security for supply operations to support Marines and Sunni tribesmen." As he spoke, he saw himself in his standard desert camouflage battle dress, body armor, knee and elbow pads, a helmet which everyone called a "Kevlar" with goggles above its brim. He remembered emailing a photo of himself dressed for desert duty to his crew at Jacques Fournier Builders with the caption, *I'll be back soon.*

"My tenth or eleventh mission—only one firefight—and I manned the M-50 in the turret of a modified Humvee. That was after they fixed the Humvees with some steel plates on their undercarriages for IED protection. Wasn't much help to me." Jake noticed a flicker of interest. "I was in the second vehicle in a column of six. Two Humvees, three supply trucks, and an armored truck mounting an M-240. All our previous runs on this ribbon of road through sand and dust and rocky gullies and burned-out villages had been uneventful. Not that I didn't see the same carnage you witnessed."

The vets still looked like truants getting a principal's lecture. One had the fidgety look of a smoker dying to light up, another was about to bang his head on the table as he nodded off.

"We were out about ten k's when my Humvee struck an IED. I remember some of it, the initial shock, air sucked out of my lungs, my head caroming within my Kevlar, my neck smacking the butt of the M-50, then, seconds later, a more powerful explosion, the Humvee rearing up, falling on its side, tossing me out on my butt. Someplace in all that, I took a blow to my arm"—Jake raised his stump—"not realizing then that I had been whacked by a shard of metal. I got medevacked after a few bad guys with RPGs were taken out."

Blood and guts got the attention of two or three vets; the others remained either too bored or tired to react.

"Where did they send you?" asked a gaunt vet wearing a khaki field hat, a spark of interest in his eyes.

"Eventually to Walter Reed, outside of DC. With all the other maimed and depressed and stupefied who populated the amputee wards. Anybody else been there?"

"Not in your ward. Surgical," the same vet replied. "Took one in the belly," he said, lifting his grayish shirt and tee to show a six-inch scar across his stomach. "Lost a kidney and was there for two months. Fuckin' shithole as far as I'm concerned."

Jake said, "I heard it got renovations after vets complained." Jake took a swig of water and listened as the vet further described his wound and troubled hospitalization. Jake remembered his own early weeks there, the pain when his morphine was reduced, the ringing in his ears, how his bruised larynx left him a voice that seemed both tremulous and guttural. As for his stump, it healed faster than his reconciliation with his reconfigured body. He couldn't bear to feel or see it in a mirror and, like other amputees, wore a skin-colored, sock-like covering over the bandages. He wouldn't dwell on that.

"I don't know about you," Jake said, directing himself to the same vet. "Nobody would have said I was a good patient. I hated the boot camp supervision in the ward, the limited privacy, the stink of disinfectant, and a nursing staff often with a take-a-number attitude. My head was in a bad place. I even resisted occupational therapy that was designed to help me cope with eating and hygiene and day-to-day life missing an arm. And for reasons I can't explain, I flatly refused a prosthetic. They told me that was a manifestation of PTSD."

The vet with the flag bandana challenged Jake. "If you fuck up, it's always PTSD. *Always!* How about just not giving a shit or getting pissed?"

Jake didn't respond, having had the same reaction more than once.

"Anybody else get migraines?" Jake asked. "I still do. I try to avoid the triggers, drink herbal tea instead of coffee, you know the routine." Two vets looked at one another and one tentatively raised his hand. "The docs at Walter Reed told me it was from bruises on my brain, from my head rocketing back and forth within the Kevlar; they said it was the law of action and reaction. I had all of the classic symptoms—confusion, dizziness, lack of coordination, loss of memory, auras and slurred speech, accompanied by headache pain that felt like someone was hammering inside my brain to get out."

"Yeah," interrupted another vet. "I get 'em all the time. When I do, I'm done. Can't do nothing." He had a thin face, deeply sad eyes, and a mouth that was in a continual side-to-side motion. Jake noticed the vet's hands shaking badly when he raised a coffee mug to his lips.

Jake continued. "I get 'em even though I try to avoid the triggers. I don't drink booze anymore. I watch what I eat and drink, try to keep everyday business hassles to a minimum. Doesn't always work. Back then, I was given candy . . . opiates, I know now. Anybody else?" The response was three vigorous head shakes and a muttered comment from one vet to another. Jake took that as getting through. "At Walter Reed, they gave me reds, and then stronger greenies. I gobbled them down like aspirin. They gave us some warnings about addiction but we all thought of ourselves as users, not abusers. Eventually, I weaned myself off the pills, but later, after I returned to civilian life, and had some . . . issues, I fell back on the relief I got from them. Became an opiate junkie for a while. Free now, thank God."

"Where's your Purple Heart?" a vet asked sourly.

That surprised Jake. He had to think where it had been stashed. "In a drawer of my desk at home."

"I pawned mine," the vet said and looked around the table for a reaction. There was none.

Another vet said, "The VA in Providence is a good place. I go once a week for my meds and treatment. Get there by bus."

"After my discharge," Jake responded, "I came back home to Pawtucket, and was supposed to report there. Stupidly, I didn't. Back then, I was pushing people away if I saw pity in their faces, or heard assurances that I was a good man, that life was going to be great, back to normal in no time. With my PTSD, I was self-centered, harsh, angry, all at once. Did have one good buddy who refused to let go, and somehow I got on with my business, a construction company here in Pawtucket, I had then—"

"Aren't you the parole board guy that lost his wife in a hit-and-run?" he was asked by a vet who had not previously spoken.

"Yeah, that's me."

"I remember reading about you in the newspaper."

"Do you ever see vets at the parole board?"

"Yeah, too many. Domestic abuse, assaults while drunk or high, that kind of thing."

"Do you give them a break?"

Jake shrugged, and then gave an honest answer. "Maybe I do."

"Fuckin' good. Those guys just never got straightened out."

The vets opened up after that with comments and questions, even good humor, and a coffee carafe and water bottles were brought to the table and passed around for refills. One or two were interested in Jake's opiate problem, and why, and his rehab. A burly vet with tattooed wrists coming out of a wrinkled gray sweatshirt said he had been a carpenter apprentice when he enlisted, and wondered if he'd ever get back to it. Jake said that construction companies like his former shop were always looking for good workers and gave preference to veterans. The vet expressed interest for a moment before he lapsed into silence, as though the effort of making a decision about an opportunity was too much of a burden.

At eleven o'clock, Jake thanked each vet in turn for the meeting, and said while no story would be the same as his, they were still comrades in arms. He made the point to raise his stump, and they laughed at the irony. One vet clapped his hands and was joined by others, a couple even smiled.

CHAPTER FIVE

"DISCUSSION!"

Mia Sanchez, the parole board's self-anointed conscience, its "wise Latina" as she was once characterized in a newspaper interview, shifted in her chair while pushing a pair of red-framed designer glasses with tiny lenses down her well-shaped nose to stare at her laptop.

"He's served seven years and . . ."

It was the next to last petition to be decided on a long and contentious afternoon. Floyd Prebys, long-necked, his nose perched over a small, tight-lipped mouth and an almost missing chin, twisted off horn-rimmed reading glasses and pointed them at Mia. "He was falling down drunk, Mia, going the wrong way on Route 95, and smashed into those kids."

With that comment, Jake shook his head. Another argument was about to begin between the board's cultural warriors in the windowless, overheated hearing room not conducive to reasoned discussion. Its institutional pea-green walls clashed with the bluish tint cast by three banks of fluorescent tubes, a combination that converted anything pale to a sickly puce. The only touch of décor, a futile attempt to add dignity to the proceedings, were United States and Rhode Island flags in stanchions facing petitioners.

Mia didn't back down. Never did to Prebys. She was smart, articulate, dogged, and intense, and made principled arguments. Prebys was a contentious jerk.

"Tragic, I agree," she responded, her voice rising in exasperation, her long, black, silky hair swirling on her shoulders as she turned to face Prebys. "But should he stay inside for another four years? He's a regular AA member," she continued, "took counseling on anger control, earned an associate degree at the community college. His discipline violations were in his early days. It's his third petition."

A third petition by an inmate with a clean prison record and a decent demeanor at the hearing was often a ticket out, provided the petitioner's crime was in the dustpile of memory.

Acting Chair Stuart Bertozzi tried to advance to a vote.

"Let's move on, people," he said, looking at each of the three members sitting behind an afternoon's collection of empty water bottles, coffee cups, and laptops, at trestle tables forming a U. Bertozzi sat at its base, flanked on his left by Prebys and Mia, and Jake, and to his right by an empty chair reflecting a vacancy on the board since the resignation of the former chair. Mrs. Ames, the board's longtime executive secretary, a stout woman with short mousy gray hair, multiple chins, a penchant for pantsuits and floppy ties, sat next to Bertozzi, close enough to whisper. A ganglia of cords draped from laptops and mics into outlets in the concrete floor.

Prebys responded to his adversary. "Mia, he took out two high school kids a week before their graduation! You heard the parents!"

They had tearfully spoken at an earlier separate hearing for victims, urging a rejection of the inmate's petition. One mother brought in her daughter's graduation photograph, pressed it to her breast, and sobbed. Prebys turned to Bertozzi and demanded, "Let's vote!"

Bertozzi, a formal, procedurally prickly personality, was a multi-term veteran of the board as vice chair, and an eager candidate for permanent status as chair once the governor filled the board's vacancy. He might have rebuked Prebys' abrasiveness if he hadn't been relying on him as a favorable vote. Instead, he said calmly, "Floyd?"

"No."

"Mia?"

"Yes," she said, with confident righteousness, and raised her questioning eyes to Jake.

Jake, as he sometimes did, had zoned out during their squabbles, had been imagining his fellow board members as kids: "Pencil Neck" Prebys a crybaby with a runny nose, picked last for team games; Mia in a frilly white dress, adored by her parents as "precious," and teachers as "precocious;" Bertozzi the chubby kid in the third row who never raised his hand.

"Jake," Mia insisted, "he's ready for parole."

"I'm thinking," Jake replied, taking a long swig of water. Three affirmative votes were required for a felon's parole, technically under the statute a "permit to be at liberty," even with the vacancy on the board during most of Jake's months of service. If past votes were any guide, cautious Bertozzi would join Prebys as a "no." If Jake voted with them, the inmate would sit out a year before being again eligible to petition. If Jake went with Mia, making the tally two to two, the petition would be in limbo until the board vacancy was filled, at which time the inmate got an automatic rehearing.

Bertozzi waited a few seconds before he prodded Jake. "How about it?"

When Jake didn't immediately respond, Prebys complained, "C'mon, Jake! Make up your mind. I gotta get back to the office."

Jake wasn't given to indecision but somewhere in his cerebral cortex, migraine neurons had been gathering for almost an hour in what his doctor called the *prodromal* phase of a migraine. Jake blinked and forced himself to concentrate. Focus sometimes helped mitigate the onset of headaches. And now he had to admit that even as a recovered booze and opiate user himself, that he hadn't been able to conclude his evaluation of the inmate's claimed rehabilitation, or plumb the depth of his remorse during the inmate's hearing. Better to postpone and give the petitioner a fair shot at a second hearing.

"Yes," Jake said.

Prebys snorted and locked his fingers behind his neck, revealing sweat stains in the armpits of his blue dress shirt. Mia, generally sympathetic to any good story of redemption and rehabilitation, tugged at her beige fitted suit jacket, barely hiding a tight smile. Bertozzi's liver-spotted hands pushed back his chair in some pique. "Chair votes no," he said, creating the tie vote that would cause the petition to be reheard in the future. He turned to Mrs. Ames.

"How many is that?"

"Makes twenty-two," she replied quickly, her voice reeking with disapproval.

"The warden has complained about the growing backlog," Bertozzi continued. "It's a morale killer and—"

"Tell the governor to make his appointment," Jake interrupted.

"And, we get to waste more time rehearing them again," Prebys sputtered, "and you know where they're going? Nowhere! Not fair to them or to us. Maybe others don't care about wasting time, but I've got to earn a living."

Prebys had long targeted Mia's flexible work schedule as a senior counselor of women students at the University of Rhode Island as a way to attack her outspoken reformist views on incarceration and parole.

Despite his migraine, Jake might have gone to her defense but didn't have to when Bertozzi used his gavel. Jake liked Mia. Jake had been impressed that she neither flinched nor inquired when she noticed his missing right arm. Diminutive at five-four or so, she didn't fit his image of a parole board member, didn't dress down to evidence serious purpose, nor neglect to show off a provocative figure with tight-fitting clothes and a little cleavage. Jake found her attractive, even sexy, with wide full lips, dark brown eyes under long back eyelashes, and lustrous black hair that fell to her shoulders.

"Last one," Bertozzi said and swept back a strand of gray hair that had fallen from his elaborate comb-over.

"The guy raped a prostitute?" Prebys asked sarcastically. "How do you do that? C'mon, they put themselves into these situations."

"Don't go there," Mia snarled.

Jake thought of excusing himself. His migraines came and went in cycles recently, and he had experienced several that were excruciating. Migraines don't have a single trait. One can be sharp and be over quickly, the next painful with hours of confusion, bad dreams, and the like. Jake was sure the one emerging one would be the latter. Nonetheless, he decided to struggle through when Bertozzi quickly called for a vote.

Their negative votes were unanimous, and the sparring came to an end. Mrs. Ames picked up her laptop and an armful of files and left the hearing room. When she closed the door behind her, Bertozzi cleared his throat loudly to stop the members' exodus. "I've been informed by the warden that Aaron Underwood is again eligible for parole."

"Cripes, just what we don't need," groaned Prebys, shaking his head vigorously. He stood, put on his rumpled suit jacket, and shoveled his laptop into a valise.

"Who is Aaron Underwood?" Jake's mental fog was thick but not as yet impenetrable.

"He bludgeoned an old lady in Greenwick decades ago," Prebys responded, answering the question Jake had aimed at Bertozzi. "South County gets up in arms every time he petitions, politicians outdoing one another against his parole. Nobody wants him outside spooking their neighborhoods. They call him the 'Greenwick Monster'."

Bertozzi, a retired high school teacher from a South County town, frowned at Prebys but explained. "Underwood's been inside for almost thirty years. His victim shot off half of his face before she died. Literally, half his face! Don't know how he survived. Terrible scarring. Hideous."

Prebys sniffed. "'Greenwick Monster' says it all."

Mia had listened to the comments about Underwood while searching in a maroon Lotuff leather duffel handbag. Finding a ring of keys, she put on a calf-length raincoat. "Why should we care what Aaron Underwood looks like?"

Prebys rejoined. "Yeah, well imagine the most grotesque face you've ever seen, and he gets to sit in front of you for at least a half hour or more. When he sits right there," he pointed to the petitioner's chair, "be prepared for nightmares."

CHAPTER SIX

"GOT TIME FOR A STOP?" Mia asked Jake as they exited the hearing room.

"Got an appointment," he responded.

"Okay," she said with seeming disappointment, smiled, left him and headed down the corridor to security control. Jake watched the swing of her hips with the raincoat wrapped around her, and thought, even in his headache, she was a package of style and smarts.

Jake paused on his way down the same corridor, steadying himself at a slit of an eye-level, wire-reinforced window with a view to Medium Security's cell blocks up an incline. His migraine had become so painfully disorienting that he could barely make out inmates in their loose-fitting khaki coveralls, winter jackets of the same color, and boots, walking toward him, or the accompanying COs in leather police jackets and brown twill trousers, using batons to warn inmates away from the temptation of making snowballs from the piled remains of a recent storm on either side of the concourse from the cell blocks.

Jake exited through two electronically controlled metal sliding doors, turned in his ID badge at security control, narrowly avoided an inmate with a lasso of orange extension cord driving an oversized floor polisher, and was soon in the parking lot reserved for the prison's senior staff and parole board members. It was near freezing, had drizzled earlier and remained overcast with layers of shapeless, slate gray clouds, affirming the Rhode Island truism that sunglasses could be put away in March until after Easter. He saw Mia's silver Saab convertible on the other side of the lot as he unlocked his rain splattered black Camaro. He slumped inside its spotless interior, and closed his eyes. The two Imitrex he swallowed might stave off some of the headache, but the nausea, the befuddled thinking, the urge to hide from the world, would progressively worsen over the next few hours. *Concentrate,* he told himself. *On what? The prison?*

During flights over Rhode Island's prison complex from nearby T.F. Green Airport, Jake had realized that the prison complex, from two or three thousand feet, could have been mistaken for a college campus with dorms, classroom buildings, playing fields, courtyards, and parking areas; only the complete absence of trees might have seemed unusual.

Medium Security's flat-roofed, mustard-colored cell blocks were clustered at the northern edge of the adult corrections prison complex, with Minimum Security to its east and Maximum Security, including its High Security component known as the *Max* for the prison's hard cases, to its south, close by the women's prison. Jake, on his first visit and with his background in construction, viewed Medium Security as a masonry contractor's dream project: four three-story concrete cell blocks connected by concrete walkways to a central concrete concourse lined with shrubs in concrete planters, chain-link fences embedded in concrete, and concrete bases for vapor lights shining twenty-four seven. The concourse, on an incline, sliced through open spaces and playing fields of the prison's thirty acres down to a line of one-story concrete block buildings holding administrative offices, mess hall, library, chapel, visitor rooms, classrooms, gym, and industrial and trade shops. Perimeter double fencing, embedded in concrete, curved inward at the top to make a climb more difficult, was topped by coiled razor wire.

During Jake's orientation briefings, he had learned that Medium

Security had been constructed nearly thirty years earlier for up to eight hundred prisoners; it now housed over a thousand. Despite overcrowding, it had a deserved reputation of being well managed and maintained. Jake was impressed by the warden's intelligence. The respect he garnered was reflected in the demeanor of COs and inmates, as well as in the shine on the corridor's tile floors, the fresh paint on interior walls and window frames, and the spotless common areas in the cell blocks and administrative buildings.

Jake always experienced a sense of relief upon leaving the confinement of one of the prisons. Those inside, including men on whom he had earlier passed judgment, remained trapped in an oppressive tension-filled daily grind, one of morning, noon, and night body counts, the clangs of metal doors, the barely hidden odors of men living and shitting together, disinfectant, the day-to-day brutal monotony of being under constant surveillance, echoing voices, the tension of sharing a cell with a jerkoff, or living in fear of pissing off gangbangers, racists and perverts, seeing life pass by through fences and bars, with a maximum of five names on a visitor list.

His fingers went to massage his temple as he experienced a burst of headache and he wondered about lifer Aaron Underwood. *How horrific is his face? Worse than in Walter Reed?*

Halfway through his weeks of recovery in the amputee ward, he had mistakenly gotten off the elevator onto the segregated floor for burn victims. A line of patients in wheelchairs with attached IV's were at the elevator; their hideous facial injuries stunned him. In shock and embarrassment, he turned his back on them—*turned his back* was engraved in his memory—as he retreated into the elevator. Those maimed faces, and his shame over his reaction, drilled a hole in his soul that never quite closed. Despite his loss of an arm, Jake claimed a future with a goal of normality; those burned vets would be forever shunned and pitied. For long thereafter, his dreams often included their ruined faces.

A sharp rap at his car window roused him; its dark tinting prevented Mia seeing Jake's pain-racked face. He lowered the window several inches but kept out of her direct line of sight. "You're still here?" she said with concern in her voice. "Are you okay?"

"Fine."

"I can't believe their reactions to Underwood," she said. "We should be bending over backward to make sure he gets a fair hearing." When Jake didn't respond, Mia continued. "I wanted you to know I am going for chair," she said, which didn't surprise Jake. "Stuart wants it, of course. How long has he been on? Ten, fifteen years, and the only improvement in the process has been electronic records and the laptops. Never speaks up for improvements to the parole system, which we desperately need." She stopped her election speech. "Has he spoken to you?"

"Yes. He said he deserves the chair for all of his years of board service."

"And?" she prompted.

"Said I would think about it."

Board terms were for four years; Jake, serving in a vacancy, had two years left on his term. Bertozzi had admitted that while he and Jake had differences in how they approached parole, he respected Jake and appreciated what he had been through. With Prebys' anticipated support, he said Jake would be a deciding vote when the new member joined the board. Jake remembered wincing at the thought of voting with Floyd Prebys.

"Prebys is a Neanderthal," Mia continued, "but I could deal with him for the year he's got left and then I'd get him off." "Jake, you've heard what they're doing in the federal court system instituted by Judge Sullivan. The results aren't all in yet, but every indication is that increased supervision and partners for parolees makes a huge difference in recidivism. I'd lobby for that . . . and realistic caseloads for counselors."

"All good," replied Jake, struggling to get out the words.

He sometimes voted with Mia, even if she occasionally gave off vibes that she was the only board member with the educational background and cultural sensitivity to evaluate petitioners in the context of their sex, ethnicity and economic class. With her smarts and credentials, Jake sometimes wondered what she was doing on the parole board. *Conviction, social consciousness, what?* In recent weeks, their relationship had warmed; they had met several times for coffee and tea at a deli and bakery down the road from the prison.

Their first time, Jake was uneasy, talking into his mug of herbal tea, checking his watch, until he felt the pull of her personality and enjoyed himself, and readily accepted her next invitation, which had gone better and the time after that, even better. He guessed she was, like him, in her late thirties. He cynically wondered if the lack of wrinkles and full round cheeks were Botox-related, learned something of her personal life, that she was a divorcée, a Brown University grad with a doctorate in sociology from Yale, lived somewhere on Providence's East Side, and stayed in shape with regular exercise at the Jewish Community Center. Once or twice as she fluttered her eyelashes over her coffee, Jake thought she might be coming on to him; as a one-armed widower, he had been flattered. Now, he wondered if their meetings were part of a pitch for his vote.

"The governor and I go back to when our union endorsed him last election, and he'll ask again. If he is supportive, you, and whomever is his appointment, are the votes I need."

By statute, the vacant seat on the board was designated for someone with at least ten years of police experience, active or retired. Until recently, it had been filled by a cop from East Providence of Cape Verdean ancestry who resigned after a heart attack. The members speculated that his replacement would be another minority cop. Since Mia was the board's Latina, an African-American seemed likely.

"Not on anyone's team, Mia," Jake said as a wave of headache struck him. He pressed the ignition button with the finger of his left hand, the windshield wipers whipped back and forth, and the Camaro's powerful V-8 engine roared. He put the car in reverse using the steering wheel controls for a handicapped driver. "Got to go."

"Jake, just keep an open mind. We'll talk some more. Soon. By the way, I'm having a few friends over for cocktails next Tuesday. I'd love to have you join us. I'll send you an email with my address."

Surprised and hurting, and not ready for the effort he would need for a cocktail party, Jake couldn't find the words to politely refuse. He didn't do cocktail parties. "If I can. I'll let you know," he said, thinking he'd blow off the invitation later. He drove cautiously, without haste, out of the slushy parking lot as he was already late for an important meeting at Livia's with his business partner and sometimes lover, Livia Antonelli.

CHAPTER SEVEN

"HI YA, JAKE," over the buzz of taproom conversations.

The bartender was shaking up a cocktail behind the taproom's antique thirty-foot-long Brunswick-Balke-Collender mahogany bar. Jake had rescued it from an Elks Lodge in Pawtucket in the process of demolition. Jake admired its craftsmanship, the careful joining of varied wood panels, the intricate carvings at its corners, the ribbon of edging holding its oak top, perfect for the new Livia's American Bistro.

It had taken forty-five minutes to travel just six miles. A truck had skidded and overturned on Interstate 95, causing a traffic snarl before the I Way Bridge at the head of the Narragansett Bay. The sun chose the last five minutes to break through the clouds, reflecting a brilliant orange and gold glare in the Camaro's side and rearview mirrors. Jack's eyes watered at the glare, increasing his discomfort. He took the Providence downtown exit on to South Main Street, through Kennedy Plaza to Washington Street into Livia's parking lot. By then, he regretted not using the car's Bluetooth to beg off from his meeting and continue on to Pawtucket to haul himself into his bedroom and surrender to the darkness.

Jake managed a smile and a wave for some familiars in the happy-hour crowd of lawyers, stockbrokers, lobbyists and bankers congregated in the taproom. He crossed into the brightly lit dining room being prepared for evening customers with tables covered by white cloths, bishop cap napkins and shiny tableware. He pushed through the kitchen's swinging door, acknowledged greetings from the sous chef and the busboy, and opened a door marked *Private*. The office was furniture crowded, with two chairs behind butt-to-butt desks, his to the left, Livia's to the right. His desktop was clear, hers cluttered by a computer, a cupful of pencils and pens, neat stacks of paper, and framed photographs, including one of Livia and Jake at the restaurant's re-opening. A lumpy sofa faced the desks. Jake didn't bother to remove his windbreaker as he sat behind his desk, leaned back, and closed his eyes.

"Hi, there," Livia exclaimed exuberantly, startling Jake into sitting upright. She swept into the office in a dark-blue-with-white-polka-dots hostess dress accented by a strand of Mikimoto pearls rippling over her ample breasts. A braceleted hand swept back a curl of blonde hair from a perfectly proportioned oval face and blue-violet eyes that, from their first meeting in rehab Jake knew, sparkled or sparked, depending on her mood and company. "What kept you?" she continued. At his lack of response, she dialed down her tone. "Migraine?"

"Yeah. But don't let that stop you."

His curt response produced a frown. "We could do this some other time."

"Get it over with."

She hesitated before she sat at her desk. Jake's face was screwed down, his mouth clamped shut, an expression he wore when in the throes of a migraine. Over the past year and a half, as they completed their respective rehabs, they had become business partners and later lovers of convenience, meaning they liked going to bed with one another. As time went on, Livia would have opted for a deeper, more meaningful relationship, but both knew and freely discussed that the ghost of his murdered wife, Hope, blocked Livia out of the deepest recesses of Jake's emotional life. Still, their relationship was satisfying. She thought it eventually might develop into something more, who knew? Jake thought it worked, for the present. He always had an active libido and had little troubling finding companionship and sexual comfort among the women he had dated mostly through friends—before he went on active duty.

Like most boys of those teen years, Jake learned about sex from older boys bragging. There were no father-son talks in his first-generation French-Canadian family. Only once, while Jake was in high school on a job, did his father suddenly say something about Jake staying out of young ladies's panties until he was older, and that any future sex be protective.

So, he learned from the conversations of the older boys with whom he caddied at Pawtucket Country Club, and from some of the pornographic magazines they had hidden in the rafters of the caddy shack. And then there was the reality of Paula Bibeault.

In those days, it was common for the young female teens of his neighborhood to host parties, which consisted of spinning forty-five rpm records, serving Cokes and potato chips and popcorn, in a basement rec room. There would be some petting, of course, for recognized couples of the time, but it never got into more serious stuff. Even when they played "post office," which consisted of someone picking out a name from a hat and the resulting couple going into an adjoining dark room together, they just exchanged chaste kisses and hugs. Nothing very sexy except when it came to Paula. If a boy was lucky and he got Paula into the room, as soon as you walked in, she grabbed your crotch, and had no objection to her partner's hand exploring her more mature figure. Paula liked guys, and it was just assumed she was a likely candidate for further exploration in a car's back seat at drive-in theaters or parking areas by the Seekonk River. She was knocked up before her high school graduation, but that didn't stop her. Later, she managed to get through Rhode Island College Nursing School, and Jake lost track of her until he went to his dermatologist two decades later and found that Paula was the dermatologist's nurse. She was then the mother of five and seemingly content with her life. She lived in the old neighborhood as did many of their contemporaries, and had kept in touch with many of the girls Jake had known. She enjoyed telling him the gossip about her now-fortyish friends.

One day she said to Jake, "You were always a catch, Jake, because you were good looking, had that Steve McQueen smile and never bragged about your conquests. You were sort of lost in yourself back then." For Jake, Paula had been one of his bridges to adulthood, and he had fond memories.

||||||||||||||||||||||||||||||||||||||||||||||||||||||||||

Livia collected a spreadsheet with columns of figures, and pages of design sketches.

"In a nutshell," she said, "it'll take about two hundred fifty grand for design, construction and furnishings." She rolled her desk chair closer to him. The expansion project would punch through a wall into an adjoining empty retail store and give Livia's badly needed space for ten additional dining tables. It could also be used for private parties. She quickly ran through design costs, construction estimates and schedules, the cash flow expected from new business, and the estimated time for payback of Jake's investment. Livia was entrepreneurial by nature and Jake believed the numbers she presented.

As she went on, Jake's migraine reached its peak of blood-pounding pressure. He could hear his heartbeat, "pulsating tinnitus," an Army doctor had called it, caused by turbulent blood flow in or near his ears. He blinked several times during her spiel, giving Livia pause, but a lift of his chin urged her to continue.

"We should do it soon if we are ever going to. We're moving the needle up every month," Livia said, showing Jake design sketches. Jake feigned interest. If not for the migraine, Jake would have had enthusiasm for her project, an echo of his years in construction. Today, it was whatever she wants.

He owed her; she had been his mentor during their rehabs. Livia Bronchowski, née Antonelli, and once again Antonelli after an emotionally draining divorce, had been a foodie personality with a popular Providence restaurant, a cookbook, and a Food Network show in the works when her world collapsed in a haze of cocaine.

"When do you need the cash?" he asked.

"The design is almost finished. I can fund that out of receipts, so fifty grand in the bank now would do it, the rest as we go along. We'll be up and operating in early September if we move on it now."

"I'm good. I'll drop off a check." Jake said weakly. "Now go bother the chef. I need that sofa."

She stood then leaned over and brought her lips to his forehead, then stood. "The office is yours." She smelled good to Jake. As she opened the door. Jake smelled the kitchen preparing for the evening's menu, which included calamari as an appetizer. She said, "Dermott was in for lunch. Wants you to call him."

"Okay." The restaurant was Dermott Francis Xavier McSorely, Esq.'s second home. He was Jake's oldest friend, his high school buddy, the popular kid who provided the crowd with fake IDs, got Jake drunk for the first time, and was an early contact to a world outside Jake's tight-knit Quebecois community. Dermott was the one friend who refused to give up on him when he suffered through migraines and PTSD upon his return to Pawtucket, then again during his bouts with booze and opiates after Hope's murder.

Jake slowly made his way to the sofa. Bending was torture; he put his hand down on its cushions so he wouldn't end up on the floor. The sofa was barely long enough to fit him length-wise at six-one, and almost wide enough for his muscular shoulders to rest comfortably. He almost smiled as he settled onto the sofa. *Livia could convince Santa Claus to drop down chimneys in July.*

Jake had purchased the downtown site for the restaurant, less as a business investment and more as a favor to Livia, with the proceeds of the sale of some Pawtucket real estate and his construction business to his employees. The building had been suffering a slow collapse. He had hired Jacques Fournier Builders, operated by Jake's former employees, to build out the space, and worked with Morris Nathanson, the Pawtucket-based, world-famous restaurant designer for Euro-Disney, Capital Grille, and Smith & Wallinsky Steak House, to create a décor that melded a jazzy zing with traditional dark woods that complemented *Livia's American Bistro* menu.

While the restaurant had been beautifully designed and built-out, it had been Livia's ability to self-promote in a tough restaurant town, her embracing rapport with customers, and her sense of food offerings and pairings that had made the restaurant popular. But the business needed to grow in order to compete and to keep pace with demand.

"Livia's Back," shouted an outsized banner over the entrance, when the restaurant reopened a year earlier. Her well-publicized rehab gave off a touch of chic notoriety that she hadn't discouraged.

<hr>

A jolt of headache sat Jake up. Concentrating on one thing, when he could manage it, often helped him get through a migraine. He recalled the festive reopening with its throng of former patrons, politicians, and media. After the ceremonial scissor cut the ribbon across the entrance, Livia handed Jake a fistful of business cards that read "Jake Fournier, Restaurateur". He protested, "Who would believe that?" She responded, flashing her winning smile, "You are my partner! But don't worry, no one is going to ask," and nobody had. The cards placed in his wallet were now worn.

"Restaurateur?" he said aloud. "Check writer was more like it." But good for Livia—it was better than being like him, without ambition or challenge, running on the emotional fumes of revenge and rage over Hope's murder. Time may have bottled up his raw anger so he could manage day-to-day, but if the stopper was pulled for any glimpse of opportunity for revenge, it would bubble up, flare and destroy. He was determined never to allow time to erode Hope's tragedy into just a sorrowful remembrance. Hope, and his unborn son, deserved better. He would not give up his search for their killer. Never.

CHAPTER EIGHT

OPERATIONS AT RHODE ISLAND SCRAP shut down at five o'clock. The crew wasn't encouraged to hang around.

Sal Gianmalvo and his yard boss, Domenic "Donnie" DelFusco, were in the beat-up trailer that served as Rhode Island Scrap's office. The cigar smoke was so thick they were barely visible to one another across Sal's desk. They had been talking about Ricky who was expected to pick up his payment for last night's special.

"He follows orders," said Donnie, a more compact and swarthy version of his boss. "You gotta give him that. And he looks the part. Ya don't fuck with a guy with a barrel chest, legs like tree trunks, shoulders like a gorilla's." Donnie wasn't sure how far to go with his criticism of Ricky. After all, Ricky was Sal's nephew and therefore *blood*. He was relieved when Sal replied, "Yeah, but he's a fuckin' lamebrain with that stupid-looking ponytail and that fucking beard that looks like it was pasted on his chin. And that fuckin' cockeye. Never know if he's looking at ya or over yer shoulder."

"And he walks kinda funny, like he's got a load in his pants," added Donnie.

Donnie looked through a grimy window into the yard and said, "Here he comes."

Sal let out a cloud of smoke and then tucked his chin into his heavy jowls. He brushed back his silver wings haircut, styled like Paulie Gualtieri in *The Sopranos,* and wheezed, "Got to keep him on the job, though. I'll give him a coupla extra bills for last night. Fuckin' Dragos were late."

Ricky, in a hoodie sweatshirt, jeans and work boots, knocked on the metal door. He took off his wraparound sunglasses—he wore them outside, sunshine or not, to cover his cockeye—and entered the trailer just as an ancient air conditioner over the door rattled on.

"Shut the fuckin' door," his uncle said.

Donnie got up and left the trailer and Sal shrugged for Ricky to take his seat. Sal's desk was cluttered with papers, a metal can of Magic Markers for the whiteboard that marked deliveries to the pier, roughed-up work gloves, stacked boxes of *Cohibas, Montecristos* and *Romeo Y Juileta's,* and an overflowing glass ashtray. A porno calendar and framed Patriots' jersey of the Gronk hung on the wall behind Sal, who reached inside his green cardigan sweater embellished by cigar ash blotches to pull out an envelope.

"You got a little extra."

"Musta been a rat," Ricky sniggered at the thought of how fast he accomplished last night's special.

"Huh? What the fuck is dat?" His uncle's voice boomed as his eyes widened from slits to round black buttons. "You don't wanna know nuthin'! You don't know nuthin,' neither!"

Ricky picked up the envelope that his uncle smacked on the desk. Checking its contents right away would be an insult. "Right, Uncle Sal."

"How many times I gotta tell ya, don't call me Uncle Sal in the yard."

"Okay, okay, sorry. I appreciate the extra. Got to tell ya, I got expenses."

"What expenses? Your whores? Dat fuckin' duded-up truck? Dat fuckin' dog?"

"I only meant—"

"Waz this? Ya want more for what ya do?"

Sal, pushing back from the desk, was working himself up. The blood vessels in his cheeks blossomed, which always happened when Sal got overexcited. "You ungrateful fuck! I can get ten guys who'd give their left nut for the dough!"

"Don't get me wrong," Ricky responded meekly. Like a prizefighter in a thirties movie, he shifted his shoulders, the back of his wrist grazed his beard. "But couldn't maybe I get somethin' more than specials? Ya know everybody. Everybody knows ya, respects ya."

"So, you complain to me? Who helped when nobody is gonna touch ya?"

Anytime Ricky made a push for recognition, his uncle pulled that story out of his ass, how much Ricky owed him for the job he had gotten for his sister Rose, Ricky's mom. Ricky had been doing okay, getting notice, gaining respect, when the hard asses at the AG's office filed on him after he roughed up a deadbeat during a collection. Sal got him a mouthpiece lawyer with some juice who got him off. Or about that thing a couple of years ago with the yard truck.

Okay, Ricky did owe him, but for how long?

"I'll do anything ya ask," Ricky said. "Anythin'."

"That's better. So get the fuck out of here."

Ricky backtracked to the door. *Not good to piss off Uncle Sal. Uncle Sal points his finger at you and wham!*

<hr />

Ricky put on his sunglasses as he walked to the employee parking area and climbed into his Dodge Ram. The truck was his refuge, his mobile billboard, his calling card. Its cab and bed were black, orange flames flared on each side from the grill to the cab, and a snorkel air intake for its 350 hp engine was centered on its hood. It sported double rear wheels with knobby off-road tires, a jacked-up suspension, and halogens over the cab. Anyone who saw it on the Hill, especially with Bitch hanging out the window showing her fangs, had to say "Here comes fuckin' Ricky!'" He kept his tools, including a ball peen hammer, an aluminum softball bat, a two-foot-long plumber's wrench, and a rack of screwdrivers, in a metal storage box bolted to its bed—all perfectly innocent if he got pulled over by the cops, but deadly when wielded by Nemesis.

He slit open the envelope and counted twenty-four Ben Franklins. Four more than usual. Enough for a couple of more rounds with that whore who worked out of the Action Club, maybe with her friend, the one with the gigantic tits and fat ass.

He felt a little better. In his way, Uncle Sal was taking care of him.

CHAPTER NINE

"GET MOVING, UNDERWOOD. This ain't McDonald's," said a passing CO.

Aaron checked his watch; he still had a half hour before his shift began and he was to report to the library to fill in for a sick library assistant. "Fuck you," he muttered to himself and slurped strawberry Jell-O from a cup.

The CO returned two minutes later, hands on hips. "C'mon. I'm not gonna tell you again. They gotta clean up in here."

Aaron ignored the warning. He had been ruminating on the Max. Last night, he had his recurrent nightmare: shattered images of that sultry summer's day he entered the Max as a manacled and handcuffed sixteen-year-old in prisoner's orange overalls, work shirt and beat-up sneakers, prodded along by guards down dimly lit corridors through steel doors to its segregation unit.

Even now, he could vividly recall the cell he was pushed into that had a metal bed frame hooked in place by chains to a stone wall, a rolled-up mattress, a table without a chair, and a tiny window ten feet up, good only for a patch of sky on a clear day or a black shadow at night.

For weeks, that cell was his hell, or at least his purgatory. It trapped daytime heat, turning it into a sweat box that lasted into the night. Once a day—guarded, cuffed, manacled, and harassed by those he passed—Aaron was pushed down a corridor to wash and use a common toilet; a slop bucket was provided for the night. His skimpy, barely edible meals were slid into the cell on a tray through a slot at the bottom of the metal door, along with a cup of Tang at breakfast and KoolAid at lunch and dinner. He became severely dehydrated and his deformed mouth made drinking difficult, until a sympathetic guard slipped in straws and, later, a sippy cup.

Aaron reached for and drank from a sippy cup that, to this day, was available to him with each meal.

He had brought his tattered volume of Robert Frost's poetry to keep him company if the library wasn't busy. It had arrived one morning in the Max, along with the page-worn paperback *Goldfinger*, the James Bond thriller, on his meal tray. Aaron, with only one eye, struggled to read *Goldfinger* in the dim light of the cell's single bulb fixture, but did so, over and over again, imagining voluptuous Pussy Galore in her sexy outfits, his hands squirming on his privates. The hardcover collection of Frost poems had remained unopened for weeks. Poetry? He had memorized Joyce Kilmer's *Trees* in junior high. But poetry? Whose joke was that?

Aaron shook his head at the thought. How would he have known then that Robert Frost's poetry would become his personal book of scripture?

He finished his meal of chicken strips, white gravy, carrots over white rice, by wiping up gravy with a slice of bread—another meal that he couldn't remember without looking at its remains on his plate. How many meals in Medium was that? Round figures would be three a day, times three hundred sixty-five, times thirty? At least he was relatively safe in Medium, not like when he was released into the Max's inmate population, confronted by manic lifers, sociopaths, gang members, neo-Nazis, and rapists. Then, a barely controlled terror had filled his belly, squeezed his throat into silence, and seeped into his brain, causing tremors, headaches, and blackouts. With no depth perception and little balance, Aaron rarely managed a meal line without bumping into a wall or a guard or another inmate for which he was cursed, threatened with shanks, elbowed in his good ear, scorned, insulted, shunned, and abused. A predator said loudly for his benefit that his "face is ugly, but his ass is smooth" but didn't make a move. None did, and Aaron soon realized his best defense, his best chance for survival, was to put his horrific face in theirs. Later, he added a deliberate lack of personal hygiene to his defenses.

"Hey, what don't you get?" demanded the returning CO.

Aaron shrugged. "I gotta hang out for a few minutes before I get library duty. Give me a break." His crooked jaw and damaged lips made his few words barely intelligible. He cocked his eye at the CO, another defense mechanism he had long ago perfected.

"I come back here and you're not gone, you got a problem." The CO left him.

A hollow threat. Aaron and the guards in Medium Security had an understanding. The COs moved double bunks into his handicapped cell for informal, less bureaucratic bookings, to punish inmates for unruly or disrespectful behavior not deviant enough for a detention cell. In fact, prolonged exposure to Aaron's face, his silent treatment, his farts and body odor, and wank offs were thought by many inmates to be a punishment worse than short-term segregated detention cells. In return, the COs dealt harshly with overt harassments of Aaron, and allowed for special accommodations: he ate his meals with the handicapped prisoners in a separate room off the mess hall, was permitted a tape player, then a CD player for music in his cell so long as he used headphones, was provided thick,-black framed glasses with a darkened lens over his missing eye's socket when outside his cell, and a hearing aid which was eventually discarded when his partial ear lost all hearing. To further enhance his chance of survival, Aaron was allowed substantial leeway to be odious; he didn't shower except on Saturday, when ordered to and alone, was rarely barbered and only when his hair became too oily and stringy for the COs, his teeth were a blackened disgrace, his breath could stop a clock. He wasn't mandated to be in the exercise yard or gym, and he was overweight and flabby.

The CO returned, hands on hips again. "I'm goin'," Aaron responded.

Aaron's rubber-soled shoes scuffed the long corridor from the mess hall to the library.

Twenty-nine years earlier, after six months in the Max, he had been transferred, with the two books that were his only personal possessions, to the then newly constructed Medium Security prison where he was placed in a handicapped cell that was four feet longer and two wider than a standard cell. Assigned to grounds maintenance, he lasted barely two weeks when it became apparent that his right hand with two fingers missing, his limited peripheral vision, his hearing half that of others, and bumbling gait made him useless for manual labor. Guards complained his presence was a distraction that reduced inmate effort and discipline. That ruled out the industrial and vocational shops like the stamping plant that made Rhode Island license plates, the auto body shop, the garment shop, and the prison kitchen. Eventually, Aaron was assigned to the library where he kept track of books on loan and shelved returns, and picked up the library's book deliveries and mail. He was industrious and became invaluable to librarians as an eight-fingered typist, later a PC keyboardist, taking on recordkeeping and other tedious duties.

Aaron didn't mind working extra evening hours because it gave him unsupervised time on the librarian's computer. The librarian for the past five years, a sympathetic but basically unmotivated bureaucrat, had transferred many of her functions to Aaron and allowed him to use her computer PIN— strictly against the rules—in order to track orders of books and magazines and to make electronic entries for those received and discarded. Through her indulgence and frequent absences, he became the only inmate in the prison complex with access to its computerized central files system for which security was practically nonexistent. During one of his illicit searches three years earlier, Aaron came upon e-filed parole petitions, parole counselors' recommendations, and parole board minutes and decisions. Aaron mined the data for parole predictions which he gave to Lester Hickman, a sadistic lifer who ran the parole pool in Medium Security. With his goons, Hickman in return provided Aaron with additional protection from inmate harassment.

Beating the system that had taken away any vestige of a normal life gave Aaron a sense of inordinate superiority over other inmates. Sooner or later, he might figure out how to tinker with petitioners' files, manipulating those for a few of the worse abusers and jerks.

Like that protected fat guinea wop, Fat Frankie Gilletto.

<hr>

Fat Frankie entered the library a few minutes after Aaron settled in. A scattering of inmates were in the law book section, scribbling away at notes for their *habeas corpus* petitions which seldom, if ever, were granted. A handful more sat at three heavily scarred, oak reading tables. Fat Frankie didn't see Underwood inside the clerk's cubicle until he placed his return books at the slot in the plexiglass window.

Aaron craned his neck to the right and saw Fat Frankie. A muscle twitched on his good cheek. He associated Fat Frankie with the rank odor of vomit. And from three decades earlier, vomit with Grandma Underwood's corpse. He turned fully in his chair, took off his glasses, and gave Fat Frankie a good view of his ravaged face. To him, Gilletto, too, was repulsive—a short shit, bald as a cue ball, with fat rolls under his chin, fleshy cheeks, a nose like a pumpkin stem, and lips like Mr. Potato Head.

Fat Frankie shoved two books through the slot. Aaron checked each for misuse, entered "returned late" and "pages dirty" on the keyboard, whether they were or not, and turned the computer monitor so it was visible to Fat Frankie. For a reason nobody remembered, library use violations resulted in reduced canteen chits and could get into an inmate's record, a black mark against good time and privileges.

"Fuck you!" Fat Frankie muttered in response. "Too fuckin' late. Won't be long before I'm out of here. I got a record that's a parole board's wet dream while you'll fuck around in here until you croak."

Aaron usually ignored insults, but not from this greaseball who had vomited—*vomited!*—on him. Aaron grabbed Fat Frankie's hand, yanked it through the slot, bent his wrist against the sharp edge of the plexiglass, drawing blood. Stunned, off balance, Fat Frankie gasped, crashed against the cubicle and fell to his knees.

The lone CO on library duty dropped his *Sports Illustrated*, stood, wrestled his black belt over his paunch, pulled out his baton, and approached the cubicle as Fat Frankie gained his feet, clutching his wounded hand in his other. Aaron stood and said, "Asshole shoved books at me and got his hand jammed in the window."

The CO wasn't looking for aggravation, not with the rumored protected Fat Frankie. Nor did he relish the idea of the paperwork that went with an incident report. Instead, he made a show of command by sticking his baton into Fat Frankie's gut. "Back off, Gilletto. Get a Band-Aid at the medical station and get to your cell or I'll write you up. Now!"

Fat Frankie was wide-eyed as were the inmates at the reading desks and in the law book section. Tonight, the word would be out that Fuck Face had Fat Frankie on the floor and got away with it.

"I remember," Fat Frankie managed to blurt out as he was prodded away holding his wrist.

Aaron sat, his anger still seething. Later, he'd search for a way to screw up his prison file. *Get him rejected by the parole board?*

CHAPTER TEN

JAKE AWOKE TO VOICES and noises from Livia's bustling kitchen. He realized where he was and that he should get to his condo to continue with the postdronal phase of a migraine, when headache was replaced by fatigue, nausea and listlessness.

He drove north on Interstate 95, passing highway signs for the Paw Sox stadium, the Slater Mill Historic Site, and the Blackstone Valley National Park, before he swung the Camaro on to the School Street exit and into the maze of one-way streets in Pawtucket's densely packed downtown that left visitors complaining that once entered, you could never leave.

He came to The Slater, the first apartment project built by Jacques Fournier Builders, a one- and two-bedroom lofts conversion of an abandoned textile mill along the Blackstone River, with financing scraped together from personal savings and a loan from the Pawtucket Credit Union. The Slater's success led to the formation of Jacques Fournier Properties and a half dozen more multi-story, brick- and stone-faced condo and apartment complexes by the river. They were designed for commuters—by rail and Interstate 95—to Providence and Boston, and members of the city's vibrant arts community looking for work-live spaces.

He recalled Mia's question during their last tête-à-tête after a parole board session. "Why do you live in Pawtucket?" in the context of, "Why not live on Providence's historic East Side?" He had fumbled for his reasons and listed, "Grew up there . . . my business is there . . . convenience."

He couldn't get the words out to articulate the truth: that his French-Canadian bones were in Pawtucket. After Hope's murder, it was his place of refuge. Dermott, ever the philosopher, had once chided Jake, saying that nostalgia was always about the present. And maybe it was for Jake when pleasant memories were a good substitute for a grim future.

To Jake, Pawtucket still evidenced the clannish, parochial *Pah-tuck-et* of his youth, a working-class, gritty city proudly nicknamed the "Bucket" for its mix of immigrant stocks, the Irish, French-Canadians, Scots, Poles, and Portuguese, with a scattering of Italians and Cape Verdeans. The wave of Latino immigration had yet to come. The city's husbands and fathers were workers who got grime under their fingernails and calluses from their tools and machines, drove nails and trucks and buses, were mailmen, cops and firemen who took the family to church on Sunday, who frequented local taverns and the Narraganset Race Track, while its wives and mothers were the first to work out of the home earning money for amenities and to send their kids to Catholic schools. They were hardworking, hard to please people, and inured to hard times, especially after the textile mills and machine shops closed and Interstate 95 plowed through its downtown, dividing, then destroying, its once vibrant commercial heart. Still, families identified their ethnicities, economic status, and relationships by the boundaries of city's Catholic parishes: the Irish had St. Mary's, Saint Joseph's, Sacred Heart, St. Edward's, and St. Leo's—Dermott's parish; the French Canadians inhabited and worshipped at Sainte Jean Baptist, Our Lady of Consolation, and Sainte Cecile parishes; newish St. Theresa's was mixed.

Jake's Quebecois parents had settled on Grand Avenue in Sainte Cecile's, a neighborhood of small Cape Cods, bungalows and post-World War II ranches, with a few scattered two-families, all built on tiny lots with patches of grass in front and back, asphalt driveways, and safe streets for kids to play on. His father operated a specialty cabinetry and woodworking shop in their garage and basement where young Jake witnessed and admired his father's skills and trade with a growing appreciation for the precision of a jigsaw cut, well-carved or joined pieces, and the knowledge of woods and grains, discovering what would become a life-long satisfaction in crafting useful and beautiful things. His mother was a loving disciplinarian. Jake's beloved Memé, his father's mother who lived with them, was grandmotherly, with her stories of growing up with seven brothers and sisters on a small farm near Trois Riveres on the Saint Laurence River.

His family clung to the emotional ties of their Quebecois heritage, and passed on their insular culture to their only son. They shopped at nearby Bonaventure's Grocery and Tessier's Hardware, Doctor Cormier was their physician, Maurice Tetreault their lawyer and tax preparer, DuPuis Oil delivered heating oil, had savings accounts at Pawtucket Credit Union, then known in the parish as the French Bank for its affiliation with the parish, and Madeline Tremblais from down the street was his mother's best friend. He was taught in Canadian-French by the tireless Soeurs la Sainte Union des Sacrés Coeurs at the nearby parish school. The family spoke Canadian-French at home; on holidays they sang *Frère Jacques* and *Alouette* and *Au Claire de la Lune* around a spinet piano in the parlor. Robert Goulet's baritone was a favorite voice on long-playing records. They enjoyed Memé's *tourtière*—French-Canadian ground pork pie served with green tomato relish—*putine, cretons* and pea soup, and attended musicals and dramatic readings at *Societé Cercle Jacques Cartier* Hall. Every summer the family visited relatives in Quebec, borrowing Uncle Emile's Buick for the trip. Jake's Canadian-French was that of a native, his early American English sometimes a garble of syntax.

It was an existence as uncomplicated as a fried dough treat at Homer's Lunch on Central Avenue. It lasted through high school and a year of junior college—no Laval University in Quebec or Providence College for Jake—before he joined his father full-time in what was re-named Jacques Fournier & Son Carpentry, later to become Jacques Fournier Builders after his parents and Memé passed and Jake became a sole owner of the family business. Jake always said he was born to build. Owning property came later. His hands were large and strong, made for woodworking tools.

In that *metier*, Jake had an attachment to the music and muses of Quebec that blossomed into a deep appreciation of the songs of Robert Charlebois and Natasha St-Pier and traditional *Québécois* fiddle, guitar and accordion music from the *Chansonniers*, with trips to Quebec City and Montreal on his Harley with motorcycle buddies from the neighborhood. Like his parents, he was into *je me souviens*, a Canadian salute to Quebec.

Jake parked the Camaro in the mansion's stable, now a three-bay garage, with a fourth bay dedicated to his woodworking hobby. He climbed the rear stairs, let himself in, flipped on lights, and headed to the condo's bathroom where he stripped and took a hot shower.

He changed into a red flannel shirt with its right sleeve hemmed up, and jeans, thinking he might get through the vestiges of his migraine watching an NHL game. He went into the library, snapped on the switch for the chandelier, and sparkles of light splashed the white board.

He sat and stared at its smudged and blurred lettering, the stark evidence of his failure to find and deal with Hope's murderer. Early on, state police forensics identified the murderer's truck from paint scrapes as a Ford F-150, a model from 2001 to 2005 with a second black paint job with paint commonly used by body shops after 2007. Also discovered was a trace of white paint, possibly from an ornamental stripe, a common accent decoration of the time. The staties said they checked and rechecked auto repair shops for information on a repainted black F-150 with a white stripe, without success, and their investigation eventually cooled. Frustrated by the lack of progress, and in the throes of his booze and opiate dependence, Jake hired Garo Hagopian, a private investigator and friend of Dermott's, who for months thereafter painstakingly traced truck registrations within a fifteen-mile radius of the crime, interviewed their owners, inspected dozens of F-150's, including some with a white stripe detail, but none had been repainted or could be traced to East Providence that night. He had even questioned owners of F-150's not re-registered the following year, in case the killer's truck had been sold or junked. The task was overly ambitious and moved the investigation exactly nowhere.

Garo's diligence did, however, uncover the sustaining context for Jake's search for the killer. In a review of police records for vehicular violations and crimes in nearby Seekonk, Massachusetts, Garo discovered records of a robbery at a convenience store a mile from the scene of the collision and not five minutes before the hit-and-run. The store's inside video camera was broken, the shellshocked Pakistani clerk, now long since moved on, couldn't remember anything after he turned to pull a pack of Marlboros from a dispenser and was slugged from behind. But there was a grainy parking lot video of a pickup, likely a black F-150, peeling off from its parking lot.

The timing of the assault and video was the basis for Jake's conviction that his quarry wasn't like the hit-and-run drivers he encountered at parole hearings—a panicked kid, a drunk or doper, an average person falling asleep at the wheel who didn't have the courage to stop and identify himself or herself. Those were people who Hope, if not Jake, would have forgiven. Hope would have pled, "Jake, it was an accident. Get on with your life!" No, her killer was a bad guy, escaping from the robbery and assault at the convenience store, the only hypothesis Jake could live with, even as he heard Hope say, *"Jake, don't be judge and jury."*

He snapped on the green banker's desk lamp over the desk blotter, and opened a drawer for his checkbook. The account balance was sufficient for Livia's needs because he liked the security of available cash. The stream of income from the sale of his construction company to his employees, largely funded by Jake taking back notes and the sale of apartment buildings he owned and taking back mortgages. There was also the modest rent from Livia's and the proceeds of Hope's life insurance from Hasbro. After he made out the check, he put it in his wallet, smiled in satisfaction of his contribution to Livia's success, turned off the lamp, and closed his eyes.

The day after tomorrow would be the third anniversary of her murder. A reward advertisement would run in all the local newspapers and online news outlets as it had in the past two years. Garo, now an investigator at the public defender's office, would moonlight and monitor leads, and it would be Garo's designated cell phone number, email address, and PO box number in the advertisement.

Jake lay on his bed. He thought of calling Livia for company but didn't. Instead, he prepared himself for the likelihood of no viable response to the advertisement, for failure, again. Dermott, who spent three years in the seminary during his life's odyssey of religion, college, police, and law, once likened Jake's living of life after personal tragedy to the teachings of the ancient Stoics who believed that everyone was fated to particular experiences, and morality consisted of how well you played your part when faced with life's challenges. Failure and tragedy, in Dermott's telling, were the universal human experiences. And a good man can never give up, he would say.

Curious about Dermott's comparison, since Dermott remained more Catholic than the Pope, Jake had read up on Stoics but came away with a different take. Life was like a series of poker hands; you can draw to an ace high full house, ready to collect the pot, and you are beaten by Fate's royal straight flush. If you're lucky, you win a small pot now, and that keeps you moving on and provides an occasional burst of optimism—like Livia's presence in his life. Or, when Jake foolishly, naively, bought into Dermott's arguments that membership on the parole board would be therapeutic, help him come "out of himself," rid him of his self-pity through a focus on the lives of others. He had been blessed by Livia's companionship but unlucky with the parole board. He had realized that he possessed neither the temperament nor the moral stature to judge others. He should be interested in the causes of crime, the fashioning of the right punishment to fit crimes, the effect of incarceration, and the possibility of redemption, but he wasn't. He found it was profoundly ironic, profoundly wrong for Jake Fournier to pursue vengeance on Hope's killer.

He lay without shedding his clothes. He would read, and sleep, after he stopped asking himself where Hope's murderer was that night.

CHAPTER ELEVEN

"NO, I WON'T SEE HIM!" Aaron shouted at his sister Millie when she said she had brought an investigator from the public defender's office to interview him.

They were in a room off the corridor to the visitor's hall that was otherwise reserved for lawyers and their clients. Years before, prison administrators, concerned that one glimpse of Aaron in the visitor's hall would result in screams and fainting, had decreed any of his visits would take place in there, with a CO posted in the corridor outside.

Millie Underwood was not to be dissuaded. She was plump, double-chinned, wide-mouthed and determined, with something in her face that held a resemblance to the half of Aaron's that still functioned. After years of championing her brother's cause, she didn't let his intransigence dissuade her. After ten minutes of contention, Aaron allowed investigator Garo Hagopian to enter the room.

Garo Hagopian, although tall and broad-shouldered, had little resemblance to Aaron's idea of a PI. He looked and dressed more like a burly junior high English teacher. His sports jacket was tent-like, his trousers had multiple pleats, and he wore a starched white shirt with a pinkish tie askew at the collar. His black eyes and a high brooding forehead topped a dark, plain, open face that smiled easily. His blanket of black curly hair seemed at odds with touches of gray.

Dismissively, Aaron, after his quick sideways glance of disapproval, didn't give Garo the courtesy of eye contact. He leaned across the table, putting the ravaged side of his face close to Garo's while taking off his glasses for a full Aaron.

"Mr. Underwood," Garo began, his voice disguising his reaction to his close encounter with Underwood's damaged face, his words becoming a rote description of his professional duties. "Thank you for permitting me to meet with you. As an investigator for the public defender's office, I review cases handled by some of our lawyers, even cases years old, if we become aware of claims as to the quality of legal representation provided by our office. I've been given your file to review. If my review indicates that you may not have been adequately defended by one of our lawyers, I will present my findings to my boss, the public defender. She could approve a further investigation, even the filing of a motion for a new trial. That is her decision alone."

"What's that to me? I'm not going anywhere anytime soon." Aaron's crooked jaw and anger made his words barely intelligible.

Millie admonished her brother. "I've been after the public defender's office for years to review your case. It is finally doing it, and you are being ungrateful. Mr. Hagopian has reviewed the public records and found that maybe you were not given proper advice by your lawyer as to your guilty plea, and that there could have been some evidence that should have been produced that could have aided your defense or mitigated your sentence. He thinks there is a chance—"

"Baby sister," Aaron responded, "how many times have I asked you to leave it alone? Why do you keep it up?" He coughed as he determined to form words that would be understood by a stranger. "This is my life; this is where I'm going to be for the rest of my life. There is no way I am getting out. No new trial, no parole, no way. This is it."

"Aaron," she pleaded, "I need you to do this. I want you to do this. Tell Mr. Hagopian he can go forward."

Garo pulled a sheet of paper from a badly scuffed-up leather valise.

"To begin an investigation, I need you to sign this affidavit and form of release for confidential information from investigatory sources, including the attorney general and state police. My office will enter my name automatically on your visitor list, and I can usually see someone when I need to."

"Sign it," Millie insisted, with more authority in her voice than Aaron ever recollected.

Aaron shrugged. *Should I sign it? For Baby Sister?*

The newspapers and the people of Greenwick had created his image as the horrific, murderous "Greenwick Monster." All wanted to keep him inside, forever, dreading that he might be allowed back in town, spooking everyone. In their hyperbole, children would run screaming to their parents in panic, pregnant women would abort, the town would be forever stigmatized and traumatized. *A motion for a new trial would surely unnerve the bastards,* he had to admit. *Maybe I should also file for a parole, despite the shit that the town would stir up, just to piss 'em off.* He took the pen from Garo without embarrassing himself by putting his good eye inches from the affidavit and signed where indicated.

"Thank you, Aaron," Millie said appreciatively as Garo took back the pen and affidavit and stuffed it into the valise. The lawyer then removed a yellow legal pad and readied his pen. Again, he returned to rote.

"The duty of a defense counsel is to provide a zealous, single focused defense of a client. That includes investigation, preparation, and presentation. Do you have any recollection of consultations with your lawyer relative to an investigation of the facts of your case or trial preparation? I'd also like to know what advice you received from your lawyer as to your guilty plea."

"Are you kidding me?" Aaron started to shout, but a glance at Millie calmed him. "I met him only once, just before the trial. He told me I was guilty, that I killed her and she shot me and I was found next to her body. My fingerprints were on the pry bar that killed her, that I was the only one who could have done it. And, told me I would be on exhibit for days during the trial, like a zoo animal or a freak in the circus." Aaron touched his face with the three fingers of his right hand and leaned into Garo. "I had this. I was embarrassed, humiliated. Where could I go with this?"

Garo feigned being unfazed by Aaron's outburst. "Did you understand from your lawyer that your plea meant a life sentence? Limited chance for parole? By law, your plea had to be arrived at intelligently, voluntarily, and the effect understood."

"I don't remember what he said." Aaron's anger at Garo's probes was now undisguised. "What was important to me was my face. What I wanted was to hide myself from people, to be alone."

"And the judge?" Garo continued. "He was supposed to establish that you understood the plea, knew that your constitutional rights for a jury trial were being waived, that your plea was knowing and voluntary."

"Yeah . . . voluntary?" Aaron replied with overt sarcasm that could not be misunderstood, putting his glasses back on as though to leave. "There ain't anything you can do about it."

"Why did you go to the Gist farm?" Garo asked.

"Don't remember." Aaron's voice dropped off. Disowned by his parents, without visitors until his sister returned to Greenwick ten years ago, his memory of a life before prison was virtually gone, vanished as if written on the Magic Slate he had once been given as a birthday present. When the plastic cover sheet was lifted from the black, waxy tablet, the sheet was clear. Only two vivid memories survived—Grandma Underwood, dead, in the parlor, and a blood red moon that he could have imagined.

"Did you ever go to the Gists' farm before?"

"No."

"Why then? Because it was Halloween?"

Aaron didn't reply.

"Do you have any recollection of going into the house?"

Aaron's frustration burst. "I don't remember anything about that," he shouted, his words as mangled as his memory. What little he remembered was what he had been told after the fact, nothing direct except Grandma's voice and the blood red moon over the barn.

Aaron turned to his sister to avoid the investigator's question. *Fuck him.*

"And did you bring a pry bar?"

He didn't respond, wondering if he should admit his planned prank. He knew he had no animosity against the old lady.

"That might be important," Garo prompted.

Aaron's eye remained fixed at his sister. He pushed back his chair and snapped, "This is all bullshit. I got nuthin' to tell you. Lucretia Gist got murdered, I was found there, everybody said I did and I confessed even though I don't remember doing anything to her."

Garo knew not to press further.

Garo's beat-up Equinox was soon on a busy Interstate 95 heading to the public defender's office on Pine Street in downtown Providence. Clouds that rolled over one another promised nothing good and veiled the city's distant skyline.

Garo felt his breakfast rise in his gut and pulled over into the breakdown lane to recoup as he considered Underwood. *Hideous, angry, and abused for years.* Would he be able to overcome Underwood's negative reaction to him? Could Underwood's memory be refreshed, as Garo had observed in cases of victims of clerical and boarding school abuses? What motive did he have to smash an old lady's skull? Had the state neglected its duty to provide him medical treatment? Was the plastic surgery of the time advanced enough to do him some good? How long would it take to make a case for the public defender? Would she agree to file a new trial petition, and would there be any chance of success?

He came to the same conclusion he had reached during the first few minutes of the interview. Underwood's attitude didn't help his cause. But who could not have empathy for Underwood's ugliness, or be outraged by the apparent injustice at his trial? Somebody had to step up and help this guy.

CHAPTER TWELVE

THE LAW OFFICE of Dermott F. X. McSorely was on the second floor of a converted three-decker in a trash-littered and dog-poop-ridden district of taverns, bodegas, cell phone distributors, liquor stores, and payday loan offices near the statehouse. Cheap office space was coveted by those who needed occupancy near the seat of state government for a quiet chat, a sleepover when necessary, or any liaison convenient for General Assembly members and their staffs.

Jake pulled into a fenced-in parking lot behind the building to find Dermott's two allocated spaces filled by his beat-up, mud-spattered Cadillac Seville and a new black and shiny Lincoln MKZ. Jake backed the Camaro out of the lot and parked in front of a nearby New York System wiener joint. He climbed the steps of the tenement's stoop and followed smudged placards with arrows that directed him past the office of a union lobbyist, up a narrow staircase, and down a hallway to a door with frosted glass lettered with Dermott's name.

The empty and unstaffed waiting area opened into an office filled by a desk stacked with manila files, two straightback chairs and a metal cabinet topped with files so high that adding one more might topple them. Its single window had a view of the statehouse if you craned your neck.

Jake called out, "Someone's Lincoln's in your spot." Dermott's response came from behind the door to a room the size of a broom closet that had a cot for when Dermott didn't make it home to his Pawtucket apartment, which was often.

"Hey, no problem. Belongs to Rico Zompa. On the first floor. Lets me use his secretary when I need to."

Jake slung his jacket off his shoulders to a chair that also supported several weary looking redweld files. One at a time, he grappled them to the floor and sat.

"So, what's up?"

Dermott entered, unshaven, his curly red hair in disarray, his freckled round face pale, his tongue wetting his wide lips, stuffing his rumpled shirt over his belly into baggy trousers.

"Hey, *Fourn-yay*," Dermott said, pronouncing Jake's surname like a Canuck from Sainte Cecile's. "*Comment allez-vous?*"

Jake had seen Dermott drunk and sober and he gauged his friend's condition as hungover. "I gotta hit the can. I'll be right back." Dermott departed for the bathroom down the hall. Jake sat and waited impatiently. Dermott returned, hoisting up his stomach with a tug at his belt.

"Thanks for coming over," he said and collapsed into the desk chair's cracked imitation leather, pushing aside papers as his elbows plopped on the desk's blotter to cradle his chin and jowls. He smiled gamely. "What d'ya call an old, crooked lawyer?"

"What?"

"Your Honor. What does the lawyer name his daughter?"

Jake nodded encouragement.

"Sue. One more. What do you call a cheap circumcision?"

"What?"

"A rip off."

Jake shook his head, wondering if Dermott was warming up to emcee an Irish Club event in downtown Pawtucket, a venue in which he was known to lead choruses of rebel songs and grab a mic to crack politically incorrect ethnic jokes.

"What's up?" Jake asked as his friend blew into a handkerchief.

Instead of an answer, Dermott responded, "You remember the game tonight?" He had tickets for Providence College-Georgetown, the last Big East basketball clash at the Dunkin' Donuts Center.

"Yeah."

"Good." He turned to a coffeemaker to warm what was likely day-old sludge in its carafe.

"I know you don't want any of this," he said as he poured the black liquid into a stained mug. "I still don't know how you can drink that herbal ilk." He turned to the window and squinted. "Hate even to bring it up," he said.

"What?"

"Frankie Gilletto."

"Frankie Gilletto?"

"Yeah. Ran a pawn shop over on Broadway. Serving time for having unregistered guns in pawn."

"So?"

Dermott turned back to face him, folding his fingers in a schoolboy's clasp and leaning in to Jake. "Anyway, his mother is dying and he's coming up for—"

"Don't go there. You promised not to."

"I know, I know." Dermott took a sip of the coffee, grimaced and shook his large head before he leaned back and stared at the crumpled, dimpled ceiling tiles that could have been installed before Jake was born. "But here's the story. I'm in deep. The NFL games, then the Super Bowl last month. Who would have guessed the Pats could lose? Had them and gave up six. And they go down by thirteen?"

"If this is going where I think, I'll forget about it."

"Well, I can't. That's the problem. His cousin is Chris Gilletto. Runs the union local at the pier. The pier operator is my biggest lobby client, so I got to deal with Chris at the statehouse, where he's a power with the Providence delegation. Chris also is very close to my bookie, who is also his bookie, and somehow it comes down to everyone knows I got the Speaker to put you on the parole board, and they figure we're *goombahs* like they are and that family will do what it has to do. So Frankie is coming up and it's a first time so he might not make it, and that would be too bad for him and his mother, who has dementia, by the way. So, Chris asks me to represent Frankie and I tell him that if I did, you gotta recuse yourself if I do. Chris doesn't understand recusal. So anyway, he gets pushy. Says he's got to get his cousin out."

Dermott's hand swiped his eyes and his grin disappeared. "If he got out, that would be good for me, Jake. Very good."

"How much are you in for?"

"If he's got a bad record, no sweat. If he's clean, look it over. Please."

"Did you promise anything to Gilletto?"

"No way, never happened. I told him if I said something, you'd probably bust me in the mouth. Which I hope you don't do, by the way. But if he does get out, I could take some . . . silent credit."

"I can't believe this. I'm going to recuse myself."

"Geezus, don't do that. Whatever you do, don't do that."

"Got to. I don't have to explain why. Every other session, someone does because of some connection."

"He'll figure I screwed up his chance. Listen, Jake, he needs three votes to get out, right? Only two to get him to a second bite of the apple after the governor makes his appointment. Just make it two if he gets another one. If he gets two, consider making it three. Supposedly, he's been an angel inside. That isn't the end of the world, is it?"

Jake's silence signaled rejection. Dermott had a lot of good qualities— at that moment, Jake had trouble remembering what they were—offset by the fact that he drank too much, gambled too much, and gabbed too much.

Dermott didn't give up. "*Mea culpa, mea culpa, mea maxima culpa,* Jake," the former seminarian continued. "I'm sorry, I'm sorry, I am really sorry. But, Jake, I need this."

Jake stood to leave and picked his jacket off the chair. "I can't. You know that. You promised never to ask."

"Geezus, Jake, get off your high horse. This is Dermott who's asking. Don't be a stubborn prick." Dermott's face flushed with embarrassment, resentment, anger and frustration as Jake reached the door.

"See you at Livia's at six, unless the invite is cancelled."

"Don't let the door bang your tight ass on the way out," Dermott murmured, and then shouted as Jake reached the stairs, "At least, think it over?"

CHAPTER THIRTEEN

THE SUN HAD BROKEN through a lumpy gunmetal gray cloud and brightened Rhode Island's multi-domed, white marble statehouse. Jake's Camaro was stopped by a uniformed cop as school buses disgorged middle school students for the obligatory civics class tour. Jake remembered Sainte Cecile nuns chaperoning his own sixth grade class tour through the statehouse's ornate chambers and reception rooms.

Since leaving Dermott's office, Jake had calmed considerably. His best friend was barely surviving in the netherworld of influence peddling, lobbying and *quid pro quo* politics, with a law practice consisting of legal crumbs from cronies in the General Assembly, coupled with his part-time political appointment as a bail commissioner and justice of the peace. His professional life had to be altogether demeaning for someone as intelligent and socially nimble as Dermott, who had gone to law school to be an advocate for the downtrodden, the wrongly accused. Now he had been reduced to begging his best friend to help a Mob fence.

The Camaro was waved on by the cop and was soon across the bridge over the Amtrak rails and the historic Providence and Worcester canal. Jake drove in a haze, still thinking about his best friend's dilemma and plea. It was Dermott who had stayed with Jake during the weeks and months following Hope's murder, when Jake was drowning in self-pity and frustration, and in alcohol quieted by opiates. Booze and opiates

welcomed him again with open arms and he was overly comfortable in
their embrace and had become a drunk and pill-popper, a disruptive,
bothersome nuisance to state investigators' flagging efforts to capture his
wife's killer. One night, almost a year after the date of her death, Jake,
driving erratically on East Avenue in the Oak Hill section of Pawtucket,
was stopped by a cop who, luckily, was a high school classmate of Jake
and Dermott's at St. Raphael Academy. After a field sobriety test, he called
Dermott instead of a backup. The next day, Dermott signed Jake into
residential rehab.

"You would have been a good father confessor," Jake had told Dermott
during his rehab. Later, Jake came across a quote attributed to Muhammed
Ali that got to the innards of their relationship, and had it inscribed on a
piece of faux ivory he gave to Dermott: *Friendship is the hardest thing in
the world to explain. It's not something you learn in school. But if you haven't
learned the meaning of friendship, you haven't learned anything.*"

Jake eased the Camaro into his reserved space at Livia's parking lot.
Two of the kitchen staff were outside on smoke breaks. He replied to their
greetings and went through the kitchen and crowded restaurant and took
a stool at the end of the bar in the taproom. The bartender poured San
Pellegrino into a glass over ice with a slice of lime for Jake as Livia popped
up at his side. Above a long plaid skirt, she wore a white blouse covered
by a red blazer.

On its lapel was a gold and silver Graff pin shaped like an artist's
palette, a gift from Jake. One look at Jake and her dazzling hostess smile
changed to a concerned expression. She hugged him.

"You okay?"

"Fine."

"Did Dermott catch up with you?"

Livia was a mother hen to Dermott, whose tab was rarely totaled.
When it was—and if he had the cash—it was whittled down to what was
available. Livia was sure Dermott never guessed he hadn't paid in full.

"Yeah."

"Is he okay? Seemed kinda twitchy."

"He's fine."

"You're quite the conversationalist."

"Sorry," Jake replied, flashing a wan smile. "After lunch, thought I'd check out the construction plans and schedule. Let the guys know I'll be around. I'll be like your clerk of the works."

He knew that comment would redirect her focus as the addition to the restaurant's space was all-consuming, and she left him for their office to get the plans. *Good!* Sooner or later, she'd remember the anniversary of Hope's death, or read the reward advertisement and become especially affectionate. She was like a nurse in that respect, and sometimes he found her efforts suffocating when all he wanted was to rage.

"Damn," he said aloud, realizing that he was again being critical of someone who was loyal and cared for him.

Livia's luncheon menu always included popular French-Canadian appetizers of crepes, pork meat pies, ragout of the day, and pea soup, all in honor of Jake's heritage. The thick pea soup was his usual when he sat at the bar, he could practically inhale the stock and boiled ham in it. Today, however, he ordered a bowl of Rhode Island "chowda" thick with quahogs, potatoes, onions, tomatoes, and a hearty cumin seasoning, with a side of French fries with vinegar. He was reaching across the bar for the San Pellegrino when he felt a firm grasp on his left shoulder.

"Jakey! Hey, good to see ya."

Jake hated "Jakey."

He forced a grin of hospitality as Joe Twomey, Speaker of the Rhode Island House of Representatives, took the stool beside him. As a sign of historical deference, nobody called him Joe anymore, only *Speaker* or *Mr. Speaker.*

The Speaker's thin-lipped, almost impish smile was in full flower. His blue eyes always seemed to dance with an interest and intensity that made constituents and panderers alike believe they had gained his full and supportive attention. A blue-hued tie, white shirt, and tailored dark blue suit, with three points of a starched handkerchief—like a sail—peeping out of his breast pocket, complemented his Irish good looks. "Funeral at the cathedral," he said in a distinctive tenor.

"Had lunch before heading up to the statehouse, Jakey. Saw you duck in here. Avoiding the customers? Wish I could sometimes. But I can't, not in my game."

His game was being the single most powerful politician in Rhode Island, who had his say on all legislation, vetted all appointments, even those within the authority of the executive branch. It had been the Speaker, at Dermott's request, who saw to it that Jake was appointed by the governor to the parole board, notwithstanding Jake's lack of academic credentials, police background and his recent abuse history. The Speaker stilled a few objections from Progressives and Republicans with Jake's war record, the tragedy of Hope's death, and his rehabilitation. It was a just a little feel-good business by the Speaker for Dermott who was his first cousin and a fellow Pawtucket guy.

At a loss for a mutual conversation subject, Jake asked, lamely, about the legislative session that was about half over.

"Sales tax issues coming up," the Speaker said. "Governance and funding of education again, legalization of marijuana again, gun laws . . . again. Then the budget. Governors get lots of ideas in election year on where to spend money." He paused. "Glad to run into you. Wanted to mention something."

"Shoot."

"When the governor makes his appointment to fill the vacancy on the parole board, I assume it will elect a permanent chair? Any interest?"

"Me?" Jake answered with incredulity. "No."

"You'd be good!" The Speaker was on a riff. "Give some stability to the board since you got two years more in your term and we hear there are some . . . personality challenges among the members?"

Jake shook his head at the offer. "Thanks for the thought, but no thanks."

"What do you think of Mia Sanchez? She's had a partial term and got reappointed last year, has academic credentials, supported the governor in the last election."

"I like her. She'd be an active chair."

"Maybe too opinionated? Doesn't get along?" Before Jake replied, the Speaker squinted. "Any idea how she might vote if Aaron Underwood comes up for parole?"

"No." Which was not the truth.

"That's an issue," he said. "Friday, the House is scheduled to vote on a resolution asking the board to pass on Underwood if he does apply. They don't even want to wait until he applies. No legal standing, of course. But . . . what are ya goin' to do?" He grinned. "The sponsor is my deputy whip. Represents Greenwick. The prospect of the 'Greenwick Monster' on parole is getting his constituents worked up. I won't vote, never do unless something is a squeaker, which this isn't. Puts me in the mix, though. If it passes and the board grants the freak a parole, they'll be a lot of unhappy legislators."

The Speaker flashed his signature smile at Jake. "With Underwood, we got to deal with keeping someone in. Most times, it's about getting someone out."

Jake sipped his San Pellegrino and tensed for the nudge-nudge that he now expected.

"I never pass it on, of course. People think what they want to think." He glanced left, then right, then moved closer to Jake before continuing. "I have a supporter, Chris Gilletto, union guy. Helps keep the Providence delegation in line. Unruly, ill-disciplined bunch. I never know what they'll do. A guy like Chris doesn't understand that politics has no place at the parole board. His cousin Frankie is up for parole. I told him I can't get involved and he gives me a sob story that Frankie's mother is sick and Frankie's kept his nose clean inside for almost three years so he should get out. Chris is all about politics, so he thinks all a parole needs is a push from the right direction." He smiled at the absurdity of politics impacting a parole board decision.

Jake joined with a smile while thinking, *First, he flatters me about being chair, then while insisting that he'd never interfere, even for a close political associate, all the while he's signaling he'd be obliged if Chris Gilletto's cousin was granted parole. And maybe Underwood shouldn't. No wonder he's the Speaker. What a wily son of a bitch!*

Jake slid off his stool, saying he had to review the build-out plans for Livia's additional space. The Speaker said, "A party room is a great idea. I'll be supportive of that. I had my fundraisers for me and for my people in the House, this place is convenient, food always good and Livia is a great hostess."

A sincere comment or more flutter?

The Speaker put out his hand to Jake who responded with his awkward left handshake. "Maybe the chairmanship ends up with the governor's appointee. Wouldn't be my choice," he said ominously as his hand went to Jake's right shoulder, hesitated, and moved to his left. His charm oozed again. "Just think on it. Plenty of time. And," he added softly, "see what you can do about Dermott. Dresses like a homeless guy, and some of his clients—? Sleep with dogs and you pick up ticks."

Jake's eyes followed the Speaker toward the coatroom. If Jake had been irritated by Dermott's approach on Gilletto, he was now angry at the Speaker's orchestration. Just being seen socializing with the Speaker at Livia's or other watering holes, and visits to the Speaker's office during House sessions, kept Dermott in the lobbying business. Any pressure from the Speaker, known never to forget a favor given nor a payback for anyone who crossed him, would be an additional strain on his already compromised best friend.

Livia returned with rolled-up plans under her arm and a tray with a bowl of chowda with oyster crackers.

"What did he want?" she asked. Livia's ex was a former state representative and an intimate of the Speaker, so she didn't trust him, even though she appreciated the patronage of the politicians and lobbyists that the Speaker brought.

"Said I'd make a good parole board chair. Blarney."

"You would, too. "

Jake smiled and reached for his wallet and handed her the check for the contractor.

"Thanks," she said. "We'll open right after Labor Day. I promise you. On time and on budget. I know it will work. And, I am having so much fun!" Her smile was dazzling. She put her arms around Jake, kissing his forehead. "Thanks, partner. We'll do good! I guess I'll see you later. Dermott said you're going to the PC game tonight."

"Yeah," Jake replied, wondering how much of the evening would be spent fending off a renewed approach by Dermott on Gilletto's parole.

CHAPTER FOURTEEN

IF CHRIS GILLETTO HADN'T had very good reasons to visit Medium Security that afternoon, he wouldn't have taken the time. Not with what he had going on at the Providence pier as the business agent for Local 17, Heavy Equipment Operators.

Gilletto drove a pimped-out, union-owned Chrysler 300 to the prison, sucking Tums for his *agata*. All the pains in the ass had been in his office. Sal Gianmalvo started it, complaining about the overtime he paid at Rhode Island Scrap, money that was skimmed for the Local's mob- controlled executive committee. Gianmalvo needed the yard grunts to work to contract and stop screwing off. Chris promised he'd talk to the men. Then, on a tip, or just to be pissy, Customs was all over a shipload of clementines from Morocco, searching for drugs. The owner and shipping agent were going apeshit as the fruit began to spoil, all the while taking up dock space needed for Chinese scrap freighters. To make things worse, Gilletto's bookie had called looking for his vigorish when Chris, losing nightly on spreads on NBA games, had a particularly bad case of the shorts.

The visitors' hall in Medium Security always reminded Chris of the cafeteria at Mount Pleasant High School where he had spent two wasted years on his "career path" to become a wiseguy. The room's floor was polished, had high ceilings, fluorescent fixtures, and was decorated with colorful murals of comic book heroes, famous Americans of all skin colors, Disney characters, and Narragansett Bay lighthouses. Soda and snack vending machines lined the yellow masonry rear wall. A raised platform with a CO's desk faced twenty or so Formica topped tables with attached metal seating. There were no windows. The air was stale and still.

Chris spotted his cousin and was immediately conscious that his height, chiseled features, hazel eyes, aquiline nose and shock of oiled black hair made him elegant by comparison. His clothes distinguished him from the other shabbily dressed visitors at the tables—today, that meant the expensive camel hair overcoat over his arm, a custom-made silk and wool sport jacket from Raphael the Italian tailor on Broadway, and light slacks and handmade loafers. An open collar white shirt revealed a tuft of chest hair and a gold chain.

Fat Frankie, from his assigned seat on the inmate's side of a table close to the CO's desk, watched Chris stride toward him.

"Waz up? How am I doin'?" Fat Frankie asked impatiently.

"Ya don't ask about yer mama?" Chris replied with an argumentative superiority. Since he was there to put a squeeze on his cousin, he sought to quickly establish position. Besides, he was fond of his widowed aunt who lived on Federal Hill next door to his mother, also a widow. As the older and healthier of the sisters-in-law, his aunt cooked for both families, lots of pasta dishes made with Chris' favorite gravy, one reason why he still lived at his mother's, along with it being free and convenient.

"Okay, okay, how's she doin'?"

"So so. Always complainin' about her feet."

"Okay, so I asked. Tell her I'm home soon. Now what about me? What's happenin'? I'm goin' nuts in here!" His bandaged hand went under the table. "So, I gotta know how dis is goin' down."

Chris was slow to respond. Had to be careful. Fat Frankie's reputation on the Hill had soared for being stand up when he refused a deal from the AG to rat out the Brow. He'd taken a trial, and lost. Of course, if he *had* ratted, Fat Frankie would have been laid out in a wooden tuxedo at Nardillo's Funeral Home long ago.

"Depends," said Chris, noncommittal.

"Ya know I'll do right when I'm out," Fat Frankie said.

In addition to paying his cousin for getting him parole, he owed him another ten g's a year for looking out for his mother, and throwing some bucks at friends in the police department.

"I gotta tell ya," Chris replied, frowning, sitting back, his arms across his chest, getting ready for his pitch, "I got a lot invested in you, Frankie. It's gettin' close but I'm not takin' any more chances of gettin' fucked over. I gotta have somethin' in my hands. Now!"

Chris, who had pissed away the up fronts long ago, had been working a scam in promising his cousin a rare first-time parole. Bullshit, of course, but he had it figured that if his cousin did get out, it was payday. If Fat Frankie stayed in, well, Fat Frankie must have somehow screwed up. Chris' plan for today was to scoop whatever he could now so that his bookie didn't send out his collectors.

"I don't like to talk in here," Fat Frankie whispered. "For all I know, this table is wired."

"Yeah?" Chris put his hands beneath the table and fished around, then tapped the table top with his fist. "Look at it. Plastic in a steel frame. Think they got a wire stuck in it? Never happen." Chris' head moved forward. "I'm tired of your bullshit, Frankie. I got to know my interests are being protected. Are you protecting my interests, Frankie?"

"I am. I am." With his parole hearing coming up, he couldn't take any chances with his cousin who was dangerously unreliable and volatile. "I got somethin' for you. Something I put away." Chris leaned into Frankie's whisper. "Something like what I used to wear, ya know?"

Diamonds!

Fat Frankie wore diamonds—on rings, in his earlobes, on watches and bracelets. Half the jewelry stolen, in Providence and right up to Boston, washed through his fence, and he sometimes kept pieces for himself, particularly diamonds that couldn't be traced. Wearing diamonds signaled to his customers two things—he had the wherewithal to buy, and was protected.

"I gotta couple for you that will pop out yer eyeballs," Fat Frankie said. "And a guy in New York that wants them. I'll make the deal as soon as I'm out, and you'll be one happy wop."

That was a mistake. Chris resented the slur, even when it came from another wop. He was proud of his Italo-American heritage, although other than Columbus and Garibaldi, he couldn't name a single national hero. But only a few weeks ago, he'd punched out a Portagee at the docks who told that joke about why flat tires are Italian because—*dago wop, wop, wop.*

Chris inched closer to his cousin's sweaty face. The overheated room, the other visitors in their Salvation Army clothes, the cries of overactive kids at a nearby table, were getting to him. He spread his legs wide and slowly placed both elbows on the table as his forehead furled and mouth tightened.

"Now, Frankie, or I fuckin' ice your deal."

Fat Frankie croaked back, "In the garage. Under the shit hanging in the rear wall, behind a loose board. Four nice ones in a little blue cloth bag. Yours. But just between you and me, okay? I'll buy them back when I'm out. Worth at least four grand. Between us, right? If the Brow thinks somebody got somethin' before him—"

That made sense to Chris. While it wasn't cash, the Brow was always first in line of any payoff and he could hold out until the parole hearing, then pawn the stones if he had to.

"You had better not be shitting me, Frankie."

"Why should I? You're my ticket out of here. Right?"

Chris stood, put his coat over his arm, ready to leave. "Don't fuck up, Frankie. We're this close," he said putting his point finger on his thumb, "but it could go south if you fuck up in here."

Fat Frankie said weakly, "Tell Mama in a couple weeks from now, her *bambino* is coming home."

Chris passed through security and strutted out to the parking lot, smug in his smart move on his cousin; his bases were covered. If Fat

Frankie ever checked, he'd find out Chris had spoken to the pols in the statehouse, including the Speaker and Providence city counselors, asking for support letters to the parole board or a call to anybody with juice. He even gave a push to that Irish dickhead McSorely at the statehouse, figuring if McSorely represented Fat Frankie, his buddy on the parole board might do something for him. But McSorely told him that his buddy couldn't vote if Dermott appeared for Fat Frankie. *A fuckin' recusal, whatever that is.* Still, he had been just short of threatening when he told McSorely that he needed that vote. He'd remind him. Couldn't hurt.

CHAPTER FIFTEEN

A CONCRETE DRIVEWAY SPLIT 40 and 42 Swan Street on Federal Hill—40 being the home of Mrs. Luigi Gilletto, mother of Frankie Gilletto, and 42 the residence of Mrs. Gino Gilletto, Chris Gilletto's mother. A two-stall, masonry block, pitched-roof garage straddled the lot line. Chris parked in front of the stall for 40. He fiddled with the rusted garage handle which didn't budge; the handle at 42 also stuck. "Fuck."

In the kitchen at 42, his mother and aunt sat at the table, anxious for any news from his prison visit.

"Frankie says he'd be home within weeks," Chris reported, which earned him generous hugs. His aunt and his mother fervently believed that it was the *evil one* who brought Frankie—"such a good boy"—his troubles. Almost immediately, the sisters began planning a welcoming event for Frankie's return, with Chris nodding his agreement to their choices of food—"what Frankie likes"—and their admonitions to him to "take care of Frankie." "Sure, sure, don't worry!"

Chris returned to the garage door at 40 Swan with a can of WD-40. He doused its handle and after a half dozen twists, it popped, the door creaked open, and the garage exhaled months of stale air—mixed with fumes from an oil-stained floor, bags of hardened cement and Quick Crete, stacks of paint and solvent cans, and acidic wood rot. Neither

sister had a use for the garage. Chris snapped a switch by the door for
the overhead light which failed to go on. "Shit," he said, and retrieved a
flashlight from the Chrysler's trunk.

A circle of light played on the rear wall where hand tools hung on nails
and racks, and shelves were lined with glass jars and cigar boxes filled with
nails, bolts, screws and miscellaneous junk over a workbench. He pushed
aside sawhorses, ladders and cartons of Elmer's glue, brushes and painter's
tape to better examine the wall. *What did Frankie say exactly? "Behind all
the shit on the rear wall"?* Chris wasn't sure of Frankie's exact words.

So he tossed aside tools and hardware and pulled at a few boards that
were loose. The others were nailed tight. *Nada.* How high could his cousin
reach? Maybe Frankie stepped on something beyond Chris' reach. Then
he realized that his cousin hadn't said which side of the garage. Maybe
it was on 42's side, stuffed with remnants of his father's masonry and
painting business—trowels, plywood sheets, a hand crank cement mixer,
concrete forms of various sizes. He checked and found the boards behind
its workbench were also nailed in tight.

Not here, not there. Is the fat fuck lying? Or did somebody beat him to
it? Chris' frustration increased at the thought of being screwed! "What
da fuck?"

He returned to the house to ask the two widows if anyone had been
in the garage since Frankie left. Had Frankie asked for anything in the
garage? Was anything thrown away?

They answered with questions of their own, like he was a *sciocio*, a
dummy. Nobody had been in there, and so what is there, was there. "Are
you going to clean it up? Are you going to park your car in there?" If he
wanted the garage cleaned up, he should use the "Spanish" people from
the pier, like the ones that took care of snow removal on the driveway
and the sidewalks and mowed the strip of grass in back, and not get his
clothes so dirty.

Chris tried to shake off impatience and failed; he returned to the
garage, found a chisel and a pry bar in the discarded pile of tools, and
started to pull off boards at the rear of the 40 Swan side. Dust and grit

roiled up from between the boards and masonry blocks, blackening his face, his hands and clothes. *Maybe,* he thought, *the stones fell between the boards and the masonry blocks.* To get them, he'd have to tear off the roof, maybe tear down the walls, *maybe the whole fuckin' garage!*

For that, he needed grunts.

CHAPTER SIXTEEN

THE LAST REGULAR SEASON Providence College Big East basketball home game at the Dunkin' Donuts Center, locally known as "the Dunk," would be attended by eleven thousand of the Friar Faithful roaring with each Friar basket or defensive play. Livia's had gained a reputation as the place to eat and drink before and after games, and would be jammed with the boisterous and bumptious.

Dermott was at the two-deep bar in the taproom facing a raft of beer pulls and tiers of gleaming booze bottles, engrossed in a plate of calamari with banana peppers and red sauce. Dermott's plaid sports jacket needed a press, a Friars black and white baseball cap covered his untrainable red hair, his behind overflowed his stool. He spotted Jake in the mirror over the bar. If he harbored any lingering resentment at Jake because of their earlier spat, it was hidden in his greeting.

"Hi ya," he shouted, waving a longneck of Bud Light. "Sit down." Showing crooked bottom teeth, he shrugged to his right. "Scored another ticket and got Garo to leave his computer and come." Garo had become a computer nerd since his divorce.

Garo Hagopian acknowledged Jake with an upraised fork that quickly returned to a plate of *penne bolognaise*.

Jake squeezed onto the stool revealed by their sideways moves and ordered a fried oyster appetizer. The observant bartender quickly served him his usual San Pellegrino while Dermott loudly extolled the Friars' recent play to all within ten feet, between mouthfuls of calamari. When Jake's oysters arrived, Dermott, still in his spiel, speared two before Jake could pick up a fork. Jake placed his left hand next to his plate to protect his meal.

To their faces, Jake referred to overweight Dermott and the wide-girthed Garo as the "tons of fun." As Jake heard it from Dermott, Garo, a few years older than Dermott, had stayed in a Staties uniform long enough to attend night law school at Roger Williams University—where the two met—at the expense of taxpayers, as did Dermott, then a Pawtucket cop. After a bout of testicular cancer and a failed marriage, Garo didn't have the energy for the solo criminal law practice he had envisioned. Instead, he got a PI license and joined the public defender's office as investigator. According to McDermott, Garo picked up the reputation of being "St. Jude, the Patron of Lost Causes." Jake thought that was appropriate; Garo continued, on retainer, to investigate the cold case of the hit-and-run murder of Hope Fournier.

"Gotta go," Dermott announced over the bar chatter in the Pawtucket accent of missing r's and last syllables. He blotted his chin with a paper napkin, and as he slid off his stool, he scanned the crowd for anyone he had missed greeting. Jake stood to leave, but Dermott touched his shoulder and laughed.

"Jake, like I gotta go. Not you gotta go. Hey, how'd the Irish jig get started? Too much ta drink and never enough pots ta piss in." He disappeared towards the restrooms, shaking hands along the way.

Jake indicated to the bartender that the tabs were on the house, and upon Dermott's return he and Garo murmured thanks. The three retrieved their jackets from the coatroom and stopped at the reception podium to say goodbye to Livia. Jake gave Livia a kiss and said he'd see her tomorrow.

Inside the cavernous arena, Jake was not surprised that their seats were three rows behind the Friars' bench, it being a point of pride for Dermott to be prominently seen at every important sporting event in Providence. To which he never, ever bought a ticket.

"Who gave them to you?" Jake asked over the crescendo of Jumbotron blasts as the Friars took the court.

"Hey, a payback. Guy I helped out had to go to Florida because his mother took sick—and here we are." He kissed a ticket stub. "Thanks, Mom," he laughed. Garo and Jake raised their eyebrows at each other as they stood for a flag-toting ROTC color guard and the national anthem. The Friars were quickly up by ten and held the lead 'til halftime; Jake enjoyed the game while Garo didn't evince much enthusiasm. Dermott left them for schmoozing and beers as a halftime show of a CYO pre-teen scrimmage was announced. Jake was surprised when Garo shifted his bulk toward him and said, "Not to mix business and pleasure, but you got Aaron Underwood maybe coming up."

"So I hear."

"He was in for ten years when he was first eligible—he was twenty-six—and there was such a stink that the General Assembly made it twenty-five years inside for anyone serving a life sentence before being eligible to petition. So, after twenty-six years inside, he had his first hearing and didn't make it, then a year later and again the following year—both denied. So if he tries again, it would be his fourth attempt."

Jake considered parole petitions to be confidential. Dermott had complained that Jake was as closed-mouthed as a quahog when it came to parole board business.

"Why are you interested in Underwood?" Jake asked.

"Underwood's defense attorney was from the list of part-time public defenders they used back then, a WASPy white shoe, later disbarred for more than once showing up drunk in Superior Court. Back then, half the lawyers on the list were guys like him—no practices, living off the state's tit, representing deadbeats in open-and-shut cases where they would get a thousand or two just for showing up. They used to say 'Cop a plea and collect your fee.'"

"And you're telling me this why?"

"Our office is reviewing cases this guy handled. Underwood's file ended up with me. After I read the trial summary, I got interested."

"We don't get into trials. Not our job."

Garo ignored the hint. "Here's the thing. It was a shambles. Lots of public anger in Greenwick over a vicious murder of an old lady. Judge Glancy was over the hill, prosecutor rushed the case, and Underwood's lawyer appears to have engineered his guilty plea, probably so he wouldn't have to spend time to investigate or prepare a defense. With half his face shot away, you can imagine the pressure on Underwood, at sixteen, with everyone telling him he killed the old lady. Told me all he wanted to do was hide from the world. Since then, never admitted he did it. Never!"

Jake feigned interest in the kids on the court and groaned when one launched a three-pointer that rimmed out.

"I met with him and his sister this morning. If you saw his face you'd understand why he pled out. Its hideous and scarred and puckered up like a prune . . . or like it had been in cold water for a day. Since he's not escape bait—where could a face like that go?—he's become the trustee of trustees with all sorts of privileges. Works in the library and the librarian and COs let him roam around admin and the cellblocks in Medium, picking up books, delivering . . . what have you."

Dermott, his Friars' cap now askew, rejoined them exhaling beer, with one in his fist. "Gonna take 'em by ten at least," he bellowed to no one in particular.

"At least," replied a Friars fan in the next row.

"Twenty!" yelled another.

Jake tried to put the subject of Underwood to bed. "Maybe Underwood's better off inside. Seems like he's got a life—"

"Underwood?" Dermott perked up and squeezed around Jake to ask Garo. "Is he coming up again? Are you involved? No way he's going anywhere. Not the Greenwick Monster."

Garo's response was interrupted as Dermott and the other fans got to their feet for the opening play of the second half. Behind Dermott's back, Garo leaned into Jake. "I think I can make a convincing case for a motion for a new trial. Up to the PD of course."

Dermott overheard Garo. "Jesus, Mary and Joseph," Dermott said. "Why get into it? Hide the poor bastard away. Please!"

CHAPTER SEVENTEEN

JAKE LEFT LIVIA'S POSTGAME euphoria before eleven; Dermott remained with two drinking buddies who were state representatives, muttering to Jake, "*Veni, vidi, velcro.* I came, I saw, I gotta stick around."

Jake drove to Pawtucket, listening to a CD of the French Canadian group *Les Bon Hommes de Nord,* driving under the speed limit because he knew his concentration was lacking. Just being with Garo, not even talking about tomorrow's reward advertisement, brought back memories of Hope.

Would she be with him tonight? Even when Livia shared his bed, Hope would sometimes lie with him. He'd feel her presence and sense her perfume, experience her slim, curving body wrapped around his, her breath and hands on him, her mouth exploring his. He would twist and turn with desire.

Jake couldn't sleep. If he was true to her memory, to his own concept of justice, he had to stoke the fire of his vengeance on the anniversary of her death. He had to remember her in life and relive her tragedy in death.

Hope Jameson came into Jake's life when Jake's construction business, post-Iraq, was thriving but his social life was not. That changed one morning at Gold's Gym when a newcomer walked onto an adjacent treadmill, an attractive brunette, ears plugged by the white ear buds of an i-Pod, hair in a ponytail that called attention to her high cheekbones, full breasts and a tight behind. They smiled at one another each morning for a week, gradually getting into conversation, leading to a coffee at nearby Seven Stars Bakery in Hope Artiste Village.

Across the table, Jake had felt the impact of her greenish-blue eyes, gleaming teeth, and skin that seemed so pale it was almost translucent. She was employed as an intellectual property lawyer at Hasbro, the toy company with its corporate offices in Pawtucket. Her conversation was animated, occasionally cocking an eye at something he said before her full-lipped smile that made Jake smile as well.

He was immediately comfortable with her, before long joking with her, offering an exaggerated quirky syntax of a "Canuck," the French Canadian idiom he had grown up with, transposing a noun and an object or phrase within a sentence, as in "Throw me down the stairs, my hat," or "The next time you cut through my yard, go around," or slipping a verb into a noun as in, "Let's give Father Girard the clap." She laughed and that made him happy.

After three coffee dates, Jake got up the nerve to ask her to dinner. In another week, he was invited to dinner at her apartment on Wayland Square in Providence; they brushed friendly good night kisses and it went no further.

Jake's love life was then nonexistent. He hadn't dated because of his uncertain voice, and an imagined physical awkwardness in lovemaking overwhelmed his needs. That was, until one night after dinner with a lot of wine at her apartment, they kissed awkwardly on a sofa like teenagers, then passionately, each exploring the other's face, and moments later, she unbuttoned his shirt and didn't flinch at his stump. In fact, she kissed it. That single act released the shame and tension that gnawed at him since the moment he realized he was no longer a complete piece. That night, they became lovers.

In the days that followed, his passion for Hope had no bounds. He dreamed about her between dates, what they would do for each other's pleasure. He couldn't wait to have his hand on her smooth body; she reciprocated with a passion that startled Jake, and maybe herself. The image of her naked body after lovemaking—glistening with a musky perspiration, when he would tell her how beautiful she was and she'd smile back at him—swept away any vestige of hesitation.

They married six months later, had a honeymoon at the Chateau Frontenac in Quebec City, and purchased five acres in Seekonk with a farmhouse and barn Jake thought he would, one day, convert into his office. Renovations to the house accelerated with her pregnancy. Because a kid needed a father with two arms, two hands, Jake even researched prosthesis. New devices were myoelectric, battery-powered, converting electric signals of muscles above the stump into movements of the prosthetic that was intuitive, natural-looking, and reactive.

On a rainy Thursday night during her seventh month of pregnancy, they met for dinner at the Waterman Grille by the Seekonk River in Providence. She'd had a checkup with her obstetrician that afternoon, brought copies of the sonogram to show Jake their soon-to-be born son, and was enthusiastic about a baby shower planned by friends at Hasbro. Jake also had good news; he had overcome financing issues for a planned rehab of the rundown Governor Foley Mansion, a porticoed, late nineteenth century three-story residence on Park Place, the "quality's" enclave in the old downtown of Pawtucket. He planned three spacious upscale condo units.

In addition to the project being lucrative, he imagined its renovation would energize other projects in the downtown of the city. *A good day*, he thought and over coffee, Jake held her hand. He remembered it as dry and soft, and he thought that they would make love later, maybe for the last time before the birth.

The next half hour had a clarity that never diminished. He had followed Hope's red Mini Cooper—into which she now barely fit—in his Chevy Silverado four-by-four truck to the Henderson Bridge over the Seekonk River into East Providence, the shortcut to Seekonk. It was cold and drizzling, he had the defroster on high, the road was a shiny slickness, oily where potholes had been recently filled. He was maybe two car lengths behind her when the blinding lights of an oncoming pickup sideswiped the Mini, sending it twisting out of control, and with a thunderous crash, it crumpled around a utility pole.

Jake slammed on the brakes, ran to her rescue, conscious of the Mini's crushed front end, shattered windshield, and the rippled sheet metal over its compacted frame, the dying engine's hisses and grindings, the cascading sparks from electrical wires tumbling onto the Mini's roof, the deployed airbag. The driver side door handle wouldn't budge. He screamed as he pounded at the window and looked for signs of movement from under the white plastic of the air bag, then he kicked in the window on the locked passenger door, vaguely conscious of the smell of gasoline. He snapped shards of glass as sharp as shark's teeth out of the window, the glass cutting deeply into his fingers, to open the door and boost himself inside where he pushed at the inflated air bag until he heard someone behind him, then felt hands grappling his chest, pulling him out of the Mini seconds before the car was lifted into the air in a flash of fire.

He was treated at City Hospital in Providence, the regional trauma center, for his cuts and broken fingers, burns on his hand and arm, and a concussion. "What about Hope?" he had asked, over and over, coming in and out of consciousness. Hours later, he was told that she was dead.

<hr/>

Jake thrashed on his bed, his need for resolution intense. Vengeance was a bottomless pit. He knew evil would come of it even when he raged, but long ago, had crossed that bridge. Not something the Stoics would approve.

CHAPTER EIGHTEEN

REWARD: $100,000 FOR INFORMATION LEADING TO THE ARREST AND CONVICTION OF THE HIT-AND-RUN DRIVER WHO KILLED HOPE FOURNIER.

The proof of the advertisement in the online *Journal* had an ominous black border. Above Hope's photograph, huge black type summarized the hit-and-run without the gory details, and included the reward website, a P.O. box address, and Garo's cell phone number soliciting any tip, suspicion or inquiry that would be dutifully vetted for any trace of legitimacy.

Online, it was less eye-grabbing than it would be in the broadsheet *Journal* that Jake would read at the Vet Center after a planned bruising workout at the Y on Union Street. He walked around the corner to Operation Safe Return on Main Street. It was too early for most vets to arrive, so Jake didn't expect company at its Starbucks-like coffee, tea, and water bar and newspaper rack. Jake took the *Journal* from the rack, and sat at a table by the window. He always felt clumsy turning newspaper pages with his left hand while pressing others with his stump, so he usually avoided page-by-page reading in public. But this morning, the need was there to experience the impact of the ominous reward advertisement.

"I saw the reward advertisement," Paulie Caprio said, looking over Jake's shoulder.

Jake looked up. Paulie, in jeans and a New England Patriots sweatshirt, his round face screwed up in an attempt to show sympathy, was a veteran of the Afghan war. He had returned with an opiate habit that led him into drug distribution and a year in Minimum Security, and was on parole granted at the meeting before Jake became a board member. In recent weeks, he had attached himself to Jake like a mussel to a shoreline rock. Jake didn't mind; he respected Paulie's efforts at sobriety, taking his meds so as not to experience anything close to a bipolar event, his willingness to find a job and get on with life.

"Your wife was beautiful, man," said Paulie. "I'm sorry for her and for you."

Jake closed the newspaper. "How's the job going?" Through Livia's efforts, Paulie was employed in the kitchen at Victor's, an Italo-American neighborhood restaurant on Mineral Spring Avenue in North Providence.

"Okay. Helps I'm Italo and got family up there."

Paulie got to what he was excited to talk about. "Hey, I hear the Greenwick Monster—Aaron Underwood—is coming up for parole. Wait until ya see him! Most God-awful thing ya can imagine because it is real! Worse than Freddie and the Chainsaw stuff. Nothing works on one side, where it's all scars, while the other is almost okay, except always in a grin. A walking nightmare. Scared the living shit out of me first time I seen him."

"Then I pity the poor bastard," Jake replied without thought, and returned the newspaper to the rack.

Paulie's brown eyes gave off a nervous intensity; a broken front tooth caused a slight whistle in his words. "He's got this way of sneaking up on ya," Paulie said, following Jake. "Ya know what I mean? One moment he ain't there and the next he is, never talkin', just lookin' at ya from the one eye in the part of his face that ain't chewed up. A wonder somebody hasn't iced him."

Jake shrugged off the description.

"Is that woman professor still on the board?" Paulie pitched his voice lower as though he was about to reveal a confidence. "Well, she's gonna faint away with this guy." He shivered, whether from recollection or to be dramatic, Jake couldn't tell. "Better get her prepared. Maybe for her they should put a bag over his head when he comes in. And this guy, where can he get a job? Can't make a livin' scaring people, right? They don't have freak shows any more. Or go out? Can't take him to the market or a movie. No mother is going to want him seen by her kid."

"Paulie—"

"Maybe some sort of horror or sci-fi or video porno gig?"

Jake turned away. "You want to walk?"

"Nah, got to stay here for the morning preach." That was a session with the center's psychologist known by all the vets as The Preacher. "And I said I'd help with the prep for the lunch, some pasta casserole they want to try. But let me tell ya, when Underwood sits in that chair and gives you that half a face—"

CHAPTER NINETEEN

AT ABOUT THE SAME MOMENT, Aaron Underwood was placing returned books on shelves in the prison library. Each one taken from the book carrel with his good hand was carefully pushed into place, symmetrically lined up, spine facing out, alphabetically by author's last name. He was behind schedule, having met earlier with the public defender's investigator in the lawyer's room. He remained perplexed by the investigator's restless standing, sitting, standing again, hands in and out of his beat-up valise at the end of the table, while asking questions about Aaron's public defender lawyer's performance and his guilty plea. In an hour he was scheduled for the mandatory pre-parole petition conference with a parole counselor when he would decide whether to apply for parole.

The prior night, while his jerk cellmate was in the gym, Aaron had read aloud familiar Frost poems. The poetry soothed him with its rustic images of country life, the earthy smells, colors and seasons, enough so that he began reconsidering the positives of a life on the farm, a home, with Millie. Frost's lines remained with him as he pushed the book carrel to his cubicle:

"Home is the place where, when you have to go there, They have to take you in."

His home, where he would be taken in, would likely be limited to the farm. Still, he considered that if he had a mind to, he could raise chickens as he did as a kid, have a pet, read anything he wanted, have a computer of his own, watch all the porno he wanted to, wank off when he needed to, and most importantly, he'd have privacy—no asshole cellmates, daily counts, clanging steel doors, shrill voices and screams in the middle of the night, and the mind-numbing regimentation that had been at the core of his existence for almost thirty years. At some point, the geographic restrictions would be lifted and he would walk down Greenwick's Main Street, frequent its stores and public buildings, scaring the shit out of the liars and hypocrites who'd left him to rot inside. His sweet revenge.

And there was something else to weigh. In addition to Millie's entreaties, his online examine of recent parole board decisions gave him a glimmer of hope that the new woman member, Mia Sanchez, would be empathetic. As to Fournier, the newest member, his record was insufficient to evaluate.

Still, any "yes" votes would be a victory of sorts. Despite the daunting prospect, maybe it was worth a shot. He'd play it cool and evaluate what the counselor might say.

<hr />

Aaron and his accompanying CO arrived at the parole counselors' offices. He was waved inside a tiny, goldfish-bowl office with Plexiglass dividers at eye level; the CO remained seated outside. Aaron was surprised and dismayed that his assigned counselor was Nelson Lansing, the same one as the prior year, the author of a parole report that described him as "aggressively passive," "resentful" of prior parole board prior rejections of his petitions. The counselor also reported Underwood's animosity for the residents of Greenwick whom he had called "liars" and "enemies" in his interview. That had earned him a "no" recommendation. Aaron resolved not to hit the same hot buttons this time.

He sat across from the parole counselor and sensed that Lansing masked his unease in being in Aaron's presence with officiousness and a quick recitation of the points required to be made to inmates regarding parole petitions and procedures.

Aaron listened patiently, removed his glasses, and said in response, "I didn't give you a story last time I was up for parole—like 'I'm sorry,' 'I found religion,' or 'I took a course.' I didn't mess around, and the same is true now."

"With your record, if you'd showed some remorse . . ." The counselor fingered the keys of his laptop. Aaron wondered if he already inputting a "no.""Remorse?" Through his deformed lips Aaron forced a snicker that came out like a horse whinny. He cocked his head to stare at his clasped fingers in his lap. He knew where he should be headed: *Be sorry for the victim. Admit you did the crime. Keep your temper. Above all, be nice and respectful. All that bullshit!*

"I wish she had not been murdered," he said, "like I wish I had not been born. You should put in your report that there's a better chance of me never comin' back here than ninety-nine point nine of these guys. If I had the other half of my face, I'd already be out of here by now."

Lansing turned away, seemingly letting down his guard for a moment, *maybe*, thought Aaron, *recognizing the truth to his plea?*

Encouraged, Aaron thrust his broken face at the counselor. His voice cracked with emotion as he choked out, "Am I a menace? Will I break the law? That's what they should decide. My record has been clean for almost thirty years. Instead, it's all about my face. Last time, and I meant it, I told them I'd wear a mask and keep a leg locator on, whatever. Got nowhere. One member even said I was insulting them. Look, I'll abide by any restrictions," he said, and thinking that he had to retain a sliver of integrity, "but I will not say I'm sorry I killed her, because I don't remember that I did."

The counselor reverted to self-importance as he pushed aside his laptop. "If you got parole, you'd have to live on a disability check from SSI. Not sure how much that will be."

Aaron wondered why in only one year the counselor had forgotten his sister's wealth. "Millie has enough for both of us. Owns the farm free and clear. Made a pot of money when she sold twenty acres where they built that casino over by the highway. Got to go there sometime." Aaron knew a parolee is restricted from visiting casinos.

That engendered dismissively raised eyebrows. "So you're going forward with a petition?"

Aaron hesitated. "Yeah," as his deformed hand picked up his glasses and put them in place. His voice lowered in deference. "Look, you seem to be a decent person. Show them there is an honest, decent guy in the system, somebody with a conscience, who knows that I am ready to get out, that I won't be a problem."

To Aaron, the counselor appeared momentarily conflicted, perhaps pleased by the unexpected compliment and Aaron's changed attitude. Then abruptly, the counselor closed his laptop. "That's all," he said and called the waiting CO, leaving Aaron crestfallen, believing that the son of a bitch would be a "no" again.

The counselor tossed an empty coffee cup into a basket behind his desk and fought off an urge to go through the rigmarole of security doors and security checks, to the designated area outside for a cigarette. He loosened his tie, put his elbows on his desk, his fingers supporting his chin. It would be easy, safe, and not unexpected for him to again check "no" in the recommendation box on the parole decision form. The only letters of support in Underwood's file were from the prison librarian and Underwood's sister, against a bunch from Greenwick. Then, he had the unexpected thought of giving Underwood a favorable or neutral recommendation, based on his clean record and the interview in which Underwood didn't display anger.

He evaluated his personal risks, if he should make such a recommendation. A move like that would be controversial, and attention would be focused on the honest, decent guy in the system who had only two years to go to be pension-eligible. *Why risk it?* No, the Greenwick Monster would be getting a "no," but he might say something positive in his write-up. Meanwhile, he had to get though the day writing up three more parole reports and conducting two more interviews. The last interview was with a fence, Francisco Gilletto, a first-timer, no lawyer listed for him, coming up for hearing next week.

This first timer, not represented by a lawyer, wouldn't take that long.

CHAPTER TWENTY

AT PRECISELY ELEVEN THAT MORNING, *Aaron's Anguish* was posted on YouTube from off a dark web virtual private computer network that made its source untraceable.

Amateurish and not always in focus, the video lasted all of forty-five seconds, a full color shot of Aaron Underwood's face shown in a shaky pan from its permanently grinning half to its mass of scar tissue. His shattered mouth and lips were barely moving, as though muttering; his one eye engaged with something above the camera. Below his hideousness, a text crawl declared that Aaron Underwood had been hidden away in a Rhode Island prison for almost three decades and would remain there, uncared for, for the rest of his life unless the public demanded his parole or pardon. Viewers were implored to contact the governor and prison officials, and flood their websites with messages of concern, and join the fight to free Aaron Underwood.

Within minutes, the video had gotten through content moderators at social media platforms and began to rack up hits and furious posts on FaceBook, Snap Chat and Instagram. *Aaron's Anguish*, a portrait of a life lived in grotesqueness, quickly became the day's hot social media imperative.

When the prison's website crashed and the governor's office was deluged by vitriolic messages demanding Underwood's parole, an assistant warden and a captain from the prison's Security Investigation Unit were dispatched to the library where they took Aaron into the vacant office and showed him the video on a laptop.

Aaron's anger was palpable; his hands shook in rage. He hadn't bothered to read the message stream when he croaked, "You can't let that be shown. I never allowed that. It's a breach of my privacy!"

They explained it was already out on the internet.

"You're trying to kill my parole, create hysteria against me," Aaron shouted in a raspy screech. He managed to get to his feet, his hands before him, pleading in a barely understandable voice, "Just leave me alone."

Tears welled as he was hustled away to a detention cell in the Special Management Unit of the prison.

Stuart Bertozzi was enjoying a cup of homemade minestrone after spending the morning at the Exeter Golf Course with his retired teacher cronies when he received a call from the warden of Medium Security. After he hung up, angry and frustrated, Bertozzi, along with his wife, watched the video. She was horrified and he became livid. His above-the-fray position on an Underwood petition had been undermined by the incompetence of the prison staff in allowing the video to be recorded and aired.

Bertozzi telephoned Mrs. Ames to prepare a statement from the board, just in case, to the effect that "Underwood would be treated like every other petitioner, and the board would proceed with justice and fairness, as it did with every petitioner. He emailed the other board members with the URL to the video, reminding them that they should refer press inquiries to him as acting chair, through Mrs. Ames. Then, pending further input from the warden, he decided to take advantage of the sunshine to prune dead shoots from the rose bushes along his backyard's fences. Upset by the video, he worked with vigor.

In the woodworking bay in his garage, Jake was fine sanding a jewelry box for Livia. Joinery of different woods in delicate patterns and detailed marquetry in veneers gave him a sense of accomplishment that, since Hope's death, no other pastime could bring.

Garo called and alerted Jake to the phenomenon of *Aaron's Anguish*. Jake watched the video on his phone, was disturbed by Underwood's ruined face, as rutted and destroyed as those he remembered from the burn ward at Walter Reed. He went indoors to his laptop where he viewed it again and read several online, passionate posts the video elicited, but found himself singularly unmoved. The video, he thought, was a brazen attempt by Underwood, or someone on his behalf, to pressure the parole board. How was it that a self-confessed murderer merited such public support, while disfigured heroes of Iraq and Afghanistan, who would never play up their ghastly injuries, were forgotten by an ungrateful nation?

Jake's sense of injustice became primal. As far as he was concerned, Underwood's petition should be considered on his record in prison, along with the viciousness of his crime, and the likelihood of a repeat. He became determined that social media emotions would not influence his vote.

CHAPTER TWENTY-ONE

TWO LATINO DAY LABORERS from the pier had been at the Gilletto homes on Swan Street since early morning with a truckful of tools, followed soon after by a dumpster, delivered compliments of his buddies in the Providence Public Works Department.

To the grunt who understood English, Chris Gilletto said, "You guys clean out the garage and pull down all the boards inside the rear of the garage, and if you see anything that looks like it shouldn't be there, maybe a cloth bag for instance, you give it to me."

To his mother and aunt, he had lied with his explanation that rats had eaten through the garage masonry, might be between the boards and the walls.

"Rats!" they'd exclaimed, hands flailing in front of his face. "We never had rats. Must be those new people," referring to the families from Guatemala living in a block of crowded tenements on the other side of the fence, the same houses where Gillettos had lived two generations earlier.

The grunts quickly peeled off the boards and found nothing as described, leaving Chris to swear a blue streak as he combed through the debris before it was tossed into the dumpster.

Chris ordered the grunts to remove the garage roof. The sisters-in-law, wrapped in coats and shawls, watched the tear-down efforts with avid interest from the small backyard porch at 40 Swan, swapping stories about when Luigi and Gino built the garage, their partnership in good and bad times.

Nada! But Chris wouldn't stop. The grunts took sledges to the masonry walls which crumbled easily. Dust choked the yard and Chris checked every piece of board and chunk of masonry, to no avail. Then when he was, just about to give up, he spotted a dirty purplish cloth bag in the debris, its closing strings knotted tight. With great expectation, he took the bag into the Chrysler, unknotted the strings, and poured four multifaceted stones into his palm.

Each was as big as his pinkie's fingernail and they sparkled brilliantly in the sun. He smiled, put them back in the bag, brought it upstairs to his bedroom closet, and put it inside of a shoe. He came downstairs and hugged his mama and his aunt.

The garage demolition caught the attention of neighbors, and when the Gilletto sisters-in-law walked to Scalia's Market on Atwells Avenue for some odds and ends of groceries and neighborhood gossip, they were accosted by nosy friends who compared notes, argued points, and concluded that Chris was going to build a new garage to welcome his cousin home. The sisters confirmed their neighbors' intuitions. *Why mention rats?*

"My Chris, what a good, generous boy," said his mother proudly.

CHAPTER TWENTY-TWO

BY LATE AFTERNOON *Aaron's Anguish* had gone viral. The principal suspects in the warden's investigation of how the video had been made, and by whom, had been questioned and results evaluated.

Millie Underwood denied involvement and was clearly surprised and angry when shown *Aaron's Anguish* on a laptop brought by uniformed Staties sent to the Underwood farm. She protested to the point of pounding on a Statie's chest with her fists.

"You people are bent on keeping him in prison. Why can't you leave him alone!" They reported back by phone that she appeared clueless about the video, or social media in general, and didn't own a cell phone or a computer.

As for the prison librarian, she had been out for almost three weeks with lower back pain. When the Staties visited her home in nearby Warwick, she had already seen the video and answered their probing questions in a fury.

"Are you suggesting I had something to do with it? How dare you! Of course not! And I can't believe Aaron knew anything about it. He's very private. Doesn't raise his head unless he has to." She continued to give the investigators an earful about injustice, topping it off by saying she was coming back the next day to make sure Underwood was not ill-treated by an angry administration.

The COs who had monitored Millie Underwood's visits were interrogated by the SIU, but their union steward promptly filed a grievance that halted questioning. "C'mon, why would a CO do it in any event?" the steward complained, as he alleged harassment. "To what advantage? Take the chance of losing your job? For Underwood?"

If not for his sister and the librarian and the visit-monitoring COs, all bets were off. Security's computerized visitors' log was checked for all visitors. Other than Millie Underwood, no one else was listed, leaving the investigators to conclude it could have been any CO among the two hundred working in Medium Security who had used a prohibited cell phone.

The warden released a statement after some prodding by his staff, and the governor's office maintained that Underwood, under a life sentence for a gruesome murder, had been well-treated during incarceration, was eligible for parole, again, after being denied three times, and that the parole board—not prison authorities—would determine his fate. That prompted an angry Bertozzi to release his statement for the parole board. Both were promptly and predictably lambasted on social media message boards, and on a quickly created "Free Aaron" website where supporters were enlisted in "Aaron's Army." The website had the promotional sense to adopt the *Phantom of the Opera*'s mask as its unofficial logo and the hashtag #Free.Aaron. Its self-proclaimed leadership urged the socially conscious to flood the phone lines and email addresses of Rhode Island politicians, and solicited volunteers for rallies at the statehouse and a vigil at the prison. The Free Aaron movement seemed gratuitous and unorganized, but it was soon mobilized. And it was angry.

—————————

Mrs. Bertozzi noticed a television transmission truck parking in front of her home. Concerned, she ran outside where her husband was putting away his pruning shears in a garden shed. Miffed by the intrusion, he walked around to the front of his house as a Channel 8 female reporter and videographer, already shooting, approached him on his driveway. Grim faced, not realizing that he gripped the handles of the shears as though threatening to snip off a head or arm, Bertozzi responded to the reporter's first question with a shout of, "Get off my property!" as he snapped the shears closed. Much to his embarrassment and anger, the video of the confrontation was shown on the six o'clock news and was later posted on the Free Aaron site with unfavorable comments.

While controversy roiled around his imprisonment and disfigurement, the principal character in the Aaron's Anguish drama languished in his detention cell, mortified that his face had been captured for viewing by those outside of his narrow prison life. He was unaware that his freedom had become the focal point of a campaign supported by a legion of sympathetic viewers. All he knew was that he was in lockdown because some prick, a CO he thought, secretly put a cell phone camera on him.

CHAPTER TWENTY-THREE

"FUCKIN' RICKY."

Sal Gianmalvo sneezed. His huge nose was a vacuum for the trailer's lint, grit and dust. He caught another sneeze halfway through, snorted instead, and slammed the morning's *Journal,* folded to the reward advertisement, on his desk, scattering cigar ashes. He was sure Ricky got his dumb from his old man, a small-time sniff-ass who slapped Rose around, beat up the kid one too many times, and even killed the kid's dog out of spite. He had been iced years ago after he gave the Brow some shit.

Sal opened a box of Montecristo's, snipped off the tip of a seven-inch Churchill, and fired it up. He took in a lungful, coughed, and blew out a cloud of smoke. Ricky was damaged goods, always a problem for Rose—fights at school, training school after an assault, small time muscle shit—but he was family, and Rose had nagged Sal to do for Ricky about the time the Dragos came along with their proposition to the Brow to dispose of "baggage." Back then, Sal thought it was better to have blood involved in the racket, so Ricky got hired for the specials.

His desk chair creaked as he sat back and sucked his cigar. Donnie DelFusco was outside and Sal watched him approach Ricky to summon him to the trailer. Sal didn't need problems like Ricky. The fuckin' Chinese didn't use so much scrap in the last few years. That made the Dragos' specials appreciated.

He placed his cigar in the ashtray as Ricky knocked and entered.

"Sit down!" Sal yelled. He wiggled out from behind his desk and threw the newspaper at his nephew. "Here you go, hot shot! The fuckin' hit-and-run!"

Ricky picked up the *Journal* and saw the reward advertisement. Same as last year, and the year before. He read it slowly; he wasn't an especially good reader and was out of practice.

"Geezus," he said. "Again? Fuckin' ancient history."

Sal lumbered around the desk, his index finger jabbing the air in front of Ricky's face. "Yeah, well, *ancient history* or no, I'm reading dis shit's back." His eyes narrowed to a squint. "Where's that jerkoff you were with?"

Ricky's face squeezed together as if in thought. "Aldo Baldolucca? He shits his pants just thinkin' about me. Don't worry."

His uncle moved his bulk to sit on the edge of the desk; Sal's deepened scowl flattened the smirk on Ricky's face.

"I don't worry, asshole. You ever see me worry? Never. I don't let things get to the point where I gotta worry. I think ahead so nobody fucks with me, ya hear what I'm sayin'? Everybody knows: don't fuck with me. And if they do, fuck happens. So here's da t'ing, why don't ya get ya head out of yer ass and make sure Baldolucca's reminded he shouldn't be tempted to drop a dime."

Sal hacked a cigar cough and turned away from Ricky. "You take care of dis t'ing, see. I don't want to hear no more about dis, ya get me?"

Ricky left the trailer, *Journal* in hand, put on his wrap-arounds and stomped over to the compactor.

Two yard guys working on a junker saw his hulking presence, exchanged glances, and got out of his path.

The weather had warmed to around fifty; a starkly bright sun glinted off the scrap metal strewn around the yard. Ricky took off his baseball cap and loosened his hair.

"Fuck!" he said aloud. *Three fuckin' years and the shit is still out there.*

Three fuckin' years! Bad karma. Should never have used that fuckin' junker truck from the yard.

He wound a chain from the flatbed's winch around the front axle of a Buick junker, and wondered where Baldolucca lived after doing a year for possession of weed and meth with intent to sell. Before Baldolucca went to prison, Ricky had let him know he was a dead man if he opened his trap, and Aldo had kept quiet. Still, Ricky had to find him. Shit, more than that; he had to make sure he would never rat him out. Maybe rough him up? He'd confront the prick tonight.

Would that be enough?

CHAPTER TWENTY-FOUR

"WHERE THE FUCK IS HE?" Ricky complained aloud.

Marlboro butts filled the Ram's ashtray. It was after eleven and Ricky was parked across from a dilapidated three-decker with six utility meters attached to its dented aluminum siding. One mailbox bore the smudged name "Baldolucca."

After a couple of drinks at the Action, Ricky decided to take Aldo out. As long as Aldo was around, Uncle Sal would be on Ricky's ass. Sal was right: fuckin' Aldo was a liability. Sooner or later, Aldo would get caught up in something and go for a prosecutor's deal or claim the reward. If he disappeared now, who'd care? But first, Ricky had to make sure that the fuck hadn't already ratted him out. He would take it slow, get the scene settled in his mind, case it out clever-like, figure out when and where, be Nemesis.

At eleven-twenty, a Taurus that needed shocks bumped into a parking area next to the tenement. The driver got out, locked the car, and walked toward the front stoop.

Ricky left his truck and called out, "Aldo, how da fuck are ya?"

His voice froze Aldo Baldolucca who barely managed to catch his breath, turn, and reply, "Hey Ricky, a surprise. What's up wid ya?"

Ricky approached, his right hand raised to give Aldo a knuckle bump. "Same old shit, ya know. Been thinkin' I ain't seen ya since ya got out. How ya doin'?"

Aldo returned the bump. "Okay, workin'."

"Gonna invite me up?"

"Sure, sure," Aldo replied without enthusiasm, and unlocked the tenement's front door. "Watch your step. The fuckin' old lady who owns the place never replaces the landing's light bulbs."

Ricky followed his prey up a narrow, dimly lit staircase to a third-floor front apartment. The staircase had all the familiar smells of a city tenement: old paint, overcooked food, layers of dust, and cigarettes. As they climbed to the third floor, the back of Aldo's neck became a convenient target of opportunity. Ricky saw himself grabbing that skinny neck with its bulging Adam's apple and wringing it like a chicken's. The thought passed. *Be cool. Don't leave fingerprints in the apartment.*

Aldo unlocked the apartment door and snapped a switch lighting ceiling track bulbs. Clothes were scattered on tables and chairs, skin magazines lay strewn on a stained carpet along with beer cans; trash from takeouts left a rancid odor.

"Didn't expect company," he said in excuse as Ricky sat on a once-beige sofa, careful not to touch its wooden arms or the table in front of him. "How 'bout a beer?" Aldo left for a tiny kitchen and returned with two Bud Light cans. He popped their tops and gave one to Ricky. They mocked a toast to each other and took long swigs. Aldo sat in a soft chair across from Ricky.

"How's your parole goin'?"

"Nothin'. I report once a week to this broad downtown. They check me for drugs and I tell her I'm doing great. Job makes the difference. Takes five minutes once I get in to see her. Sometimes I got to wait an hour though, 'cause she's got a shitpot of guys. Never bothered to check here although she's supposed to. Four more months and that's it."

"Where you workin'?"

"Restaurant in North Providence on Mineral Spring. Victor's. Family place. Hires out of the poke. Gets guys on the cheap, but it's enough. Kinda like the food part. Might stay with it."

Ricky took Sal's newspaper copy of the reward advertisement out of his jacket pocket and tossed it at Aldo. He watched Aldo's face turn from surprise to fear. Aldo returned the newspaper to Ricky before another swallow.

"Fuckin' years ago," Ricky said as he refolded the newspaper and placed it back in his jacket. "Think he'd give it up by now."

"Yeah." Aldo finished his beer with a belch and wiped his mouth on his sleeve.

"Still out there," Ricky said. "Hundred grand. For that kind of dough, I'd turn myself in." Ricky laughed and Aldo tipped his empty to show he appreciated the humor. "I don't worry about it. Never worry is my motto. I know you wouldn't rat me out. Never."

"I'd never rat," Aldo replied a second too quickly. "Look, I was inside for a year and didn't rat." He put the can on the floor next to his chair.

"That's what I said, too. 'Aldo is stand up, would never rat out a buddy,' I said."

"Who to?"

"My uncle. Sally G. Doesn't want somebody to finger his shop as an accessory, get it?"

"Tell him no worries. I'd be an accessory too and they'd stick me back inside."

"Just thought I'd remind you . . . put my uncle's mind at ease."

Ricky smiled, seeing sweat glistening on Aldo, the fuck's, forehead. *A worm, a weak fuck. Maybe, I should pop him now? No, better to wait, find a better place, quiet, be smart like Nemesis.*

"Come to think of it, I could say you were drivin', not me."

"What's this shit? Who would believe I was drivin' your uncle's pickup with you workin' at the yard?"

"Hey, don't get excited," Ricky smiled, enjoying the worm's reaction despite inhaling a whiff of his treachery. "I'm bustin' you. Anyways—"

It was time for Nemesis to squeeze. He put his beer can on the carpet, reached into his jacket and pulled out a slick Glock, one of his favorite pieces.

Aldo jumped in his skin. "Fuck! What's this?"

"If I thought you would rat on me," Ricky fingered the gun and his grin became a death head's, "I'd have to take you out. But you're stand-up. Nothin' for my uncle, or me, to worry about, right?" Before Aldo replied, Ricky added, "Heard you got pussy whipped inside."

Aldo felt his face tighten, his back stiffen.

Ricky stood, stuffed the gun in his waistband, picked up his beer can, and swaggered to the apartment's door. "See you around, huh?"

"Yeah, anytime." Aldo followed him to the door, opened it, waited for footsteps on the staircase, locked it, and slotted its chain lock.

Aldo snagged a corner of the tattered shade in the front window and caught a glimpse of Ricky sliding into the front seat of a pickup, one of those big four-by-four Dodge Rams. He heard its engine catch and watched it leave the curb; only then did his breathing return to normal. Quickly, he was into the kitchen and the fridge's vegetable drawer where he had hidden the weed he desperately needed. He rolled a joint, lit up and returned to lie on the sofa.

The toke calmed him. Christ, in a lifeline of bad luck, it was his worse luck that he had been with Squillante that night. His supplier insisted he needed muscle for the drop to some spics who were gun crazy, and got him Squillante, a *cavone* that the supplier knew. *Fuckin' guy looked the part of muscle; black tee, ponytail, tattoo, huge fuckin' shoulders, even with his cockeye.* Ricky picked him up in a junker truck, a Ford F-150, from his uncle's scrapyard. *Said to call him Nemesis, not Ricky. Fuckin' weird!*

The drop in a parking lot over the state line in Seekonk was no trouble, even after Nemesis strutted around, showed off the gun in his belt, getting the spics hyper.

Later, they celebrated the deal going down with some high-end weed in the parking lot, with Ricky getting smoked and bragging about his muscle work. "Never pay for nothin'," he boasted.

A few minutes later, Ricky pulled the truck into a Cumberland Farms convenience store. "Cigarettes," he said. Aldo didn't know he was going to prove he "never paid" until Ricky rushed out of the store with his hands full of packs of Marlboros and peeled the truck out of the lot.

It had started to rain and Ricky, going too fast into the curve near the bridge in East Providence, skidded, fishtailed into a car—a Mini—that went off the road. Ricky managed to bounce the truck back into the right lane, straightening it out, barely missing a large pickup following close behind the Mini.

Later they checked the damage to the truck, which amounted to a crunch in the left fender and scrape from the left front wheel to the driver's door. They agreed nobody would care about damage to a yard junker, maybe nobody would even notice. Then, at a tavern where they met Aldo's supplier to split the cash, the *News at Eleven* flashed the crash scene. Ricky nudged Aldo to watch and said matter-of-factly, "Hey, somebody bought it."

At that moment, Aldo's life changed.

Aldo had another toke and two more beers and watched porno movies, but his mind was filled by Ricky. *Why did he show up now? And take the beer can with him? To finish the beer or not leave a trace of his presence? Geezus, with a gun.* Was that just to put a scare into him? Should he blow town *now* before the crazy bastard decided to off him? But where to? With no cash, and he'd have to break parole! *Fuck!* Did he have a better chance surviving if he got his hands on the reward, waited out parole, *then* scrammed?

He barely kept himself from popping the pills that were secreted in the lining under the sofa. Only the meeting downtown in a day or two with his parole officer stopped him. He could get away with weed because he had a medical marijuana card for his nervous condition. His parole officer didn't mind the beers or the legal pot, but if a urine sample revealed he had taken the serious junk he had hidden, a cache for sale, she'd slap him back inside for two hard years.

"Gotta do it," he said to the empty apartment.

CHAPTER TWENTY-FIVE

AARON WAS RELEASED from detention after a suggestion from the governor's office that continued segregation would stoke adverse media coverage and partisan outrage. He entered the food line late for the noon meal to withering stares and even a few approving nods among grimaces. *What is goin' on?* he wondered.

He finished his meal alone in the handicapped mess and returned to his cell to find his cellmate's belongings had been removed. He lay on his bunk, closed his eye, and went into his memory bank to where he kept images of Frost's poems. The warming sunshine, the air smelling of spring, the early green of the playing fields behind the fences along the concourse on his way back to his cell gave him his needed lines:

The sun was warm but the wind was chill
You know how it is with an April day.
When the sun is out and the wind is still,
You're one month on in the middle of May.
But if you so much as dare to speak, . . .
He chose not to speak to himself about parole.

It wasn't until Millie's visit later that afternoon that Aaron learned that the video, instead of inflaming those hostile to his parole, had created a tidal wave of support for his release. In the lawyer's room, closely monitored by an unfamiliar, unfriendly and suspicious CO, his sister gleefully told him of being interviewed by reporters with video cameras who seemed sympathetic to his release. *Aaron's Anguish*, she gushed, had been viewed by millions of people on the internet who were on his side. Worldwide, people were demanding his parole, or a pardon, and offering funds for advocacy and reconstruction of his face!

As proof, she had brought the morning *Journal*. The newspaper's coverage of the Free Aaron movement and Aaron's Army astonished him. He hadn't bothered with news from the outside in years. Now he couldn't wait to get to the librarian's computer.

On his way down the concourse for dinner, he saw a hawk circling high above the Max. He had heard a rumor that birds sometimes nested in its cupola, but in all his years in prison had never seen any. *Is the hawk nesting or looking for prey?* Either way, he remembered a line from Frost *"And made us happy in the darting bird,"* and took its appearance as a good omen.

His optimism didn't last long. On his way back from his cell block to the mess hall, he was accosted by two older COs who made dismissive remarks about Aaron's "television debut," how he could have used some makeup, and repeatedly asking, "How did you do it, Underwood?" and "Who helped you?" *Pricks!* In his cell, he made up his mind that he'd push for parole. That meant doing anything that would keep his face and cause in public view. Win or lose, after years of just enduring his fate, he had a goal, a purpose!

CHAPTER TWENTY-SIX

UNUSUAL HAPPENINGS IN CLOSE-KNIT Federal Hill get talked up quickly, especially when they involve wiseguys. At the Social Club, a Mob hangout that reeked of tired smoke and spilled beer, the gossip reached the Brow who conducted business in the quiet of the Social Club's basement, the walls of which were lined with lead sheets to avoid electronic surveillance.

Chris Gilletto received an in-person summons—the Brow only communicated through messengers—as he sat down for dinner with his mother and aunt. After that, he barely got any food down. Chris made a few phone calls and found out he had a problem; the story about a present for Frankie hadn't washed to the *regulas* in the Social Club. The *regulas* knew that Chris Gilletto wasn't likely doing anything for Fat Frankie.

Chris passed the verbal protocol at the sliding window in the Club's side door and ordered a beer at the bar, noting that other than a couple of head shakes, he was purposefully being ignored by card players, pool players, and those watching a porno video on a huge flat-screen television. Nobody said anything about the demolished garage.

Not a good sign.

After fifteen minutes, a well-known associate of the Brow appeared in the doorway behind the bar and gave Chris a shrugged order to follow him downstairs.

Geezus, Chris thought, *the Brow himself,* a bear of a man with a forehead that shadowed his eyes so that you couldn't see into them.

Fortunately, before he had left Swan Street Chris had stuffed the cloth bag in his jacket pocket. He would make peace if he had to.

But it wasn't the Brow he saw through the veil of cigarette smoke. Luigi "Lucky" Barracelli, one of the Brow's intimates, lounged on a lumpy leather sofa, one arm casually propped along its back, facing a pool table where two hulks Chris recognized as Lucky's guys—one had already served five years for a plea of manslaughter—stopped their play and rested their chins on the butt ends of cue sticks. Barracelli motioned Chris to a hardback chair across a low table; a glass of something amber was in front of Barracelli, next to a filled ashtray.

Chris eased himself into the chair, trying to show a *whadafuck* attitude while taking in Barracelli's hawk-like face and his black, empty eyes. With a cigarette parked in a corner of his lips, Barracelli would have been a Hollywood version of a mobster, except that he wore a green short sleeve golf shirt open at the collar, and sported a toupee with a sweep of black curls that was much too youthful. Chris had heard that if you stare at that toupee, you should make out your will.

"You knocked down Fat Frankie's garage," Barracelli said. He took a deep drag on his cigarette, exhaled smoke at Chris, and stubbed it out, with emphasis, in the ashtray.

"Whole garage, Lucky, my side, too. Rats," Chris began in reply, "fuckin' rats."

"Frankie used the garage for business, off-line business, ya know that? We know. Kept stuff there to take care of people that needed to be taken care of, so the shop didn't get into it, and he didn't pay us for other stuff he kept there for himself. We let him do it."

"Didn't know. We're not exactly buds."

"Ya lived next door to yer cousin forever and ya don't know? C'mon, I'm no *testa di cazzo*? The garage goes down because Frankie told ya somethin'."

"Nah. Like I said, it was the fuckin' rats. From the goddamn spics over the fence. Our mamas, they're scared crazy of rats."

Barracelli's eyes remained cold. *Geez,* Chris thought, *he's a made man, a guy born without a conscience, and he's pissed. Forget the fuckin' scam on Fat Frankie. Tell him a story that sounds right, and fuckin' hope and pray.*

"Ya got it right about one thing. When it got demolished, come to find out the guys doin' the job found this." He reached into his jacket's inside pocket, which caused Barracelli to jump across the table and grab Chris' arm. "Lucky, let me show ya," Chris pleaded as a pool player's arm crushed his neck.

Barracelli blinked an *okay,* and the pool player relaxed his hold on Chris.

Slowly, Chris withdrew the cloth bag and croaked out, "Has a couple of stones in it. Huge fuckin' surprise! I'm going to see Frankie tomorrow and ask what the fuck?"

Barracelli grabbed the bag and dumped its contents onto the table; three sparklers rattled on the tabletop; the fourth and largest that had been in the bag remained at home in Chris' shoe, just in case.

"You was goin' to do what?" Barracelli barked.

"See what da fuck was up."

Barracelli slammed his hand on the table, scattering the diamonds, knocking two on the floor. Chris bent forward to pick them up but was restrained by a cue stick at his throat.

"So, you was doin' some business."

"I brought 'em in, didn't I? Why would I do that?"

"Because yer a fuckin' moron. You got them talkin' up there," his eyes arched upwards. Barracelli sat back, his eyes threatening mayhem even as a crooked smile emerged.

"So here's what's goin' down, asshole. Since you," his finger wagged in Chris' face, "and Frankie been fuckin' around . . ."

"No fuckin' way, no fuckin' way," Chris managed to get out before the cue stick tightened at his neck.

". . . the protection he's been gettin' just got more expensive. Another ten now, another ten when he's out. You give him that message. Cash, no fuckin' stones. But leave these with me for . . . a deposit."

"The guy's inside, how's he gonna come up with cash?"

"For you numbnuts to figger out."

"Sure, sure," Chris said quickly. "So, if he don't pay?"

"Then you pay. You're a guarantee. Bad for him if he don't, and bad for you." Barracelli's eyes locked into Chris.

"What da fuck, Lucky, he's only my fuckin' cousin. I don't know what he's got."

"Can't choose yer relatives and can't screw around with us."

The cue stick was released when Chris nodded his assent.

"See ya, Chris," snickered one of the pool players as Chris climbed the stairs to the bar. He was already wondering where he would get the cash if Frankie didn't pay. It wasn't like Chris kept a stash somewhere or had a bank account; all he had was a roll of flash cash, what he wore, what he drove, that's it! Everything else went to his bookie.

Got to get Frankie out so he will pay!

<hr>

Chris walked home on streets narrowed by lines of parked cars. It would be easier to squeeze Frankie to pay now, if he thought he was getting out. First things first. Frankie had to hire Walter Kramer, the lawyer with a rep of being successful at the parole board. Months ago, Kramer had demanded ten grand as a retainer and cheap-prick Frankie had said no. Now, Chris needed Kramer to get his cousin out. If Frankie didn't pay Kramer his retainer, Chris would have to pay, and his only ready source of cash was the Local's pension fund. He'd have to write up a lump sum retirement for one of the fake enrollees he had on its rolls, something he didn't want to do because he was already into the fund big time. *Shit!* How did he get to be his cousin's guarantor?

Chris went up the back stairs at 40 Swan and into the kitchen, opened the cabinet over the stove, and poured himself a large *grappa*. Next to the cabinet hung his mother's icon homage to the Madonna. "Hey," he said, saluting the Madonna with his glass, "How 'bout some fuckin' help?"

CHAPTER TWENTY-SEVEN

JAKE BEGAN HIS MORNING at six-thirty at Gold's Gym, which he frequented when his at-home routine was getting stale or he needed a change from the Y. *Aaron's Anguish* followed him.

In the weights area, steamy with sweat from three other lifters in a cacophony of crashing bar bells, a mounted flat-screen television showed repeated stills from the video. Jake averted his eyes but couldn't miss the commentary from the musclebound lifters on mats near him. One complained, "Only time Rhode Island gets on the fuckin' national news, and it's about a monster."

Returning to his condo, Jake went to the library and flipped through cable news channels. The reaction to *Aaron's Anguish* was still mushrooming. Cable news talking heads, social media celebrities and progressive politicians kept opining on the injustice of keeping Underwood imprisoned. Not one mentioned Underwood had pled guilty to murder.

A local station's early news covered the planning of a pop-up rally at the statehouse later in the day. An attractive young woman with a Providence College sweatshirt spoke to the camera, wide-eyed and shrill in her demand for justice for Aaron Underwood. "He lives without human dignity, and is treated like trash." She was cheered by friends wearing Phantom masks.

Their spontaneous enthusiasm heightened Jake's reluctance to accept Underwood's injury as trumping a gruesome murder and parole board precedents. If anything, his attitude hardened with every uninformed opinion or naïve protest.

After one o'clock, when he walked down to the vet center, the sun had finally won its battle with the rolling March clouds, leaving the sky the color of washed-out denim. The air was crisp with just a tickle of wind. Jake had promised a vet from Central Falls that they would play cribbage, a game he enjoyed and, like the vet, had learned from parents.

As Jake entered, Paulie Caprio, with the hangdog look of someone about to go off track, tugged at his arm. "I gotta talk to you," said Paulie.

Jake assumed Paulie had seen the video and wanted to talk about Underwood, or was about to rattle off some excuse as to why he quit his job or got canned. Lacking patience, Jake said, "I promised to play cribbage with Al Thibeault . . ."

"I know. He told me. And I kinda asked if that could wait until we talked. He'll be back in an hour."

Jake readied himself for a confession. He took a handful of stale Munchkins from the food counter, a bottle of Poland Spring from the fridge, and motioned Paulie to a table by the front window. His view encompassed Main Street's brick office buildings and stores selling exotic ethnic foods and local farm produce, hairdressers and nail salons, and a bank branch. Jake and Paulie pulled out metal chairs with stenciled lacy backs—ice cream chairs, Jake remembered they were called.

Sitting facing Jake, Paulie stared at a spot a foot over Jake's head.

"I don't know if I should be a go-between but—"

"Go-between?" Not what Jake had expected. "Better spit it out."

"A guy I work with. Aldo Baldolucca. We're closing up last night, just us, everybody else is gone and he comes over to me. He's been jumpy all night, screwing off. Somebody dropped a tray of dishes and I thought he was going to flip out."

"And?"

"So, he lights up a joint and says, 'Your buddy from the vet center, the guy whose wife got killed in a hit-and-run, has reward ads.'"

Jake tensed. It must have shown in his face because Paulie stopped, his jaw quivering. "I knew this was a bad idea."

"Go ahead," Jake said quietly.

"When I started working at Victor's, Aldo was already there. Asked me how I got the job. I said through you. Then one time I mentioned your wife's hit-and-run and the reward adverts you ran, and I thought then Aldo looked like he'd seen a ghost. I said you'd been a . . . mentor . . . to me. For weeks after that, nuthin' more than a 'howahyah' now and again. Then, last night, he's got sweat dripping down his face, and he's my best buddy, and asks if I could set up a meet with you. I ask him why, and that I didn't want to mess with you. He said it could be worth my while if I did."

Paulie's hand slapped the table. "I said I didn't need anything from him. If he had a good reason, I'd ask you, but if it was shit, I'd bust him one. So he says it's about when your wife got killed. He didn't come right out and say it but maybe he knows who—"

The large screen television across the room flashed on and CNN boomed across the room. Jake turned and saw three talking heads discussing *Aaron's Anguish*—shown only in still pictures—and medical treatment for prisoners. Jake's breathing slowed and he felt a tightness in his lips.

"When does he want to see me?"

"How about now? Down at the park. He's waiting. Said it had to be today or it'd be too late."

CHAPTER TWENTY-EIGHT

THE MIST FROM THE PAWTUCKET FALLS swirled over the river like smoke, creating fantastic images falling into themselves. Every so often, a breeze would flick a streak of mist here or there, allowing the sun to form fleeting rainbows.

Aldo Baldolucca leaned over a metal railing, staring down at the eddies of dark current that fell into the Falls. A leaf, a shred of paper trash, a twig, a blade of long grass, all languid in their pace floating on the river until swept over the precipice in a flash of green and white water and lost in foam. He heard footsteps on the cinder path behind him and turned. Coming toward him were Paulie and a guy with a serious, narrow face, a day's beard, and a zipped jacket that hinted at a muscular body. One sleeve of the jacket was stuck in a pocket.

"Aldo, this is Jake Fournier." There was no response from either party. "I'm goin'. See ya later at work, Aldo."

"Tell Al we got to postpone the cribbage," Jake said.

"Okay." And Paulie was quickly out of earshot.

Jake sat on a bench facing the Falls and appraised the short, skinny guy in a satiny windbreaker with a Patriots logo, dirty jeans, and a greasy Red Sox cap from under which unkempt hair escaped. The guy's skin was yellowish and he was unshaven; his eyes were bloodshot; his prominent Adam's apple must have been a lifelong embarrassment.

"Something you want to say to me?" Jake demanded.

"The reward. What do you need to collect?" Aldo's voice didn't hide his anxiety.

"What have you got for me?"

"A name." Then, unconvincingly, he added, "Sorry about your loss."

Jake curled his lip at the false sympathy. "Heard lots of names from scumbags trying to cash in, get rid of a somebody they don't like, or fear. I don't like that shit."

Aldo's Adam's apple bounced when he gulped. "I'm not one of those. What do I have to do?"

"Two things. First, something that convinces me to take you seriously." Jake surprised himself with the flatness in his voice. "Second, an arrest and conviction. The reward is for information leading to an arrest *and* conviction."

"Does that mean testimony?"

"I'm not a lawyer or a prosecutor."

"Suppose somebody just supplied the name, and you work it out?"

Jake shook his head and stood. He planted his feet like a boxer in front of Aldo, not threatening but not yielding space. "A hundred thousand has got to be earned."

Aldo, even in his trepidation, understood Jake's logic. "Look, if I give you the name and he finds out, he'd off me. He's . . . connected, get me?"

In Rhode Island, "connected" means to a politician or the Mob. Jake took it to be the Mob, and it was a lame excuse for not coming forth with information. Despite his incredulity, Jake replied evenly, "If I had a name and something substantial to back it up, enough so that the cops investigate and arrest and the AG had a case, there could be something down, something more after arrest, the rest upon conviction."

Aldo turned away and stared down at the flow of river water into a cauldron of rock and spume. "How do I know you will pay?"

"Don't waste my time," Jake replied through clenched teeth. "Convince me and you might get some cash in your hands while I check it out. Otherwise, fuck off."

Aldo stretched his arms above his head, rolled his head around his neck. Jake heard the cartilage crack. "How about I describe the truck?"

"Yeah?"

"Black. Beat-up . . . ah . . . a white stripe along the fenders over the front wheels. Maybe a Ford F-150."

Jake choked back a reaction. The media had reported the likely truck model and the black paint, and the description had appeared in the reward advertisement. But neither the media at the time nor the reward advertisement had mentioned a white stripe.

"Where's the truck now?"

Aldo hesitated in his lie before answering, "Don't know."

Jake braced his shoulders in menace, took a step forward that positioned his face inches from Aldo's. "And you are full of shit. I should turn you over to the cops and let them sweat you, let some ambitious prosecutor make his case and put two douchebags away, one for the killing and one for refusing to talk. If you're on parole or probation, you can kiss that away."

Aldo stepped back against the railing as he felt sweat or mist on his neck. "Okay, I got something else. The plates on the truck."

Jake stepped back so Aldo could breathe.

"Not like Rhode Island plates. Kinda . . . orangey."

"Orangey?"

"Yeah."

Jake's mind flashed to Garo's futile hunt through the files at the Registry of Motor Vehicles. "From where?"

"Dunno. I just kinda remember the ugly color."

Jake's hand went to Aldo's shoulder and felt him shudder. "I got no time for this. How about I beat the shit out of you right now? If you got a name, give me it and where he is, and something more than an "orangey" license plate. Then maybe you get some dough. But if it's bullshit, you never again have a night safe from me . . . never!"

Aldo sucked in a breath. "I want ten g's and you get the name, where he works, some other stuff I know. I'll pick him out for ya. Take it or leave it."

Jake's hand left Aldo's shoulder; he might have slapped him hard but Jake heard his smarter self say *Back off, this puke could put away Hope's killer.* The white stripe, the license plate that fit into Garo's futile search, he knew something. *Could this son of a bitch have been a passenger?*

"Can't do business," Jake said slowly and put his fist in his jacket pocket, turned, and started down the cinder path toward Main Street. *If this rat doesn't crack now, I'll kick his ass.*

"I'm all you got," Aldo called after Jake halfheartedly, thinking maybe he asked for too much. Maybe he should get what cash he could and get outta town.

"What do I have to do?" Aldo shouted again at Jake's back.

Jake stopped, didn't turn. "Give me the name, where he lives, works, everything you know about the hit-and-run."

"How do I know I give you the name, you don't turn me in or come after me?"

Jake turned, his fist out of his pocket, a finger trained at Aldo's face. "You don't. But I won't. Shit or get off the pot."

"When do I get the cash?"

"Four o'clock, here, on Monday, and only if I think what you give me is worth it."

"Ten?"

"Two, if it's good information. If it isn't, I'm your nightmare. If what you give me checks out, you get another three, and I'll keep you out of it . . . if I can. Until it goes to trial. I'll stash you out of town, at my expense, my private witness protection plan. On conviction, you get the balance of the reward."

Jake reached into his back pocket, took out his wallet and found a *Jake Fournier, Restaurateur* business card. His cell phone number had been penciled on the reverse side. He took three steps toward Aldo, saw his Adam's apple bob, and handed him the card, which Aldo put into the liner of his cap.

Aldo drew in a deep breath, nodded.

Jake walked up Main Street toward Park Place, pondering the possibility that on Monday he would have a name. He remembered the convenience store assault uncovered by Garo's tenacious work. If Baldolucca knew about that, Jake had his clincher.

The stopper on his reservoir of vengeance had been pulled.

CHAPTER TWENTY-NINE

CHRIS GILLETTO, UNSHAVEN, his eyes like cracked cue balls, wearing a sweatshirt, jeans, and sneakers, stood at a visitors' room table in front of his cousin. He struck a belligerent pose, having decided that the only way to deal with the situation was to blame Frankie for everything that had gone to shit.

"You fuck," he snarled under his breath. "You got into a scrape with that fuckin' monster. Everybody's heard that. Probably in your fuckin' record, too. And, you let my stones fall between the boards and blocks of the garage. That meant the roof had to go."

"What?"

"Yeah, it's gone. Took it down."

"I got no garage?" Frankie choked out.

"Hey, it was a shitbox! It had to go. Had to tear the fuckin' thing down with the roof gone. Rats got into the blocks, fuckin' rats the size of cats."

Frankie gulped. "You got the bag, the stones?"

"Yeah."

"And I got no garage?"

"Yeah."

Fat Frankie sat back, incredulous.

"So, here's what you gotta do to get out of here." Chris sat down facing his cousin. "After all I done, after what I paid out, with all the fuckin' calls

I made, ya probably fucked up parole by that dumb play messin' with the freak." A lie, but what did Frankie know? "Only chance ya got now is hiring Kramer."

Fat Frankie winced in bewilderment. "What are you saying? I need Kramer? Because of Underwood? Because you knocked down my garage?"

His cousin hunched closer. "You really need him now 'cause I got told by Lucky that you gotta pay another ten, in or out, and another ten when you're out. Don't ask why. I don't know why. Maybe to pay up for your protection in here after this shit with the freak everybody's heard about, or the Brow got pissed when ya last minute fucked up."

"Another twenty on top of what I paid?"

"Ya gotta pay, Lucky said. In or out."

Fat Frankie's face paled.

"Ya don't pay and yer still in because ya didn't hire Kramer, ya know what that means?" Chris whispered. "You won't be able to shower without some meatball dropping the soap. Or have a peaceful sleep. With Kramer and what I've done, ya got a chance to be out. Without him, just fucked."

Ten for Kramer and another twenty for the Brow, Fat Frankie would have to tap his other stash of gems and cash that was stuck behind loose bricks behind the oil burner in the cellar at 40 Swan. But he couldn't reveal the location to Chris.

"You tell Lucky this. It'd take me a couple of weeks to reestablish connections when I'm out, collect what I'm owed. So, he'll get his cash. Meanwhile, the diamonds from the garage, you give 'em to Kramer. Tell him the rest comes when I'm out."

Chris didn't want to admit that Barracelli had three of the diamonds and he wasn't going to give up the one for his bookie. "No way I give up my stones. Anyway, he won't want stones. Lawyers take cash only. I've spent all the dough I'm goin' to. And, I'm tellin' ya, with Lucky on your case, yer ain't in no position ta negotiate."

Fat Frankie had no choice but to play along. "You get me that fuckin' mouthpiece. Upstairs in my Ma's room, she's got this big jewelry box on her dresser. Got a false bottom. Take the base off. I got three g's in cash there, some pearls, couple of rings, looks like a bunch of cheap shit but it's not worth five or six broken up. Give Kramer the cash and the jewelry. I'll buy it back when I'm out. He'll have his ten. Everything else in the box is hers and worthless shit. Leave her stuff alone, or she'd notice it's gone and go crazy."

"And if you don't get out?"

"He's got the cash and the stones. I'll deal with Lucky. And I'm getting fuckin' out, ain't I?"

"You were for sure until you fucked up. Now, we'll see."

"And you owe me a fuckin' garage!" Frankie said.

"You threatenin' me?" Chris pushed back his chair in a show of anger. "You owe me! Three years of taking care of your business, your mother! Don't fuck with me, Frankie, or you're gonna feel somebody's dick up your ass."

Chris left his cousin after Fat Frankie backed off on the garage, figuring he could retain Kramer for the cash in the jewelry box with a promise of the balance, and give the rest of the jewelry to the bookie as a "hold." If Frankie didn't get out, Chris would dip into the pension fund to pay Kramer off. His cousin would have to take care of the Brow by his lonesome, inside or out.

By the time he was past security, Chris was thinking about how he would hit on Dermott McSorely in the limo ride to or from the Mohegan tonight or tomorrow, scare the living shit out of him with some story he'd come up with. Maybe say he bought McSorely's chits; the bookie would cooperate if he got a pay down from Chris.

CHAPTER THIRTY

JAKE AND LIVIA occasionally spent an off-season weekend at her place on Thames Street, a Newport high-rise condo that shadowed the restaurants, bars, and docks of its waterfront. They usually would leave Providence after the departure of the dinner crowd at their restaurant on Saturday nights, and return on Monday morning. This time they decided to leave on Saturday noon and stay a bit longer.

She cooked dinner: snail salad, lobster florentine, and tiramisu. Before bed, they watched *Saturday Night Live*. Jake had been particularly laconic, and Livia guessed he was frustrated by the lack of response to his ad. After their lovemaking, Jake considered telling Livia about his encounter with Aldo Baldolucca. Then he changed his mind. Telling her, or Dermott, or Garo, would give the sketchy scheme a legitimacy he still doubted. When he got a name and whatever else on Monday, he'd lay out a plan, tell Livia, get Dermott and Garo involved, maybe try to interest the Staties. If Baldolucca wasn't forthcoming, Jake was determined to squeeze him dry of anything he knew—and by any means.

They were up early on Sunday, Livia to attend Mass at St. Mary's while Jake had coffee at a nearby Starbucks. "Living in sin," as her mother called it, didn't stop her from attending Sunday services. Jake hadn't been in a church since Hope's funeral.

Livia prepared a full breakfast of scrambled eggs, sausage, toast, banana bread, and fruit and then they took a long walk to First Beach and back. The morning clouds had moved to the northeast, leaving a warming sun and a deep-blue sky with a stretch of yellow on the horizon toward Jamestown across the bay. Livia wore a PawSox baseball cap, her hair in a ponytail through its slot, filled-out white slacks, and a green vest, looking very smart to Jake.

Upon their return, Jake relaxed on a cushioned chaise on the condo's balcony, comfortable in a dark-blue fleece and jeans, his face buried in the hardcover of *Team of Rivals* by Doris Kearns Goodwin, a Christmas gift from Livia who said he could do with something thick and inspiring.

He gave it a good effort, but his eyes quickly closed and he dozed, to be awakened by seagull cries as a trawler chugged by. A light, salt-edged breeze with a hint of seasonal change blew off the Bay as the temperature rose into the low sixties. He was making a second effort at the book when Dermott arrived noisily and unexpectedly. Jake couldn't remember him ever showing up at the condo off-season.

When the sliding glass door to the balcony opened, it was clear Dermott had brought with him a bag of trouble. His rumpled plaid sportcoat did nothing for a complexion that was pasty, maybe jaundiced. His eyes were puffy over purple half-moons, his shave had been hit or miss, and no attempt had been made with a comb. *Hungover, or something worse?*

Livia asked if Dermott wanted anything to eat or drink. He seemed to agonize over his response and uncharacteristically waved her offer away. Getting the message that Dermott wanted a private conversation with Jake, she closed the slider.

Jake roused himself to sit straight into the back of the chaise. "Where have you been?"

Dermott sat in a wicker chair that faced the sun-speckled harbor and put on sunglasses as he settled in.

"At Mohegan with the pier operator's guys, a couple of legislators . . . leadership guys." He looked up at the sky, maybe wistfully. "What a ride," he said with a touch of pride. "Got there before dinner last night, won a few big pots at Texas Hold 'em right off the bat and hit it big at craps, and

I'm up about forty big ones, crowd cheering, booze flowing, people placing bets on my rolls. I just kept goin'. Quit about two when I couldn't even see the dice, when I was ahead sixty. I got comped a suite and upgrades for the party, which bought a shitload of good will. This morning, after we had some bullshit business meeting to write off the trip, it was back to the tables, and Lady Luck jilted me. Two hours and it was gone. Zip!" His voice trailed away.

Jake knew all too well that gambling was in Dermott's genes. His dad had eked out a living as a bookie and tout at the old Narragansett Race Track in Pawtucket, supplemented by selling cheap life insurance, running his book in the back room at Duffy's Tavern on Broadway, and as an occasional eulogist and pallbearer at Kelly's Funeral Home for Pawtucket's bereaved Irish.

"So, what's up?" Jake said, thinking that Dermott looked like he couldn't afford the four dollar toll over the Pell Bridge.

"Gilletto."

"Not going there!" Jake replied crisply, even as he wasn't surprised at the repeat bump.

Dermott whipped off his sunglasses and leaned in to Jake. "Listen, for Chrissake. Just listen to me."

"I can't. Told you." Jake's lips tightened, his eyes became lasers.

"Chris Gilletto came with us, never said a word about what I asked you before, so I thought it was over. Then, as we get into the limo to come home, Chris tells me he's bought what was left of my chits from my bookie. He wants his cousin outta prison! The guy's coming up for a hearing this week. If he's out, I get time to work out my debt, or at least postpone. He left it open as to what happens if Cuz stays in."

Jake stood, refraining from grabbing his best friend by the shirt, lifting him off the chair and throwing him down. Dermott cringed under his stare.

"I came home broke. I had paid the bookie down some when I was on top but I still owe. But it's not the money to Chris. He wants his cousin out, figures you'll help me if I get squeezes. I told him no way and he ignored me."

Jake turned away and gripped the balcony railing with his left hand as though he could have ripped it out of the floor. A seagull swooped by, its rough *caws* bouncing off the brick walls of the condo building, its eyes a mean yellow.

On the bay, ranks of mini whitecaps were rolling toward the harbor, a pair of twelve-meter yachts, bow to bow in full sail, knifed through the greenish-blue water. Jake blinked as he experienced an aura dancing over the rocky shore of Jamestown in the distance. "Tell him that if he pushes, you'll go to the Staties."

"Can't do that! One word from him and I'll lose the pier operator's business. That's all I got . . ."

"I'll loan you the money." He had done so before and knew that Dermott resented the obligation, even as he never gave more than lip service to the idea.

"Are you fuckin' listening? I'm telling you, he wants the cousin out! Not the fuckin' money! I can deal with what I owe . . . if the cousin gets out." Meaning, Jake feared, he'd get cash or credit somewhere, gamble to win enough to pay off the chits. And lose. Then, a collector from the Hill would show up one night and Dermott would be beaten or killed.

"He's got me by the balls, Jake. You gotta help." With his eyes tearing, Dermott said, "I'm not supposed to ask?"

Years of friendship, loyalty, payback were being levered. Dermott blurted, "You fuckin' owe me!" To Jake, it sounded like something deep in Dermott's craw had been eating him and finally crawled out.

Jake watched Dermott's face as he gaped in surprise at his demand. Up went both of Dermott's hands, their palms facing Jake.

"I didn't mean that, Jake. You know I don't. I'm scared shitless what happens if I don't produce." He choked out, "Sweet geezus! He could sic a collector on me and I lose the pier! He wants his fuckin' cousin out!"

Jake's throat tightened. He didn't have the voice to relieve his best friend's fears, or his embarrassment at his plea.

"There's no way that he'll get three votes for parole if he's a first-timer."

"If you vote yes, I'm clear! Up to him to get the other two. I'll have time to figure something out with him on the chits."

So that's the deal, Jake thought.

Dermott waited for a response as Jake stared at him, without providing one. Then, Dermott wiped his eyes with his fingers, stood slowly.

"Sorry, Jake." He spat over the railing, opened the slider, and left.

CHAPTER THIRTY-ONE

AS EVENING CLOSED in over Newport, Livia was at the wheel of Jake's Camaro, driving cautiously, uncomfortably, not used to the Camaro's powerful engine. There was no conversation. This time of day, the light changed over the bay. It could be yellow, purple or gray and often it would drizzle and become a hard rain, or like tonight, a mist that moved across the Bay like a curtain with a sunset behind it. Jake didn't pay any attention to it as he suffered through the migraine, and whatever thoughts he had were of Dermott.

Instead of taking the Pell and Jamestown bridges over Narragansett Bay into West Bay, she drove north on less travelled Route 138 to the Mount Hope Bridge over to the East Bay mainland. Jake roused himself to open his eyes as they crossed the elegant green latticed span into Bristol near the campus of Roger Williams University. Livia asked if they should stop at the Lobster Pot or Roberto's in Bristol, or a fast-food place. Jake, not ready for food, managed to get out his "no."

Close to nine, they arrived at her East Side apartment. Jake's headache had moderated and he insisted he could manage the drive on to Pawtucket. She left him in the car, and blew him a kiss.

Fifteen minutes later, he entered the Governor Foley Mansion through the back stairs. Despite his lingering migraine and the scourge of listlessness, he went to the library and logged in on the parole board laptop, determined to learn more about Gilletto.

Francesco Gilletto had been booked three times for possession of stolen goods, charges never prosecuted, before drawing the short straw two years ago. Gilletto stood trial on the Superior Court's gun crime calendar, had been convicted, and sentenced. While in prison, his rap sheet was clean except for a single disorderly incident early on. His mother's age and illness were verified by a doctor; he had a raft of letters in support of his petition, including one affirming an offer of employment as a bookkeeping clerk at the Port of Providence, and the favorable recommendation of his parole counselor, one Nelson Lansing who said that while inside, Gilletto filled all of the necessary conditions for release, and noted a job awaiting and a pledge to live with and take care of his sick mother.

Jake stood, stretched, followed by two sets of runner's presses against the library's door frame. He considered the ramification of a *yes* vote.

As for the other members, hardass Prebys would be a no, Mia a yes, assuming Gilletto wasn't a jerk at the hearing. Bertozzi? Jake knew he favored inmates who had a family to go back to, a real job, who were older, and whose crime was not violent. On that score, with a favorable report from the parole counselor, Gilletto had advantages. But Bertozzi was also tough on anyone connected to criminal gun sales. Jake counted him as a likely no.

If Bertozzi voted no, a yes vote from Jake would make the tally two to two, and Gilletto would get another hearing after the governor's appointee was sworn in. Could Jake justify a yes vote for a mere postponement? He'd likely be off the board by the time Gilletto came before them again and not have to deal with Gilletto's freedom.

Jake never went round until deciding. And rarely did he second-guess himself.

If Dermott was in his place, Dermott would leap to his aid, no questions asked, even faced with his own perils. Jake had to reciprocate. If he didn't bail out his friend, Jake would have to deal with yet another instance of guilt and shame.

CHAPTER THIRTY-TWO

RICKY WAS GOOD with a jamb. As a kid, he'd popped car locks in twenty seconds. At the scrapyard that skill was useful, too; some asshole was always locking a junker before it got cleaned out of stuff not going through the shredder or into the compactor. Without keys, a grunt would either bust a window—which could earn you a good arm gash if you weren't careful—or you got Ricky to push a jamb between the window and frame and flip the lock.

The grunts would say, "Fuckin' Ricky is good for somethin'."

Pop! The driver's-side door of Aldo Baldolucca's Taurus opened. *Thank you, Aldo, you fuck,* he thought for parking at the rear of the lot by a thick screen of bushes and trees still bearing clumps of dried brown and black leaves. He folded the jamb, pocketed it, and pulled on latex gloves. He felt the first drops of rain.

The car's interior smelled of dirt, fast foods and weed, mimicking Aldo's apartment. Ricky unlocked its rear door, slid into its bench seat, pushed down all the door locks, and squeezed down behind the driver's seat. It was tight but he could leverage himself so that he'd be up and behind Aldo when it was time. And he'd be able to see when Aldo exited the rear door of the restaurant.

As he lay concealed, Ricky pictured the scene: *Aldo unlocks his car, gets in, the garrote goes over his neck, he squirms, kicks out, his arms restrained by the steering wheel, and in a minute of yanking and struggle, it's over. Aldo's head is a purple pumpkin.* Maybe Nemesis whispers something so Aldo, the rat, knows who's killing him. His body goes into the trunk, Ricky drives the car to the Rhode Island Scrap, he sucks out the gasoline, it gets compacted, and it's over. Aldo Baldolucca just disappears. Nobody cares. *Nemesis rules! No worries, Uncle Sal.*

He checked his watch. Almost midnight. *The fuck should be out of work any time now.* Only one other car left in the lot, about forty feet away, close by a dumpster. *Must belong to another employee. Shit,* he thought, *suppose its driver comes out at the same time? Have to be careful, let Aldo settle in, even turn the engine on, whoever was in the other car wouldn't hang around in this rain. Yeah, be careful. Hey, the windows are fogging up.* Good that he couldn't see in, but would Aldo notice?

〰〰〰〰〰〰〰〰〰〰〰〰〰〰

Hungover, sleep deprived, his stomach upset, maybe coming down with something, with Squillante and the one-armed Fournier on his mind, Aldo Baldolucca had another bad night at Victor's. He screwed up orders for the Fry-o-later—the fish fillets, the calamari, and the veal parms in too long and dried out or not cooked through and soggy—waitresses shouting at him for side dishes of pasta and gravy, the boss yelling at him to shape up.

As he finished mopping the kitchen floor, for the last time he thought, he said aloud, "Shape up, my ass. Tomorrow you can take this job and shove it!" He threw his grease-spotted apron into the laundry hamper. He would have Fournier's dough and his paycheck for his getaway. He shouted, "Paulie, let's get out of here."

A splatter of rain cloaked the slam of the restaurant's rear door. Ricky saw two figures sprinting toward the cars and heard a "See ya" from the other guy. A key went into the driver's door lock, it opened, and Ricky felt Aldo slide into the bench seat. Aldo flipped his baseball cap to the passenger side of the seat and turned the ignition key. Headlights from the other car swept the Taurus as Aldo's right hand went to the console's transmission knob.

Ricky was as quick as he was silent. The garrote looped over Aldo's neck, was yanked upward, Aldo's head snapped back into the headrest, his mouth opened, his eyes bulged in their sockets. Blood streamed from his bitten tongue and coursed down his chin as his fingers grabbed the steering wheel to pull forward, then clawed at the wire biting deeper into his neck, severing his windpipe. Blood gushed from his neck a millisecond before he went into shock, his straining legs thrust forward, his right foot floored the gas pedal, his right hand jerked the gear shift out of neutral into drive. The Taurus shot forward.

The dumpster took the head-on impact.

Ricky was stunned by the car's lurch forward, the collision, the explosive inflation of the air bag that smacked his temple. His head bounced backwards, his fingers gripping the garrote trapped under the hard plastic. As the engine raced, sputtered, pinged and died, he managed to wrench his fingers free and mouthed, "What the fuck!"

Despite his confusion and hurt, he grasped a rear door handle, the door squeaked open and he pushed himself out head first, landing hard on the wet asphalt, scraping his hands, cracking his forehead. He staggered to his feet, dumbfounded that his hands hurt and were bleeding, that blood was dripping into his eyes. The driving rain doused his face and blurred his vision as he leaned against the crumpled car.

The driver's side front door was blocked by the dumpster; condensation made it impossible for Ricky to see inside. He wobbled around the car to where the front passenger door had sprung open and saw the inflated air bag that enveloped Aldo. *Dead? Where's the garrote? Under the airbag?* Ricky kneeled on the seat, took the jamb from his jacket pocket, and stabbed the airbag; his first blow scudded off the hard coating. He struck again, harder, and, he heard and felt a whoosh in the blowback of gas as the bag deflated. His right hand found Aldo's face under the bulky and still firm plastic. He didn't feel a breath or the garrote.

Ricky had no time to fish around for it. As he rolled out of the passenger seat, he noticed something white sticking out from inside Aldo's baseball cap he'd left on the seat. He picked up a business card that read *Jacques Fournier, Restaurateur.*

Fournier? The fuckin' reward guy? He turned the card over and saw a handwritten phone number. "Fuck!" He stashed it into his jacket pocket and limped away as the rain, whipped by a biting wind, struck him in with a relentless fervor. *Gotta get out of here,* Ricky thought. *Be smart like Nemesis. Don't run; stay off the main drags; use back streets to the Ram.* His truck was parked at an all-night Stop & Shop a half mile away.

<hr>

At his apartment, Ricky threw off his sodden, bloodstained clothes, stuffed them into a trash bag, and crashed on his bed with a fifth of Yukon Jack. Bitch greeted him with some agitation—maybe it was his sweat or the blood—and had to be quieted by shouted commands and a can of dog food.

"Fuck! Fuck! Fuck! Fuckin' Aldo! Why couldn't he just die?" Ricky complained to the bottle. If only he hadn't let him turn the ignition key. Didn't happen like that in the movies. If it had gone as planned, by now that asswipe would have been embedded in a metal block ready for the pier and a trip to China.

But so what? Nobody saw him. He and Aldo never palled around, and he never visited Aldo at the ACI. *The fucking garrote?* Nobody knew he had one. Bought it in New York years ago for the right opportunity when he was made. And he'd worn latex gloves, so no fingerprints. Who might think he might silence Aldo? Maybe Uncle Sal, and he wasn't going to spill any beans—might even approve.

He rubbed his scraped forehead, bruised fingers and palms and lifted his right leg, the one that hurt. His knee was bleeding where it was scraped raw. His ears still rang from the airbag explosion, his fingers were bloodstained. *Blood?* The latex glove had split when he fell. Was his blood on the asphalt of the parking lot or in the car? He had no idea if a smidgin or a spoonful was enough for a DNA trace. *Shit!* He had a record, maybe they had his DNA or at least his blood type.

Then he remembered the latex gloves. He sat up. "Where's da fuckin' gloves?" He opened the trash bag and went through the pockets of his jacket and jeans. One was there, where was the other? Did he drop it as he trudged to his truck? He had them on when he touched Aldo's face, he remembered. Could be fuckin' anywhere, maybe in the Ram. He'd check in the morning. Just not in the parking lot. Latex gloves? A million sold every day. Even if found, what could they show? Any prints would have been on the inside and obliterated. *But DNA? Fuck!*

He took a long swig of Yukon Jack. He was okay, he thought, and remembered Fournier's business card.

CHAPTER THIRTY-THREE

THE TAURUS WAS DISCOVERED by the restaurant's refuse removal truck early the next morning. North Providence cops arrived shortly afterward with screaming sirens and an emergency vehicle. Their call to the DMV provided the Taurus' registration for one Aldo Baldolucca, 621 Atwood Avenue, Cranston. Only when the airbag was removed, revealing a deep neck wound and a garrote, was the car treated as a crime scene and the Staties and Medical Examiner's Office were called. By then, the persistent rain, the refuse crew's boots, and police shoes had obliterated any blood on the asphalt by the car. State police detectives dispatched from the nearby Lincoln barracks took one look at the body's wounds and the garrote and didn't need a medical examiner's report for a cause of death. To them, a garrote meant the Mob.

The owner of Victor's, Victor Palmeri, arrived at his restaurant and identified the body of his employee, Aldo Baldolucca. Palmeri said that he had left the restaurant at ten-thirty, leaving Baldolucca and Paulie Caprio to clean up and close. In his paper-strewn office off the kitchen, Palmeri loudly complained, as he went through a file cabinet to find Paulie's file, that his wife persuaded him to employ ex-cons and parolees as kitchen help.

"My fuckin' business will be in the toilet for weeks because I married a do-gooder!"

Armed with Paulie Caprio's Bureau of Criminal Information record, two plainclothes detectives were dispatched to Carvour Avenue in North Providence where Paulie was rousted and questioned for almost an hour. They didn't tell him, at first, that Baldolucca was dead, only that they needed to know where Paulie was last night. And then, what about his buddy Aldo Baldolucca?

Paulie scowled. "Buddy? Nah."

He agreed with comments made by his boss that Baldolucca had been jittery, screwing up. He said he and Aldo had closed around twelve, it was raining hard, he saw Aldo get into his car, before he, Paulie, drove out of the parking lot. Paulie said he went home, watched some TV, and went to bed. No, he didn't see another car in the lot or anyone else in the lot or inside Baldolucca's Taurus.

Paulie blanched when the staties revealed that Baldolucca was dead, but not how, and that there would be more questions so he should be available later in the day. Paulie said he had to go to work; one statie, heavyset, square-jawed, and mean looking, told him he had the day off. Somehow, despite his confusion, Paulie managed to avoid Jake Fournier's name in connection with Baldolucca; he knew sooner or later it would come out, but he had to give Jake a heads-up. He owed him that.

As he drove to Pawtucket, he couldn't help considering the possibility that Jake could have taken Aldo out.

━━━━━━━━━━━━━━━━━━━━━━━━━

White faced and unshaven, Paulie arrived at the Governor Foley Mansion at eleven-thirty; Jake had been at his laptop reviewing parole petitions for tomorrow's hearings in Medium Security. Paulie's urgency wasn't disguised as he blurted out in the hall what he had learned from the staties, being "the last person known to be with the victim." He sat on the library's sofa and said with pride that he hadn't mentioned that he had introduced Aldo to Jake only two days earlier. His hands shook and he choked as he got out his important question.

"You didn't have anything to do with it, Jake, right?"

"No."

Jake slowly walked across the room to sit at his desk, hiding the depth of his disappointment. He had been so sure Baldolucca would cough up a name that he had withdrawn two thousand in fifties from Pawtucket Credit Union and had worked out a scenario as to how he would flash the cash, ask him about the Cumberland Farms assault as a test of veracity, elicit the name of the killer and whatever else he could get from Baldolucca. With Baldolucca's death, Jake had only hearsay statements that the killer was "connected," and the F-150 had an orangey license plate.

"They'll be back at me, Jake. For sure," Paulie said nervously, despite being reassured. "I don't like being their last to be with."

"Don't worry. Neither of us has anything to hide. Tell them what you know, including that you introduced me to him on Saturday. I'm doing the same. I don't know if he was telling the truth or not, and he never told me who killed my wife. There will be questions like, what did he tell you. What did I? Answer with the truth. Did Baldolucca say anything to you about me?"

"Only that you were a tough guy."

Jake reached into his back pocket, opened his wallet, found a worn business card of Dermott's. "Call my lawyer. He'll get you a lawyer to represent you. I'll take care of the cost. I appreciate the heads-up, but I'll take it from here."

Paulie didn't seem to be any less upset when he reached into his jacket pocket and handed Jake a business card. "This is a statie's card. Name is Harrigan. He'll be batshit that I didn't mention you, Jake." He drew himself straighter. "Well, tough shit," Paulie said proudly, "Vets stick together."

CHAPTER THIRTY-FOUR

DERMOTT, HOPING THAT JAKE had changed his mind about Fat Frankie Gilletto's parole, immediately answered Jake's call to his cell phone. Despite his growing disappointment, he listened without interruption as Jake told of his encounter with Aldo Baldolucca, and Paulie's visit. When Jake finished, Dermott asked, "You think this guy was on the up and up?"

"From what he said, maybe a passenger? I don't see him as the driver or trying to score some cash. I planned to find out if he knew about the Cumberland Farms assault before he got anything."

"So, what's-his-name . . . Baldo what?"

"*Bal-do-lucca.*"

"Contacts you through this Paulie Caprio from the vet center. Decides to rat out somebody and collect the reward." He paused. "Kind of a coincidence that he's hit within hours of meeting you."

"Can't help the timing."

Dermott's voice slid into a professional tone. "Your Paulie will tell the staties everything that's happened, or what he's imagined, sooner or later. Probably sooner. Better for you to get out in front with them. Remember, they have no love lost on you. Maybe you should have called them after you met Bal-do-lucca?"

"After three years with no results, I should fall all over myself to call them?" Jake unburdened himself in a tirade against how the staties' let their investigation of Hope's murder become a cold case; Dermott didn't interrupt until Jake simmered down and said, "I could say that I doubted him, which I did, what with three years gone by. I wanted to see if he was for real before making the call."

"Doesn't wash. If you got the cash from the credit union, you thought it was legit. By the way, what's your alibi for last night?"

"Me?"

"You dumb Canuck! Because you're on the parole board, you think you get a pass? You met with someone you think can name Hope's killer, right? You think Aldo what's-his-face is maybe a passenger. You're frustrated, revengeful, you waylay him in the parking lot at that restaurant to beat the driver's name out of him. He doesn't come across and you kill him." Dermott paused. "Or maybe you do think he's the driver and you kill him. Or, because he was the passenger, you kill him. Don't think you are in the clear, boy-o! You have motive, opportunity, means."

"But I only got the cash this morning."

"Being clever. So what's your alibi?"

"With Livia until maybe nine or so, then I went home."

"Anybody see you come home, maybe the people in the upstairs condos?"

"Not that I'm aware of."

"Where's the cash?"

"Here. In my desk."

"Who else knows about Baldolucca besides Caprio? Livia?"

"No, I didn't want to involve her or you."

"Too bad."

Jake got angry. "I should have planned an alibi better, right? Is that what you're saying? Should have stayed with Livia or had her come over?"

"Calm fuckin' down!" Dermott replied sternly. "You don't have an alibi if the kill was after ten. Best thing you got going is the forensics. Always something left at the scene, a bloodstain, a fingerprint, something, and you haven't been in his car or touched him."

Jake remembered that in the park on Saturday, he did. "Grabbed his shoulder. He had on a windbreaker with a Patriots logo."

"Well, that's fucking great. Let's hope he had an extensive wardrobe. So how was he killed? Knife, gun?"

"Paulie didn't know." He picked up the statie's card Paulie had left with him. "One of the staties who questioned Paulie was a Sergeant Francis Harrigan. Know him?"

"You don't get any luck, do you?" Dermott said. "He's a stiff. So, do you own a gun?"

Jake hesitated. "Yeah. But not registered. When they shipped my stuff home from Iraq, it came inside a set of fatigues, never bothered to register it."

"Who knows?"

"You do."

"Where is it?"

"In the safe in the library."

"Leave it there."

"Any other lectures?"

Dermott's voice betrayed impatience with his friend, and now client. "Listen to your lawyer. I'll call the staties, set up your interview. You'll tell them what you know. Keep it straight, don't try to turn it. Harrigan probably has heard about you, probably thinks you are, can I say it, an asshole. Otherwise, lay low. Okay? Usual routine, whatever, and don't talk to Paulie. He'll be under a lot of pressure, and you don't need his association right now."

"He can't take a fall for me. I gave him your cell number. Get him a lawyer."

"I will, but don't worry about your con."

"He's not my 'con', just a guy I counsel."

"The staties might figure that he did it for you, that you worked together on this."

"Shit. Didn't think of that. Can I call Garo?"

"Not yet. Garo works for the state, even if he kept his PI license. Got to think on it. Probably okay but—"

"So what should I do?"

"Don't talk to anyone about this, not even Livia. She'll be questioned and I want her honestly to say she hasn't talked to you."

"Got the parole board meeting tomorrow morning?"

Dermott waited a full ten seconds for Jake to say something hopeful about his vote on Gilletto. His resignation to Jake's silence showed in his voice.

"Go. Keep your yap shut about this."

Upbraided like that at any other time, even by Dermott, Jake would have snapped back. Not today.

"I'll be back to you if I can arrange a meeting with the staties at your place," Dermott said. "Until then, just, please, don't do anything rash. Please?"

CHAPTER THIRTY-FIVE

DERMOTT'S TEXT TO JAKE said to expect the staties around six or so. Detective Sergeant Francis Harrigan and Corporal Stanley Pulaski rang the doorbell at five-thirty and were greeted by Jake in a sweaty tee, gym shorts and Nikes. He had been pounding the Everlast weight bag hanging from a ceiling in the mansion's basement with an eight-ounce glove on his left hand.

Jake sized them up in a quick look as they passed by him into the hall. Harrigan had a decade on Pulaski and acted very much the senior as first inside the hall. Both matched a statie profile: six feet tall, serious frowns, brushcut hair, overcoats.

Jake escorted them into his rarely used living room where the setting sun streamed in through damask curtains chosen by Livia. Their raincoats were placed on a chair, revealing dark suits, white shirts, and striped ties, Pulaski's brighter than Harrigan's. Harrigan was square-jawed Irish, with large ears close to his head and cool blue eyes that took the room in with a glance; Pulaski had high Slavic cheekbones, a narrow chin, brown eyes, looked intelligent, and had an amiable smile. Neither accepted Jake's offer of water or soda as they sat stiffly across from Jake on the sofa. Harrigan was ready to begin, but Jake insisted they wait for Dermott.

Harrigan, his voice flat, turned conversational. "I remember your wife's case. Wasn't on it myself, but I remember it."

Jake nodded. Every cop in the Scituate and Lincoln State Police barracks remembered the Fournier hit-and-run, for all the good it had done. Jake steeled himself not to respond. Let them lead with their uneasy small talk until Dermott arrived.

Which he did, five minutes later, Dermott noisily knocking, walked in, calling out to Jake. He gave Jake a high-five and followed him into the kitchen for a requested Diet Coke, which Dermott wouldn't drink if dying of thirst in a desert. There, he whispered that Jake should be careful of his answers, and that being early to an interview was a statie trick of the trade to get a few minutes alone with an interviewee.

"They aced me by beating me here. Should have warned you." Then, he cautioned, "Harrigan is one of those tough, belligerent Irish cops that Italians and Canucks hate at first glance. By the way, the feeling is mutual."

They returned to the living room. Dermott settled in an armchair facing Jake so he could signal by facial expression if need be.

Pulaski had his iPad on his lap. "Let's start off with how you came to meet with Baldolucca."

Jake rattled off how Paulie Caprio told him that Baldolucca chatted up Paulie to set up a meeting.

"And you agreed?"

"I might have held off since the reward advertisements in the past had produced no viable leads, but Paulie said that Baldolucca was waiting for me down at the park by the Slater Mill."

"Did you consider that Caprio might have been involved with Baldolucca, maybe in some kind of scam?"

"No. Paulie was just a conduit, doing a favor for a co-worker. I think he's doing okay, got his head on straight. I think he was also eager to do me a favor."

Pulaski made a note. Jake wondered if the notation was what he had just said, or an appraisal of his comment on Paulie.

"So, you met Baldolucca at the park. When was that?"

"Around three on Saturday. Paulie introduced me and left us."

"What did Baldolucca have to say?"

Jake craned his neck as though trying to get the picture straight in his mind and slowly described his encounter. Pulaski interrupted him when Jake said that if Baldolucca had good information, Jake would evaluate it and decide if it was worth following up with some cash.

"So, did he tell you anything else useful?"

"He knew there was a white stripe on the truck that killed my wife, something not known, I believe, outside of law enforcement. That was critical for me to take him seriously. He also said that the license plate on the truck wasn't like a Rhode Island plate. Said it was orangey."

"Like out of state?" Pulaski asked. "Yellow with blue legend is New York. Jersey is yellowish."

"He said orangey, not yellowish. Then he demanded some cash before he said anything else. I got a little hot then, and told him that I should just turn him over to you guys so you could sweat him. That got his attention because he was on parole. He said that if I could show him ten thousand, I'd get the name and other information about the killer and that it had to be right away. I could see he was nervous, I'd say scared, maybe desperate, so I offered two grand and said I'd meet him in the park today at four, if he delivered who, where he was . . . that kind of thing."

"So, he wanted you to come up with some short money, is that it?"

Dermott answered for Jake. "My client didn't say that. He's not here to guess. He can only tell you what he heard."

Jake wondered at the comment. It didn't seem helpful because it produced a scowl from Pulaski, and Harrigan shot Dermott an unfriendly glare. Was Dermott just marking out boundaries?

Harrigan's voice reeked with cynicism. "Let me get this: you were going to fork over two grand to a con you had just met, that could have been bs-ing you?"

Jake stared Harrigan down. "If you mean why didn't I call you? By the time I got through to someone who even remembered the case, Baldolucca'd be gone. What was I supposed to do, sit on my ass when I had the first legitimate lead in three years?"

Dermott interrupted. "This guy knew about the white stripe and supplied a reason why we couldn't run the pickup's plate through the registry. My client can afford the money and he had a lead and you gotta think this guy's a jittery punk ready to rat out someone, so time was of the essence."

Harrigan dismissed Dermott's defense. "So, during this conversation, where were you?"

"On a bench, at first. Baldolucca stood by the railing near the falls. When he clammed up, I got up in his face and grabbed his shoulder. Wanted him to know I had strength, a grip, despite my injury, that I was a serious man."

"You threatened him?"

"He didn't say that," Dermott interjected.

Harrigan let out a long peevish breath. "Look, counselor, we can do it here or at the barracks. We know your client's issues and we respect them, but we got a homicide here. Anything else, Mr. Fournier?"

"Baldolucca said that the driver was connected."

Pulaski looked up from his note taking, Harrigan's eyes narrowed. "What did you take that as meaning?"

"The Mob."

"Did you believe him?"

"Had no reason not to."

Harrigan shook his head, either in disbelief or to show he was a tough cop. "Which brings me to the question, Mr. Fournier, where were you Sunday night?"

"I was with my business partner, Livia Antonelli, until nine or so. I came home, went to bed. You can reach her at Livia's on Washington Street."

"Anyone see you come home?"

"I didn't see anybody."

"Any calls, emails, anything that shows you here?"

"Not that I'm aware of, except I did go online to review some parole petitions. You might be able to trace that. Until around ten p.m."

"Too early to help you." Pulaski said.

Harrigan rubbed his thick chin and too obviously was thinking how far he wanted to push Jake in an initial interview. Dermott's lips were pursed as though primed for argument when Jake asked, "How was he killed?"

Harrigan replied, "It will be on the news tonight. He was garrotted."

"Garrotted?" Dermott yelped. "In the car?"

"Leaving that for forensics. Right now, we're interviewing anyone he was with during the prior forty-eight hours. So far, we know that includes the people at the restaurant, Paulie Caprio, and your client."

Dermott wiped the back of his hand across his lips; as his hand slowly left his face, he was smiling. "Can't see a one-armed guy killing anyone with a garrote."

Harrigan gave Jake an up-and-down look of appraisal and replied sharply, "Mr. Fournier looks healthy enough to me." Harrigan stood and picked up his coat. "We're through for now. Might have to ask you to come in, Mr. Fournier."

"Okay by me, so long as Dermott's there."

Harrigan nodded at Jake, ignored Dermott, and started for the hall. Pulaski closed his iPad, gathered his raincoat, and joined Harrigan. Jake followed and opened the front door, reiterating that Paulie Caprio was merely a conduit to him, to which he got no reaction. Jake returned to the living room, as Dermott's tongue flicked his lips; the flag was up for some liquid refreshment.

"A garrote job," he said, his eyes bright, "would you believe it? Should take you out of the spotlight."

"That's not what I got from Harrigan."

"He's a cop. Not going to give up on anyone yet." Dermott laughed. "And you get to be interviewed wearing a tee shouting 'I got muscles.' Great!"

"The garrote?"

"To them, it means the Mob is involved. At one time, a garrote was used as a lesson, to make a point. Old school. Youngbloods would never use it." He shook his head. "Then, you tell them that Baldolucca said

Hope's killer was connected. The organized crime squad will have the bit between its teeth, notwithstanding Harrigan's suspicious cop mind. They'll ask questions on the Hill about the deceased, stir up the pot."

He stood and started toward the front door. "I'll follow up with somebody I know pretty well who works at the staties. Right now, it's time to add to my tab at Livia's."

Jake followed him into the hall. "Will you tell Livia what's happened?"

"Yeah. Remember, don't call her. I don't want her to embellish the facts."

Jake nodded and a guilty thought came to mind. *Gilletto is coming up tomorrow.* "Gilletto?" he said.

"Do what you gotta do," Dermott replied weakly with a shrug.

◊◊◊◊◊◊◊◊◊◊◊◊◊◊◊◊◊◊◊◊◊◊◊◊◊◊◊◊◊◊◊

That night, early local television news reported a murder in the parking lot of Victor's Restaurant in North Providence. Because of all the station's comments that the weapon was a garrote, police sources suggested the murder was a Mob hit.

That produced *agita* at the long bar at the Social Club. For two knee-crushers throwing back straight shots of Early Times bourbon, the garrote job on Baldolucca replaced speculation over the teardown of Fat Frankie's garage. "*Who's* dis fuckin' Baldolucca?"

"Small time."

"Did he owe?"

"Don't know."

"A snitch?"

"Don't know."

"Anybody he pals around with?"

"Don't know."

"A fuckin' wire? Like the Moustache Petes used in the movies? Some fuckoff wanting to show his balls, move up?"

"Yeah."

"So, nobody knows dis guy and because of the wire, the goddamn staties will be sticking their noses up where dey don't belong. I got my hand on my putz until dis is hung up."

In the soundproofed room below, a command was given to a circle of intimates. "I wanna know!" The table shook when the Brow's curled fist beat on it. He was rarely there after ten, and here it was close to midnight.

"We asked around. Nobody knows dis guy."

"Find the fuck who did it, or find me somebody who we can throw at 'em. *Capisce?*"

CHAPTER THIRTY-SIX

DURING THEIR FIFTEEN-MINUTE hearings in Medium Security, six victims or their family members forcefully argued against paroles for inmates who had committed heinous and unforgiveable acts, insisting that the perpetrators should serve out terms that were already too lenient for abuses suffered. One tearful victim exhibited scars on her arms and legs from burns from a cigarette while being gang-raped. The last to be heard was a thirteen-year-old boy, afraid that his inmate father, convicted of second degree domestic assault, would again abuse his mom, his sister, and himself.

After the family left the hearing room, Bertozzi offered that the father shouldn't be released while his children remained at home. All nodded agreement. When finished, Bertozzi looked at each board member in turn. The four had been chafing to bring up *Aaron's Anguish*. He began by saying, "You all read the statement I put out. That's as far as we go, as far as I'm concerned."

A flood of comments came, with Prebys the loudest. "The media frenzy is absolutely disgusting. Last time, it was just the town. Now it's every progressive politician and the town. Couldn't believe it! How could that video get taken? Where? And the outcry! You'd think Underwood was a war hero. This guy is a confessed murderer."

Jake grimaced at how close Prebys' outrage matched his own, and decided to remain silent.

Mia stuck out her chin. "Whoever filmed Underwood did a public service! He's been inside for almost thirty years, no trouble, wears the wounds."

Prebys ignored her. "I'm getting angry calls from my family, friends, clients to make sure he stays in. Even from a few from the other side who want him out. It's so emotional, all over the top."

"The video has struck a chord with the public," Mia said, "and we ought to listen." She turned to Jake for support, but he remained silent.

Bertozzi said gloomily. "My wife made me unplug the home phone because of all the calls we've been getting. Then Sunday after Mass, had a bunch of people tell me that Underwood should stay in. Our priest must also have an opinion, because his sermon was all about compassion, and one earnest young couple came up to me to say Underwood should be paroled because of his face."

Prebys rejoined, "I'm for invoking the six-month rule, right now, whether or not we hear from the warden. Underwood had to know he was on camera, a violation of the rules. That would kick the can down the road for a year. Get us out of the media's gunsight."

Bertozzi closed his laptop and stood. "Ten-minute break. I need a few minutes with the warden."

—————————————————

Jake had downed too much bottled water during the longer-than-expected victims' hearings and left for a tiny office with a toilet down the corridor from the hearing room. The board had long ago commandeered it for its private use. He had his key in the door lock when he heard Garo's voice, "Hey, Jake. Got a minute?"

Garo heaved himself towards Jake from down the corridor. Not having heard back from Dermott as to whether he could discuss the Baldolucca murder with Garo, Jake was reluctant.

"I'm back into hearings in a few minutes."

Garo ignored the brush-off as he reached Jake. He wore the same sports jacket as at the PC game; the waistband of his chinos buckled under his girth.

"If this is about Underwood . . ." Jake said, shaking his head "no way" as he entered the office. An overhead light blinked over three plastic scoop-seat chairs, a metal desk that held mugs, pencil holders, yellow legal pads and telephone books. A large, round wall clock ran ten minutes fast. Not to be denied, Garo followed him and sank into a chair; Jake sat on the desk's edge facing him.

"Did you watch the video?" asked Garo.

"Yeah."

"That's all you've got to say?"

Jake let out an impatient breath. "Maybe Underwood wasn't well advised or his trial was screwed up, and that's your department. But Lucretia Gist was murdered, and Aaron Underwood pled guilty. How she suffered is part of what we consider. Along with his record and whether he would be violent again, his face doesn't get him much leeway with me."

"Underwood's a conflicted and complicated character. I can tell you he's got no answers when it comes to the night of the murder. Just repeats he can't remember anything after leaving his house."

"He'd better remember if he comes before the board. And, so much for the remorse box. Anyway, I told you I'm not getting into it."

"I'm not asking you to."

"Yeah?"

Garo smiled. "Okay, so hear me out for a few minutes. I pieced this together from the offer the prosecutor made to the judge before the guilty plea was accepted. The old lady was as deaf as a post and was found in a room in the back of the house with the television blasting. No evidence of a forced entry, so we don't know how Underwood got in."

Jake put up his left hand to stop Garo, to no avail.

"You should hear this, Jake. You'll sit in judgment on him. Underwood is found on the floor next to the body. His face is a bloody mess. Double barreled bird gun, a scattergun, on the floor. Shoots a load of BB's like from a Red Ryder BB gun when you were a kid, only lots of BB's. Both barrels fired. One blast was in the ceiling, the other likely took off half Underwood's face. The two fingers of his right hand could have been lost in either shot. So how did she get two shots off? The fatal blow crushed her skull, likely she's immediately unconscious and dying. A pry bar is found on the floor next to them, his fingerprints on it, hers on the scattergun. But Jake, there is no record that anybody checked for fingerprints anywhere else in the room or house. Nobody saw the need to spend any serious investigation time on this, too obvious, right? Open and shut."

Jake replied with evident impatience. "So, they were less than thorough, but he's there, and she's dead from a whack from a pry bar lying next to her with his fingerprints on it. What's missing from that? Garo, I got to take a leak and get back inside."

"So, I ask ya, what came first?"

"What?"

"Does the kid somehow get inside, the deaf old lady manages to get off a round, which blows his face off and his right hand's fingers, and he still whacks her? Never happened! And despite her wound, she fires off two shots, squeezes two triggers, and his face and fingers are blown away? No way. By the way, there is nothing in the reports as to whether it was established Underwood is left- or right-handed. And how did he hold a pry bar with his fingers missing?"

"I don't follow."

"Think, Jake, think. Makes a difference on the angle and place of the head wound as to how it was swung and where her skull was crushed—right hand, likely left temple, left hand, right temple, unless her head was turned at some odd angle."

"Okay, they should have."

"The blow that killed her cracked her skull like an eggshell. The staties figured the blow triggered a spasm in her trigger finger that blew off Underwood's face. But that doesn't account for a second blast. There were two separate triggers on the scattergun. Is it really possible she got off two shots at him before or after she got whacked?"

"You have a theory?"

"Don't know yet," Garo admitted. "But here's something really peculiar. According to the staties' file, a couple of kids who said they were doing tricks or treats on Halloween found them. And not little kids, but junior high kids in the same class as Underwood. And you'll like this . . . one is now the Greenwick police chief. Name of Bain, the guy leading the opposition for parole. Bain's father was the chief before him and was the first police presence on the murder scene."

"Still nothing," Jake shrugged.

"The staties' complete file, including forensics, went to the AG for the grand jury indictment and trial. I got all that from the Research Division, which is usually on the ball. Haven't gone through it all yet, just what I told you. But nobody can locate the local file. Big case like that, biggest probably in the town's history, and they can't find the file? The whole story stinks, and it's not just my gut. Things don't add up. Anyway, I say Underwood didn't get the justice of a fair trial or a good lawyer. And we're all entitled to that."

Garo thought that last comment would strike home. *Where was Hope's justice?*

Jake resisted Garo's theories with the implication that the parole board should revisit the evidence and the trial, and started for the toilet door. His hand was on the knob when Garo said, "Okay, assume he did it thirty years ago, what keeps him in prison is his face. The board has paroled a lot of murderers, some who served less than thirty years."

"Yeah, and it might in his case, if convinced he was sorry and wouldn't do it again." Jake opened the door, unshaken in his belief that Underwood's parole petition had to be evaluated using fact and precedent—not emotion.

He decided against answering Garo. Instead, he said, "Did you join Aaron's Army?"

CHAPTER THIRTY-SEVEN

THE BOARD HEARD AND DECIDED twenty-three petitions from repentant drug dealers, other petty criminals, probation violators, and abusive partners, most of whom claimed to miss their wives or girlfriends or the desire to provide for their offspring, all of whom, including multiple parole violators and crime repeaters, pledged never to return to prison. The members worked quickly and were ready for Francisco Gilletto by one o'clock.

The portly, brow-wiping attorney Walter Kramer entered the room with Fat Frankie Gilletto and a CO. Fat Frankie's opinion of his last-minute, pricey lawyer was that he was a fuckin' know-it-all, an expensive double-breasted suit, with fat rippling down his neck and his tasseled loafers. An hour earlier, they had met in a lawyer-client room; Kramer told Fat Frankie that he was fortunate that his cousin Chris convinced him to take on the case at the last minute, that he put together a presentation in less than a day, and warned—warned—him to keep his emotions and language and facial expressions under control. Kramer said he would open with a statement covering all the legal bases for a parole, and then Fat Frankie would answer likely questions, which he briefly went over. Kramer also made the point that he was still owed six thousand for his fee that Chris had promised to pay promptly. *"What happened to the jewelry?"* Fat Frankie wanted to ask, but didn't.

Fat Frankie settled his bulk in the petitioner's straight-back chair and watched Kramer and the two older men exchange Rhode Island pleasantries—Red Sox prospects, Providence College in the NCAA's playoffs, the Celtics, the crummy weather, "How's your kid?" The other two were the woman whom Kramer said might be sympathetic, and the guy that Kramer didn't know. Neither bothered to look up from their laptops. *Look at them,* Fat Frankie thought, *so this is who passes judgment on me? An old guy with a potato face and a bad comb-over with a gavel in his hand, another one with thick glasses on a long nose born sucking lemons, a prissy woman in a tight black suit, got a figure, not a bad looker, and a younger serious guy, expressionless, with a lot of combed-back hair over his ears and a furled forehead, likely a hardass. What's with the sleeve in a jacket pocket?*

The comb-over opened the hearing with a tap of a gavel. "Opening statement, Mr. Kramer?"

Kramer stood, rebuttoned his gray suit jacket, opened a redweld file, ponderously removed clipped packages of documents, thumbed through them, and placed them on the table in precise stacks. Portentously he cleared his throat, and began.

"Just a few words, members of the board. My client, Mr. Gilletto, absolutely merits your consideration. I'm sure you have carefully examined my client's clean prison record,"—he touched one pile—"the quality of his community support,"—another pile—"his mother's medical records as to her dementia, and her desire to be assisted by her son"—another pile touched—"and his future employment"—the fourth pile he similarly blessed. "I remind you that this was his first offense, and any fair-minded person would agree his sentence was harsh."

Kramer went through the highlights of each stack with emphasis on Frankie's mother's medical condition and Gilletto being her only son.

"You will find that Mr. Gilletto fulfills every important condition for parole under the statute, and I urge your due consideration. His suffering mother awaits him. Thank you." He sat, wheezing from exertion.

That's it? Frankie thought. *Maybe eight or nine minutes max? For ten g's?*

"Mr. Gilletto, do you want to make a statement as well? If not, we will proceed with our questions."

"No statement, sir," he replied with the smooth politeness Kramer had instructed.

"Very well. Mr. Prebys?" the Chair said with a nod to Prebys.

"What kind of a job is a clerk at the Port of Providence?" Prebys asked, making the job sound dinky.

"I would help with bookkeeping," said Fat Frankie. "I'm good with numbers."

"A new opening or something that's been advertised?"

"Pay isn't so much, I was told, so the job has been hard to fill."

"Okay," Prebys said, evidencing little interest, folded his arms, and sat back in his chair.

The woman, earlier described by Kramer as likely sympathetic because of his mother's dementia, had been peering at him over her glasses.

"As I understand it, you were in the pawnshop business, is that correct?"

The long-nosed guy snickered loudly. "How do you spell that....*p-a-w-n* or *p-o-r-n*?"

The woman and the Chair scowled; the other member didn't react.

"I was a licensed pawnbroker for over twenty years. Broadway Pawn and Coins. Bought and sold gold and estate jewelry, watches, lots of coins."

"Can't go back to that, can you?" the woman asked flatly.

"No, ma'am, lost my license."

"Because you had possession of stolen guns?"

"They were in my shop in a pawn when I got caught up in a crackdown on all the Providence pawn shops. I hadn't been . . . careful with the regulations." He stopped, having been warned by Kramer not to get into his case or his defense. "My mother is getting on, all kinds of things wrong with her, dementia . . ."

"You served almost three years?"

"Yes, ma'am. If I get out, I'm not coming back. I'm fifty-two and I want to spend the rest of my life outside. I'll live with my mother, I'll take care of her, she's got no one else." He heard himself sounding sincere.

"Any relatives, friends that you would look to for guidance, assistance, if you are released?"

She must be a complete dope. "Father Scalini at Holy Eucharist. I think he wrote you a letter in favor of my release. My family is in his parish. I don't drink no more, I won't gamble, not even a scratch ticket."

He felt pressure on his thigh from his lawyer's knee that signaled "Don't overdo it."

"Thank you," she said, scanned her laptop's screen, and sat back.

The comb-over nodded at the remaining member, the new guy. Fat Frankie's eyes went to his. They were frosty, black as coal, penetrating, forcing a look away.

"No questions," he said, and Fat Frankie almost sighed in relief.

The comb-over took over. "The board takes gun trafficking very seriously, a crime against the community. Guns go anywhere, everywhere. Kids get them as easily as buying bootleg cigarettes. Those guns could have killed in a gang turf war . . ." He rambled on.

Fat Frankie tried to look interested but wanted to say that gangbangers didn't use guns like his cache of three compact Glocks. They wanted something mean looking, heavy, and scary like .44 magnum automatics to stick into their droopy pants. Then, he remembered something— remorse.

"I'm very sorry. I learned my lesson the hard way. I was stupid. Never should have taken them in, ruined my business, my life."

He stopped, mentally reviewing his list: *job, mother, being polite, remorse.* There was something else. *What is it?* He felt the sweat popping on his forehead. That wouldn't look good.

Bertozzi looked to his right and left. "Any more questions?" There were none. "You'll be informed on our decision," and he nodded to Mrs. Ames, who had entered during Kramer's initial spiel. *What was I supposed to say?*

Fat Frankie remembered! *A thank you!* "Thank you for listening to me. I promise I'm going straight. I got a job waiting for me and I'll take care of my mother." He stood and turned to Kramer, who shook his hand weakly before returning his files to his briefcase. Kramer said his goodbyes to the board members and preceded Gilletto and the CO through the door to an anteroom.

|||||||||||||||||||||||||||||||||||||||||||||||||||||||

As they waited in the anteroom for the CO to unlock the door to the corridor, Kramer whispered to his client that the hearing had gone well, that he was optimistic, and that Frankie better come up with the rest of his fee, fast. Frankie's reaction was, *It goddamn better have gone well, for ten g's.*

CHAPTER THIRTY-EIGHT

PREBYS CLOSED HIS LAPTOP and yawned. "Got a favorable recommendation from his counselor. Let him serve the two months to make it an even three years, then out." He inspected the ceiling and missed Jake almost blurting out, *What? A gun possession rap and Prebys votes for parole?*

Mia squelched her rebuttal to Prebys' expected no vote and said, "He's got a clean record, a favorable recommendation from his counselor, sounds remorseful, got a job, and a mother he says he can take care of. Yes."

Bertozzi, flabbergasted by Prebys' vote and now frustrated and irritated, broke the tradition that the Chair vote last. "I don't hold with selling guns! He can wait a year and come back."

Jake swallowed hard. He had prepared for his yes vote that would mean a postponement, but not a *yes* that would grant a gun seller parole. He needed time to gather his thoughts, recalculate what a yes vote meant legally and morally. Then, he concluded, sometimes you just have to pick a side.

"I—"

Wham! The metal anteroom door reverberated as though struck by a sledge, and then all heard muffled cries, a sharp bang at the door, a thud and a clear shout of *"Officer down! Code blue! Code blue! C thirteen! Officer down!"*

Bertozzi gripped the edge of the table to steady himself, remembering an incident from the prior year when an inmate grabbed a chair and threatened to heave it at the board, the on-duty CO struggling to restrain him, shouting "Code blue" into his shoulder mic.

"Stay put," Bertozzi ordered sharply as Mrs. Ames and Mia pushed their chairs back to allow them space to move quickly out of harm's way; Jake, seated closest to the anteroom, was halfway to its door. Prebys, ducking under the table, screamed, "Call a CO!"

Bertozzi didn't have to. A CO burst in from the anteroom, baton raised, hair disheveled, out of breath. "Sorry, folks. Under control."

"What's going on?" Bertozzi demanded.

"Not sure yet, got a CO and prisoner on the floor."

Bertozzi followed the CO back into the anteroom, returning in less than a minute to a spat between Prebys and Mia as to whether to continue the vote. Bertozzi slammed his gavel.

"Adjourned," he said. "We'll get a report from staff. Seems that Aaron Underwood pushed a bookcart in the corridor into the petitioner. We are adjourned."

"Underwood?" Prebys and Mia chorused.

―――――――――――

Fat Frankie had followed Kramer into the corridor, back to back with the CO fumbling with a ring of keys on his belt to relock the anteroom door. A smile of self-satisfaction at his smooth-as-silk performance was beginning to gel a second before he had sensed motion in the corridor to his right. He had turned and taken a bookcart's charge full on. His buttocks smacked into the CO's rump, pushing the CO into the unlocked door that opened under the pressure, the chain with key in the lock pulling the CO forward. Fat Frankie had grabbed at air, tumbled with the CO onto the anteroom's floor and against the inner door where together they flopped like freshly boated bluefish. The CO had shouted into his shoulder mic as Fat Frankie's attempts to roll his bulk off the CO got him tangled with the CO's legs; they screamed at each other and tussled to gain leverage to stand, as two other COs with batons raised rushed in from the corridor. Fat Frankie was jerked up by his shirt and pushed into the corridor where he was now cuffed and his face flattened against the wall.

"It was Fuck Face!" Fat Frankie had shouted repeatedly, just as he had three years ago in his first altercation with Underwood, until silenced by a baton that smacked his behind.

|||||||||||||||||||||||||||||||||||||||||||||||||||||||||||

Jake walked across the parking lot, Prebys, short of breath, seething in frustration, a step behind him.

"Can't believe it. I heard that monster has the run of the place, but the silver lining is that's it for Underwood. The six month rule applies. He's history. And as for Gilletto, the vote should stand."

"I didn't vote," Jake reminded him as he continued briskly toward the Camaro. "Bertozzi said we would continue the vote on Gilletto after we get the warden's report. As to Underwood, we should wait to determine if he is punished for the incident."

Prebys' breath evolved into a snort, his face a fierce red. He caught up to Jake, grabbed him by the right shoulder, spinning him around. "C'mon, if Mia and I can agree on something, what's your problem?" Prebys' weak chin made an effort to be forceful.

Jake stopped, took Prebys' hand and flung it from his shoulder, applying more pressure than necessary, "Easy, Floyd, don't get into something you can't handle."

Prebys' car was quickly out of the parking lot while Jake lingered behind the wheel of the Camaro. At least temporarily, he had been saved from a demeaning, legally corrupt, and morally dubious vote. Was he now off the loyalty hook? If the six-month rule was invoked against Gilletto, Jake could resign without letting down Dermott. *It could work out,* he thought. Would Garo be disappointed if he left before Underwood came up? Shouldn't be, since Jake made it clear that he wasn't likely to vote in favor for his parole.

He pressed the ignition button and the engine started with a growl when he saw Mia waving at him from an open window in her nearby Saab. He rolled down his window.

"Things are getting bizarre," she shouted. "Why would Underwood risk an opportunity for a hearing? Can't understand it." Then she added, "Are you coming tonight? Don't think I got your RSVP. Business casual dress, six to eight."

Jake had forgotten to respond to her cocktail party e-invitation. Maybe because an East Side cocktail party was unfamiliar territory? Or because Mia might come on to him? He hesitated before he said to himself, *Why not?*

CHAPTER THIRTY-NINE

JAKE SWUNG THE CAMARO out of Medium Security's parking lot onto Pontiac Avenue, with Alanis Morissette sounding sweet on the CD player. The morning's events were playing out in his mind when a shiny red Ford Fusion swung sharply into his lane from a car dealership, causing Jake to stomp the brake pedal. *Idiot*! New car, new driver? Staring at the Fusion's rear, his attention was drawn to its license plate, a beat-up, loosely attached on an angle, orange plate. *Orange?*

Jake accelerated the Camaro and closed to within ten feet of the Fusion as it made a turn onto the ramp heading toward Interstate 95. Tiny black lettering spelled out "USED" and "RI" above four black numbers on the orangey plate.

"Used?" Jake shouted.

Jake pulled over before the exit to Interstate 95 north, touched Garo's pre-set number on his cell, and sat back as it synced into the Camaro's bluetooth.

"Used plates are temporaries," Garo said, "for dealers and repair shops and junkyards to pick up or road test."

"The truck could have been one of them."

"Long shot, but I'll get on it. Those guys are not nature's noblemen, some are connected."

"Bill your time for this."

Garo paused before saying, "Okay, and I heard from Dermott. I got retained on the North Providence garrote murder."

"Dermott told me not to call you because you work for the state."

"Must have forgot or figured it out because he put me on it."

"Will you have time for both, particularly the used plate?"

"Yeah, I got a couple of vacation days coming to me. But I do need something in return. Your open mind."

"Underwood?"

"I know what you said earlier, and I respect that, but I'm asking you to look at whatever I come up with."

"Aaron Underwood pled guilty, Garo. You can't get over that. The crime was vicious. The parole board isn't a pardon commission, and I'm not a goddamn therapist."

Garo huffed. "That malarkey may be okay for routine cases. Underwood isn't routine." After a moment, he added, "And now you know how it feels to come under suspicion without an alibi."

CHAPTER FORTY

LIVIA WAS AT THE REGISTER with the cashier, going over luncheon receipts. Excited as Jake was to tell her about the orangey plate, he was ushered into their office. Jake took the sofa and she stood by her desk, hands on hips, frowning, looking down on him.

"A state police detective," she said, sounding pissed, "name of Pulaski, came in this morning. Inquired as to when you left me Sunday night. Did you say anything about this Aldo somebody, or about new evidence in your wife's case? I said no." Jake could see she was building up for a quarrel. "By the way, why didn't you tell me about this guy you met hours before we drove to Newport? I have to hear about it from Dermott? We were together the whole weekend, Jake, the whole weekend!"

"I was trying to stay cool about it, not get anyone else involved."

"Not good for us, Jake. All weekend?"

He apologized and told her about Paulie Caprio, the meeting with Baldolucca in the park. "I should have told you. When the staties questioned me about Baldolucca, Dermott told me not to call you because you are my alibi, such as it is, I thought that he'd talk to you first."

"Which he did and told me not to contact you," she replied slowly. She shook her head, still frowning and not forgiving. "So, I told the cop that when you left me about nine, you had a migraine that had been going on for hours and said you going home and to bed."

"Did I say that?"

"Yes," she replied firmly, "you did."

"That's all?"

"I didn't like his tone. Pushy and accusatory, as though I knew something more. Which happens to be wrong, because you didn't confide in me." She took a step toward him, sat on the sofa's arm, leaned in to him, and exhaled. "Dermott said this Baldolucca might have been a passenger in the truck that killed Hope. Knew some details. If you believed him, that could establish a motive for his murder."

"I went home, checked my laptop and went to bed," Jake insisted. "The guy was killed with a garrote in the parking lot of the restaurant where he worked in North Providence." She winced, and he patted his right shoulder. "The garrote takes me out of the picture. But the staties on the case, this guy Pulaski for one, are not letting me off as yet."

"Jake, I was just thinking out loud about how it could look to a cop." Her tight smile belied her relief. More than anyone, even Dermott, she knew of the violent, often detailed, deaths he dreamed of for Hope's killer. Too often she had awakened during his nightmares and lay with him to soothe him.

Jake took her hand, about to tell her about the orangey plate, when interrupted by a sharp rap at the office door.

Dermott entered, his stained Kelly-green tie was a St. Patrick's Day leftover, his wrinkled blue suit had stood up a date with the dry cleaner. Jake gave Dermott the sofa, moving to behind his desk. "Fuckin'. . . oops, pardon my French . . . oops, pardon my choice of nationality, but the Irish can be pigheaded." Dermott loosened his tie and left it askew. "We're nice sort of people until we wear a uniform." He laughed in self-deprecation. "Harrigan will retain you in the 'interest' file unless and until something comes up on the garrote or forensics, or another motive is discovered."

"But it was a garrote," said Jake.

"Harrigan thinks you're the type that could do it, despite your obvious handicap. Told his squad you got muscles popping out all over, the victim was a scrawny guy, weighed less than one-forty. A couple of staties have been doing one-arm exhibitions to show that for a guy as musclebound as you, it is physically possible. Being a smart guy, you purposefully used a garrote to throw off suspicion."

Jake raised his left hand in defense as Dermott continued. "But, more importantly, they got no one else. And no witness. They've canvassed the neighborhood. Nobody saw anything or anybody suspicious. With that rainstorm, nobody even heard the crash. For a suspect, they go into the guy's history, and there's you, *mon ami*. Unless there is a source or something from forensics, they've got no one but you and . . . Paulie Caprio, who also has no alibi. He stays a prime suspect as maybe your accomplice. So, they'll pressure him."

"He'll be okay. He knows nothing."

"Whatever. They'll press him to say something incriminating. He's gotta be very itchy right now because they got a search warrant for his apartment and found some weed in his refrigerator. Claims he has a medical marijuana card, but couldn't produce it. He called me and I got him a lawyer."

"How do you get all this inside stuff?"

"A buddy, like me, a former seminarian, in admin with the staties. Still has a moral compass."

"I told Paulie to be absolutely truthful."

"And maybe he will be, but eventually he'll say something that'll get twisted. Until then, every denial will be taken as jerking them around. I got Lev Goldstein to represent him. Good guy. By now, he's on the case. By the way, I need a five-grand retainer for me, two for Garo's time and effort would do it. Lev will want two or three."

"No problem. Paulie doesn't deserve this. What am I supposed to do?"

"Absolutely nothing out of the ordinary. Keep your yap shut, please. Go to the gym, the parole board, but stay away from Paulie. Can you do that?"

Jake nodded and finally got to relate his sighting of the orangey license plate.

"I've seen them!" Dermott exclaimed. "They smack them on for a test drive, right? Hold them on with magnets. On and off. I bet hardly anybody keeps a record of who's driving one or a make or model. But maybe somebody remembers one coming back with a crushed fender."

"Finally, a bit of good news," said Livia, who had been patiently listening to Jake and Dermott. "I've got to get into the kitchen for tonight's menu." She bent at the waist and kissed Jake's forehead. "Be careful. Listen to Dermott. Please!" she said and left them.

"Gilletto," Jake said, as the door closed, breaking the confidentiality rule of the board by revealing that it had been two-to-one for parole, and up to him, when chaos broke out in the corridor. "The vote was postponed until the incident is investigated. Shouldn't be long."

"He's got two votes? Without you?" Dermott's face came alive with possibilities.

"The six-month rule might apply."

"Oh, I love these unwritten rules."

"Do you want to know how I would have voted?"

"No," Dermott replied too quickly, leaving Jake with the impression that Dermott didn't want to risk embarrassment. Instead, Dermott smacked his lips. "If I was Chris Gilletto, I'd get busy on the governor's appointee to the board—if he can find out who that is."

CHAPTER FORTY-ONE

IF IT HAD BEEN physically possible, Aaron, cuffed and flattened against a corridor wall by COs, would have closed his grin.

He had not seen Gilletto since their altercation in the prison library. Aaron had picked up a carton of new books from the mailroom and was on his way back to the library in the corridor outside of the parole board hearing room when Gilletto suddenly appeared, blocking his way. Aaron realized that Gilletto had just left his hearing, and the son of a bitch was smirking. Smirking! Enraged, Aaron rammed the bookcart into Gilletto's gut.

When Aaron was hustled away to detention, he admonished himself for losing control, and as a result likely his freedom. He got an idea when he heard Gilletto's lawyer. "Probably didn't see my client with that one eye," he shouted to the COs.

By the time the SIU investigator came into Aaron's detention cell, he was prepared, claiming that he had been in a hurry, hadn't noticed Gilletto emerge from the anteroom until it was too late to avoid a collision. "Sorry," he said with as much sincerity as his voice could muster, "but shit like this happens when you only got one eye."

Later, the CO who had hit the floor with Gilletto told the investigating SIU that Gilletto was on Underwood's blind side when the bookcart struck Gilletto, or maybe Gilletto was surprised to see Underwood in the hallway and walked into it. Either way, the CO saw it as an accident, which was reflected in the report to the warden.

After discussion among the warden and his assistants, and a nudge from the governor's office, it was decided to continue with Underwood's parole hearing in the morning.

CHAPTER FORTY-TWO

AS JAKE DRESSED for Mia's cocktail party, he wondered what "business casual" was these days. He decided against a dress shirt and a tie, in favor of a dark brown turtleneck sweater, gray slacks, and a gray tweed sport coat that had been purchased with Hope four years earlier. Jake stood in front of the bedroom mirror, thinking he looked presentable. He ran his fingers through his hair to give it something of a less stylized, more youthful look. *Why?* he thought.

He checked emails for Mia's address and soon found himself on Wayland Avenue, only a few blocks from Livia's apartment, in a well-to-do residential area of single-family homes on treed lots set back from the street. Some homes had wide verandas, others with Queen Anne embellishments, still others were neo-Georgians from the 1920s.

Her house was Mediterranean style with a red tile roof and a pebbled driveway that cut through a lawn of winter killed grass bordered by shrubs and raised flower beds to a garage. The line of cars at the curb stretched down the long block. Jake made a U-turn and parked closer and across the street. The night was cold, overcast and damp, as a whiff of winter remained. He marched up three stairs from the wide sidewalk to a flagstone walk to the front door and heard the buzz of conversation and music before he rang the bell. When it wasn't answered, he entered.

The central hall was crowded with well-dressed young- and middle-aged guests in conversations, holding drinks and picking at hors d'oeuvres from trays held by female servers. *University types, stockbrokers, lawyers, realtors,* he thought, *all likely somebodies in town.* A staircase facing the entry led to a second floor. Jake didn't recognize anyone and was about to venture into a living room when, in the crush of guests, out of the corner of his eye he saw an extraordinarily appealing Mia. Her hair was curled back into a bun, she wore a figure-enhancing, knee-length red cocktail dress, a gold necklace with a turquoise stone settled neatly in her cleavage. Her makeup was perfect, and her smile was gracious and inviting.

She reached him and placed her arm through his and murmured, "I'm sooo glad you came, Jake. C'mon in. There's lots of people you should meet."

She fluttered her eyelashes as she led him into the living room where a substantial open space suggested furniture had been removed to enhance party traffic and cocktail chatter. He felt her pressure on his arm as she introduced him to two men in their early fifties holding martini glasses. One she introduced as Howard something, the other as Charles something. Both looked professional, and both extended their right hands only to pull them back upon seeing Jake's disability.

Charles started. "So, you're on the parole board with Mia."

"Yes," Jake said simply and was asked by a server what he wanted to drink. Jake indicated a San Pellegrino with a slice of lime would be fine.

"How long have you been on?" Charles asked. Jake noted his piercingly bright blue eyes, a long jaw, and that he spoke through a large honker.

"Just a few months," Jake answered.

"Any background in criminology or sociology, like Mia?" Howard's dry voice gave off indications of a Yankee lineage. "And she does brighten a room."

"There was an opening and I volunteered."

"Of course," Howard said to Charles as though Jake hadn't spoken. "She's exactly the sort of person that we need involved in volunteer social services. You know she'll take it seriously, you know that she's got judgment, you know that she can handle herself."

Jake thought, *Like I can't?*

His San Pellegrino arrived and he sipped his drink as the conversation stalled until Charles said, "I don't believe I'd be equipped to do it. I don't have preconceived notions on guilt and innocence, or whether someone deserves a break."

"And what do you do, Howard?" Jake asked.

"I teach at Brown. English Department." Howard looked at Charles and chortled, "And I'm very judgmental."

Charles laughed. "Well, I'm judgmental, too, I guess. Have to be. I'm a banker. But that's basically credit scores and reputation. I don't have to deal with life and death in a prison."

Jake felt an irritation growing. "Have either one of you ever been inside a prison?"

"Not me," said Howard, smiling. "They've never found me out."

Charles' eyes sparked with interest. "I have, years ago. I took a tour at Medium Security with a group from the Chamber of Commerce learning about governmental services including the penal system. Quite frankly, I don't know how anybody makes it through there."

Howard interrupted. "You know, Mia told us a bit about this situation with this murderer Underwood. I saw that video. I suppose you've got the same issues she has?"

Jake took another sip before he replied. "The video certainly has gotten an audience and some folks seem to want his parole to be more a question about his face and how he was treated than what he did or might do. Some forget he pled guilty to a horrendous murder. We have to evaluate whether that someone, under stress or whatever might have been the trigger, would do it again."

"I say keep him in. Why take the chance?" Charles said.

Howard disagreed, "I say it's time—"

Mia arrived at that moment. Being the good hostess, she said, "Boys, I'm taking him away."

Jake smiled pleasantly and was led into the dining room overflowing with guests with plates in hand, picking at platters of vegetables and cold cuts or dipping into chafing dishes. Jake indicated to Mia that he would pass on the spread and was promptly introduced to two URI professors, both female and both smartly dressed and chatty. It had been a while since he had been in one-on-two friendly conversation with comely female strangers. After pleasantries, the taller, prettier one said, "Jake, I know this is impertinent, but how did you lose your arm?"

"I was in the military."

"Where? In Afghanistan or Iraq or—"

"Iraq."

"Never should have been there," said her friend with a *tsk, tsk* voice. "If we had simply minded our own business, things like what happened to you wouldn't have. It was Bush, Cheney and the oil people, that's the only reason we were there."

"Well, after 9/11," her taller friend commented, "we all lost our heads a little bit. We had to get back at those people. If we're not careful—"

"Those people? Who are 'those people'?" the other replied as Jake drifted towards an offering of charcuterie at the serving table. He finished his drink, and nibbled a few pieces of hard sausage and edged out to the hall. He was thinking it was time to leave when Mia's hand was placed possessively on the small of his back. She guided him through the hall to a library. Abruptly, Jake felt fatigue. He glanced at his watch and the numerals danced on its face. A migraine was coming, and he was angry because he was complicit, having left his pillbox of Imitrex on his bedroom's bureau.

"Jake, I hope you can stay for a bit. Most of these folks are leaving now, but some of my special friends will stay for coffee, cordials, and dessert." Jake decided he could brave the migraine.

A waitstaff of two served cookies and a sliced date cake in the library. Jake recognized one guest: Mark Plotkin's photograph appeared over his twice-a-week column in the *Journal*, and Plotkin was the kind of guest he might have expected at a party thrown by Mia Sanchez. Jake sat on a leather sofa with Mia at his side. Plotkin was holding forth as though testing out a column.

"What interests me is how the opposing sides are shaping their messages," he said, suggesting that his insights merited attention and approval.

"The Free Aaron partisans are cosmopolitan and spontaneous, adept at their use of the internet's unstoppable pull to draw in national politicians and celebrities. They now have Susan Sarandon reprising her Academy Award portrayal of a nun serving death row prisons, joining Alec Baldwin on YouTube in support of parole, Stephen Colbert and Trevor Noah and others keep advocacy alive for late-night viewers. Their cause attracts young people, college students in particular, who get their news and form their views from social media interaction, and have the time and opportunity to rally for Underwood's release on campuses and at the statehouse, and participate in the vigil outside the prison. They are connected and can pop up at any time, any place."

Jake heard murmurs of assent.

"An example of their star power will be on display Saturday afternoon with a Free Aaron rally planned with Terrell Williams at the Temple to Music in Roger Williams Park. Everyone know who he is?"

His answer came from the youngest of the listeners, a woman who appeared excited and keenly aware of Williams. "The rapper with a conscience," she said, "multi-time Grammy award winner. Singer, composer, great keyboardist, a social media star, born and raised in South Providence. He'll attract a huge crowd."

"Thank you," Plotkin said as though she had stolen his next few paragraphs.

"On the other side," Plotkin continued, "Greenwick's police chief is not exactly a media star talent, and his message is that Aaron's Army's soldiers are softheaded do-gooders and Underwood is a vicious murderer. Not exactly inspiring. The closest the opposition has to celebrity are talk radio hosts like…" his thumb at his open mouth in a gagging motion, "Buddy Callahan."

That brought out a few "I can't stand him" comments.

"These guys beat the Underwood piñata daily. They conflate the possibility of Underwood's parole with the inability of state government to deal with the frustrations of disgruntled, defensive, ordinary Rhode Islanders." Callahan, according to Plotkin, had organized counter demonstrations at the prison and at the AG's office, urging his listeners to be assertive toward politicians, pushing them to keep Underwood locked away.

The monologue was interrupted as a cart of cordials, ports, and iced wine was wheeled in.

Jake was all too aware of Callahan. Two years earlier, Jake had been featured on his drive-time program and in Callahan's echo chamber of the dissatisfied to berate the staties—also a *bête noir* of Callahan—for the lack of progress in Hope's murder investigation. Jake had been warned by Dermott and Garo that Callahan's program was a food fight on radio. After that one appearance, Jake agreed that Callahan was self-centered, morally tone deaf, articulate, sharp-witted, and dangerous.

Drinks were served as Jake's migraine became a serious challenge. He excused himself, intending to use the half-bath off the hall to splash water on his face. Mia followed. "Migraine?" she asked. "Oh, Jake, I should not have pressed you to stay. You were just being polite."

"I wanted to stay, believe me."

"Look," she said, her face showing concern. "I know this sounds impertinent, whatever, but why don't you take a few minutes and lie down before you go? I've had migraines for years myself. Never know when something is a trigger, like stress or I'm off my diet, or not getting enough sleep. What do you take?"

"Imitrex and I forgot to bring it."

"I take Fiorinal."

Jake remembered the brand name, an older medication containing barbiturates. He hadn't swallowed a barbiturate in years.

Mia continued. "I take one when I think I've got a migraine coming on and it helps. I'm no doctor, but my guess is two would do it for someone your size. No more powerful than a large dosage of Ambien. It's started to sleet. The roads will be icy. Lie down. If it doesn't help, I'll drive you home."

Jake knew he should say no to both offers. But the thought of being able to close his eyes at that moment overcame pride and caution.

She led him upstairs and opened a door to a bedroom with an adjoining bathroom and a king-size bed that was crisply made up with a pale blue coverlet. Nightstands were set at either side with table lights, which Jake saw as flickering. Across the room was a dressing table with bottles and sprays, supporting a sturdy mirror. He sat at the edge of the bed.

"Mia, go back to your guests. Don't want to be a problem. I'll close my eyes for a few minutes, then I'll roll home."

Mia left for the bathroom, returned, and put a glass of water and put two green capsules on the night table.

"Jake, don't worry. You shouldn't drive. Take as much time as you need. I'm here to take care of you." She cradled his face in her hands and looked him squarely in the eyes. He didn't resist and breathed in the lemony scent in her hair and skin as he swallowed the capsules and closed his eyes.

He lay on top of the bed and before he knew it, the Fiorinal had knocked him out.

CHAPTER FORTY-THREE

CONSCIOUSNESS RETURNED RELUCTANTLY. He found himself under a cover without any idea where he was. He stretched his left arm and felt the width of the bed. It didn't seem familiar. His mind went to memories of perfume, to breaths, and a sought-after low spot in the bed beside him. He rolled over on his stump and touched a body. *Livia,* he thought. *I must have made it to her apartment. But how did I get here?*

The body moved closer. He touched something flimsy, silky and warm, a camisole maybe, and he realized where he was. His eyes opened, his tongue flicked his lips, found his mouth was as dry as cotton; his headache had left but not the numbness, indecision, and stupidity. He felt the body curl into him, fit into his back, and he sensed breaths on his neck and shoulder, and realized that his jacket and trousers were gone.

"Jake, are you awake? Are you okay?"

"What time is it?" he asked.

"After four. When I came in to wake you and drive you home, you were out cold. I got you comfortable. There was a sleet storm outside. Impossible to drive. In the morning, I'll make us a breakfast and get you home."

Jake turned on his left elbow, braced himself to face her and felt her lips hungrily pressed on his. He thought he would be too numb to reciprocate, but he did feel the pulse of desire. Her kisses and tongue went down onto his neck and chest and to his stump. She was touching him, caressing him with hands that knew their business, and he responded, not totally convinced he wasn't dreaming of Hope's fierce lovemaking.

It was as if she had grabbed his tie and led him to her bed. He felt her hands on him, and knew that he was hard as she fondled him.

"Jake," she said, almost in a purr. "Just relax. You don't have to do anything. Nothing at all. Let me take care of you."

She straddled him, engulfed him. This was something that Livia, no, this was something Hope might do. Mia's breaths became shorter and shorter, dissolving into a moan. He found himself in a rhythm with her hips and body, her hands on his shoulders, pressing down, her breasts so close to his face. He grasped her buttocks, and opened his mouth as she held him at the edge, and they gasped together as they climaxed in his deepening thrusts.

Jake had slept after the sex and awoke confused again as to his whereabouts. He sat up and put his face in his left hand and felt the heat of shame and desire. He wanted to say something about the passion that had been there, just as it had been with Hope. In the dark, he could make out the room's furniture, the outline of a window, a lamp. Mia moved, her hand caressed his stump, something that Hope sometimes did.

"This was a mistake," he blurted.

"No, Jake, no, it was good as I knew it would be. It was just something that happened. I never expected it, but I don't regret it. It was nice, Jake. You were nice. Nothing to regret. Go back to sleep and then I'll drive you home."

Jake struggled to stand. He was lightheaded. Where were his jacket, shirt and trousers? His eyes fixed on a shaft of light, might have been a streetlight.

"No, I can drive," he said, finding his clothes neatly folded on a chair.

She propped herself up on an elbow, her breasts filled out her silky pajama top. "Jake, we have time to see if this can work for both of us."

CHAPTER FORTY-FOUR

THE WEATHER WAS NOT as bad as Mia had suggested. In fact, while the side streets to Pawtucket were slippery with black ice, the main drags had been salted and sanded. He arrived at Park Place just as a red line of dawn pushed away the dark. He went to his bedroom, tucking away his dark, guilty thoughts for another few hours of sleep. He woke only to be plunged into recollections of how Mia's skill and passion reminded him of lovemaking with Hope—and his infidelity to Livia.

By eleven o'clock, the remains of the sleet had evaporated in a warming sun. Jake went for a long, mind-clearing jog. He worked up a healthy sweat over a familiar seven-mile route from Park Place to Armistice Boulevard, then along the Ten Mile River trail in Slater Park, onto the bike trail through East Providence, over the Seekonk River to Providence's East Side, down Blackstone Boulevard, and back towards home.

As he reached Park Place, he heard, then saw, a chanting, placard-shaking crowd milling about on the front lawn of the Governor Foley Mansion. Buddy Callahan, in a baseball cap and windbreaker with a bullhorn, stood under its portico. A media truck from Channel 11 had its transmission antenna raised; video cameras were visible in a crowd that was middle-aged, white, and hanging on his every shouted word. A Pawtucket police cruiser was parked across the ribbon of parkland in front of the Pawtucket Foundation's office.

Jake climbed the granite steps of the Spanish-American War memorial, a cast iron statue of a Rough Rider with a slouch kit, bedroll and rifle by his side, facing the mansion; no one gave a second look at the tall guy in a hooded sweatshirt, running pants, and sneakers. Shouts of approval and placard waves came regularly during Callahan's harangue against the "elitists" and "left-wing whack jobs" who comprised Aaron's Army and the Free Aaron movement. He called for renewed pressure on the parole board members to vote for "the people." He finished to applause and strident shouts of approval, surrounded by backslapping and hugging supporters.

Callahan's message irritated Jake, but more so, he was angered by the trespass on his property. His stubbornness kicked into gear as he pushed back his hood and elbowed his way forward through the crowd to the mansion's front walk. He was climbing the steps to the portico when a woman's voice rang out, "That's him!"

The balding, red-faced Callahan saw Jake and thrust a mic into his face as camera lights winked on.

"Look, everyone, this is Jake Fournier from the parole board. He's been a victim of shoddy police work, knows what the people deserve and need in terms of personal security." He turned to Jake. "Don't inflict this monster on us, Jake. He killed an old woman and got what he deserved."

It was not a time for reasoned argument. Instead, Jake removed his sweatshirt to reveal a sweat-stained tee and his right arm stump, gave the crowd time to notice, and said without emotion, "You may not realize it, Mr. Callahan, but you and these folks are trespassing on my private property."

Clearly surprised by the rebuke, Callahan retorted, "You're a public person. Before all this and now as a parole board member. The people have a right to protest."

"That's why we have parks. One right over there." Jake lifted his stump in the direction of the Rough Rider. A woman in front seemed to audibly gag as she turned away.

"We're here to let you know the people have a say on this. Which way are you going to vote?" Callahan angrily demanded, gaining encouragement from voices in the crowd.

"I'll vote whatever way I think is right. Trespassing on my property isn't going to pressure or sway me, and it doesn't do your cause any good." With that, Jake found a key in his running pants, unlocked his front door, and went inside, leaving behind shouts of "Monster Lover."

He leaned against the closed door and was surprised that no one hammered on it.

After the crowd dispersed, Jake went outside with a trash bag and picked up soda cans, plastic coffee cups, a placard shouting "Don't free a killer," and McDonald's wrappers. Two newly planted geraniums under a front window had been crushed, and the groundcover of *verbiea* disturbed. A Pawtucket cop left his cruiser and helped him with the trash.

"I'm gonna tell the chief we ought to stake out here. Some of these people are hotheads." He stuffed an armful of cans and papers in the trash bag. "None of my business, but I've seen the video. Time to let the bastard out. Lots worse get out all the time."

"Thanks," said Jake.

Jake watched Channel 11's *News at Six*.

The lead story was the governor's appointment of recently retired state police Major Jackson McNally to the parole board. The appointee was pictured, during a voiceover, in a Smokey the Bear uniform. The governor's statement recited McNally's long experience as a decorated, respected cop and the state police's highest ranking African-American officer, and gave his assurance that "Public safety will be his first priority as a member of the parole board." To Jake, that sounded like a vote for law and order with Prebys and Bertozzi, and one against Mia and parole for Aaron Underwood.

Jake's own moment of newsmaking was mercifully short, with the camera panning the crowd, an interview with a protestor who did herself no favors with her display of missing lower teeth and ignorance, and a final shot of Jake under the portico, his stump raised, in his challenge to Buddy Callahan. Jake, the reporter noted, was an Iraq war veteran who has lost an arm in that conflict, and who had more recently engaged in a single-minded search to find the driver who killed his wife in a hit-and-run.

Jake felt good about how it came out until Garo and Dermott made a joint call from the taproom at Livia's.

"How did you get caught up in that?" Garo asked.

"How was I not to? They were on my front lawn!"

"Not a good move, old boy," Dermott said. You could hear the frown on his face. "You don't need publicity right now. Not with the Baldolucca investigation still open. When you get riled, you can come off like a know-it-all dickhead. Remember that!"

"Thanks. Did Livia watch it with you?" Jake asked. "I'd like her opinion."

"No, she was with customers," Dermott replied.

Garo said, "Here's an update on Baldolucca. Bunch of arrests for small time stuff, pled to selling pot, a meth charge was dropped in the plea agreement, got a year in Minimum before he got paroled six months ago. He was a street drug guy, not a Mob guy. So, why get offed gangland style?"

"He knew who killed Hope and said her killer was connected. That's why."

"Hope's killer killed Baldolucca?"

"Yeah," Jake replied slowly, realizing that was exactly how he figured it went down.

Garo seemed dubious. "I'll mine the data further, find out if Baldolucca palled around with anyone connected. Tomorrow morning, I'm going to the DMV to check out who worked with used plates back then. After that, I'm heading down to Greenwick."

"Greenwick?"

"I made a contact. The probate clerk is also the town clerk. Remembers the murder, lived right down the road from the Gist farm." Garo paused. "Say, what are you doing tomorrow afternoon?"

"You know I can't get into your investigation."

Dermott said, "If it keeps you out of the limelight, no problem."

Garo added, "There's nothing in the law that says a parole board member is prohibited from a little bit of personal investigation or sitting in while some questions get asked. Might do you good. After today, you—"

"I got a lot going on," Jake responded.

Garo replied, "You've got a lawyer, an investigator, a clear head, and money. Underwood had nothing like that, nobody to stand up for him."

That hit home. Despite that, Jake said, "But I'm innocent and didn't plead guilty. What are you asking me to do?"

"I talk to the clerk, you listen and give me some insights later."

"I don't see that it advances your cause or gets me anywhere."

"Maybe a little understanding?"

CHAPTER FORTY-FIVE

RICKY WAS WRAPPING a chain around the front axle of a battered Jeep that could have seen combat. *Last junker of the day,* he shrugged. Thirsty for a drink, when he was summoned by Donnie DelFusco to the trailer. He removed his sunglasses, stuffed his ponytail under his baseball cap, and knocked.

Uncle Sal was sitting in a beat-up soft chair, his feet on a stool, cigar chomped between his teeth. "So, that guy Baldolucca got hit Sunday night?"

Ricky had prepared. *This shit's nothing to Nemesis.*

"I heard. No surprise wid that fuckup. Musta been some street shit deal that didn't go down. At least, no more worry that he'd get tempted."

Sal's cigar had burned down close to its band and gone out. He paused to relight it, puffed twice, and blew a cloud of smoke at Ricky.

"The guy used a wire. A fuckin' wire! Who would use a wire? On some street guy? Nah. Only an asshole would use a wire." He pointed the cigar at Ricky. "Just a fuckin' coincidence, right?"

Shit, the wire! Nemesis used it because he wanted it to be like in *The Godfather.* That's how you get rid of a rat. *Sal should know dat.* Ricky's voice caught when he replied, "Just one asshole hitting on another asshole. Jerks like Aldo stir up a lot of bad blood."

"Nobody knows about the two of ya? And the hit-and-run?"

"Nah."

"If you had something on with the fuck, and the Brow finds out, you got a big problem."

The Brow? Ricky was stunned, and just managed to get out, "I'm sayin' nothin' to do with me. Just street shit."

Sal said flatly, "We got some business coming in soon. I'll let ya know."

"Sure," Ricky replied with relief. "Anytime."

"And if ya hear anything about this guy, like somebody calls ya, I wanna know."

"Fuck," Ricky muttered as he returned to the yard to hoist up the Jeep. *Nobody would have known nuthin',* he thought, if it had gone as planned. Aldo would have been just another missing person who jumped parole.

His only loose end was that business card and the glove that he must have dropped on his way back to the Ram. He had checked the card's handwritten phone number and found it was different than the one in the reward advertisement.

How the fuck could Baldolucca get a card like that? Only if Aldo had made a contact, but if he'd been ratted out, the cops would be sniffing up my ass by now. And a rat like Aldo would have run if he'd nailed any cash. Nah, Aldo might have been thinkin' about it but didn't get to say nuthin'. I offed him just in time. Just have to keep it together, be careful, let Nemesis take care of it.

Sal watched his cigar burn down in the desk ashtray. He shook his head. *Ricky's as believable as fuckin' Pinocchio. Look at 'im, his cockeye and stupid looking beard. Fuckin' Ricky did it! So, Ricky, ya gotta go.*

Rose would be a bitch about Ricky's upcoming vacation; lots of crying and screaming. Sal would have to come up with some bullshit story to satisfy her, tell her Ricky was on the lam, maybe out of the country, someplace like Cuba or China, where he couldn't call or write. She might believe him, and if she didn't, it was because she'd figured out that Ricky had done somethin' really stupid.

Ricky had to go. If he got picked up for Baldolucca, he'd rat for sure. Be a *quaquaraqua*, a stoolie. Sal picked up the cigar and his index finger snapped off the ash. He would make the case to the Brow that a "missing" Ricky be offered up for Baldolucca and maybe that fuckin' hit-and-run, leaking it to the Staties that it had been "taken care of."

Sal didn't want to do the job himself; Ricky was blood. Maybe he could get the Dragos' guys to do the job. He'd contact Jonny Drago. Would cost a coupla big ones but worth it.

CHAPTER FORTY-SIX

JAKE EXERCISED, SKIPPED BREAKFAST, and was in the stable by eight-thirty to finish Livia's jewelry box. The joinder was neat, the mix of boxwood and pearwood on the top and sides a pleasing match, the strip of jade along the front edge worked, and its interior mahogany dividers and drawers slipped in and out neatly. He screwed on brass hinges, then cleaned off his workbench, swept up the dust and shavings on the floor, washed up, and walked over to the veterans' center.

Paulie Caprio accosted him at the entrance. "Thanks for the lawyer. I need it. Hope to hell the guy I got the medical marijuana card from was legit."

"Paulie, that's for your lawyer, not me."

That went by him. "Geezus Christmas! A fuckin' garrote!"

"So I hear."

Paulie followed Jake to the water and soda refrigerator by the coffee bar. "They said I should stay away from you since I got staties on me. Told him if you came in, I'm not avoiding you."

"Take the advice. You don't need to be seen with me until all this clears up."

Both looked up as Harrigan and Pulaski filled the center's Main Street entrance, stepped inside, looked around, and spotted them. Their raincoats, suits, and demeanors screamed cop.

Jake watched their approach, angry at what he took to be their brazen provocation in showing up at the vet center, maybe to catch Paulie unaware or to throw their weight around.

Pulaski came up close to Paulie. "Tried your apartment and thought you might be here. Find that medical marijuana card yet, Paulie?"

"Still lookin'," he replied. Paulie was a deer in the headlights, his face ashen, fingers twisting in his hands, his eyes finding his sneakers. "My lawyer says I should call him if I get questioned."

"Sure, go ahead."

"You didn't need to come here." Jake moved between the staties and Paulie before Paulie got himself in deeper. "You heard him, he's got a lawyer."

"Trying to tell us how to run this case, too?" Harrigan's huffed.

"So tell me, any luck on the orange license plate?" Jake asked.

Harrigan's puzzled expression and hesitant response gave away his lie. "Turned it over for followup."

Jake's irascibility ratcheted up. "How's this for cooperation? How about I show you exactly where I met Baldolucca. In person." Jake reckoned he could deflect some heat off Paulie. And what the hell, they really wanted him. And maybe it was time for a payback. "Suppose you wait outside for a couple of minutes, and I join you when I finish up here?"

"Sure." Harrigan's smile came out as mostly a sneer. "Don't want to leave any bad impressions with—" he looked over the ten or so heads that turned away as he spoke, "—these upstanding citizens."

The two cops left and waited on the sidewalk of Main Street. Jake grabbed Paulie's elbow. "Call your lawyer," Jake said to the trembling Paulie. "Don't try to help me out. Stick to the truth."

Jake smiled as he pulled out his cell phone, hit the Uber app and tapped in an address and time.

A cold wind raked the sidewalk. Had to be close to freezing. The two staties had turned up their collars, Jake zipped up his jacket and put his hand in his pocket.

He walked briskly, the cops a step or two behind, up the incline of

Main Street to the China Inn, a favorite restaurant of Jake's, past a stodgy looking high-rise housing for the elderly, around the corner and up to Summer Street, past the renovated Y, the magnificent marble columned Greek porticoed Sayles Library, and the Georgian style Telephone Company building, then north to Exchange Street past the Cape Verdean Society Hall, to face another elderly housing high-rise. Jake thought of angling into an alley behind a deli with a smelly dumpster, just to see if the cops would follow, but didn't press his luck. The staties followed apace, with Harrigan once calling out, "Where we going?"

Jake gave an over the shoulder response. "To where we met, okay?"

He continued to Roosevelt Avenue, past the art-deco City Hall, and Slater Mill, the anchor for the newly dedicated Blackstone Valley National Park, and to the grassy area by the rushing Blackstone. A direct route from the vet center would have been a three-minute walk, tops; this downtown excursion in the cold had taken closer to ten and the staties, recognizing that Jake had ragged them, registered an impatience bordering on anger.

A newish green Honda was idling at the curb in front of the park. Jake motioned to the driver to lower the passenger side window. "Uber?"

The driver nodded and Jake got in the back seat.

"What's going on?" Harrigan, red-faced and slightly out of breath shouted at Jake.

Jake rolled down the window and said loudly, to make sure the driver heard and would remember, "You know I need a lawyer present when either one of us is approached for questions, yet you follow us on our walk." Jake took a pedometer out of his pocket. "Two thousand, three hundred thirty-eight steps. Out-and-out harassment for you to follow us around the city."

Harrigan sputtered, "You're every bit the guy with the bad attitude I heard about," his face nose-to-nose with Jake's.

Jake shrugged. "See that bench over there by the river? That's where I met Baldolucca. Said I'd show you where."

"You're gonna have to come in."

"That you do through Dermott. By the book. Thanks for the airing," Jake said curtly and closed the Uber's window.

"A parole board member hiding behind his lawyer," Harrigan shouted with disgust. "We'll be talking."

In the sideview mirror, Jake saw him smacking a fist into his palm as the Uber car drove him away. Jake had no doubt that they would be talking, after which he would be written up as ill-tempered and uncooperative, which was not far from the truth. Unstated was the threat of a planted press inquiry, yes, a parole board member has been questioned in the investigation of Baldolucca's gangland murder, along with a reminder that Jake had undergone a very public opiate dependency rehabilitation after his wife's murder and his criticism of the staties.

Jake found he didn't particularly care if the media took the bait.

CHAPTER FORTY-SEVEN

GARO PICKED UP JAKE at Livia's Bistro. The sky had opened up in a downpour that sounded like drumbeats on the Equinox's roof. Jake, in a Paw Sox-logoed windbreaker and baseball cap, dashed inside the Equinox and was struck by a strong pine tree scent from the air freshener hanging from its rearview mirror.

As they drove up Washington Street through downtown toward the highway, Jake, in high spirits, boasted of his earlier bettering of Harrigan and Pulaski.

Garo shook his head, even as he appreciated Jake's gambit. "You don't listen, do you? Baiting staties? Dermott's so right, you are a hardhead."

Interstate 95 South was slick surfaced, the Equinox was pelted by the driving rain and water thrown up by eighteen-wheelers. A northeast wind buffeted it along open stretches. Over the noise of its defroster, Garo groused about his tedious morning in the insufferably dry, overheated lower basement of the decrepit Registry of Motor Vehicles building across from the state house where no one, he complained, seemed to have the authority or ingenuity to discard or digitize years of yellowing paper motor vehicle records.

A mousy-haired woman with a muffin top and sour demeanor was in charge. Reluctantly, she had removed an empty Dunkin' Donuts box and plastic coffee cup from a smeared tabletop, and disappeared into a line of ceiling-high racks to find the requested records.

She had taken her time, but eventually returned with two large cardboard boxes filled with "used" registration applications for the year of Hope's death, and two extras: one each for the years before and after. Attached to the applications were copies of required licenses to sell new and used cars.

Garo explained to Jake the job he had faced. He had discovered online that Rhode Island licensed thirty new car dealers, over three hundred used car dealers, and to his surprise, over two hundred auto body shops and salvage yards that had "used" registrations for vehicles they repaired and sold. The sheer numbers and his time limitation forced him to prioritize his search on applications and registrations to locations in Providence, North Providence, East Providence, Pawtucket, Cranston and Johnson. First, he eliminated new car dealers as being less likely to have one driven by an employee or customer after nine o'clock on a rainy night. He segregated what was left into used car dealers, auto body shops, and salvage yards, the type of businesses often used by those connected as ideal fronts for washing money, and a place for wiseguys to hang out. He had pulled forty-two applications and registrations, now tabbed by yellow sticky notes, that demanded more careful inspection. He wanted to copy them, but the bitter attendant said the copy machine didn't work. So, he had to write down the info.

Fortunately, while most signatures were scribbles, each was notarized so the applicant's name was either printed or typed in the notarial acknowledgement. Some were familiar, Garo told Jake, connected guys like Nick Giambi and Felix "the Cat" Maffeo. A few family names he would have to check into.

Gonna start with the scrapyards tomorrow, biggest first. That's Rhode Island Scrap run by Sal Gianmalvo whom I remember from my days in the staties."

"Thanks, Garo," Jake said. "I appreciate everything you do."

When Garo got to the state employees' parking lot, he saw a ticket

tucked under the wiper, *Illegal parking in a handicap space.* He'd missed
the wheelchair logo in the crappy asphalt that was in a puddle.

Garo's bill just got an additional "miscellaneous expense."

━━━━━━━━━━━━━━━━

The Equinox left the highway at the Route 2 exit and stopped at Allie's
Doughnuts where Garo purchased a box of handmades and put it in the
back seat. Jake didn't ask why.

They drove west toward Connecticut on a highway that quickly went
from four lanes to two, lined by road slush rapidly melting into brown
puddles. They passed thickets of red-budded trees, clumps of yellowish
forsythia, firs that sheltered patches of dirty snow and zigzagged upward
toward the rain clouds, muddy farm fields and weathered outbuildings.
Closed roadside vegetable stands appeared every quarter mile or so. As
they passed a sign that read, *Welcome to Greenwick, Friendly Town, Friendly
People,* Garo said, "The next left is Slocum Road, where Lucretia Gist's
murder took place. Maybe we can check it out on the way back."

Jake was noncommittal.

Rain, heavy as hail, swept the Equinox as it rolled into the village.
Not a stoplight in sight. Two lines of one-story commercial buildings
faced a wide main street, with cars parked at angles on both sides; a white
clapboard church with an ornate steeple overlooked a patch of village green
with benches, trees and a monument dedicated to the heroes of some long
forgotten war, as did a stonefaced library. The town hall, between a pottery
shop and a diner, was grayish granite, with twin turrets that made it appear
to be more like an armory than a municipal building. Garo parked in its
parking lot and left the SUV, carrying the box of donuts and his beat-up
valise. Jake dutifully followed him to a flight of stone steps smoothed by
a hundred years of foot traffic. Rainwater dripped from the flag that hung
limply over its entrance.

Inside, three frosted balls of a flamboyant ceiling fixture illuminated
a spacious wainscoted foyer with a floor of octagonal black and white
tiles. A transom over an open door to the room on the left was marked

"Town Clerk" in antiqued gold script. As they entered and approached a chest-high counter, Garo wiped the rain from his face and hair with a handkerchief, and flashed a wide smile at a fresh-faced young woman who smiled back.

"Is Mrs. Hoxey in?" he inquired.

"Yes, are you Mr. Hagopian? She's waiting for you in her office. Just off the staircase, by the bulletin board."

They retraced their steps and walked past a darkly stained wooden staircase with wide risers and ornate banisters under an arrow pointing upstairs to "Town Council" in the same antiqued script. Jake paused at the town bulletin board, with tacked-up notices for council and commission meetings, along with library hours, a VFW ham-and-bean supper, and cake sales by ladies' auxiliaries at local churches.

Garo coughed to get Jake's attention, knocked and entered the room, followed by Jake.

"Ah, Mr. Hagopian?" Rising from behind a desk piled with stacked folders was a thin, pleasant-faced woman, her gray hair swept back neatly. She wore a dark blue blouse and tweed skirt, and a smile.

"Thank you for sparing me the time," Garo said. "This is Jake Fournier, from the parole board."

"Yes, you said he might be with you." As they took seats in front of her desk, Jake glared at Garo. What had Garo said to her about Jake to gain this interview?

Garo placed the donut box on her desk. "Thought your staff might like something for their afternoon break."

"Isn't that welcome?" she sighed with a smile. "Nobody can resist Allie's." She put the box to one side of her desk and continued briskly. "We found the records you asked for. My years as Town Clerk and Probate Clerk is an advantage when you want to find old records." She opened a manila folder thick with papers that cracked with dryness, unclipped a number of them, and spread them on her desk. "This is the probate record for Lucretia Gist. A distant cousin was the only heir-at-law, so she got the Castle."

She stopped, looked up, realizing the need for a clarification. "That's what we called the Gist homestead: Gist Castle, a large bungalow, with a peculiar looking turret on one side."

Garo and Jake sat back.

"Well, she—this cousin, I mean—said she wanted to live in the house during the pending probate—can't imagine why after that terrible murder—and the judge said it was hers to do with what she wanted, so long as she posted a bond. Which she did. Soon, everyone was talking about how the cousin tore the house apart, then, the barn and the outbuildings. Her son joined her going through it. Never reported finding anything of value."

"What were they looking for?" Jake asked.

"As I told Mr. Hagopian, everyone in Greenwick thought Old Lady Gist—" She hesitated. "I should really start at the beginning to give you the picture. My family's farm was just down Slocum Road, maybe a quarter of a mile from the Gist's place. She was a recluse, odd, and deaf as a doorpost."

Garo interrupted. "You knew Aaron Underwood?"

"I was one of Aaron's few friends, maybe the only one. We took the same school bus into the village. I was a year or so younger, and he was . . . nice . . . never teased me like the other boys. I would describe him as awkward, painfully shy, the butt of jokes. Unfortunately for him, he had a widely spaced front teeth and clamshell ears that stuck out of his hair. The bullies taunted Aaron for his goofy looks, said he was the spitting image of, oh, what was his name, the cartoon character on *Mad* magazine's cover?"

Garo replied, "Alfred E. Neuman."

"Yes," she said, "that's it. And he was." She shook her head in remembrance and sat back. "Aaron was picked on as the tongue-tied class dunce. I felt bad for him. I don't know what happened up there that Halloween, but I can tell you that the notion that he was there to steal her gold was just incredible to me . . . is even now."

Mrs. Hoxey saw Jake's reaction to *gold* and explained her reference. "Lucretia Gist was a miser. When she came into the village in this old car she drove, she'd wear shabby clothes and shout down people in her deafness, and everyone believed that her father, an arch-conservative, had a stash of gold coins not turned in as required when FDR took the country off the gold standard back in the Depression. People said the coins were stashed away in the Castle, but I don't believe that's why Aaron Underwood would have been there." She stopped. "In my opinion, that is."

Garo turned to Jake. "What I learned in my prior conversation with Mrs. Hoxey is that Lucretia inherited gold coins that the father kept with a coin dealer in Philadelphia. She had a standing order for some to be sold to collectors, with the proceeds deposited into her account at the South County Trust Company. Gold was maybe four hundred dollars an ounce back then and a gold coin's value, depending on the denomination and condition, could be worth a lot more to a collector."

Mrs. Hoxey flipped through the pages of a file. "Lucretia's probate inventory states that the dealer held several hundred coins in different denominations, ten-, twenty-, fifty-dollar gold pieces, at the time of her death. All were graded as *fine*, valued according to the inventory at over two hundred thousand dollars, a lot of money back then. The coins that were with the dealer went to the cousin, but the local suspicion was that there were more coins hidden at the Castle, because a Gist never would have let a stranger have possession of them all."

Garo leaned in to Jake. "The way I see it, either the dealer had all her coins or some were still in the house, or were found by the cousin but not reported to the probate court, or never found. One thing we know for sure is that Underwood, injured and lying on the floor near her, didn't get them."

"Well," Mrs. Hoxey continued, "eventually, when the probate closed, the cousin left Greenwick and she sold the farm on the cheap to folks from New York who'd heard the rumor of coins. They continued to search, and finally abandoned the place. Became a dilapidated eyesore, windows boarded up, chimneys falling down. About ten years ago, the town took title in a tax sale. By then, and this is shameful, the place become polluted when somebody decided to dump oil and chemicals out behind the barn.

House is still there, a wreck. The town hasn't done anything with it, not with the pollution problems. A wonder it hasn't been torched by now."

Garo said, "I don't want to put you on the spot, but you said that you doubted Underwood's involvement in her murder."

"I never did believe that the Aaron Underwood I knew could have bludgeoned her. He may have been slow, but he was a gentle kid. His family was hardscrabble poor—we used to say that the Underwoods harvested rocks instead of potatoes. They were a little strange, too, reclusive, attended a tiny church north of the village run by a firebrand preacher. Took everything in the Bible literally. Other than going to school and church, Aaron wasn't allowed off the farm. Another thing I remember was talk about bad blood between the Underwoods and Lucretia Gist, something about her refusing to lease some of her land to the Underwoods to farm. Back then, it was practically unheard of, and a sin, to let good farmland lie fallow."

She stopped her narrative. "May I have a minute to bring out the donuts to the staff?" She left and returned promptly. "They are appreciative," she said and returned to her desk. "So around here, at the time of the murder, nobody could come up with any reason for Aaron to be there except to steal the coins to help out his family, he had that pry bar with him to pull up some boards or flooring and something went wrong. Of course, Aaron never said. Then, years afterward, we heard about the boys' prank."

Garo repeated, "Prank?" Garo repeated.

"Well, Joe Tingle eventually told the story. Joe has the cleaners in the village. Has a loose tongue after a few drinks. The story was that Billy Bain—he's our chief of police now—and Joe put up Aaron to pulling a prank. He was going to pull the hub caps off her jalopy at Gist Castle that night. Billy and Joe went up there to check on Aaron. With Billy's father being the sheriff, they could likely get away with anything. Anyway, with Aaron pleading guilty, the boys' involvement with Aaron being at the Castle was kept pretty much under wraps. And we didn't know of the planned prank until much later on."

Garo's eyes danced with thoughts. "The father was sheriff for quite a while?"

"Decades. Never asked for a raise, which was much appreciated here. Later, the family hit the lottery, so he continued on."

"Lottery?" Garo asked.

She smiled. "Well, not literally. Some out-of-state relative died and left enough to send Billy to URI and to buy that big white house with the veranda and fruit trees out front that you passed coming in on 102. Billy lives there now. He took over as sheriff, now chief of police, when his old man retired. Got to be going on fifteen or so years ago. I never understood why the son wanted his father's job. Doesn't pay much. Maybe it is the uniform."

CHAPTER FORTY-EIGHT

JAKE AND GARO SAT in the Equinox with the heater and defroster on max. The temperature had dropped to just above freezing. The rain had stopped and the sun was setting with a yellowish brightness.

"So, tell me how you did it?" Jake said.

Garo smirked. "Well, I checked into what happened to Lucretia Gist's estate and ended up talking to Mrs. Hoxey. When I asked for the probate file, her voice lit up, and I guessed that if I was especially courteous and not at all my sometimes obnoxious investigator self, and I brought a bribe of Allie's Donuts, I'd get more than a retrieve of dusty records."

"It's all interesting," Jake said, "but I don't see what difference the coins or his background or the prank makes. Underwood was *there*, his fingerprints are on the pry bar, and she fired the scattergun which took off half his face."

Garo countered. "Opens up possibilities. Nobody knew of the prank at the trial except the two kids and, likely, the chief of police. Nothing in what I found in the trial transcript or the staties' records. Never got the local's file, and now I can guess why. Underwood had a reason to be there other than the coins or a family squabble. So there goes the robbery or anger motives for murder."

Garo thought for a moment before he continued. "Suppose someone got in the house before Underwood, while the deaf old lady is watching television, gets her to tell where the coins are hidden, does the old lady in with a pry bar, and later when Aaron discovers her, that same someone lets him have it with her scattergun, then places Aaron's fingers on the pry bar to throw the blame on him. It could have happened."

"You have a great imagination. Yeah, *could* have but—"

"Or how about this? The chief for sure had the opportunity to search the house for coins. Bain and Tingle discover the bodies, call the father, the father arrives, goes inside, has to search the house for anybody else involved—right? Maybe gets the idea to also search for the coins? Can't you see what an effective defense counsel would do armed with that insight? The possibilities? Credibility crumbling before a jury?"

Jake let Garo continue to spin theories as they drove from the village. After all, Garo was his investigator, too.

||||||||||||||||||||||||||||||||||||||||||||||||||

They parked on Slocum Road where they found the rutted track up a knoll was fenced off by barbed wire. Jake got out of the Equinox to survey the shambles. A circular window, with one pane missing, flashed back the setting sun. What had to be the remains of the turret and porch were barely visible through a growth of small trees and bushes.

"What?" He heard Garo on his cell phone shout from inside the Equinox. "That son of a bitch!"

Jake returned to the Equinox but Garo, intent on his conversation, ignored him. He considered that Garo would spin out more scenarios, but one thing for sure, the Aaron Underwood that Mrs. Hoxey described didn't fit the profile of the murderers who had come up for parole during his few months on the board. A fifteen-year-old kid, awkward, who looked like Alfred E. Neuman, who was shy, "slow," without a reputation for a bad temper or some sadistic tendency, or even truancy, bludgeoned an old lady? On a prank?

Garo scowled as he stepped out of the car toward Jake. "Our office was told today that Chief Bain is going to speak at a special victim's hearing. You know what bullshit that is!"

"I don't know."

"Jackson McNally, your new parole board member, pulled it off, in cahoots with the AG. Hasn't been to his first meeting and he's already calling the tune. Goddamn it! Bain isn't a victim entitled to appear under the parole statute: he's an advocate to keep Underwood in prison."

Jake's eyes remained trained on the hulk of Gist Castle. The appearance by Chief Bain was certainly contrived, and an early indication as to how the board was going to operate with McNally as a member, even under Bertozzi's continued chairmanship. No way could he stay under such circumstances.

Grim faced, Jake said, "What would you have me do? I'm thinking of putting in my resignation."

"Hold off," Garo said. "On second thought, seems to me that since Bain has offered himself up as the voice of the victim, you're entitled to ask him a lot of questions about the prank, why he was there, about his old man."

"Maybe, but that's up to Bertozzi. He may cut me out right away."

"My report will be on the PD's desk day after tomorrow. But, knowing her, she might wait to see if he's paroled, save the time and money on a new trial motion. Dunno."

Jake shrugged. "Okay, I owe you. I'll do my best to get your questions asked. But I gotta say that Underwood isn't my highest priority right now."

"I'll start on the scrapyards tomorrow."

CHAPTER FORTY-NINE

MILLIE VISITED AARON every other day, the maximum number of permitted visits allowance even for family, and kept him focused on the online and media uproar over his destroyed face, his incarceration and his parole petition. In addition to copies of the *Journal,* she brought photographs of the family home, repaired and painted and virtually unrecognizable to him, its second floor bedroom that would be his, the barn, and even the fields and meadows that stretched east from the casino and west to Slocum Road. He imagined what it might be like to live there, walking the remaining acreage, the freedom of ten acres. Somehow, it left him both fearful and dissatisfied. He would still be in confinement, even without walls.

"I've been on the radio," she said with a prim smile, "been interviewed at the farm by CNN and MSNBC, and I think I did okay. I've been saying what you suggested, what it is like to have a disfigured face that hasn't been treated in prison. These people seem to get it, are sympathetic. They've got this big rally planned on Saturday at Roger Williams Park, with a pop singer, Terrell Williams. Everybody seems to know him."

"Are you going to speak?"

"Yes."

"Then read this for me." He gave her a sheet of paper with a poem in a large block printing, an idea he had to connect with his Army. When she finished reading, she folded the paper and put it in her pocket. "I will, Aaron. They'll love it."

That night as he lay on his bunk, Aaron recalled Hagopian pushing him to remember that Halloween. *And did anyone else know why he would have gone to Gist Castle?* A prison psychiatrist years ago had told him that his memory lapse resulted from emotional and physical trauma; it was the way his brain prevented blocked-out bad memories from taking over his life. But nothing was said about how he could regain a lost memory. In fact, the shrink told him it was best to let his memory go, and accept what he had been told.

Aaron read Frost's poetry to ease into drowsy relief. His eyes closed as a memory leaked. Bainsy and Tingle, his frequent tormentors at school, were involved, and he had been smart. Somehow, he had come up with the perfect prank on Old Lady Gist. That was as far as he got. But after thirty years, it was something.

He determined that until he had a clear mental picture, he wouldn't admit to remembering anything about that night.

CHAPTER FIFTY

"QUITE A SHOW you put on with Buddy Callahan," Prebys sneered when he and Jake arrived at the same time at the security desk in Medium Security. Jake ignored him and clipped a security badge to his shirt pocket. In smoldering silence, they entered the hearing room and both were surprised by the presence of a tall, broad-shouldered man standing next to a clearly disquieted Bertozzi.

Jackson McNally had arrived.

Dermott's verbal sketch hadn't done McNally justice. He made a strong impression in a dark suit, white shirt and subdued tie, *a statie civvies uniform,* Jake thought. He was square jawed and handsome, maybe six-two, with dark-copper skin that contrasted nicely with his gray eyes. His close-cropped salt-and-pepper hair had a distinct part on the right side.

Bertozzi made introductions. McNally's eyes sized up Jake, then Prebys. Jake welcomed him and McNally, noting Jake was missing an arm, didn't put out his hand, but smiled as Prebys gushed, "I'm so glad you are here. Your experience is just what we need," he said to the obvious embarrassment of Bertozzi.

McNally took the chair next to Jake's and across from Mia, who had been studying her laptop with intensity since Jake's arrival. They had not spoken since the cocktail party.

Bertozzi, formal as usual, banged his gavel to open the session and said that until the new member felt comfortable with the board's routine and procedures, and if no one objected, he would continue as acting chair. McNally smiled and nodded. Mia glanced coolly at Jake.

As an initial matter of administrative business, Bertozzi announced that the warden had concluded that the corridor incident between Aaron Underwood and Francisco Gilletto had been an accident, and therefore no violation of the six-month rule had occurred.

"Nothing to invoke," he said, "against either one. Unless there is an objection, we'll vote on Gilletto's petition today as a final item." For McNally's benefit, he explained the six-month rule. "This is a little unusual because the event occurred after Gilletto's hearing."

Jake added, "But before we finished voting."

McNally interrupted, rather aggressively. His voice was timbred.

"I remember Gilletto's trial, and I've read his petition file. We arrested Gilletto, aka 'Fat Frankie', a known Mob fence, after a tip from an informant. I'm comfortable in voting on Gilletto's petition."

"Nothing on you, Major," Jake said quickly, "but you didn't see or hear Gilletto. You weren't even appointed then. I don't believe you should vote." He addressed Bertozzi. "Shouldn't that be the rule for voting, appointed to the board and been through the hearing?"

Bertozzi's eyes sparked with interest. Then, his mouth drooped as he considered how denying McNally a vote might appear to the governor's office.

"We don't have a rule or a precedent on the point. I'll leave it up to the board."

McNally's mouth tightened as he leaned forward, stared at Bertozzi, and said pointedly, "I expect to vote."

"Jake's right," Mia said. "Major, you really don't want to begin your term on the board with an issue like that."

"I appreciate your concern," he said, sat back and clasped his hands in his elbows as if to signal discussion was over.

Bertozzi called the vote and Prebys and McNally were in favor, Jake and Mia against. All looked at Bertozzi. "Unusual, but in view of the Major's background and familiarity with the prisoner, I'll go with it. I vote yes," and he nodded at Mrs. Ames. "I want Gilletto to be available if anyone wants to hear from him. Okay? Let's get started."

In the next two hours, twenty petitions, mostly perfunctory first or second tries, were heard and acted on. Jake voted with the majority in each case, except for one in which he voted to parole a veteran with a give-me-a-chance smile. Jake's vote earned a petulant glance from Prebys. McNally didn't vote on any petition, saying he hadn't prepared himself sufficiently.

By eleven-fifteen, the only remaining business was Gilletto. Mrs. Ames left the hearing room and returned to announce that Gilletto was in the anteroom if any member wanted him back for questions. Nobody did.

Bertozzi addressed the board as to the procedural status of Gilletto's petition and was immediately upstaged by McNally.

"I like the idea of having him on a short leash through parole. How did you see it?" he asked Prebys, who was too obviously flattered by McNally's attention.

"As Stuart said, we were voting when Underwood and Gilletto had their—what did you call it, Stuart?—their 'incident'? I had voted to keep him in until he made three years, just another ninety days or so. Mia was a yes, Stuart was a no, Jake hadn't yet voted."

Mia coughed and explained. "Despite his serious offense, I thought he should be paroled based on his clean record, a job waiting, and his mother's dementia. If we follow precedent—"

Bertozzi broke in sharply, "Those guns were going somewhere. Major, the board has always dealt forcefully with inmates convicted of buying and selling guns." There was little doubt as where he was coming down. "Does anyone want more time?" he asked. When no one responded, Bertozzi started with Prebys.

"Yes, again!"

Mia said, "Yes."

Bertozzi nodded at Jake. Mired in self-contempt for what he was about to do, Jake took in a breath that was interrupted by McNally's out-of-turn voting "yes."

Jake's mouth opened; he struggled not to show his relief that bordered on physical. Jake having been saved from illegality and disloyalty by McNally's preemptive vote. Jake's eyes went to Bertozzi who was demonstrably angered by both McNally's violation of procedure and his vote that would parole a gun law violator. "Jake?" Bertozzi finally asked, his voice showing the strain of self-control.

"He has his three votes for parole, so I'll pass."

Bertozzi directed a comment to McNally. "When the votes are there for parole, no need to continue the vote unless someone wants to make a point." He swallowed hard and grasped the gavel as though still formulating his response. "And I do," he said slowly. "Those guns on the street could have been used in murder or assault. And he is a first-timer. Can't go along with that. Chair votes no." He turned to Mrs. Ames. "Send him back to his cell," as he slammed his gavel in frustration.

The unease in the room was palpable. Even Prebys was quieted. Then Bertozzi said, "The AG has requested that the board permit Chief Bain from the Greenwick PD to speak to us on behalf of Lucretia Gist, Underwood's victim." He nodded at McNally and continued, stiffly, "I understand the idea came from Major McNally." He paused, and Jake noted the tremble in his hand holding the gavel. "While I believe this request is within the discretion of the chair, and we do have subpoena power we never use, I've decided to put the issue to a vote."

Mia was astonished. "How can Chief Bain represent a victim? The statute's very clear: Statute says 'victims or their representatives' and 'representative' has always meant close family members or domestic partners. The statute says nothing about the police."

McNally's authoritative voice answered before Bertozzi could respond. "The case is so old this victim doesn't have any relatives left to represent her. Since the town has a position on his parole, we ought to hear from it, in lieu of the Gist family."

Prebys nodded agreement.

"No, no!" Mia continued, ignoring McNally. "The statute is clear. It's a terrible precedent. We'll have police chiefs and state police in here all the time if we allow this."

Jake knew she was legally, morally, and procedurally correct, but he had to weigh her justified concerns against his obligation to Garo to interrogate Chief Bain. *Goddamn, another conflict.*

"Ordinarily, I'd vote against it because Mia is right on the issue, but this has become an extraordinary situation. Okay by me."

She shot Jake a disdainful look.

"Okay, all in favor, say yes." Prebys, McNally, and Jake were in the affirmative, Mia in the negative. Bertozzi didn't vote. Jake wondered why. "I'll be back to you as to a time and place."

"I can't believe this, Stuart," Mia complained. "You, of all people, bending the rules, years of precedent? You've always been a stickler on procedure." She continued to vent her frustrations while collecting her laptop, handbag and coat. "I'm not going to participate. This is a grievous, likely illegal, move and I'm not going to be part of it." The threat of adverse publicity in her tone was obvious as she stomped out of the hearing room.

McNally sniffed at her dramatic exit and addressed Bertozzi. "On Underwood, and this six-month rule business, do we vote on that?"

Prebys jumped at the thought. "We could have our own opinions on whether the six-month rule applies for that incident or the video. How could it have been produced without him in cahoots? Clearly that's against prison rules."

Bertozzi thundered his reply. "No rule infraction is on the record as we sit, so there is nothing to apply the six-month rule."

McNally asked, "Is this rule written down somewhere? Or one of your—"

"Look, we just gave Gilletto the benefit of the doubt as to the anteroom incident," Bertozzi said. "A double standard on Underwood on that would be picked up by the media. As to the video, as the warden said, there has been no conclusion to the investigation."

"Don't see this as a double standard at all," McNally muttered.

"Good," replied Bertozzi abruptly, "then you won't lose any sleep over it. Session over." He stood, closed his laptop, and abruptly left.

CHAPTER FIFTY-ONE

PREBYS TOOK HIS JACKET and briefcase and walked around the tables to put out his hand on McNally's shoulder who, noticeably to Jake, reacted by stiffening.

"We need some backbone and direction, Major. We waste too much time with nonsense." After eyeing Jake's reaction, Prebys left.

Jake finished the water left in his bottle, closed his laptop, preparing to leave when McNally addressed him coolly. "Heard you're involved in that garrote case in North Providence. I ran into Frank Harrigan yesterday. Thinks you showed him up."

Jake bristled. "Involved? Do you mean questioned?"

"All I'm saying is that you're in the mix. We all know how you criticized our investigation of your wife's hit-and-run, that you said publicly you would find the killer and do justice. Like you were Judge Dredd."

"I was justified by the way you guys mishandled it."

"Sooner or later, the media will get the story."

"When it's leaked by you guys."

McNally pulled his ample shoulders back, adjusted his tie, stood, and despite having sat for over three hours, he now appeared as crisp and as commanding as ever. Jake tucked his laptop under the stump of his arm, picked up his jacket and headed for the door. He was surprised when McNally asked, "What about Underwood? Did you see the video?"

"Yeah."

"If he gets out, won't be long before he'll be thinking about getting back in. These guys can't adapt. Did you see that movie *Shawshank Redemption?* Remember that old con, Brooks, I think, out for a couple of months, has nightmares, afraid all the time because no one was telling him what to do. Couldn't bear it. Committed suicide."

Jake remembered the powerful scene. He could imagine something similar happening to a long-timer, and Underwood was clearly a long-timer.

"We just have to call it as we see it." Jake said. "And straight," immediately regretting straight, because in his vote he had just been no better in his respect for rules and the law than McNally.

McNally's lips curled, his chin touched the knot of his tie.

"Here's my take on granting parole. No hankies for me. If a record is good, I see a chance for rehab, stability, I vote for parole. Give me a chance to vote no because of whatever, I'll do it. I'm going to worry more about putting a murderer, a gangbanger or wife beater or child abuser back on the street than someone who forged a check. Pretty simple. Protect the community. That's what I told the governor and the Speaker when I was interviewed."

Jake made no response. *Governor and the Speaker?* Who likely gave him guidance for his vote on Gilletto and Underwood? The governor wanted McNally to protect his political backside, and the board got an alpha dog when it needed consensus to operate efficiently. McNally's appointment added another reason for Jake's resignation. McNally would surely be overbearing and too full of himself.

"Yeah, well," McNally said in a throwaway tone. "In that garrote case, I'd keep a low profile if I were you. You wouldn't win a popularity contest at the barracks after some of the things you've said publicly. And get an experienced criminal defense lawyer, somebody who really knows the score and doesn't piss people off."

Meaning, Dermott was on the piss-off-people list.

As it had with Harrigan, Jake's anger overcame his good sense. "I suppose I should say thanks for the advice, for a heads-up. So don't think me too ungrateful if I just say fuck you."

McNally's cold eyes flickered, then widened. Jake wondered when was the last time someone had told the fucker off.

CHAPTER FIFTY-TWO

SAL GIANMALVO WAS SUPERVISING delivery of two loads of newly arrived junkers when he spotted Garo at the trailer's steps. He paused to relight his cigar, using the moment to get his thoughts together. He tugged at the belt holding up his girth and walked deliberately over the muddy puddled ground toward the trailer.

"Ain't seen you in a long time, Garo," he said, forcing a smile, and putting out a meaty hand.

Garo took his hand. "How are things going?"

"Okay, how about you?"

The two had tangled when Garo worked the organized crime detail while a statie, and Sal was then a small timer into gambling and protection. That was before the Brow, Sal's father's boyhood friend from the same village in Sicily, decided Sal would front the Mob's scrapyard business.

"Need a few minutes of your time, Sal."

"Sure," he replied and opened the trailer's aluminum door, as a gracious host. The stairs sagged under their combined weight.

"Take the crap off the chair and give your feet a rest," he said cordially. Garo did so as Sal squeezed behind his desk and put his cigar in the desk's ashtray; the trailer, already suffused with old smoke, began to fill with Sal's acrid addition.

"Checking on something you may remember."

"I remember Christmas, the Red Sox in '04 and 9/11. What else?"

"Three years ago, somebody driving a Ford F-150 with some white trim did a hit-and-run in East Providence, killed a woman. Truck had a used plate. Husband's a friend of mine. Not looking for the registration owner. Just the driver."

Sal's flat face paused.

"Just the driver," Garo repeated.

"I thought you were with the public defender. You moonlightin'?"

"For a friend."

"I'm supposed to remember three years ago? C'mon, Garo, I'm no Einstein."

"You had two plates then."

"I think I got two plates now. When I gotta pick something up or when, once in a while, I got something worth selling and they wanna test drive. That don't happen much anymore. The operation is too big now. Stuff comes in from all over, that compactor can do six cars an hour, and I go ten hours a day, sometimes more."

Garo had noticed a newish Chevy Silverado truck with a used plate parked not far from the trailer. He took a chance with a lie.

"Plate I'm looking for had three numbers. Not too many of those still around. If a plate gets turned into the registry, they don't bother to reissue. Just give out a new number. RMV says you got two three-numbered plates."

Sal tried to cover up his eye blink with a blast of cigar smoke.

"For Chrissakes, Garo, over time I've had dozens of trucks and as many cars on those plates. We don't keep records of who drives 'em or when they leave the yard. Nobody does."

"Would have been returned with a crumpled left front fender. Maybe somebody would remember that." Garo leaned forward. "I'd appreciate a little help, Sal."

"Tell you what. I'll check. Donnie might remember if somethin' came back crapped up." Sal took his cigar from the ashtray. "Hey, how 'bout a couple of these Monte Cristo's?" He tapped a cigar box.

"Don't smoke."

"Too bad. These are the best." He opened the Monte Cristo box and handed three to Garo. "Take 'em anyway. Give 'em to a smoker."

Garo thanked him for the cigars as Sal stood. Interview over.

"I gotta get back in the yard," Sal said, maneuvering around the desk. "The help these days, geezuz, half don't speak English. They fuck up all the time. If I find out anythin' I'll let you know. Got a card?"

Garo pulled out his wallet from a back pocket and deposited on the desk a creased business card from his PI days.

"Glad things have worked out for you," Garo said as he opened the trailer door and surveyed the piles of scrap, a half-dozen filled dumpsters, twenty or so junkers, a continuous belt with metal buckets going up thirty feet into the mouth of a shredder, the two yard cranes, and a huge compactor.

"Can't complain."

"A lot of the guys you ran with didn't have the same good sense."

Sal took that as a reassuring compliment. "Things turned out good."

"Wouldn't want it any other way."

Sal's eyes narrowed with suspicion.

Sal immediately made a call on one of the drawerful of burner cell phones in the trailer's desk and asked for a meet.

An hour later, Sal's blue, diamond-finish Cadillac SUV pulled to the curb in front of White's, a diner near the old US Rubber plant off Promenade Street. Shaped like a streamliner railroad car from the thirties, its aluminum siding pitted and dulled by weather and age, White's was hauled each morning from a vacant lot on the Hill to service cops, factory workers and Water Department's crews from four a.m. to seven p.m. A neon sign over the door flashed *Eat*.

Sal got his bulk through the door, looked down the row of empty tables by the windows, and saw a hawk-faced, unshaven man. Sal ordered a black coffee as he waddled by the counterman and sat across from Lucky Barracelli, who showed no sign of recognition. Sal didn't speak until his coffee was delivered. It tasted burnt, likely drawn from the bottom of an urn, so he poured in enough sugar to layer the mug's bottom.

"I got this problem."

"Yeah?"

"My nephew, Ricky, the guy who does the specials. I think he took out that fuck with the wire."

Barracelli's eyelids flickered. "Yeah?"

"Garo Hagopian was at the yard this morning. He's working a hit-and-run case from three years ago."

"He's being a pain in the ass all around town."

Sal gulped his coffee. "Said that who did it was driving a truck with a used plate. Back then, I let Ricky borrow junkers—yard trucks or cars—when he needed, before he got that fuckin' pimped-up beast he drives now. Sometimes he took it without letting me know." He stirred his coffee and looked at Lucky over its lip. "Ricky was the driver, the fuck that caught it, Baldolucca, was a passenger. They were on some job."

Barracelli's black eyes shot through Sal's. He put one hand on the edge of the table as though preparing to leave, the other to possibly go for Sal's throat.

"Listen, it was a situation," Sal tried to explain. "I came in one morning and I see the yard's pickup, a Ford F-150, and its left front is crumpled. Turns out, I find that Ricky had it out. I ask him and he says he did and had a fender bender with a pole. Didn't think much of it until reading a story a coupla days later, about cops lookin' for a black Ford F-150 in East Providence for a hit-and-run. Shitload of publicity on it. We were starting' the specials by then, so I needed him. I got the pickup compacted and out of the yard and I sat him down."

Barracelli's response came slowly, his voice so low Sal had trouble hearing him across the table.

"You wait three fuckin' years to tell me?"

"He's my sister's kid. What was I supposed to do? Never thought it'd come up like this."

Barracelli shredded a paper napkin, scattering the pieces on the table.

"Somebody woulda taken him out already if it wasn't for respect for you. Now, because ya didn't take care of business, our friend has a problem. We got staties blowing smoke up our asses on account of the wire. What a fuckin' stupid trick!" He picked up the shreds one by one, balled them up, and shoved them into Sal's lap. Sal didn't expect the insult, he had his pride, but didn't react.

"Who else knows?"

"Nobody." Sal had it figured that it would be his call on how Ricky went down. His responsibility, too. He stirred his coffee, poured in more sugar, thinking he would lay off the job to someone Lucky directed him to, like the Dragos. "I thought maybe Ricky gets offered up for the garrote job and the hit-and-run so everybody's happy."

"We'll think about it. Our friend isn't going to be happy. Too close to the yard. The yard is important to him, to us."

"Look, the only witness to the hit-and-run is dead and when Ricky goes, it's over. Maybe he should go with the next special."

"You didn't hear me?" Barracelli growled. "I said we'll think about it."

"I can operate the crane and the compactor," Sal said. "Did it all the time back then."

Lucky Barracelli shook his head. Sal wasn't getting the message; how and when were no longer in Sal's control. He was in deep shit for not controlling his nephew. Never know what that means when the Brow is pissed. Lucky knew the Brow had been approached by the Dragos the previous week with a new opportunity, for more money and less risk than compacting of stiffs. That would cause Sal to lose the cash from the specials. He could still run the scrap business—if the Brow let him.

CHAPTER FIFTY-THREE

FOR THE REST OF THE DAY, in the shop, in the mess hall, walking back and forth to and from meals, Fat Frankie felt the stares—some mean and suspicious. When would the all-important brown envelope be thrust through the bars? They all wanted to know, especially those with something on the betting line.

Just before the dinner count, a trustee came by and handed Fat Frankie what he'd been waiting for. He took it to his cot, sat, looked at it intently, and opened it with a fingernail.

He withdrew a two-page form, printed on one side. At the top was his name, his sentence, a description of the parole hearing procedure. Impatiently, he went to the second page. A box was filed in after the word Parole: *Granted.*

"Whew." He waltzed around his cell, waving the form in the air. "I did it!" Was his cousin Chris at all responsible? *Hard to believe numbnuts pulled it off.* No, had to have been his sterling performance before the board. Maybe Fuck Face ramming into him had somehow helped. Okay, now, he had to come up with some change for the Brow. As to his cousin, he would fuck him over. Then, he read the two typed lines after *Conditions*: "To begin ninety days from date" and "Supervised and restricted to Rhode Island without written permission from his parole officer for balance of original sentence."

What the fuck is that? Are you shitting me? I gotta wait three months and get permission to go to New York or Florida for two more years?

⁃⁃

Aaron was returning to his cell block from dinner when Lester Hickman touched his arm and his two goons came up on either side.

"Gilletto's out. A fuckin' first timer? You fucked that up, Aaron. You didn't get it right. Cost us a lot. So," Hickman whispered, "ya owe me. On yer way out of this joint?"

Aaron turned his ravaged face to Hickman, using his oldest defense to end a conversation. "Not sure I'm leaving. I need three votes. I never got one before. Why should it be different now?"

"Yer hearing will be big time, more bets than when Luciano was up the second time," Hickman said. Aaron recalled that Alfredo Luciano, a made man who served fifteen and made it out on his second try, was presently residing at Gates of Heaven Cemetery in East Providence, the result of a misunderstanding with the Brow as to who was who in the Mob hierarchy. "So if ya got a deal wired with all this bullshit, I gotta know."

"Don't take bets on me."

"Nah, ya know it doesn't work that way."

"I'm just sayin', I can't handicap myself." His stomach clenched. Hickman, a sociopath, would be vengeful if Aaron failed to give him something, even if it was a roll of the dice.

"That disappoints me, Aaron. Really does, after all I done for ya. Hurts Jersey and Quint, too." His head shifted to indicate the goons and their pace slowed. "Maybe there's somethin' we can do to change yer mind?" Hickman smiled and grabbed Aaron's three-fingered hand. It wasn't the feel of flesh to seal a bargain; it was to break a finger or two, if he had to.

Aaron panicked, but had an idea. "If I give you my prediction, and it comes out right, you gotta put the kibosh on Gilletto's parole. Some kind of problem before he's out, something that would keep him inside."

Hickman rubbed his grizzled chin. "I get it. Ya figure this is it, yer outta here at last, last chance to get at that fat prick."

"I didn't say that."

"That's good enough for me. But I gotta tell ya," he said, again squeezing Aaron's injured hand, "I gotta know fer sure at least a day before they vote on you. One way or the other. In or out." He stared into Aaron's eye. "No bullshit."

Aaron shrugged. "Nothin's for sure. You know that."

"Get it right, Aaron. Lot's gonna ride on it. Hate to lose big, Aaron. But, I gotta say, fuckin' accidents happen, don't dey?" Hickman turned to his cohorts who nodded. "All the fuckin' time."

CHAPTER FIFTY-FOUR

JAKE HAD AN EARLY DINNER with Livia at a back booth in the dining room under a poster touting Providence's fabulous WaterFire illuminations on the Providence River.

They hadn't slept together since Newport, and both realized that they had compartmentalized their lives in that brief space of time, Jake with the parole board and Baldolucca's murder, and Livia with the restaurant. Their verbal communications were so hesitant that Livia welcomed being interrupted several times by customers and waiters. Livia kept their conversation on the progress on the construction project; Jake sensed she was trying to control her emotions.

For his part, Jake failed to muster the courage to confess his faithlessness to Livia with Mia. For all Livia's affection for him, he knew her strong personality demanded, above all else, loyalty. Her lover had to be all in; his confession might destroy their mutual respect and partnership. Not what he wanted, not now.

When Livia left the table and returned to say she had to be at the podium to greet guests, Jake felt relief. They agreed to get together over the weekend.

Jake's cell phone vibrated at eight thirty-five while he was getting into his car in the restaurant parking lot.

"I know everything that Aldo Baldolucca knew." The voice was male, muffled as though spoken through something masking, like a handkerchief. "If ya want it, it will cost, and first ya got to show me yer interested and can follow directions. Tonight, exactly at ten, circle Kennedy Plaza three times. Go slow. But don't stop. At eleven, drive up to the Hill, go under the Arch, ya know where dat is? Go twice between eleven and eleven-fifteen. Do it and I'll call ya with details for a meet."

"Who's this?"

"Aldo Baldolucca was my . . . friend." The exaggerated hesitation made Jake guess lover. "Nobody should die like that. I want the bastard that did it to die. If I smell cops, it's over. I disappear. What kind of car ya got?

"Camaro. Black."

"Be there tonight or forget it. If you make it, you'll get another call soon." The call ended.

Jake checked the caller ID on the cell's screen and called back. Three rings and a female answered, "Yeah?"

"I was just talking to somebody—"

"Well, this ain't just somebody, honey child. Dis is a pay phone at Kennedy Plaza. Ya sure ya weren't looking for me? I got juicy pants for a stud like you."

Jake didn't call Garo or Dermott; it was premature, and if he had called, they would be cautionary, and he didn't want to be careful because the call had the smell of the real thing. Finally. Nor would he call those SOBs Harrigan and Pulaski. They'd think it was some kind of dodge to throw them off his trail on Baldolucca's murder. And they could screw it with a surveillance.

His private cell number was the link to credibility. Jake remembered that Baldolucca had his business card with the cell number scrawled on the back. He must have given it out, to whom, his boyfriend from prison? Or a *goombah*, like a Paulie? Either might make sense. To find out, he'd have to start by making a tour of downtown Providence.

CHAPTER FIFTY-FIVE

RICKY STOOD IN A CLUSTER of fir, oak, plane, and maple trees in Burnside Park off downtown's Kennedy Plaza, deserted except for a few of the ever-present homeless sitting around the Bajnotti Fountain with their shopping carts of belongings. Nothing to indicate cops.

His pulse quickened as ten o'clock drew near. Precisely at ten, a throaty roar had him turn toward the yellow bricks of the Commerce Center complex as a black Camaro turned into the incline past the Rhode Island Foundation headquarters, and disappeared down the hill towards the Biltmore Hotel. It reappeared in front of City Hall at the western end of Kennedy Plaza to pass a row of RIPTA busses, the Federal Court House, and the post office to return to Commerce Center. Minutes later, after the Camaro completed a second loop and then a third, Ricky watched it turn in to Washington Street. Ricky smiled. Jake Fournier was on his way to Federal Hill. He had taken the bait.

Ricky left Burnside Park, crossed to WaterPlace Park to Citizens Bank Plaza, got into his truck and, playing it cool, took an elaborately long route past the statehouse, up Smith Street, down Chalkstone Avenue over Route 6 to Dean Street, and found a spot to park by Gasbarro's Liquors on Atwells Avenue. He sauntered down the Hill's bustling sidewalks where restaurants' outside tables were warmed by gas heaters. Ricky blended in as a Hill guy, wearing a black fleece jacket, sunglasses despite the hour, his long black hair pulled back under a baseball cap, his bearded chin in his chest. His eyes didn't stray right or left, he didn't try to pass anyone on the sidewalk as he hunkered along. At ten minutes of eleven, he had walked three-quarters of the way to the Arch and hadn't seen any cops except for the obligatory cruiser parked near the crosswalks of DePasquale Square. At five 'til, he spotted the black Camaro coming towards him behind a couple of duded-up Mustangs and Chargers cruising the Hill for show. In the reflection of the smoked glass front window of Restaurante Milano, Ricky watched the Camaro pass behind him and under the Arch.

Ricky crossed the street to a Dunkin' Donuts. Five minutes later, with a mocha iced coffee in hand, he watched the Camaro slide by him and under the Arch heading to downtown.

"Hooked," he said aloud, and paused, unsure of his next step, but satisfied that Fournier was doing Nemesis' bidding.

He left the downtown to work out his anxiety in the familiar surroundings of the Action Club.

CHAPTER FIFTY-SIX

IN JAKE'S DREAM, a single bulb provided a shaft of light on a hawkish, dirt-smeared face with inset black eyes, lips shut, the expression one of arrogance and contempt.

With Jake's full hand slap, the prisoner's head snapped back. Blood dripped from a nose that was already pulp; his expression, angry, insolent, remained. Jake had to change that. He struck an orbital bone fully with his fist. The killer's eye puffed up; while it started to close, his expression still said "I'm not sorry for what I did, for your pain, for your loss. I am outside of your power; let me loose and I'll inflict as much pain as I can."

Jake had a pry bar in his hand. He would bring it down, crush the skull, break the jaw, knock out teeth, wipe away his face . . .

He jolted awake. Pry bar? Never had a pry bar in Iraq. That had to have materialized from Garo's recollection of the Gist murder.

The dream further confused Jake's revenge with a memory of a field interrogation of an Iraqi insurgent, planting IEDs in Anwar Province, who was captured by Jake's squad shortly after a device detonated and killed a pregnant Iraqi woman. The insurgent mocked Jake and his co-interrogator, his head pivoting back and forth, muttering "Allah Akbar," spitting saliva and blood at him, his hate surpassing his pain. Jake would have pulverized that face if not held back by his partner.

Jake knew that wartime incident was shameful; when he finished with Hope's killer, would he feel the same? No, the killer he envisioned was a hulk, stupid looking and without conscience. He deserved to die.

When would he get the next call?

CHAPTER FIFTY-SEVEN

JAKE WASN'T COMPLETELY SURE of his motivation the following noontime when he headed down Providence's Elmwood Avenue towards Roger Williams Park for the much-ballyhooed rally featuring the appearance of Terrell Williams. It wasn't Williams' music that attracted him. Rather, he wanted to understand how much of the Free Aaron buzz was real and how much social media flummery. Plus, he wanted to keep occupied while he waited for the call from the tipster.

The weather was unkind for an outdoor rally in late March, always a chancey time for anything outside. The temperature hovered at forty and the overcast was low and a heavy gray. The Camaro rebuffed wintry gusts off Narragansett Bay. Jake dressed in a fleece hoodie that covered his forehead under a windbreaker, jeans, sneakers—both for the weather and to not be recognized. His beard was two days dark and he wore wraparound sunglasses, the cheap drugstore kind with a bluish tint.

Traffic on the Park's serpentine roads was slowed by knots of pedestrians and bicyclists bundled within down jackets, pullovers and parkas. Yellow school buses, orange cones and police tape prevented nearby on-street parking, and he was waved by a traffic cop to a lot close to the Betsy Williams Cottage, which meant a ten-minute walk around a series of ponds to the Temple to Music, the park's festival area. He followed throngs of college kids wearing identifying sweatshirts and holding placards with

Instagram or SnapChat photographs of the startling face from *Aaron's Anguish*; a few wore *Phantom of the Opera* masks. Drumbeats, boomboxes, air horn blasts, and "Free Aaron!" chants resembled a political rally or a rock concert.

The Temple to Music, a marble edifice that reminded Jake of a war memorial arch, squatted behind a limpid moat within a tipped bowl of curved embankments. Raw winds whipped around the bowl as Jake gained its upper lip, looking down into a milling crowd.

A young serious-faced woman in a Brown University sweatshirt offered Jake a fact sheet on Underwood's situation, with instructions on how to contact the governor and the parole board to express outrage. On the stage under the Arch were two rows of seats filled by people huddled together against the cold, and off to one side, a four-piece band, heavy on the bass guitars and drums, played a song that Jake recognized from an old *Highwaymen* album by Cash, Nelson, Kristofferson and Jennings. Past the far lip of the bowl, where the park's famous antique Looff carousel played calliope music, police sawhorses and cruisers with red, white and blue flashing lights blocked the roadway from a throng of anti-Aaron protesters, armed with placards and bullhorns; their blasts were carried by the wind into the bowl.

A black stretch limo fronted by two Providence police motorcycles came up and parked on the road close by Jake. The cops got off their bikes, the doors to the limo opened, and Terrell Williams emerged, dressed in a purple windbreaker and tracksuit, his trademark fedora pushed back on his head. Three hulking bodyguards escorted him through excited admirers down the embankment to the stage where he was hugged by all. A "Free Aaron!" chant began, and Williams joined in the rhythmic hand clapping, encouraging the crowd while pacing the stage. With its attention drawn to Williams, the crowd ignored the Providence mayor standing behind the superstar. Over the noisy excitement within the bowl, Jake caught a drift of boos from the anti-Aaron protestors.

The mayor made his plea for Underwood's cause, then introduced Millie Underwood, wrapped in a dark red parka over a long skirt that reached her boots, her gray hair tossed by the wind. She held the mic in trembling hands and her first words were lost in the wind and a feedback.

". . . been asked by my brother Aaron to say 'thank you.' You have given him hope. By the way, that is our state's motto, Hope. But for people like Aaron, it has been in short supply. Because of you and thousands like you, through social media his plight has become well-known, in fact of international concern. His life until now, because of suspicion, fear and bigotry, has been a life without human dignity or empathy. You will change that."

Applause, cheers and more "Free Aaron!" chants.

"I urge you to contact the prison, the governor, state politicians, the parole board, to free my brother."

More applause, cheers, and chants.

"During his thirty years in prison, my brother has become a lover of poetry, particularly the poetry of Robert Frost, and is himself a poet. He has asked me to read some lines of his own dedicated to all his supporters. It's entitled *A Prisoner's Thanks.*" She read her lines slowly in a thin voice.

"*One day, I will see the light*
Unfiltered by iron, fence and wire
And to you who see and share my plight
Know freedom is all I aspire.
As I lay inside dark walls tonight
My thoughts will be of you
One day I will with all my might,
Say thank you, thank you, thank you."

"From the bottom of my heart and my brother's heart, thank you."

The crowd erupted.

"A Frost reader, a convict poet? Classic," Jake muttered as he felt the pervasive vibes of good feeling and renewed determination.

Williams embraced Millie, waving to urge the crowd to continue its appreciation. Then with a hand mic, in a hip-hop cadence and without notes, set up his targets and knocked them down, one by one, starting with the governor who Williams said should pardon Underwood, then the state attorney general, the Greenwick Town Council, Buddy Callahan, and the Rhode Island penal system.

Jake was impressed how he glibly rolled off names, and that he didn't use notes. It was his crowd. His applause lines hit on pitch, and produced spontaneous enthusiastic rifts of "Free Aaron!" chants and placard bounces.

As Williams finished, Jake heard the throaty roars of motorcycles. Three abreast, a posse of bikers came thundering along the road around the lip of the bowl, their leather jackets, helmets, and Harleys' chrome shining despite the overcast sky.

Jake, assuming they would be anti-Aaron and fearing the worst, was surprised by the red, white and blue "Bikers for Aaron" banner held by the first row of riders. They continued on toward the carousel. As they slowed, anti-Aaron demonstrators rushed forward to the police lines with their placards held like lances. Jake witnessed one demonstrator move right up to the first rank of bikers, placard at the ready, just as Jake, and everyone else in the bowl, heard the distinctive sound of a gunshot.

It was loud, clear, and there was no doubt in anyone's mind—certainly not in Jake's, as an Iraq War veteran—that it was a gunshot. Terrell Williams and the mayor were hustled off the stage by bodyguards and cops, and rushed up the bowl's incline to their limo.

The crowd, stunned at first, looked every which way for safety before panic and confusion took over. It became a shouting, screaming mass of people breaking toward the departing limo, pushing around the moat and up the incline, heedless of the pleas for calm by someone at the Temple's sound system. Children were hoisted on parents' shoulders; carriages and folding chairs were overturned and left behind; people stumbled and fell; placards and signs were abandoned. Jake had a flashback of Iraqi fugitives fleeing an onslaught of their village.

Jake was bumped and pushed but managed to keep on his feet. He helped a mother with two small girls up the embankment, turned back and saw what the excited crowd stumbling toward him didn't—cops with batons flying in a melee of uniforms and leather and placards; people and bikers hurtling forward; a cop going down; bikes roaring and turning away. Cops manhandled bikers and demonstrators toward patrol cars and a paddy wagon. Sirens began to slice the air from outside the park as a patrol car pointed towards the gate to the Cranston side of the park, followed by a straggly line of bikers. A Channel 8 van was there to video all, and countless cell phone cameras would have already uploaded images of the turmoil.

Jake helped remaining stragglers up the incline, stashing his sunglasses in his jacket pocket. The bowl was almost empty when he came face-to-face with a young woman struggling toward the road as she spoke into a cell phone. Something said *reporter*, and he instinctively turned away. From behind, he heard, "Mr. Fournier?"

Jake slowed but didn't stop. She followed, and caught up to him. No sidestepping or trot would shake her off.

"Mr. Fournier, right? Mr. Fournier?"

Jake's face clouded as she took cell phone photographs of him.

"You're Jake Fournier from the parole board?"

"No comment," he said, realizing that sounded stupid.

"Should you be here? This is a pro-Underwood rally."

"I was curious because of all the media hype."

"Not influenced?"

"No. Not by crowds or speeches."

"How about that gunshot?"

"As a veteran, I've been in situations with guns. They only aggravate the situation."

"So, you being here doesn't suggest support?"

"It signals nothing of the sort. And I've got to go."

CHAPTER FIFTY-EIGHT

JAKE DIDN'T WATCH the six o'clock news, but he got a call from Dermott.

"What an effing mess!" Dermott said. "A biker with a loaded gun is not somebody you want at your rally! It started when the pack got to the anti-Aaron group. Someone got past a cop and whacked the biker with a placard, then a couple of bikers went into them. Then the shot. But get this: we know who did it because the a-hole shot himself in the foot, right through a leather boot, even with the chains and buckles, and blew off a toe."

Jake's laugh slowly rolled off his tongue. *Thank God!* Relieved the shot did not come from a gun directed at a supporter of one side or the other, he didn't tell his friend about being at the rally or the *Journal* reporter or being photographed, thinking, hoping, there might be an outside chance the encounter wouldn't make the Sunday newspaper.

"Want to join me tonight?" Dermott asked. "I've got a gig at the Irish Club, a lot of Guinness and song, and it would be good for you to get out."

"I'm hunkering down. Wherever I go, people will be looking for a hint on Underwood's parole or want to give me advice, and I'm tired of it. And I can only take so much Irish blarney. You won the rebellion, I know, but that was over a century ago."

"Ah, but that's not what it's all about. It's about the hundred times we lost our country and our women through treachery and money-grabbing and being layabouts. You Canucks did lose it once to General Wolfe at the Battle of Quebec. Wolfe versus Montcalm. You were conquered, and that was it. You Canadian Frenchies have no songs of revolution, a few poems, maybe, and *putine*. You have nothing to say about the Irish being raucous."

Jake switched subjects. "What have you found out about me and Baldolucca?"

"The organized crime squad figures it was someone in the Mob, maybe a wannabe. Always some of those around. I still say that someone will get offered up. The Mob doesn't want the heat. It'll be somebody dead or on vacation."

"So I'm in the clear?"

"You're still in play. You will be, until someone surfaces."

"I assume they're going to want to talk to me again." Hesitantly, he recounted his interaction with Harrigan and Pulaski.

Dermott's reaction was predictable. "You don't get it, do you? You're becoming a righteous blowhard, and if that's how you want it, you'll get screwed. Just what do you think you're doing?"

Jake mumbled through an apology, even as his friend's anger persisted, burning in his throat.

"I bet the only thing that's keeping you from being questioned in Scituate right now is this Underwood thing, which I would guess is soon over."

"Probably sometime this week."

"So, listen to me for once. Stay out of the limelight. Focus on what Garo can come up with on the license plate. I like a couple of names on his short list." He lowered his voice. "Anyway, I think he's going to have a lot of time to work on it."

"What do you mean?"

"I guess he didn't tell you. Garo was approached by the Security Investigation Unit, the SIU, at the prison as to if he had filmed *Aaron's Anguish*. Seems that they electronically update the visitor's log at Medium Security bi-weekly and his name finally popped up."

"Did he do it?"

"Don't know, he's got the ability to, and I'm not gonna ask him. But he was a PI, after all. Knows that kind of computer and internet shit. I think his days at the public defender's office might be over since he's no longer welcome in the prison complex. He's on paid leave as of right now. Can't serve two masters but that's Garo. Justice haunts him."

"Speaking of justice, I'm resigning from the parole board. It'll be delivered right after the Underwood vote."

Dermott exploded. "Are you listening? Not yet! The longer you stay on the board, you get a better chance that something breaks on Baldolucca from forensics or a source. If you resign now, the staties will be all over you."

"I'll be fine."

"As I remember your parents, they were nice people, reasonable people. Where did you get such a fucking thick head?"

<hr />

Later Jake opened his laptop and found the file on Underwood that Garo had emailed: a fact sheet gathered from the state police, Medical Examiner's Office, AG and Superior Court files, laced with information from the town clerk, logically organized. He read through it twice. Nothing changed his mind as to Underwood's guilt or parole application.

But it had focused his thoughts on the role of the parole board, its unwritten human dimension, what the members could do to round out the criteria's hard edges and do justice in an imperfect system.

Jake had concluded that parole kind of worked when left to itself without politics and social media pressures. Petitioners had to show something to earn parole, attend counseling sessions, get GED diplomas, maintain relationships with families, maybe have a job offer. Compare that with probationers that judges let off who never saw the inside of a prison and went back to their old haunts, to gangbanger friends, uneducated, unemployable, and minimally supervised by overworked case workers. Worse, he had learned, seventy percent of probationers and parolees were "banked," in the jargon of the probation and parole staff—meaning inadequately supervised, if at all. So, no surprise that seventy percent of probationers and parolees would be rearrested in three years. At any one time, up to a third of the population in the prison system were probation and parole violators. And sooner or later, they would apply for parole.

Jake went to bed early after texting Livia a lie that he had a migraine and he'd call her in the morning, still hoping that he wouldn't be a story in the morning's *Journal.*

He had another restless night. Too much on his mind. It was almost two when exhaustion finally caught up. He had hoped for a call from Baldolucca's friend, and was now convinced that that person was likely Hope's killer, posing as an informant, a rat. He'd be ready when he got the next call.

CHAPTER FIFTY-NINE

GUN SHOT HALTS RALLY was the banner headline in the Sunday *Journal*. Jake read the account at the kitchen table. The chaos at the park and its aftermath were vividly described by a *Journal* team of reporters, replete with comments by participants filled with anger, suspicion and resentment.

Jake's photograph appeared on an inside page; he looked grungy in his hoodie, his head at an angle, his face unshaven. Although she had quoted Jake accurately, the reporter suggested his presence at the rally was a conflict of interest, or at least inappropriate, for a parole board member. Bertozzi apparently hadn't answered a phone call from the reporter for a comment, Mia also failed to reply, of course, and McNally said he was surprised that a parole board member would attend such an event. Prebys, however, let loose.

"Totally improper. The public expects us not to take sides until we have all of the information on an inmate. I would not have gone, I can tell you that."

Jake thought, *You prick!*

In unexpectedly warm weather, Jake jogged two loops around downtown Pawtucket's bicycle path. He called Livia upon arrival at his condo, detailing the rally and its aftermath and his involvement with the late Aldo Baldolucca. She didn't interrupt, although she was obviously put out because he hadn't sought her advice or comfort the prior night.

He heard little forgiveness in her voice as she rattled off her list of concerns. They ended with, "You are turning into a mystery man. You go to that Terrell Williams rally without telling anyone—not me, not Dermott or Garo. You're in the Sunday *Journal* and you don't tell me before I see it. What's going on?"

He almost told her of the phone call from Hope's killer but lamely said, "I just didn't want to worry you."

"Jake," she said, her voice beginning to crack. "Before my ex left, I could feel the distance growing. Sure, I was on cocaine, but it was him, too. He—we—stopped talking. He didn't want me to feel the weight of his bookies and the banks breathing down his neck, and I wasn't any help. Don't do that to me."

She paused. "Are you okay?"

"I'm fine. Tired, frustrated, feeling used, but I have it together. I was so close to finding the guy who killed Hope and then how Baldolucca got killed. And I'm in the spotlight because of Underwood's parole and a suspect in Baldolucca's murder. What I should have been doing is keeping you close."

"Jake, remember one thing, please. What we have is based on trust. On honesty. We have both been through a lot. Don't let your purpose obscure that. If it does, we will lose something precious."

"I know." She agreed to come to his condo for dinner and a sleepover.

CHAPTER SIXTY

THAT AFTERNOON, in a tank top and briefs, Ricky was sprawled on his bed. His attic apartment was stale and smelled of dog, and he was sweating out his third beer. *How, where, when to take Fournier down?* Had to be soon and flawless.

Nemesis would have a victim come to him. Facing the rear gate of Rhode Island Scrap on Plainfield Street was a nondescript strip shopping center with a large parking lot. He could stake it out from behind the plastic slats in the yard's gate. Somehow, he'd get Fournier from there to inside the yard, knock him off, compact him, and send what remained to China.

He remembered the black, shiny Camaro that Fournier drove. Park it anywhere in that neighborhood of Rhode Island Scrap, it wouldn't last ten minutes before some asshole broke in or stole the tires, or a cop checked it out. Got to deal with that.

Ricky lifted the beer can, finished its contents, and swiped his chin with his wrist. Outside, Bitch, not the only pitbull in the neighborhood, was chained to a clothesline post and in turn, barked and loudly whimpered. Ricky's eyes went to the *Journal* he'd purchased for news on Baldolucca—nothing—but this Fournier guy was news.

Ricky read the story on Fournier's appearance at the Terrell Williams rally for Underwood. If Fournier disappeared, the cops would go apeshit trying to find him. But maybe somebody who didn't like the way the parole might go could be blamed. Ricky would send an anonymous threatening letter about Fournier to the cops. *Nemesis smart!*

He tossed the empty in the direction of an overflowing basket beside a small refrigerator and fell back on the sagging mattress. *Lay it all out,* he thought, *get it in order.*

First, Fournier would be induced to come. And to bring cash. Maybe he already had it together, if Aldo was about to snitch. *How much? Play it safe, ask for what he was to give Baldolucca. Gotta think on that, not get greedy.* Also, he needed to give Fournier another taste to get him to Plainfield Street for sure. *What would it be?* Sal said the PI dick asked for help in looking for a black Ford F-150 with a white stripe over the fender. *Can't tell him what happened to the pickup. Can't involve Rhode Island Scrap.* Was there something else about the truck that would be known to Jake as the only other witness?

He got up for another beer. As he opened the refrigerator, a weak light within went on. And he remembered that the yard's Ford F-150 had a bar of lights over the cab, halogen spots, and he was pretty sure a couple had been on that night. Anyone seeing the pickup from the front should remember the bar of lights. He cracked open the can and took a long drink. *That could be the hook.*

He went back to the bed, his thoughts still circling over when to do it. Since Sal would have a delivery from the Dragos soon, why take the chance on Sal finding out he was in the yard on his own deal? *Better to pull off a two-fer.* Get Fournier in the junker before the Dragos arrived. No doubt Fournier would be closely monitoring his cell phone, so as soon as Ricky got a call from Sal for a special, *badda bing!*

He sat up, feeling the familiar rush. Nemesis was ready.

CHAPTER SIXTY-ONE

THE GOVERNOR CALLED AS BERTOZZI, who was sitting on a couch in his den, watching a late Celtics playoff game against the Cleveland Cavaliers.

After the call, Bertozzi couldn't concentrate on the game. He had his marching orders: Move up Underwood's petition and get the matter quickly resolved. Do that and he had the governor's support for chair.

With perspective sharpened by two fingers of Glenlivet, Bertozzi considered the governor never directly said how he wanted the vote on Underwood to go. Shrewd! To Bertozzi, the governor's appointment of law-and-order McNally signaled his preference: the board's decision on Underwood would be the tipping point in his favor for chair.

Bertozzi sipped his expensive Scotch and justified himself. He had previously opposed parole because Underwood didn't show remorse. Was it any different this time? He might wrestle with the moral dimensions of his no vote on Underwood, despite his clean prison record, board precedent and rules, and that damaged face. But it would be over. Three votes against parole for sure, maybe four if Fournier remained unshaken. That would elect him chair.

His wife called him to come up to bed. Instead, he poured himself another Scotch and remembered that someone, years ago, told him that Rhode Island politics was a blood sport. Some blood was going to be spilled over Underwood's petition. It should not be his.

CHAPTER SIXTY-TWO

JAKE GRILLED STEAKS. A glass of prosecco and Livia softened as he'd hoped. After dinner, they watched two episodes of *The Crown* on Netflix, and went to bed. Jake found himself relieved that the expected call from the killer hadn't happened while Livia was with him.

When he woke, Livia had left the bedroom for the kitchen. Last night's lovemaking had been slow, gentle, more friendly than a hungry passion, as though both sensed something palliative in their touchings.

He thought of Hope. Their physical connection had been deeply possessive, exploring, a taking in of each other. It was rarely that way between Jake and Livia. Mia seemed to have awakened something deeper in his physical needs. *Is it just the sex?* he wondered.

He thought of things he did for Livia—gifts of jewelry, financing the restaurant, trips they enjoyed. Unspoken was that the memory of Hope lingered. If he brought justice to Hope, would his relationship with Livia deepen from affection? Or would his needs, emotional and physical, take a different turn. *Mia?*

〰〰〰〰〰〰〰〰〰〰〰〰〰〰〰〰〰

Later, over scrambled eggs and English muffins with lime marmalade, Livia expressed enthusiasm about turning the new space at the restaurant into a mini-gallery for local artists on a revolving basis. "The cost goes up for directed lighting but Jake, I think it would be great."

Jake appreciated being asked his opinion but knew it was *pro forma*. Anything for Livia when it came to the restaurant.

CHAPTER SIXTY-THREE

MINIMUM SECURITY'S ADMINISTRATION BUILDING reminded Jake of a Pawtucket parochial school: brick façade, white trim, multipaned windows, raised flowerbeds refreshed with mulch, flags waving in a stray breeze, and no fence. Jake picked up his ID badge at the security desk and walked down a long corridor with a polished but worn tile floor. Room 107 was narrow, set up so that an inmate would sit at one end of a table to face board members lined up two on a side, with Bertozzi and Mrs. Ames at the other end. Two inspirational posters—*Courage* and *Dignity*—supplied decor.

He entered and sat and looked across the table at Mia. He felt uneasy, even sheepish, wondering how she and he would interact. There had to be a good reason for her attendance after her threat to boycott Chief Bain's appearance. Was it him? She appeared to be ready for battle, her chin firm and posture unflinching. She finally glanced at Jake, then shook her head, and he rationalized it had more to do with his vote to hear Chief Bain than something personal.

Then Prebys burst into the hearing room, red-faced and shaking with anger, holding a newspaper in his hand at shoulder height, pointing it at Mia. "The *Journal*'s editorial says we're interviewing Chief Bain today. Asks by what authority? I didn't think you'd actually leak it, Mia."

McNally looked bemused at the accusation. Bertozzi, ever the conciliator, the peacemaker, interrupted. "Could have been anyone—the AG, the chief himself. I called the reporter this morning and explained our authority to have anyone we want appear by subpoena. This was just an easier procedure. Hopefully, she'll write that up."

Mia responded. "I told you it would get picked up by the media. Anybody can read the statute. It says nothing about third parties like the police getting a hearing by claiming to represent a victim. The Free Aaron partisans are entitled to know."

"Cut the crap," Prebys huffed. "Mia, it was you." Then he turned on Jake. "Gotta be fifty demonstrators outside when I came in. How many, Jake, at your hip-hop rally?" He tossed that off with new confidence. "I guess you're no longer undecided?" He turned to Bertozzi. "Don't we have a rule about a board member publicly taking sides before a vote? We sure have rules about everything else."

Jake ignored Prebys. Bertozzi had earlier admonished Jake by text about his appearance at the rally and the *Journal* story. Jake had accepted the criticism without excuse.

McNally broke the tension when he opened his laptop and said with authority, "Let's move on."

"In light of the weekend's events," Bertozzi began, his voice tight with emotion at McNally's demand, "it's been requested that we hear Underwood's petition as soon as we can. His complete file is now available. Further delay will just inflame a situation that is growing out of hand. I'd like to go ahead with Underwood's hearing tomorrow. You can see him and hear him and make up your mind, and we'll have as much time for discussion and decision as we may need. Any objections?"

Prebys smiled. "Not from me. I'm over prepared."

McNally said, "Okay by me. Good idea."

"I object," Mia shouted. "It's a rush to judgment. Do it and your political agenda is going to be obvious. We need time, especially after hearing Bain. Whatever respect parole still has with the community will be dashed. Our rules require at least five days advance notice for a meeting. I'm insisting upon that. How about you, Jake?"

"I don't like the idea of an exception to the rules, especially in this case."

"They're our rules," insisted Prebys. "We can change them, we can override them when we want."

"Mia, this is obviously critical," Bertozzi said. "Another rally or demonstration could get uglier, become a riot take over by bad guys and looters."

"I am here for Chief Bain's testimony under protest, and I'll be under protest for Underwood's hearing because somebody should defend the integrity of our parole process, including our rules . . . and I thought it would be you!" Mrs. Ames glared at Bertozzi, stung by Mia's obvious contempt.

"If there's a delay and another riot, if someone gets hurt, it would be on your account, Mia," Prebys said.

Bertozzi stared Prebys down, further dismayed that he had to rely on a jerk like Prebys for a vote in the election of a chair. He needed time to think. He brought down the gavel. "Five-minute break," and left the hearing room with Mrs. Ames in tow.

Prebys immediately went to sit in the seat Bertozzi had vacated to speak to McNally; Jake, in turn, sat next to Mia. She was breathing evenly; Jake wasn't.

"It's just an extra few days, but something has to slow down the train," said Mia. "I think there is progress being made in public opinion in Underwood's case." Jake realized that these were the first words from her directed to him since he left her bedroom.

"I—"

She looked across the table at McNally and Prebys, now in deep conversation. McNally's hand shielded his mouth. "Look at them. Prebys has become McNally's puppet, playing politics with someone's life."

She lowered her voice to a whisper. "Jake, the other night I had too much to drink, never should have been lying next to you. Just stupid."

"As much my fault as yours. I'm in a relationship, Mia, and—"

"Makes it worse."

"We are still colleagues, Mia."

"But it happened," she said, shaking her head. "Let's think it through together."

"Must be some genuine affection on both sides," Jake said. His words sounded stiff and didn't begin to convey his sentiment nor moral confusion. Thoughts of their moments together flooded his mind and despite the serious questions at hand, he found himself grappling with desire.

ııı

Bertozzi and Mrs. Ames returned and musical chairs resumed. When all were settled in, Bertozzi said, "I've checked with the warden's office and his legal counsel. We do have a five-day rule, but it can be waived by a majority vote of the members."

Prebys smiled as Bertozzi continued. "We clearly have three votes in favor. Let's do the right thing and move on it. Where and time will be communicated by email later today. If you want to override me, I'll put it to a vote." He waited, heard no response, then said, "Bring in Chief Bain."

CHAPTER SIXTY-FOUR

CHIEF WILLIAM "BILLY" BAIN was ushered into the victim's hearing room by a very subdued Mrs. Ames. He took a chair and sat straight enough to be an altar boy at High Mass. He nodded at Bertozzi and greeted McNally as an old acquaintance.

McNally responded warmly. "Welcome, Chief."

Chief Bain measured up to Jake's expectation. He was in his forties, trim, perhaps five-seven, tow-headed, dark blue eyes under shaggy eyebrows, and a chin that looked like it had been carved out of brick. His gray hair was cut in a military brush; a fuzzy gray caterpillar ran over his upper lip under a nose too short for a long face. His brown uniform jacket mimicked a statie's with a silver badge over a breast pocket, and worn over a tan dress shirt and black tie. A thick black belt with an ornate, polished buckle held up creased trousers. He placed his Smokey the Bear hat on the table in front of him.

"Good mornin', Chief," Bertozzi said briskly. "Do you have a prepared statement?"

"Good morning," Bain replied firmly with a hint of South County twang. "I have some notes I would like to read."

Mia interrupted. "Let the record show that I am here under a protest as I believe Chief Bain should not be allowed to appear before us as a representative of the victim."

Bertozzi said, "Noted," and nodded to Mrs. Ames. He sat back, folded his fingers. "Proceed."

Bain reached into an inside pocket of his uniform to remove folded pages. He flattened them on the table and slipped on half-glasses that rested on his nose.

"Aaron Underwood murdered Lucretia Gist on October 31, thirty years ago. She died from a blow that caused severe trauma to her brain. The weapon used was a pry bar. Underwood was severely wounded by the victim who fired a bird gun—a scattergun—before she died. Underwood was found next to her body, barely alive himself. His fingerprints were the only ones found on the pry bar. We believe this was a robbery attempt that ended up in a murder."

He looked up from his notes to check the panel's reaction. A pinkish tongue wet his lips.

"Underwood was charged as an adult, pled guilty, and was sentenced to life imprisonment. There is no reason to believe that he didn't commit this vicious murder." He shuffled the pages. "I'd like to read a resolution passed by the Greenwick Town Council."

"We are aware of the town's position, so that won't be necessary," Bertozzi said.

McNally quickly interjected. "Why not let him read it?"

"Because I don't think it's necessary."

McNally didn't back down. "I've known Chief Bain for years. Greenwick is only four miles as the crow flies from our Scituate barracks. Been in his office many times. I've always found the Greenwick police to be cooperative, helpful in every investigation."

Bertozzi muttered, "Thank you for your endorsement, Major, but—"

Mia peered over her glasses. "I would like to hear the town's resolution. Was it approved unanimously?"

Chief Bain answered slowly, "No, there was one dissenter."

"Let him read it, for Pete's sake," said Prebys.

Bertozzi, who had been making notes, dropped his pen in resignation. "Okay, read it."

The resolution focused on the gruesome murder, its effect on the small town at the time, and the present fear of the community if a convicted murderer resided in its midst. Jake thought Mia was likely disappointed because the resolution didn't specifically mention Underwood's disfigurement; she likely would have turned any such reference into an argument for postponement or parole.

"Anything else?" Bertozzi asked Bain.

"No, that about does it."

"I have a few questions," Jake said slowly. "I want to go over a couple of things, Chief. You are obviously very familiar with the murder, one of the few folks who might remember anything. One of our jobs is to evaluate how vicious it might have been, how cruel it was. I'd appreciate your help for me to get the setting."

"Of course." Bain removed his glasses, and put them back inside his uniform jacket. "I would be happy to be helpful."

"Thank you," Jake said. "As I understand it, it happened on Halloween."

"Yes, that's correct."

"And, Aaron Underwood was then a fifteen-year-old student at the junior high school in Greenwick, correct?"

"Yes, eighth grade. He had stayed back once or twice, I believe." The Chief smiled, getting comfortable.

"I understand you were a classmate, Chief?"

"Yes."

"Prior to that night, had you ever considered Underwood capable of a vicious murder?"

McNally interrupted. "Where is this going?"

Mia responded, "If we're going to hear him, let Jake ask his questions. You said this was a special case."

Jake looked to Bertozzi. "I think I have the right to ask questions. The Chief is here representing a victim and has unique knowledge that would reflect what we might have expected from a victim. I don't believe we have ever shirked from asking a victim about an impression prior to an attack or its trauma or, in fact, much else."

Bertozzi nodded affirmatively.

"So Chief, did you think he was capable of a vicious murder?"

"He was slow."

"And a vicious murderer?"

"Not necessarily."

"Thank you, Chief. Am I also correct that you and a friend found the body?"

Bain removed a handkerchief from the trousers and blew his nose before his reply.

"My friend Joe Tingle and I were out on Halloween and we stopped at the Gists' farm. I don't remember why we were there. Back then, you know, out in the country, Halloween pranks on isolated farms were common. Nothing malicious, mind you, pranks."

"If you were doing a prank, you wouldn't necessarily get too close to the house, would you?"

"Well, I guess it would depend what we were going to do. I just don't remember. We did a lot of kid things."

"But you just wouldn't walk in someone's house, would you?"

No longer relaxed, Bain answered in a rising voice, "No, and we didn't. We noticed the front door was wide open when we arrived. We went around to the back of the house and saw lights on and the television was on loud, and we looked in but the angle didn't permit us to see much except the victim's legs on the floor."

"You knew something was wrong?"

"Yes," the Chief answered, "and we entered through the front door, went into a parlor and a dining room to the kitchen to the ell at the end of the house."

"Where you saw the victim sprawled on the floor?"

"Yes." Bain blanched at the recollection, "Aaron Underwood lay a couple feet away from her, next to the pry bar, facedown, so at first we didn't see how bloody, how hideous—"

"You knew it was Underwood despite not seeing his face?"

"I mean, not when we walked in."

"You didn't touch her or him, did you?"

"No. We thought she might be dead from the way it looked. Wasn't sure about Underwood."

"So, you immediately called 911?"

"No 911 back then. We called my dad from a phone in the room. He was sheriff then."

Jake paused to let the relationship sink in. "The state police barracks are just a few miles away, aren't they?"

"Yes, but we always called the sheriff first in Greenwick, and I wanted to tell my father that—"

"So, your father came right out?"

"As quickly as he could from on patrol, it being Halloween. I would say maybe ten or fifteen minutes, or so."

"What time was that?"

"I guess around seven-thirty, eight."

"And what did you do before he arrived?"

"What did I do? I . . . we—"

McNally interrupted. "Where is this going? There's nothing new here."

Mia said, "Oh, I'm interested. Go ahead, Jake."

"Just a few more questions to help me get the scene in my mind."

Bain mopped his brow with his handkerchief, and sat back. "She was on the floor, facing us. Her skull was caved in. We saw that there was blood everywhere. It was horrible."

"Where were you while waiting for your father?"

The Chief's eyes went to the ceiling. "We used a telephone in the parlor. I know that when my father arrived, we were on the porch, I do remember that. I also remember throwing up."

"I can imagine the scene was unsettling," Jake said. "Don't imagine you looked around the house. Upstairs?"

"No, no reason."

"Or into the barn?"

"No, certainly not. It was pretty clear to us what happened."

"Oh, you knew that Underwood had hit her with the pry bar, and she had shot Underwood?"

"Well, it seemed like—"

"Was there blood on the floor?"

"Lots. Got it on my shoes."

"And Joe Tingle was with you? Where is he these days?"

"Oh, he lives in town."

"What did your father do when he arrived? He must have been very concerned about your safety."

"Yeah, told us to get into the cruiser. He took his gun out of his holster. First time I'd ever seen him draw his gun."

"And he entered the Gist house?"

"Yeah."

"And called the state police?"

"I guess he did."

"How long before they arrived?"

"Maybe twenty minutes later. An ambulance from the hospital rescue came just before that."

"And was your dad inside during this time?"

"Yes."

McNally said to Jake, "Come on, we get the picture. A cop doing his job."

"Just one other thing. Chief, you said the motive was robbery?"

"Robbery, yes."

"Did Underwood have any loot on his body?"

"I don't recall anything unusual. Of course, he could have planted it somewhere else before we came on the scene."

"Wasn't Ms. Gist rumored to have a stash of hoarded gold coins? An inheritance from her father? That information was in the file we received." Jake's assertion as to the petitioner's file was a flat-out lie.

"Yes, that was the rumor. Who knows if she had them or not?"

"Underwood didn't have any gold?"

"No."

"If she had coins, either someone else found them, or maybe they're still there somewhere."

He laughed at the suggestion. "Oh, I don't think so, lots of folks been through that house looking."

"So, fifteen-year-old Aaron Underwood could have heard a rumor about gold coins, and on Halloween, he decides to steal the coins? Is that the theory? In the course of his robbery, he strikes the blow that kills her, and she triggers a scattergun, twice I believe, one shot that takes off half of his face?"

"Who knows what actually happened except Underwood, and he never said!"

"Oh, one last issue," said Jake. "There is something in the file to the effect that you, Tingle and Underwood together planned a prank at the Gist farm?" Another lie.

"Well, that was just kids talking. A dare, like kids do."

"Anyone else know about the prank?"

"I didn't say there was a prank. Like I said, maybe a dare."

"Could that be why you and your friend Tingle went up to the farm? To check it out?"

"I don't remember."

"Do you know if anyone ever told the state police about the dare?"

"I didn't. I can tell you that and nobody asked me about it."

McNally interrupted. "This has gone far enough!" He looked to Bertozzi, who ignored him.

"So you don't think Underwood went there for a prank, or whatever you call it, that you and Tingle planned with him? Instead, he went there to steal the rumored gold coins?"

Bain snapped back. "As far as I know." Bain hunched forward in his chair, twisted his neck in discomfort and gave a sharp response. "I don't see how that makes any difference. We found Aaron Underwood where he killed her."

He was perspiring and Bertozzi asked him if he wanted water, which he declined with a wave of his hand.

McNally, belatedly recognizing that Jake had set up the board to hear a witness to the crime scene, demanded an end to the session.

"Anything else, Jake?" Bertozzi asked.

"No," Jake sat back and closed his laptop. "Thanks, Chief. Your recollection has been quite helpful."

Bertozzi dismissed Bain, who collected his notes and hat, stood, and strode forward to shake McNally's outstretched hand. Prebys also stood and vigorously pumped Bain's hand. Jake walked across the room to Bain, and put out his left hand in a gesture that appeared to further unnerve Bain.

"Your visit today clarified a lot of things on my mind," Jake said.

Bain wasn't sure how to take that.

"Oh, I admire your belt buckle. Is that military brass?" Jake asked.

"No," he replied, looking down at the buckle. "It was formed from a fifty dollar gold piece. From my father. Gave it to me when I was sworn in as his successor. I—"

"Thanks again, Chief."

CHAPTER SIXTY-FIVE

SAL GIANMALVO TOLD HIS DRIVER to stop his Cadillac Escalade in front of LaPolla's Deli on Atwells Avenue, where Ricky was hanging out at an outside table with two other corner guys.

"Hey, Ricky, get in here." Sal told the driver to get lost, and he did, jumping out to join the corner guys.

Ricky checked inside the car, figured which door he should open, and took the front passenger seat. He was edgy and defensive.

"I had a day off, ya know."

"Yeah, yeah, had it comin' to ya, right? So, listen, nobody's called you, right, about this North Providence thing?"

"Nah. Nobody."

"Yeah," Sal said flatly. "Who the fuck knows, right? Anyway, you keep your nose clean. I don't want any trouble. Ya gotta job tonight. Get your ass over there at one. Got it?"

"Sure, sure."

Sal smiled and cuffed Ricky on an ear, almost as an endearment.

"Right, Uncle Sal. Right as rain."

"Okay. Get outta here."

Ricky left the Caddy, relieved that Sal and he were back in business. Sal's driver returned. Sal asked him, "What the fuck is 'right as rain'?"

CHAPTER SIXTY-SIX

AFTER THE HEARING, Jake went directly home. Mia had indicated that she'd like to talk, but he declined, wondering if the topic was to be Underwood, their tryst, or both.

He changed into jogging clothes, taking his cell phone with him in case the call came in. At three o'clock, as he was crossing Henderson Bridge over the Seekonk River not four hundred yards from where Hope died, his cell phone vibrated against his thigh. The number was unfamiliar.

"This is what ya do. Tonight, drive over to Plainfield Street over by the Cranston-Johnston line. Midnight. Park in the lot in front of Plainfield Liquors. Don't use that Camaro, too flashy for the neighborhood. Another car. Ya wait for instructions. Make sure you follow them."

"Look, no more runaround."

"Bring the cash Aldo was going to get."

"That was two thousand, the rest after he—"

"Fuck that. I gotta have five if ya want what I've got to tell."

Jake agreed without argument.

"No cops, nothing that looks like it's a hit on me. If ya do, I'm gone. Here's a teaser for ya—the truck that killed yer wife had bar lights over the cab and a white stripe. Remember? And I'll save you time. I'm hanging up and this phone will be shit."

Jake had begun to formulate his question on the Cumberland Farms assault, but the connection ended. Jake redialed and there was no answer. The white stripe was right, but that could have come from Baldolucca. But a bar of lights over the cab? Something new? He closed his eyes and strained to recollect the truck driven by the killer on the curve, its blinding headlights, going too fast, compensating too far left. There were lights over the cab, lights that swept his truck as it sped past him after it bounced off the Mini. Baldolucca hadn't mentioned a bar of lights during his questioning. *Who else would know?*

He slowly took up his jog again, running north along the river on Riverside Drive, and stopped at a bench across from the boathouse. Tonight, he would be confronting the murderer of Hope and his unborn son.

The next few hours after his run were mentally scheduled. The cash he had withdrawn to pay Baldolucca remained in a desk drawer in the library.

Livia's car, a white Camry with an engine whine and a rumpled rear fender, was inconspicuous enough. Could he borrow it without raising her suspicions?

Like a military police squad leader preparing for a patrol, he began to collect and check weapons for what was going to be the longest—or shortest—night of his life. From the safe, he removed his Beretta, a black semi-automatic with a rough grip and a nine-round clip. It was designed for concealed carrying, and had been purchased from a buddy in his unit, a cop in civilian life, who called the weapon "the pocket rocket." The weapon came with a holster that would easily fit in the small of his back under a windbreaker or snugly in a shoulder holster under his stub. He felt its heft, loaded a clip that came with it, slammed it shut, took out the clip and laid both on the desktop. The gun had been cleaned and oiled each of these past three years since Hope's death.

In a storage closet in the rear hall, Jake located his duffel from Iraq. He unzipped the bag, removed a rolled-up uniform blouse which was wrapped around an Iraqi scout knife—slender, sharp, flexible, with a metal grip and four inches of steel. He held it up to the hall light. A souvenir taken from a detainee who'd tried to slice up Jake's E-4, who, in turn, brandished it to the detainee's eternal peril. He would tape the knife to the inside of his stump—a body part no one was likely to pat down.

Jake returned to the library, placed the blade on the desk next to the Beretta, and went into the bedroom to rest. With his eyes closed, he began an anti-stress routine of deep breaths for fifteen minutes. He planned to avoid a migraine trigger, which meant no salt, sugar or caffeine, and staying hydrated. Then, he did a series of stretches, slowly, deliberately.

After a shower, he drank three glasses of water and logged onto his laptop and saw the expected email query from Garo about Chief Bain's appearance at the board. Then, he snapped on to the parole board laptop and saw an email from Bertozzi: the board would consider Underwood's parole the next morning in Maximum Security at eight. Early enough, Jake thought, to avoid protesters and the media. Underwood's file was also available online. Jake scanned it. No issue on his prison record, the parole counselor's recommendation was negative alluding to his lack of remorse, but with a caveat pointing out Aaron's clean prison record for about thirty years, his injury, and noting this time. Underwood seemed calm and didn't express anger at Greenwick for opposing his parole. To Jake, it still read as same old, same old, and not helpful to his petition, but it was less negative than the last.

Jake sat back, thinking the hearing and vote of the members would be anti-climactic. Mia was in favor, McNally and Prebys would vote to deny parole, and despite the recent display of independence by Bertozzi, Jake had little doubt that Bertozzi would oppose Underwood's parole. Both he and Jake were disgusted by the publicity and demonstrations surrounding the case.

As for himself, Jake hated the raw anger that he saw on his front lawn, and the noisy and egregious emotions displayed at the Terrell Williams rally. Garo's argument as to the basic injustice of Underwood's further incarceration and his own reaction to the lies of Chief Bain had eroded his firm no vote position. However, he'd wait until he saw and heard Underwood and listened to Mia's arguments. That is, if he made it through the night's confrontation with Hope's killer.

Jake called Livia at four on her cell phone. In the background was the buzz of a busy restaurant prepping for the evening menu.

"We vote on Underwood tomorrow morning early, and I've got a protest line to cross on Howard Avenue to get into the prison complex. It would be helpful if I could borrow your car—less conspicuous, easier for me to slip in and out unnoticed."

After a moment of hesitation, she agreed.

"I'll be over to pick it up in a couple of hours."

"We have got a big retirement party tonight that I have to oversee so we won't have much time to talk. I'll come over after?"

"Hon, I need some sleep and a focus for tomorrow. Got to bring finality to all this."

She didn't respond.

⁓⁓⁓⁓⁓⁓⁓⁓⁓⁓⁓⁓⁓⁓⁓⁓⁓⁓⁓⁓⁓⁓⁓⁓⁓⁓⁓⁓⁓⁓⁓⁓

Jake spent the next hour in further preparation, this time all paper. First, he wrote a one-paragraph resignation with tomorrow's date, signed it and put it in an envelope to the governor. He made a copy on his printer and put it aside. He'd bring a copy with him to the session tomorrow and give it to Bertozzi. Next, he pecked out a memo on his personal laptop of what he would want his friends to know about where he was on Underwood's parole, should his meeting tonight with Baldolucca's buddy go wrong. He printed the memo and left it on his desk—to be read by Livia, Dermott or Garo.

He checked out his will, a copy of which was in the library's desk in a drawer, next to a presentation box for his Purple Heart. *That's fitting*, he thought. After a bequest to Livia, all else went to Operation Safe Return. Dermott, his executor, had the original document, and Jake was confident any loose ends would go as Dermott thought fair and honest. *What else?* He decided to bring Livia's new jewelry box with him when he picked up the Camry.

CHAPTER SIXTY-SEVEN

LIVIA'S WAS BUSTLING when Jake arrived by Uber, not a single empty table in the dining room, the taproom full. Livia was at her best as a hostess or stopping at tables to greet familiar faces. In the taproom, Jake took a stool and opened the bar menu as Dermott squeezed in beside him. Jake was about to ask him for news on the Baldolucca murder when, in the mirror behind the bar, he saw the Speaker approach.

"The Pawtucket delegation," the Speaker slapped both Jake and Dermott on their shoulders. "Would you believe it? I've actually got a night out with the wife." He continued, again slapping Dermott. "Heard you were 'wearin' the green' last night, Dermott."

"Yeah, the Guinness was flowing. Good time had by all."

"Great, and you, Jake. Heard that Underwood is coming up tomorrow."

"Yeah."

"That video is sparking all kinds of concern." The Speaker's mouth was pressed closer to their ears. "I've now got some reps in my caucus, in addition to the progressives who have changed their minds after hearing from voters, who are now in favor of a parole. You just never know how people are going to jump."

Jake took that to mean that the Speaker wasn't on a loyalty shtick anymore. And that would be good for Dermott.

"See ya," the Speaker said, leaving them for the dining room.

"What do ya make of that?" Jake said to Dermott.

"I don't care one way or the other about Underwood, but I do care that Joe's not pissed. Gilletto got parole. And I know it has nothing to do with you. But he may not."

Livia appeared at Dermott's shoulder dangling a set of car keys. "In the lot. When can I have it back?"

"For you." Jake presented the jewelry box.

"Jake, it's beautiful." Jake took the car keys from her as she ran her fingers over the surface of the box, lifted it and examined the color and texture of the paired woods, placed it on the bar, and opened it.

"Jake," she said. "What a surprise," lifting its top tray. "I could almost fill it with what you've given me." Her eyes watered and she leaned over and kissed him fully on the mouth.

"Any little gift for me?" Dermott joked.

"Go work off your retainer," Jake said.

"Did you know that there's a blue moon tonight?" Livia asked.

"Blue moon, as in once in a blue moon?" Dermott said.

"Means two full moons in one calendar month. A good omen," Livia said.

"Good, I could use it," Jake said.

"Not only a blue moon, but around two, it will get a reddish color from a lunar eclipse. Happens about once a year, but we don't see it here often. Some religious folks believe it reflects the fires of Hell."

"That's cheery," said Dermott.

Livia laughed. "Well, don't worry, it's supposed to get cloudy."

Jake got up from his stool. "I'll return the car tomorrow. Lunchtime?" He told Dermott his plan for use of Livia's car at the prison in the morning for the Underwood vote.

Dermott said, "Take mine."

"He's all set, Dermott," Livia said.

"Okay, thought I could get at least a tankful out of a loaner." He grinned ruefully and stood. "Got to hit the Oyster Bar for a while. Party for Representative Rapucci. A friend of the working people of Rhode Island. Wish I had what he's got stashed away, workin' for the people."

CHAPTER SIXTY-EIGHT

JAKE DROVE THE CLUNKY CAMRY back to Pawtucket and quickly changed into a longsleeved black shirt with its right arm pinned up loosely, concealing the knife taped under his stump. His jeans had a leather belt sturdy enough to hold the Beretta in place, and he donned sneakers and a windbreaker. Two thick banded stacks of fifties on the outside and lesser bills underneath went into a plastic Stop & Shop shopping bag.

Jake changed his mind and decided to hide the Beretta under the wads of cash, thinking he might be frisked and it would be easy to grab it from there; no way would he let the murderer get close to the cash. In front of the mirror in the bathroom, he scratched the stubble on his face; he hadn't shaved and it seemed cool to sport a day's growth. He felt no anxiety, only the certainty that he would confront Hope's murderer. It might turn out badly, but he was committed.

At eleven-thirty, having checked the location of Plainfield Liquors on his cell phone GPS, the Camry cut across Pawtucket on Mineral Spring Avenue into North Providence where it passed Victor's Restaurant, the scene of Baldolucca's murder. *Everything in Rhode Island is close,* he thought, *too close.*

It was cold, misty, as though it might rain, the wipers cleared the windshield in stutters. At ten of twelve, he arrived at a bleak, crumbling industrial area of one-story windowless brick buildings, self-storage units, used-car lots, body shops, and a dingy strip shopping center where a Plainfield Liquors neon signed flashed. Only the homeless lived within these blocks. He drove past the liquor store's parking lot to check it out, then returned and nosed the Camry into a parking space facing the street.

The only other car in the lot, a faded Chevy Malibu, was in the shadows of a payday loan office. Jake's fingers shook as he turned off the ignition; when the Plainfield Liquor sign momentarily blurred, he shut his eyes as he felt a coming migraine.

"Lord, not now, not tonight," he said aloud.

Across Plainfield Street, Ricky peered through space in the row of plastic slats in the rear gate of the yard at Rhode Island Scrap and saw a nondescript Camry park in the shopping center and its driver inside. *Has to be Fournier.*

Ricky, with Bitch along as an added precaution and as part of his staging for tonight, had been in the yard since before ten and had seen nothing to indicate cop interest. It wouldn't take long, once Fournier entered the yard, to take care of business. Ricky would grab the cash, stash Fournier's body on the rear seat of the Malibu from which he had siphoned virtually all the gas. Later, he would take delivery of the stiff from the Dragos' guys and stuff it in the Malibu's trunk. He'd finish compacting on schedule. Take ten minutes. Then, he'd drive Fournier's Camry inside and crush it, then put it on top of the others ready for delivery to the port. *Beautiful!*

CHAPTER SIXTY-NINE

"SO DIS IS IT?" Bennie "Ears" Mezzalongo asked as the black Yukon SUV he was driving crossed into Rhode Island on Interstate 95 south. Alfredo "Choppy" Sanpietro was in the passenger seat.

"You heard Jonny. We're taking out Ricky. He's a screw-up, his gig's over. He thinks we're delivering another stiff just like usual, only we ain't. He's our stiff for tonight, why Sal is paying Jonny and us the big bucks."

"Never liked him, anyway. Can't trust anyone with a cockeye. So, this wraps it up? No more deliveries? Jeez. Easiest money I ever made. All you gotta do is pick up the baggage, drive to Providence, and drop it off."

"You fuckin' complainin'?"

"Not me," Ears replied quickly. "All I'm sayin' is, we get the call from Jonny for a pickup and delivery, all the work is done for ya, and my old lady gets her piece and shuts her trap and I get some spread-around money and—"

Choppy's fist banged Ears' hand on the steering wheel. "Watch yer speed, asshole. The staties hang out around this fuckin' curve." Ears slowed to fifty as they entered the sweeping, infamous Pawtucket s-curve emblazoned with yellow reflective caution signs and lit garishly by arc lights. "All we need on the last trip is to be stopped and get a field strip. We would be fucked, and Jonny would be apeshit."

"Okay, okay, so how we gonna do it?"

He winced as Ears picked up speed past the curve on the new Pawtucket River Bridge with its red, white and blue LED lighting on pillars that looked like wings. "Will you slow the fuck down? We don't have to be there until one." Ears eased up. "We tell 'im to load our stiff into the junker's trunk, then we pop him. We load in Ricky and leave. Up to Sal from then."

"I'll miss the cash. But I gotta tell ya, I never liked picking up stiffs. Not too bad when it's like right after, ya know, but after a day or so, fuck! Remember that guy from Mattapan? I think he was Mex. Shit, that was terrible. I had to burn my clothes."

"Yeah, that was the worst," Choppy replied, then shouted, "Slow the fuck down! We got almost an hour before we gotta be there."

"So maybe we can hit the Action?" Ears laughed.

Choppy thought for the millionth time how dumb Ears could be, how he looked like Howdy Doody with those elephant flaps of his. But a loyal soldier.

"When we get to Cranston, pull over at that Wendy's. After we eat, we go out to Sal's. Do what we gotta do."

CHAPTER SEVENTY

JAKE'S CELL PHONE BUZZED at midnight.

"Listen carefully. The car in the lot, a Malibu. Key on the floor. I'll call ya when yer inside." The cell phone went dead.

Jake looked around the parking lot for any sign of activity. A dated Malibu sedan, attracted his attention. He picked up the grocery bag, locked the Camry, and opened the driver's door of the Malibu, a shitbox with a paint job beyond faded. Its front seat upholstery was ripped, its filthy windshield cracked—a little clearer where wipers had once worked—and an ignition key on the floor. His cell phone buzzed again. "Across the street is a gate. Looks locked but it isn't. Go through the gate about fifty feet, and stop."

Jake peered through the Malibu's windshield and saw the gate. Behind it was a row of vapor lights caught in the low mist. Or was it an aura? He blinked twice.

"How do I know this isn't a setup?" Jake asked.

"Ya don't. Want to know who killed yer wife, or not?"

"I need protection from a shakedown."

"You need protection? How about me? I'm giving ya what Aldo got killed for."

"How come you know anything?"

Ricky loved this part, his false narrative that seemed to work.

"Aldo and me was tight. People might remember me, ya know what I'm sayin'? The guy ya lookin' for might figure I know somethin'. Ya get the info, when and who and where da fuck this guy is, if ya got the cash. If not, fuck off now."

"When I drive inside, stand in the headlights, and don't approach."

"Sure," Ricky said slowly. "Now, smash your cell phone against the pavement."

"Are you kidding? I just got this iPhone."

"Hit it hard. If I call the number and it's got service, it's over. Now or never."

Jake got out and whacked his cell against the liquor store's masonry wall. Once, twice, and the cell finally splintered into pieces.

He got back in the Malibu, fumbled its ignition key, awkwardly crossed his body with his left hand to grasp the gear shift, started the engine, reversed, and headed out of the lot towards the street. Headlights picked up the gate of a chainlink fence maybe fifteen feet high laced with white slats. He waited for a passing car and then drove across the street into a curb cut in front of the gate, sat for a moment to clear his head, then got out, put his right shoulder into the gate, and it slowly creaked open. As it did, Jake saw a beat-up metal sign that read *Deliveries for RI Scrap on Fenton Street* with an arrow pointing to the left.

A scrapyard. Where there could be used plates. He hadn't thought to check out a license plate on the Malibu. Now he did; it was orangey.

CHAPTER SEVENTY-ONE

ON HIS REGULAR STOOL at the Federal Bar & Lounge on Acorn Street, Sal had no second thoughts.

He gulped down his neat Johnnie Walker Blue, his third, and loudly announced he was packing it in. Sal was always a big tipper who liked acknowledgement whenever he entered a bar or restaurant. He slipped three Jacksons under the glass and left. *Fuck!* He didn't want to be personally involved in a "special:" that was in the past, but that was the way it was. Somebody had to run the machines tonight. Ricky, he'd whine, he'd plead, and what could Sal say but *Look, ya stupid fuck? Ya screwed up. I gave ya chances and what do ya do? Ya fuck up. The Brow can't let ya out of this. Ya never should have hit on that asshole. Yer a liability. Ya know what that is? A fuckin' asshole that brings down a lot of guys!* Sal dismissed the thought. No talk. The Dragos' soldiers would pop Ricky, stuff him in the junker Ricky would have ready, it goes into the compactor, and it's over.

Rose? She'd get over it. She knew her boy was a fuck-up. Ricky, the fuck, probably hadn't even called her since Sal set her up to move to Florida.

He checked his Rolex as he unlocked the Caddy. Quarter past twelve. Sal started the engine and was soon passing the Social Club. No outside lights; everybody inside, sucking around, complaining, nobody doin' business until the heat is off, the Brow pissed but already home whenever there was a hit. According to Barracelli, in a couple of days some fink would drop the word that Ricky was tight with Baldolucca, that they had a beef and Ricky took Aldo out.

Sal slowed the Caddy as he swung on to Harris Avenue, goosed it, and slowed again at the first turn into Olneyville, once an important neighborhood of Providence—lots of Greeks, Armenians, Polish, and Italos. Used to be great. Now it was filled with gangbangers, Asian gangs, spics all around. *You don't ever come to a complete stop, gotta keep moving, or some fuck jumps out of nowhere, takes a bat to your windshield. Fuckin' place is going to hell. Anybody lives here, they're crazy like the artists that found places in the old factory buildings there or stupid or doin' drugs.*

He slowed at a stop sign but didn't stop and thought maybe some jerkoff cop might be around, so next time, at a stop sign, he did stop. He checked his watch. Twelve-thirty. Drago's guys had a key to the front gate. Tomorrow he'd get Ricky's Dodge Ram repainted, pull off the tires, maybe use it as a yard truck for a while. Got to keep the Brow happy, too.

Sal's chronic indigestion flared. *Getting too old for this shit.* He needed a Zantac.

CHAPTER SEVENTY-TWO

THE MALIBU'S HEADLIGHTS revealed a hooded figure standing next to a yellow Caterpillar crane with linked metal treads, like a tank's. Behind him, within cones of yellowish light, were piles of rusty metal shapes, beat-up storage bins filled with scrap metal, and a line of junk cars. A three-story, metal-sided building stood at the end of a conveyor belt held up by a web of girders like a roller coaster track. In the shadows to Jake's left was a large metal bin of some sort—at least twenty by twenty, and walls ten feet high with an attached cab. Farther over, he made out a stacks of crushed cars. He slowed the Malibu and felt the stiffness of the blade under his upper arm. He was ready. His left hand reached into the grocery bag on the floor by his feet and felt the grip of his Beretta.

A long-handled cop flashlight beckoned him forward, held by someone five-seven or -eight with broad shoulders, stocky or all muscle, in a hoodie under a jacket. Something was gripped in his right hand, a rope maybe, that trailed off and ended behind the bin. As the flashlight waved him to a stop, the hooded figure waddled three steps forward.

"Let me see the cash," said a voice that didn't quite match the bulky menace of the figure in the headlights.

"Get that light out of my eyes," Jake commanded as he lowered the window. The flashlight intensified Jake's increasing sensitivity to light. "Back away from the car!"

Ricky took a step backward. "Show me the cash."

Jake released his grip on the Beretta and withdrew a wad of fifties, which he flipped through in the flashlight's beam. As he did, he thought he heard a low growl.

"Drop the cash," Ricky shouted.

Jake revved the engine in response. Ricky lowered the flashlight. "Okay, okay, I get it," Ricky said, "we gotta work this out."

Jake opened the Malibu's door, stood on muddy ground behind it and squinted. There was barely enough light beyond the headlight beams for Jake to discern that his adversary was holding a chain that led into the shadows behind the bin. Then, he definitely heard a distinct deep growl.

"Her name is Bitch," Ricky said with pride, "because she's a bitch pitbull. I drop this chain, yer dogfood. Bitch, come 'ere, baby, let the man see ya."

A huge dog emerged from the shadows, more of a beast from a nightmare than a dog, growling, straining at the chain, with a foot or more of chest, a block of head that seemed all jaw, and a long red tongue that shot out saliva and quivered between canine teeth. The metal spikes on a chokecollar shone in the meager light.

The beast complicated things for Jake. He had witnessed savage dog attacks in Iraq where the Sunnis bred their animals for security purposes to be vicious killers that thrived on tearing flesh apart.

"Tie it up," Jake yelled. He had to get him out of range of Bitch if he was going to take his victim down. Jake reached inside the Malibu and held up the grocery bag.

"The cash is in this bag. I'm going to put it on the trunk when you show me that it's tied up."

"Oh, yer gonna hurt her feelings," Ricky yelled back. "Okay, I'll tell ya what, I'm gonna be a nice guy and I'll chain her up to the compactor." *So that's what it is,* Jake thought, *a car crusher.* As Ricky issued a low command, Bitch gave off a reluctant whine and retreated into darkness. Ricky attached the chain to a metal ring on the compactor and yanked it to demonstrate the ring held.

Jake blinked, and then a second time, finding that his field of vision had narrowed as half of his brain began to pulsate as his migraine quickened. Within minutes, the throbbing would impair his thinking, robbing him of his ability to make quick decisions. He quickly calculated the length of chain that would allow the beast to protect and patrol the area from the compactor to the Malibu; for any close action on his part, Jake needed a few feet more, maybe to the Malibu's trunk for good measure, to be out of the dog's range.

Ricky, standing by the compactor, folded his arms across his chest like a bouncer at a South Side dive, his face full of stupidity and expectation. Jake could now see greasy hair around his shoulders and his cockeye. "Hey, don't you want to pat me down?"

That surprised Jake. He hesitated, weighing a body search against asking the crucial question about the Cumberland Farms assault.

"Hands on the door. Feet wide and out."

"Sure." Ricky assumed the position. Jake put the grocery bag on the trunk and gave him more than a military patdown: his hand went to both legs, waistband, underneath arms, down the spine. He resisted the thought of smashing Ricky's head against the car thus risking the dog's attack. The body search produced nothing but a set of keys and a cell phone which Jake returned to him.

"See, I'm not carrying," Ricky said, returning to his bouncer stance as Jake backed away towards the Malibu's trunk, hoping to lead Ricky out of the range of the growling dog. "Ya got nothin' to worry about. But this fuckin' guy yer after is the meanest prick ya ever heard of. Already got a couple of notches on his belt. Got a street name. Nemesis. Ya know what that means?" Ricky's voice became throaty. "Nobody can beat him."

"Let's get down to business." Jake put his hand in the grocery bag and flashed a wad that he placed on the trunk.

"Hey, hold yer horses," Ricky said, leaning casually on the Malibu's driver side door. "Ya gotta know what yer getting' into.

"Nemesis is comin' up in the Mob. Make it easy on yerself. Instead of going at him, 'cause what he did to your wife, tip off the cops. Dey been lookin' for who took out Charlie Morrone. Owed a shylock. Nemesis was hired to shake him down, went overboard, almost kills the fuck and Morrone is so scared, he goes to the cops. But the arrest or somethin' is fucked up and Nemesis goes free. A few months later, Morrone disappears. Nemesis whacked him with a pipewrench, wrapped him up in tape—ya know, that blue tape that ya put on boxes and shit to mail? —watched him suffocate, then took the stiff out to the reservoir in Scituate and buried him near the spillway. Gotta be there still."

Jake thought, *Why the boasting?*

"The other notch?" Jake asked.

"Ya heard about these fuckin' Asian gangs, right? In Olneyville? He's there in a deal and some kid mouths off, so he sucker punches the kid, everyone scatters and Nemesis gets in his truck and runs the kid over. Back and forth. Tire marks for sure on the body, truck is a big Dodge Ram, all pimped out, got these off-road tires and double wheels in back. He's still driving that truck."

With his headache now pounding, Jake barely managed to ask, "Did he kill Baldolucca?"

"Could be. Did ya hear how he got it? A garrote. Gotta be one tough dude to do that."

Jake squared his body, balancing his weight on his soles and asked the important question—for Hope.

"Where was this Nemesis coming from when he drove the pick-up that killed my wife? You answer that, give me the name, where he is, and the cash—" Jake lifted the grocery bag— "all yours."

"Huh?"

"Where?"

"How da fuck do I know? I think Aldo said it was from some dropoff in Seekonk?"

"No, I mean just before. Baldolucca told me something happened just before."

Ricky shrugged and then remembered. He laughed. "Stopped for cigarettes at a convenience store. Got 'em for free."

Jake's head exploded in a burst of headache as his intuition became a reality. He took a step backwards and turned to grab the Beretta from the grocery bag.

Before Jake could reach the gun, Ricky slid inside the Malibu, butt first. "C'mon, bring the cash, I'll show you where he is. It's getting late. Don't want to be conspicuous. His name is Ricky Squillante," and Ricky's hand slipped under the seat to the Glock taped there. His fingers grasped its rough grip, and he turned to Jake, gun up. "Yeah, one more thing. Nemesis was her fate. That was an accident. Your wife's number just came up that night. Yours is coming up now."

CHAPTER SEVENTY-THREE

"SO WHY ARE WE DOIN' RICKY?" Ears finished the last of the French fries and wiped the ketchup from his mouth with the back of his hand.

Choppy replied, "Sal says he can't be trusted no more. Did somethin' stupid and he's gotta pay."

"Why us?"

"Blood. Sal doesn't want to do his sister's kid. Some Old Country shit."

"So, what about us?"

"We're still in business." Choppy drained the last of his Diet Pepsi.

"Yeah?"

"Okay, dis is what I know. They don't need this Providence body-dump run any more. Micky Cerrone's got a brother-in-law in the funeral business in Lynn. We deliver a stiff to his backdoor, it stays in his cooler until it's time to take somebody to church. After the widow or whoever and the family says goodbye to their stiff and are goin' out to da cars, out comes their deceased and the mattress from the coffin, our stiff from the cooler goes in, and then the deceased goes back in, over our stiff. Becomes a twofer. And he gets a Mass, too. Or a service at the grave. Ain't that a nice touch?"

"Yeah. I didn't think of that."

"I noticed." He shook his head at Ear's manifest ignorance. "What time is it?"

"Twenty of."

"Let's go. I gotta be back home early. Promised the old lady I'd drive the kids to school tomorrow morning."

CHAPTER SEVENTY-FOUR

JAKE STARED AT THE GUN pointed at his chest. It looked larger than the Beretta still in his grocery bag.

"Sorry, pal. I gotta say I'm impressed with what ya been doing." Ricky reached into the door's map holder, took out a sap that fit in his hand and put it in his jacket pocket. "But we got to put an end to it, see?"

Ricky got out of the car, keeping Jake in his aim, and opened the rear door.

"Get in," he ordered. Jake moved slowly, sitting on the rear seat, his feet still on the ground. With the rear door between him and Ricky, there was no opportunity for a kick or a butt or a slam of the door.

"Why don't you take the money, that's what this is all about, that's what you want, right?"

"Fuck you! What I want is for you to take the piece of tape on the back of the seat. Close ya fuckin' mouth and slap it on."

Jake pressed a strip of blue duct tape, three inches wide and six inches long, and pressed it over his mouth; the stubble of his beard pinched when he breathed. As Ricky leaned in to check on its tightness, the Glock Ricky held was momentarily on the other side of the door. As Ricky's fingers touched Jake's face, Jake grabbed Ricky's hand and yanked, pulling himself up off the seat, gaining leverage to force the Glock to strike against the car door and fall to the ground. Jake pushed Ricky's hand backward to a breaking point, ready to balance himself, when he was smacked on the left temple by the sap Ricky took from his jacket pocket. As Jake's head twisted away, Ricky took the sap from his pocket and smacked Jake across his forehead, and then the back of his head. Jake didn't hear the *whap* of the second and third blows because his brain had gone to mush with the first.

"Fuck you," Ricky said to Jake's body as he went through Jake's pockets and found the keys to Livia's car. He then pushed Jake back onto the rear seat. Ricky checked his watch thinking, *Ten minutes before Drago's boys arrived with their stiff, plenty of time to put two caps into this fucker—fuck him for trying to beat Nemesis.* Headlights flashed at the front entrance to the yard.

"Who the fuck is that?" Ricky muttered as he grabbed the grocery bag. His gun was picked up from the ground and went into his jacket pocket, his hand remaining on its grip; the car keys and sap, for lack of another place, went into the grocery bag on top of the cash, and the still undiscovered gun, and left with the bag on the Malibu's front seat.

Fuck, it's Sal!

Sal lowered the window of the Caddy and squinted. Ricky was by the compactor next to a junker, shifting his weight from side to side, his head circling his neck like a boxer. Something wasn't right. Sal left the Caddy and took slow steps toward Ricky.

"What da fuck are ya doin', Ricky?"

Ricky then took a step backwards. Sal didn't appreciate the non-response nor the nervous shift in Ricky's shoulders. Sal pressed forward, leaving an arm's spread between them, and again Ricky retreated. Sal caught the tic in Ricky's cockeye, his glance at the Malibu. Sal looked inside.

"What da fuck!" Sal grabbed Ricky's arm and shouted, "Who da fuck is that?"

Bitch took the arm grab as an attack on Ricky and leaped at Sal, pivoting in the air like an acrobat as the chain held and threw the dog on the ground. Ricky shouted at the dog, grabbed Bitch's choke collar as the dog braced to resume its attack, and hung on to it, the dog gasping, its teeth and tongue glistening with slobber, the spiked collar reflecting sparks of light.

"Keep it away from me!" Sal shouted, reeling backwards. "Keep it away or I'll—"

"Sal, I can explain. I think Aldo coulda talked to this guy. I was goin' to send him off with the stiff comin' in tonight. Nobody would know."

"You asshole!" Sal reddened with rage. "YOU BROUGHT HIM HERE? How do you know he didn't leave some kinda note or told somebody?"

Ricky realized that if Sal thought it was the reward guy, Ricky would be toast. He had to be just another jerkoff buddy of Baldolucca.

"I picked him up, had no idea he was coming here so, no one knows he's here. Let me send him to China with the stiff from the Dragos."

Sal felt his heart beating faster. He took deep breaths, like the doc told him he'd feel when he had super anxiety attacks, and began to pace, swearing under his breath, looking in at Jake motionless on the rear seat. What the fuck could he do? This guy *and* Ricky both had to go. Tonight. Sal didn't have the juice for another pop without permission from the Brow.

"Tie 'im up."

"I was goin' to. I got some chain in the trunk and I'll put Bitch inside with him. She'll chew him up if he moves a muscle."

Sal motioned to the Malibu. "Get the fuckin' plates off," he ordered. God damn lucky he came early! "When dey get here, send 'em to the trailer. Got that? Don't say nothin' about—" he shrugged toward the Malibu "—dis guy."

"Right," Ricky replied, relief in his voice, as Sal returned to the Caddy and backed it across the yard to the trailer.

The chain, three-inch steel links, was awkward to swing around Jake's torso and legs but it didn't have to be tight, just so he couldn't move until he got capped. The chain had clips at both ends and after three rolls around Jake, Ricky snapped the clips together at Jake's shoulders. He then unhooked the chain holding Bitch and, using the choke collar, guided the drooling, excited dog to the Malibu. Bitch jumped onto the front seat, her ears pointed on alert, sat on her haunches behind the steering wheel, her eyes gleaming, her muzzle dripping slobber over the head rest and onto Jake's body. Ricky wrapped the chain around the steering wheel and made soothing sounds with his lips to calm her, then rubbed her neck for reassurance. Then he felt the Glock in his left jacket pocket and the sap in its right pocket.

Ricky's mind raced as he tied up Jake. *What the fuck is Sal doin' here? He never shows up anymore. So why tonight? To get a pay off from the Dragos?* No, that was never the deal; Sal got paid through some rinky-dink invoicing or maybe in cash. "Fuck," Ricky said aloud, suspicions beginning to crowd his mind. Sal didn't like loose ends. *He wouldn't pop me, would he?*

A few minutes passed uncomfortably for Ricky until a black Yukon entered the yard. It rolled right up to the Malibu for a delivery, like so many times before. Ricky advanced, waving his hands in its headlights. Ricky told Ears, who was driving, that Sal wanted them at the trailer. Ears let out a breath of frustration and put the Yukon in reverse. It stopped next to Sal's Caddy, and Ears and Choppy climbed the stairs into the trailer.

Ricky watched. Sweat broke out on his forehead and upper lip; he felt it in his armpits, the small of his back. Something was going south! He opened the Malibu's rear door, checked on Jake, and sat in front next to Bitch still panting and drooling. He swiped her sweaty coat with his hand.

"Something is fuckin' wrong, baby. Fuckin' wrong."

Bitch remained on alert, her eyes anxious, primed for mayhem.

Ears and Choppy left the trailer, followed by Sal who got in the back seat of the Yukon. Ears parked so that the Yukon and Malibu were next to each other, as usual for a delivery. Sal got out and shouted, "Get that fuckin' trunk open!"

Ricky left the Malibu and popped its trunk as Ears, Choppy, and Sal left the Yukon, leaving its doors open.

"How ya doin', Ricky?" Ears said and then went to the Yukon's tailgate which opened electronically. Choppy stood next to Sal. Ears shrugged at Ricky.

"Fat fuckin' stiff. Must weight three hundred. Dead weight." He laughed. "That's pretty good—dead weight."

Ricky walked by Sal and Choppy and joined Ears, expecting to see a sheet-wrapped bundle. He blinked. *No stiff? What da fuck!*

Ricky was hammerlocked by Ears, his neck ligaments and cartilage crushed, his arms immobilized, Sal was in his face, Choppy held a shiny gun with a muzzle silencer under Ricky's chin. Ricky struggled as Ears maneuvered him, feet first, to the open trunk; Bitch, restrained by the chain around the Malibu's steering wheel, was yelping and growling, her claws ripping up the Malibu's front seat.

"You gotta go, Ricky. You fucked up," Sal said.

Ricky squealed, "Sal, no, it's not right." His legs went limp and he fell to his knees.

Choppy reached in Ricky's pocket, pulled out Ricky's Glock, and tucked it into his waist band. "Stop the fuckin' yappin'," he shouted. Bitch howled at him from the Malibu. "I'm gonna pop that fuckin' dog. What's the dog here for anyhow?"

Sal shrugged toward the Malibu's rear door. Choppy handed Sal his gun to cover Ricky, before opening the rear door. Seeing Jake's chain-wrapped body, Choppy stepped back, his arms stretched toward Sal.

"Who-da-fuck-is-that?"

"Somebody else that's gotta go tonight."

"Huh?" exclaimed Ears.

"Wad's dis? How come ya didn't tell us about this other fuck?" asked Choppy, clearly unhappy with Sal giving him orders, the unauthorized, surprise guy in the car, and that fuckin' dog. Choppy despised anyone who told him what to do; only Jonny could do that, and like Jonny, he never liked Sal, who was rumored to be part Calabrese and therefore a born rat. "We don't got a contract on him. What the fuck do ya think this is, a freebie?"

Sal yelled back, "Hey, I'll pay. And shoot the fuckin' dog. It's got to go with Ricky."

"We need to make a call on dis other guy. Can't do it without a call."

"No time. Gotta be now."

"Fuck you! We don't do a job without Jonny tellin' us. And no two-fers."

Sal lost his cool. "I'll do it myself." Sal took a step closer to Ricky who was still on his knees, and raised Choppy's gun. "Get up, you fuck."

Ricky's legs wouldn't support him.

"Okay, right there then." And pointed the gun at Ricky's forehead.

Choppy shouted, "Hey, ya can't use my piece. That's a new fuckin' Sig Sauer! No number on it and it cost plenty! That silencer's new, too. And he's our job."

"Fuck you. Ya don't do both, ya don't get paid!"

Choppy took a step toward Sal, but Ears grabbed Choppy's arm. He said, "Too fuckin' complicated. Give him Ricky's piece and take yours back." He turned to Sal and shrugged toward Ricky. "Ya owe us for the job."

Choppy grabbed Ricky's Glock from Sal's waistband and Sal smacked Choppy's Sig Sauer in Ear's hands. An insult. This time it was Ears who took a step forward and it was Choppy who grabbed Ears' wrist.

"Forget it!" he said to Ears. "We'll get ours and Sally baby will be pleading for fuckin' mercy." He stared at Sal. "You takin' on Jonny Drago? You got no brains."

They got into the Yukon and left the yard, leaving unconscious Jake in the Malibu's back seat guarded by the yelping dog, Ricky kneeling by the junker, and Sal, holding Ricky's Glock, standing over his nephew.

Sal's eyes went heavenward and said aloud, "What a fucking mess!"

A few minutes later, the Yukon was in the parking lot of a closed Dunkin' Donuts further down Plainfield Street. Choppy was on his cell phone. Ears said, "I'm so fuckin' pissed! Who da fuck does Sal t'ink he is?"

"Shut the fuck up!" Choppy ordered and returned to his phone conversation. "It is all fucked up, Jonny" he said into the phone, "Sal has it all fucked up. His nephew, we was goin' to take him down, right? Then, we find dis other guy in the back seat of the junk car and he turns out to be somebody Sal or Ricky, with this fuckin' big dog, was taking down. Wanted us to off the guy in the car with Ricky. I know it's as confusing as fuck, but that's what it was. We told Sal we weren't doin' a two-fer."

He listened, shaking his head every few seconds. "Sal's got to knock off da two of 'em and crush 'em up?"

He listened again.

"Yeah, I suppose we could after Sal crushed up the two and the dog. But it'll cost, Jonny, Sal's no piece of shit. We don't need ramifications for taking him down. You sure Mick's brother-in-law can handle this?"

CHAPTER SEVENTY-FIVE

SAL WOULD HAVE GOTTEN an A-plus in a course on quick thinking. With the Yukon out of the yard, he lowered the gun he'd trained on Ricky. "So, see how things go down when ya fuck up? If you ain't my sister's kid, it'd be over. Over, get it? Now, ya got one chance to redeem yerself." He shrugged toward the Malibu. "Stuff that guy in the trunk."

Ricky struggled to his feet, got Bitch to settle down, dragged Jake out of the back seat, boosted him over the rear bumper into the trunk.

Sal felt a vibration from his cell phone as he watched Ricky wrestle Jake into the open trunk. Only Lucky and the Brow had the number. He was supposed to make a call back on another throwaway.

"I got to make a call. Get the crane ready, crank up the compactor." Sal's voice was strained with anger as he left for the trailer.

Sal used another burner and heard Barracelli's grunt over background noise. "What's happening over there? I just got a call from Jonny Drago. He's bullshit!"

"I was going to call." Sal told him of the complications, that Ears and Choppy took off on him, that Ricky was planning to off some asshole that ran with Baldolucca, might have been too close, who was already in the junker to be squashed.

"So what should I do? It's a situation."

"They're coming back to finish business they came for. You take care of this, Sal."

"Ricky and his guy go in the compactor? Never found?"

"It's yours, Sal."

"I know, I know. On my mother's soul, I'll take care of it."

"You'd better. Our friend is pissed. You gotta know that, Sal."

|||||||||||||||||||||||||||||||||||||||||||||||||||||||||||

While Sal was in the trailer, Ricky remembered the grocery bag in the front seat of the Malibu and, for a moment, considered an alternative move to hanging in with Sal. *I got the money, I got Bitch, I get the Ram through the gate, and I'm gone.*

Then, reality set in. Sal, or the Brow, would get to him eventually.

He banged the steering wheel and shouted, "I hope you hear me back there, you fuck! I should off you now. But I'm not. The compactor is goin' to do it. Squeeze out your innards. Crush your body. Screw off your head. You brought it on yourself, shithead."

He reached into the grocery bag, took out the sap and put it in his jacket pocket, grabbed the wads of fifties, and started to count.

"Hey, there's only two g's here. What da fuck?" he screamed over his shoulder. "You fuckin' welcher." And then, his fingers found Jake's Beretta in the bag. "Goddamn!" Ricky exclaimed, handling the gun, feeling its heft. He checked its full magazine and stuck it in his belt. He was back in business again.

Ricky's confusion raged. *Goddamnit*, he thought, *has Sal just been giving me the business for fuckin' up. Sure, I fucked up, but Sal needs me for specials, and I'm blood.*

He let out a sigh of relief. *One minute Sal's gonna off me, the next I'm helping him out. And who was he callin'? Fuckin' Sal always played it tight. Sal still has my piece, and he could have picked up another piece from the trailer. Maybe he's going to get close and put one in my head?*

Ricky opened the Malibu's door, took Bitch off the chain, grabbed her choke collar, and pulled the dog into the shadows of the compactor. He commanded her to sit, which she did, breathing hoarsely, drool dripping from her mouth.

"What the fuck are you doin'?" Sal yelled to Ricky as he approached the compactor. "Get out here where I can see you."

"Chained up the dog and took a piss." His hands went to the zipper of his jeans as he stepped into a cone of light from the stanchion by the compactor, keeping a low profile behind the bulk of the Malibu. "Sal, let me have my piece. Let me off this guy, then, he goes into the compactor and it's done."

As Sal came closer, Ricky nervously sidestepped, keeping the junker between them. Sal reached its passenger side close by the compactor. "Stop the fuckin' dance!" Sal shouted.

Ricky sidestepped again. Sal raised Ricky's gun and yelled, "You *stunard*!" He got off a shot before Ricky could reach the gun in his belt that grazed Ricky's left shoulder. Ricky cried out, fell to the ground by the compactor, and Bitch leaped at Sal from the shadows.

With a ferocious yelp, biting air with her jagged teeth, a hundred pounds of muscle sank teeth into Sal's outstretched arm and pulled him to his knees. As he toppled, Bitch was silenced as her jaws closed on Sal's throat, grinding its tissue in her fury, ripping it open. Sal buckled and flailed for air, and despite the surprise and viciousness of the attack, he managed to get off another round before he crumpled. The dog took the bullet in her neck without a whimper, and fell across Sal's bloodied chest.

Ricky staggered to his feet to see Bitch in her death throes, her jaws still clamped on Sal's throat, her eyes gleaming in defiance of the blood pouring from a hole in her neck. Sal's body heaved violently, his mouth becoming a spigot pumping out blood. Ricky picked up the Glock that Sal still held which had taken from him and put a bullet between Sal's eyes, spattering the car, the dog, and himself with Sal's blood. And again, one for Sal and one for Bitch. Then, another for Bitch. The odor of cordite hit Ricky's nostrils, the wisp of smoke coming from the gun's barrel curling like that of a cigarette.

Despite the pain and blood running down his left arm, Ricky put a bullet into Bitch's head to end her gasps, picked up his dog's body and placed it gently on the front seat of the Malibu. Then, he dragged Sal's body to the passenger's side door and put two more bullets—*thud, thud*—into Sal's chest before boosting his body inside.

Ricky's adrenaline surged; like he was Nemesis again. Sal died like any other fuck who tried to take down Nemesis.

Ricky put Jake's gun back in the grocery bag with its two g's, ran to his truck and left the bag on the front seat. Time to get the Malibu into the compactor. He checked Sal's pockets for cash; found a roll of Franklins and the remote for Sal's Caddy. He'd have to get rid of Sal's Caddy, too. Maybe another crush job, or he'd drive it over to Sal's place in a downtown high rise and park it. It would be hours before Donnie DelFusco or any of the yard guys would be looking for Sal, who usually arrived around ten. By then, the compacted junkers would be picked up and on their way to China. *Nobody knows nothin'.* He had the day off after a special, and wouldn't be around to be questioned when Sal didn't show up during the morning.

CHAPTER SEVENTY-SIX

AS HE CLIMBED into the crane's cab, Ricky's shoulder throbbed where Sal's bullet nipped him. The crane's engine was running smoothly, its control panel lights flashing the right colors, its pincers hovered over the Malibu. "A two-fer," he muttered, then shuddering at the thought of Bitch also inside the junker. Ricky pushed a control forward and the pincers dropped on the Malibu's roof with a *thunk*. Ricky had the feeling he had forgotten something in all the action, but, *fuck it.*

Jake's trip back to consciousness was through a myriad of confusing images, with the metallic taste of blood in his mouth as his short-term memory returned and he realized that he was no longer on the Malibu's rear seat. His torso and legs were cramped, and he guessed he was in the junker's trunk. His head hurt, both the migraine side and the trauma side, he heard blood pounding through his head in sync with his heartbeat. Why hadn't he taken down this guy immediately after he became sure he was the killer—*what's his name, Ricky something?* That had been his plan going into tonight, but every plan is a good plan until you've taken a head blow from a sap.

His fingers felt links of chain wrapped around his chest, his legs, his calves and ankles, but not pulled tight. He twisted his shoulders, rubbing the chain against the inside of the trunk so it slipped over his stub to his waist. With the tension gone, he followed it with his fingers until he came to clips that he snapped open, unwrapped himself, and was free. For what?

He felt his knife in its sheaf on his stump. His gun? Still in the grocery bag with the cash? Probably found by now. *What a genius ploy that had been.* So, was he coming to a gunfight armed with a knife?

Then, belatedly, he realized there was tape over his mouth. He ripped it off, peeling off a layer of lip. The jolt of the pincers landing and the metal creaks as they scraped along the Malibu's roof broke through the miasma of Jake's migraine and pain. The pincers smashed through the junker's windows and doors and tossed Jake around inside the trunk. Somehow, he managed to open the mangled trunk lid and brace himself with his feet as the pincers clutched the junker's undercarriage and lifted it off its wheels.

Ricky couldn't believe his eyes as Jake's legs, then thighs, appeared hanging out from the Malibu's trunk as the crane's arm turned towards the compactor. He reacted by pulling back on the control to stop the swing and saw Jake's torso fall back into the trunk, the trunk lid slamming into Jake's thighs. Ricky pushed a control forward and watched as the pincers opened, dropping the junker fifteen feet into the maw of the compactor. The trunk lid bounced up and down twice on Jake's thighs for good measure and remained open.

Ricky watched for any signs of movement by Jake, considered trying to get off a shot into the trunk, but the angle from the cab's window made it impossible. *Fuckin' guy,* Ricky thought. *How did he manage to almost get out?* The trunk lid slam had to have taken his legs out of commission; he was going nowhere.

Ricky left the crane and climbed into the compactor's cab, felt the vibrations of the compressor as it reached the required PSI, and thrust a control forward. The left side of the compactor squealed as it inched to the right.

"Bye, baby, bye," Ricky said aloud.

Jake, biting his lips with the excruciating pain in his thighs, was thrown forward when the junker was struck by the oncoming wall and began its inextricable push to the right. He inched himself forward, rolled forward and leveraged himself out of the trunk, landing on his bruised ribs and stump. Staggered by the sharp pain, he had no breath as he lay within a cramped space between the compactor's front wall and the junker, only barely aware that if the junker's oncoming jagged metal carcass fishtailed, it would crush him. He heard a loud crack as the junker's roof panel splintered, and glass caromed off the compactor's wall in a spray of crystals some of which embedded in Jake's face and scalp and in the hand that Jake had lifted to shield his eyes. The trunk lid split in two and sliced the air above Jake's head, and scraps of sheet metal and bumper whipped around him in all directions. The junker now hovered above him, tottering, ready to crush him, but the forward motion of the wall suddenly stopped and reversed course as the Malibu leaned into the retracting wall.

He took a deep inhalation to get control of his breaths and smelled gasoline seconds before he saw its puddle under the junker. The image of fire and explosion broke into his consciousness. The Humvee? Hope's fiery death? *Not that, God, not that!*

With what strength remained, he braced his shoulders into the compactor's side wall and inched upwards, rising to where his hips were level with its top, his right foot catching on something that ripped into his ankle. From somewhere outside and above the compactor, he heard metallic groans and creaks as the vestige of light from above was extinguished by the pancaker about to slap downward. Jake yanked his foot free, grabbed the top of the compactor's wall with his aching left hand and hurtled himself over, just a millisecond before the pancaker crashed down.

If Jake had a right arm, he would have lost it, along with his life.

The angle of the cab to the compactor made it impossible for Ricky to see Jake's escape. Ricky slammed the pancaker down a second time, raised it, and slammed it down again. *Got him,* Ricky thought, *like swattin' a fuckin' fly.*

Ricky pulled back the control, thinking he had time for a cigarette, when licks of red and yellow flame within the compactor startled him, and only then did he remember that he had not syphoned the Malibu's remaining gas. *Let it burn out,* he thought, the junker had been on vapors, just enough to get it in here, otherwise *ka-pow*! But, he'd have to put it out or it might trip a fire alarm. And then work the crane to lift the metal carcass onto the pile for tomorrow's delivery. He'd toss the trailer as if there had been a robbery, then crush Sal's Caddy or put it somewhere outside where it would be stolen or trashed, and be gone. Nobody, not even Domenic, would do anything about it until Sal appeared, which he would not. *Give him a day's start. The yard would wonder who would have dared to take Sal on. Dragos? Maybe.*

He watched the bluish flames. What a sendoff for Uncle Sal.

CHAPTER SEVENTY-SEVEN

EARS UNLOCKED AND OPENED the front gate, and Choppy drove through the yard to the compactor. Ricky, hose in hand, was spraying its inside where smoldering shards of metal and plastic gave off steam and crackles. Ears gripped his semi-automatic Smith & Wesson, snapped off the safety, then checked his back-up piece, a five-shot Colt 38, by flipping through its cylinders and putting it back in a nylon belt holster.

Choppy got out first, leaving the car door between himself and Ricky. Acrid odors of burnt rubber, gasoline, and something else putrid hit him.

"The junker had some gas left in it," Ricky said. "Flamed up. Had to put it out before it went on the pile." He shrugged toward the pile of flattened junkers on the other side of the compactor. "On the way to Shanghai."

"Where's Sal?" Choppy asked.

"Went home. He sure put a scare into me! Left the shit job to me. Like usual."

"Yeah? How come his Caddy is at the trailer?"

Ricky turned off a spigot and started to coil the hose onto a hook on the compactor. Casual. Like Nemesis.

"Left it for me to get it washed in the morning. Took one of the yard cars."

Ricky finished coiling the hose and moved into the shadows of the compactor. He realized he had to take down Drago's guys: they would be on to him about Sal's whereabouts because this was part of the deal to take him out only an hour earlier, and they could finger him to the Brow.

"Jonny says we gotta talk to him, clear everything up," Choppy said as Ears got out and walked around his open door toward Ricky. "You took care of the other guy?"

"Yeah." Ricky shrugged towards the compactor and took a step backwards, his right hand casually going to the Glock in his jacket pocket.

He had to do it now and needed no invitation when Ears came around the front of the Yukon, his right hand holding his Smith & Wesson down by his thigh. Ricky took Ears down with a gut shot before he turned the gun to Choppy getting out from behind the wheel of the Yukon. His bullet shattered the Yukon's driver's side window, piercing Choppy in the shoulder, throwing him down in the seat.

Ears dropped the Smith & Wesson and had tried to get his backup Colt from his belt holster, but had to squirm to get his body in position. Ricky was about to put another round in Ears' gut, when he heard cries of pain and anger from Choppy. With his hands filled by his Glock and Ear's Smith & Wesson, his loins throbbing with a sense of power, Ricky turned to Choppy still behind the Yukon's steering wheel, blood streaming from the glass embedded in his face. Ricky became light-headed! *Nemesis!* He raised his Glock but Choppy fired first, sending a bullet buzzing by Ricky's ear, whirling Ricky around. Ricky recovered, grabbing Choppy's Sig Sauer with its silencer from his hand and fired five rounds into him and tucked it in his waist band.

Fuck all of them! Nemesis rules.

Jake, his vision blurred, sweat streaming down his back, witnessed the carnage from the shadows by the crane, his knife at the ready. The Glock that Ricky had dropped was barely ten feet away, gleaming in a cone of light. Ricky was inside the Yukon, searching Choppy's body. Partially shielded by the Yukon's hood and open door, Jake made his move toward the Glock, only to be betrayed by a thigh that crumpled, causing him to smack his forehead into the metal tread of the crane.

Ricky blinked in amazement. "Sonuva bitch!" The Sig Sauer came out of his waistband and he aimed it at Jake and pulled the trigger. It clicked on an empty clip.

"Shit! C'mon, you fuck," Ricky screamed. In his fury, he threw the Sig Sauer at Jake, missing him. Ricky pulled out the sap, ready to crush a bone or a skull, and lunged toward the Glock still on the ground by the crane.

Jake, on his feet, adrenaline surging, managed a half step and took Ricky low on his strong side, got a leg between Ricky's legs, and the turnaround was a classic, twisting Ricky's arm back to the breakpoint, forcing Ricky to his knees, the sap falling into the mud. What was left of Jake's strength and skill went into quick boots into Ricky's chest, kidneys and back, laying him out like the corpse he would soon be. With his moment of justice before him, Jake felt energy, clarity of purpose. Jake pulled out his knife, saw its edge flash with light, and fell to his knees to straddle Ricky's chest, smelling Ricky's stale sweat. Jake had no reservations. Every revenge dream he had dreamt became a reality. Ricky Squillante, now squirming below him, the murderer of his wife and son, was a dead man. Jake's fist tightened on the knife's grip for a single downward thrust.

A bolt of unimaginable headache pain and dizziness struck Jake simultaneously. His knees clenched Ricky's ribs in an attempt to steady himself, but he lost the pressure points, sending his body forward. Ricky arched his body to tumble Jake backwards, slamming Jake's head into the crane as Ricky rolled out from under him, the knife falling to the ground near Ricky's hand.

Ricky reached for the knife and felt its grip ease into his fist. His face was flushed and wild-eyed as he mumbled, "Nemesis." He struggled to get his shoulders unpinned and pushed Jake into the crane's tread.

The gunshot and the bullet shattering on the crane's tread were a single noise. Ears had managed to get a shot off from his back-up piece before his arm fell back across his chest in permanent rest. The bullet fragmented in the tread, its pieces missed Jake but struck Ricky in the shoulders and neck. Ricky jerked backwards; Jake head-butted and jammed his knee into Ricky's groin while doubling back Ricky's wrist and turning it over with the blade pointed at Ricky's chest. Ricky fell forward; the knife's blade slid neatly into him, missing ribs with a surgeon's precision. Blood spurted, a torrent that continued as Ricky thrashed, pulling at the knife, its serrated edge catching on a rib and ripping into heart muscle. His eyes widened in disbelief. Jake let the body fall off him and took the knife from Ricky's grasp. He held it above Ricky, with the hope that Ricky would see it in his last second of life.

Jake may have been blood-soaked, wounded, suffering a mind-splitting headache, but he had the cool, good sense to search Ricky's clothing. His hands were scarlet with Ricky's blood, when he found a cell phone and the business card that he had given to Aldo—that he didn't expect—in Ricky's jacket pocket. He checked the other bodies, one on the ground for life and weapons, the other in the SUV, and confirmed they were dead. He staggered to Ricky's Dodge Ram parked by the trailer and grabbed the grocery bag containing the cash, his gun, and the keys to Livia's Camry. He placed the knife in the bag and walked back through the yard to the rear gates, and after making sure there was no one on the street, got into Livia's car and drove home leaving the gate open.

Finding his gun gave him an idea. Unless Squillante had told somebody that he was to meet Jake, or someone had noticed Livia's car and jotted down the license plate number, there was no trace of Jake's presence in the scrapyard. His fingerprints would be all over the junker, but that had gone into the compactor and been burnt; his handprints on the compactor wall might have survived the fire, but he doubted it. He had been careful in Ricky's truck not to touch the wheel or the dash. Was it possible that his involvement might be unknown to others over and above those involved in the melee? His Beretta had not been fired, he had no trace of gunpowder on his hands. A long, long shot. He'd just have to see how it would play out.

Jake arrived at his condo and parked the Camry in front of the stable and looked up. Was his imagination or migraine playing tricks on him? Was the bloody scene he had left fogging his perspective? The clouds over the mansion had parted to reveal a huge full moon, covered by a veneer of ocher. The predicted blood red moon!

CHAPTER SEVENTY-EIGHT

DONNIE DELFUSCO WAS THE DAYLIGHT clean-up man after a special, in case anything suspicious had been left in the yard. Sal had let him know that dumb fuck Ricky was to go down, and being cautious, he had wanted to make sure there was no trace of Ricky left behind. He arrived at Rhode Island Scrap at five. To his surprise, the front gate was unlocked. He drove in and parked next to Sal's Cadillac by the trailer. Ricky's duded-up Ram truck was close by. *What the fuck was Sal doing here so early?* There was a light on in the trailer and Donnie went inside. To his surprise, the place had been tossed and Sal wasn't there.

Thinking Sal might be by the compactor, Donnie left the trailer. It was raining buckets by then. He saw the Yukon by the compactor. "What the fuck is going on?" he said aloud as he trudged the muddy ground. He found one body in the Yukon's blood-spattered interior, another by the crane with a .38 in his hand, an empty Sig Sauer on the ground by the compactor, and both bodies full of holes. Ricky was curled up in a fetal position by the crane—a knife had ripped open his blood-soaked shirt.

Donnie closed the back gate and scrambled back to the trailer. He took one of the burner phones from Sal's desk drawer and called Lucky Barracelli. The phone rang and rang and rang until a tired voice answered, "Yeah?"

Donnie tried not to skip anything as he explained the situation.

"You got three down?" Lucky said, incredulously.

"Yeah, Ricky and two Dragos guys by the compactor and Sal's among the missing. And I gotta tell ya, the compactor was used last night."

"Dragos? You sure no one else?"

"Yeah, I'm sure. Ya expecting more?"

Lucky figured Sal and the fuck that Ricky wanted to off had been compacted and were in a flattened junker ready for the pier.

"When does the crew get there?"

"Six forty-five."

"Lock the gates so no one gets in. I'll be back to you."

Ten minutes later, Lucky was back on the burner. "Here's what's goin' down. I've got two guys comin' over. They'll load the stiffs into the Yukon and one will take off with it. The other guy will pick up Ricky's truck for some bodywork out of town. You drive Sal's Caddy to his apartment and leave it on the street. Door unlocked. What time do the pier guys pick up the junkers?"

"Nine or so."

"Okay, business as usual, right?"

"Business as usual," Donnie repeated. "Yeah, I got it. Nobody's to know, right?"

"Not a fucking' trace!"

"Ricky's truck is worth a few bucks."

"Did ya hear me? When it's out of the yard, it's goin' to one of our friends out of town, make sure nothing inside will be a problem."

"Okay, how about Jonny's guys?"

"He's got ownership."

"Where are they going?"

"You don't need to know, do you, Donnie?"

"No. And Sal?"

"Sal had a problem. Let that fuckin' Ricky ruin a good thing for everybody. Donnie, you may have to take over the yard. Won't be any more specials. Anybody asks, Sal's gone to his place in Florida, got health problems."

Donnie was thrilled by the opportunity. "The Brow gave the okay?"

"I'll talk to him. He will OK it. You know the operation."

"Ricky?"

"Who the fuck cares about Ricky? Anyway, he's gonna be offered up for the jerkoff Baldolucca hit. Didn't show up for work, if anybody asks, right?"

"Right!"

CHAPTER SEVENTY-NINE

AT SEVEN FORTY-FIVE, two COs, one on either side, accompanied Aaron, handcuffed and manacled, from his cell block into the rear seat of a white Ford Explorer. Aaron hadn't been inside a vehicle, nor outside of Medium Security, for twenty-nine years. He experienced both curiosity and apprehension as a seatbelt was clamped over his hips.

As the Explorer edged into Howard Drive from Medium Security's main gate, he heard his supporters on the sidewalks chanting "Aaron, Aaron, Free Aaron!" He saw a sea of placards demanding his release. Cameras facing the gates followed the Explorer's progress along Howard Drive toward the Max. Yesterday, Millie had brought him a *Journal* that described the rally at Roger Williams Park, the reaction to his poem, the gunshot that made the rally national news. It gave him renewed hope, and what he had heard and read about Aaron's Army now had physical reality and context. Here was a crowd demonstrating in the early morning chill for his cause, some singing a hymn he vaguely remembered. *Over Jordan.* When he squirmed in his seat to get a better look at how many had gathered in his support, he earned a poke in the ribs from a CO's baton.

At the main gate to the Max, demonstrators shouted "Free Aaron" in cadence. After a honk of the Explorer's horn, the vehicle was allowed into a gravel-covered interior courtyard and pulled up in front of a granite-faced building. Aaron was assisted out of the SUV. The group entered through a metal door and were guided down a labyrinth of connecting corridors into a tiny room with plastic scoop chairs, deep within the building. A stark recollection of his first and only other entrance into the Max filled Aaron's mind as he was released from his handcuffs and manacles and sat facing the door to an adjoining room. Muffled voices were audible, one louder than the others, the one Aaron thought he recalled in its harshness from his last hearing.

Aaron used the wait time to examine himself. He had been barbered, and was shaved and showered. His garb was clean, a white tee showing up under his tan work shirt, his hair was swept over his forehead and damaged ear and he wore his glasses. He felt a touch of self-confidence. All the commotion was real.

<hr />

"What happened to the other guy?" McNally asked when Jake entered the hearing room. An argument between Prebys and Mia stopped.

Mia looked concerned. Jake didn't answer McNally, only to be beset with a volley of questions from Prebys.

Jake's thighs and chest were hurting, his elbow and his scraped knees burned, his fingernails were broken, and was still recovering from his migraine. He had barely made it into the condo to throw up, had medicated himself with Imitrex and aspirin, cleaned his scrapes and the facial pricks from the flying glass. He showered, filling the bathroom with steam, scrubbing away the stain of what had gone down, of any trace of Squillante's blood, and put a Band-Aid on the cut on his forehead. His mirror reflected the puffiness around his right eye. Before he left for Maximum Security, last night's clothes went in a trash bag and into the dumpster by the stable; his Iraqi knife, wiped with alcohol, and his clean, not-fired Beretta returned to the library's safe.

"Accident," he snapped back at Prebys. That quieted Prebys but McNally frowned with suspicion.

Bertozzi, ignoring the display of temper, said, "Let's move on."

The CO stationed in the hearing room opened the door and signaled Aaron and the accompanying COs to enter. Aaron trudged in, face down, to an indicated folding chair facing the parole board members. The COs sat behind him. Not a single board member looked his way. Finally a plump woman sitting directly across from him, wearing a blue blouse and floppy tie with a pile of files in front of her, addressed him. "Good morning, Mr. Underwood."

Aaron removed his glasses in response and snapped his head upright, giving the panel the full Aaron, and was satisfied by the audible withdrawal of breaths and gasps from the two women before him.

"You have been before this board on prior occasions," Bertozzi offered as more of a statement than a question.

"Yes, sir," Aaron replied, slowly giving each member, left to right, a profile of the ruined half of his face. The two older men he recognized as being at his last hearing, the other three were new to him. The woman, Sanchez, he knew from his research of board minutes, including her votes; the member with the stub of an arm didn't have enough of a track record for Aaron to gauge his vote; the Black man was the new member and he stared at Aaron as though he wanted to grab his throat and throttle him.

"Is there anything you want to say to the board before we begin our examination?" asked Bertozzi.

Aaron had the crazy thought to tell them he handicapped their votes on parole, that his prison life was better for it. Instead, he leaned forward over the desk. Bitterness rose in Aaron's voice, recognizable despite his dry mouth and crusty lips.

"I been inside for almost thirty years. That's six wardens! In all that time, I haven't been two hundred yards from where we sit. My mother died and I didn't get to go to the funeral. I got one relative, my sister, and she's my only visitor. Not a day goes by without an insult, a reminder that I am disfigured. I got twenty, maybe more, years to live with this face. Punished enough? Do I satisfy justice enough? Yet, I've already been denied parole three times."

McNally interrupted. "Thirty years ago, you pled guilty to a coldblooded murder of an old lady living alone. In all this time, you've shown no remorse. Are you ready to say you are sorry?"

Aaron controlled his response. The words he spoke through half of his mouth came out slurred and measured.

"I have always said I have no recollection of her death. I don't know why it happened. If I did it, I would be sorry."

"Are you claiming you didn't kill her?"

"I don't remember that I did, and I don't know why I would have."

"You pled guilty."

"Yes."

"Well?"

"I was still trying to deal with the condition of my face. Everyone said I did it, even my family. Nobody believed me that I couldn't remember. Maybe then, with my lawyer, everyone telling me I did it, I thought maybe I did."

"You want it both ways," Prebys sneered. "You might have or might not?"

"All I can say to you is that I have a good record, a place to go, been no trouble ever." Aaron straightened in his chair and abruptly snapped his head upright and touched his scars. "I have this face."

The ensuing silence was broken by Bertozzi. "Just serving time is not enough. Even good time. You know that. You pled guilty to a brutal crime. Likely the old woman suffered greatly. We have to take that into consideration. The board needs to know that a petitioner understands the enormity of a crime."

"I do, sir, I understand that murder is a terrible crime."

"We have to be convinced it will not happen again."

Aaron turned his head so that his eye found each member in turn. "I can be trusted. I'd accept any limitation you decide. With a face like mine, I'm not going anywhere. All I want to do is to live with my sister."

Prebys turned away from Aaron's stare to address the ceiling. "Anyone who commits a gruesome crime, if rehabilitated, would have remorse. I don't see or hear a trace of that from you."

McNally nodded in agreement.

"I said that I am sorry if I did it."

"That again?" Prebys snorted and sank into his seat as though nothing further was required for decision.

Bertozzi nodded at Mia.

"Mr. Underwood," she said, her voice tremulous, too obviously disturbed by the ugliness facing her. "If paroled, you will eventually have contact with people who might shrink from you because of your . . . injury. Will you be able to handle adverse reactions?"

His answer was in his practiced wheelhouse. In truth, he would enjoy seeing their worst fears realized, his face in theirs. But his answer was smooth and calculated.

"Ma'am, I handle it every day. I have no shame as to my face now, not after almost thirty years. I outlived it." His left hand touched his scars. "Inmates here are not polite or sympathetic. But after a while, people get used to me. It doesn't take that long. Anyways, I would wear a floppy hat and large sunglasses when and if I ever am seen by the public or—"

Bertozzi looked to Jake who asked, "Mr. Underwood, why were you at the Gist farm?"

McNally muttered, "Here we go again," and turned to Bertozzi who raised a palm to prevent a comment. "My question goes to his lack of memory," Jake said to Bertozzi, "and its effect on remorse, or lack thereof."

Bertozzi appeared quizzical but said, "Go ahead. But, no need to rehash the file."

"It was Halloween." Aaron took a deep breath. In recent days, his attempts at recollection had produced a logical reason for the pry bar. "I was there for a prank. I was going to take the hubcaps off her car. I don't think I did. Don't remember, though."

"Anyone else know you were going there?"

"Yes."

"Who?"

"Kids at school."

"Why?"

"Because the prank was a dare."

"Who dared you?

He glanced over the heads of the board in a recollection, careful to show them his good side. "Billy Bain was one. Joe Tingle another. Their gang."

"Were you part of their gang?"

"No. I was promised I would be if I pulled off the prank."

"Why did you agree?"

"I wanted to be accepted and . . . " should he say it, yes, might as well, ". . . and there was a prize."

"What?"

"I'd rather not say."

"Mr. Underwood, it would be better if you did," Bertozzi said.

He hadn't expected to rehash his reason for accepting the dare, and was embarrassed, but continued after applying lip balm.

"There was a girl in class. A year or two older than most because she stayed back a year. Not too smart, but pretty. If I pulled off the prank, they said she would let me tongue kiss her, and feel her up." He turned to focus his eye on Mia. "Sorry, ma'am."

Prebys' elbows banged hard on the table. "For a French kiss, a clutch of breast, you killed the old lady?"

Bertozzi used his gavel. "Jake, where are you going with this?"

"A few questions more for clarification on intent."

Prebys muttered, "This is a waste of time."

"Just some kids from school knew you were going to be out at the old lady's house? Anybody else?"

Aaron raised his head in thought, remembering the lunch line when Billy Bain and Joe Tingle pushed him into the janitor's closet by the boiler room. "Maybe Mr. Cesar could have."

"Who?"

"Mr. Cesar. The janitor. Maybe he could have heard us if he was in the boiler room next door. He usually was in there, smoking, around lunchtime, which he wasn't supposed to do. After lunch, I saw him talking to Billy."

"And you didn't tell anyone else?"

"Nobody. It had to be a secret, at least until I did it, and I proved I did it. If I told anybody before, it was over."

"Do you know if Mr. Cesar was ever questioned by Sheriff Bain?" Jake looked at the board members individually.

"How would he know?" McNally snarled.

"How about Billy Bain or Joe Tingle?" Jake asked quickly.

"I object," shouted McNally.

"He can answer," Bertozzi replied forcefully.

"Don't know."

Jake asked, "The pry bar. Was that yours?"

"I brought one with me . . . for the hubcaps. I was going to pry them off, hide them, then get them back to her after she complained in the village, making a scene, and I had showed Bainsy and Tingle."

"Did you believe Lucretia Gist had a secret hoard of gold coins?"

Another surprise to Aaron. He recalled his father's anger at her, that she wouldn't let him sharecrop her land.

"My father said a lot of things about her, that she was a miser. I don't recall he said she had a hoard of gold coins."

"Did you search the house, open closets, pull drawers open?"

"I don't remember anything after I came up through the fields. But why would I?"

McNally puffed his impatience. "For the record, you refuse to admit to the murder of Lucretia Gist, a crime to which you pled guilty before a judge of the Superior Court?"

"Yes."

McNally sat back. Bertozzi took that as a signal to end the hearing and said, "Unless there are further questions?" He looked at each member in turn, then said, "You will be informed of our decision."

Aaron stood slowly. "Thank you. I am ready to leave prison. I would not return."

The two COs stepped forward, grabbed Aaron by the elbows and pushed him out of the hearing room.

‖‖‖

As Aaron was returned to the Explorer, he was looking forward to his ride back to Medium Security. He felt the explanation of his recollection of events justified some optimism. As he heard his supporters' righteous cheers, "Free Aaron, Free Aaron," he basked in their support.

"I should be free," he said aloud, and turned to a CO to shout "Free Aaron!"

CHAPTER EIGHTY

BERTOZZI ASKED IF ANY MEMBER wanted a break before discussion and vote, got no replies, and said, "Before we vote, I want to remind everyone that the warden will issue a statement after Underwood is notified of our decision. That should be an hour after our session. And no individual statements, right?" He turned his face first to Mia who ignored him by pointing her chin toward Jake, then to McNally.

"I don't intend an individual statement unless we grant parole," McNally said. "Because I'm a new member, people are entitled to know my vote. As far as I am concerned, that goes for everyone."

Bertozzi's face became a map of frustration. McNally was operating as a *de facto* chair. Then, it came to him that now was the time to call for a vote for the chair, not wait until after the vote on Underwood. Smoke out the governor and McNally and Prebys.

"Before we vote on Underwood, and because the chair will have to deal with the public outcry on whatever we decide, I'm calling for a vote for the election of our chair. If a majority disagrees, we'll wait. Otherwise, we vote now."

Jake looked around the room. Faces registered surprise as to Bertozzi's ploy. Jake, and perhaps others, realized that this was a test vote of Prebys' and McNally's support for Bertozzi.

"Premature, Stuart," McNally said slowly, his eyes trained on Prebys. "Yeah, what's the hurry?" Prebys quickly agreed.

Bertozzi asked Mia, who responded crisply, seemingly putting him down with the finality in her voice. "I think we have more important business, the people's business, to attend to."

Jake wondered about Mia's reluctance. She clearly didn't have the votes to be chair, so what difference did it make? Maybe she just couldn't bring herself to vote with or for Bertozzi.

"Jake?"

"I could do it now or later."

Bertozzi sat back. It was clear to Jake that Bertozzi, whose face revealed evident disappointment, he had lost Prebys, never had McNally, and Mia was a negative. He'd never be chair. Obviously hurt, he didn't call for a formal vote.

"Get Underwood over with," Prebys said loudly, and rudely, to Bertozzi. "I voted to deny last time and the record being no different, I vote no."

McNally joined him. "No."

Bertozzi remained grim-lipped as he said, "Mia?"

"Approve, but with conditions. Long-term counseling, limitations on movement for some period of time, and a permanent address at his sister's farm."

"That would solve nothing." Prebys challenged. "He is an unrepentant murderer. Simple as that, Mia. He's better off inside where no farmer, thinking he's protecting his kids, takes him out."

"I'm not going to debate you," she replied. "The whole country is looking at us and how we handle his petition. Fourth time up and—"

"And still not sorry for what he did, for Christ sakes," Prebys interjected. "Do those idiots out there know that?"

"His stigma counts for something. It's called justice. That's why we are here. To do justice. Maybe it's time for us to be refreshed on what the parole statute says about criteria for parole." She touched her laptop's keyboard, scrolled, and said, "I'll summarize: 'the prisoner has observed the rules of the prison,' check; 'there is a reasonable probability that the prisoner will not again violate the law,' check; 'the prisoner needs specialized medical care and services,' check; 'the release would not depreciate the seriousness of the prisoner's offense.'"

Prebys interrupted. "Got you there! Depreciate the seriousness of the prisoner's offense. He's a vicious goddamn murderer of an old lady. And, oh, by the way," he smirked, "thanks. I needed you to remind me of the standard after sitting through thousands of petitions. I must have forgotten why I'm here week after week and—"

Bertozzi used his gavel.

Jake watched as Mia, responding, choked back her tears at what was about to happen. Gone was her overt self-righteousness, any vestige of superiority. Replaced by what, her need for justice for Underwood?

"You can't just let Aaron Underwood rot away here. It's cruel and unusual punishment. You all know that! He's suffered neglect and we should not be a party to its continuing. I implore you, do the right thing! Yes."

"Okay, Jake," Bertozzi said, "where are you on this?"

"Yeah, Jake, planning to vote?" Prebys sneered.

Jake found his voice. He hunched forward. "Underwood says he is sorry if he did it." He leaned in to McNally. "I'm not aware of any law or precedent that says that a petitioner is required to admit guilt for a parole. I don't ever recall the issue coming up before. Is this precedent, Stuart?"

Before his question was answered, McNally's fist banged the table. "Jake, just what is with you? Another goddamn speech? Can't you just vote?"

"He could have pled guilty while in a severe depression related to his face, in an urge to just hide away. Now that we've all seen his face, heard his story, I understand. Okay, that's a supposition, not enough for me to make a call in his favor. But tell me, how does an old lady with a pry bar wound in her head manage to shoot her birdgun at her assailant? Not just once, twice, or get her fingers on two triggers, and fire? Chief Bain, as a kid, turns out to have egged Underwood to commit a prank on the victim and is one of the two persons on the scene, followed by his father. Apparently, nobody mentioned the prank or the other kids being there at the trial. Those facts would have pulled the prosecution's case apart if handled by a competent defense lawyer. Seems like a prank, not a stash of gold coins, enticed Underwood to the Gist farm. If the coins were stashed there, we know Underwood didn't take them, but who had the time to search the house? Bain's father and maybe the two kids or the janitor who knew of the prank. I like the sheriff who seems to have a penchant for things made from gold, like his son's belt buckle."

"This isn't a trial court, Jake," Bertozzi said quietly.

Jake felt his face redden. "Mia's right. Justice is what we are here for, to provide a human process to the statute's provisions. His grotesque face shows the injustice of keeping him imprisoned, untreated, and despised. Even if he did it, the state has something to answer for. His face is the face of injustice."

As he uttered the words, Jake suddenly found clarity; the blood spurting from Ricky Squillante's mouth had given him no relief. Justice had to be tempered with mercy, even if he had been blind to that truth. That was why he was voting to parole Underwood. Guilty or innocent, it was time to let Underwood out. Not because of Garo's anger at the failures of the justice and penal systems, nor because his own persistent vengeance had closed off years of his life, nor because of the Walter Reed wounded horribles. It was simply justice.

"Here, here," shouted Mia, "Somebody has the guts to tell it straight!"

Prebys threw up his hands. "Okay, you've had your say. Feel better? But we don't need your vote. We got three against." Prebys boasted in victory, "That's over. Finally!"

The gavel struck the table like a clap of thunder. *"Shut-the-fuck-up!"* shouted Bertozzi. "Chair votes for parole."

Air was vacuumed from the room. Mrs. Ames seemed momentarily paralyzed. Mia's chin pointed up in her astonishment. McNally was openmouthed, and Prebys' eyes bulged in disbelief and he came halfway out of his chair.

Bertozzi straightened as though a rod had been rammed up his backside. He smiled at the reactions and experienced a flush of moral relief.

"The warden deserves to know first, and I will tell him and he can call the governor. Under our rules, Underwood will be out in a maximum of six weeks. We will stipulate to the usual conditions for a longtime inmate: every other week with a parole officer for three years, home confinement with a leg locator bracelet indefinitely until the parole officer okays removal. You will no doubt want to speak your minds, but I remind you of the confidentiality of these meetings under the statute. Anyone breaking confidentiality will be referred by me to the Attorney General. The vote for parole is three for and two against. That will be the written record."

"With that settled," Jake said, "I move we vote for Chair."

"I agree and second the motion," Mia said.

"No," shouted Prebys.

"The motion has been made and seconded," Bertozzi said coolly. "I agree so it carries. Let's get on with it." He asked Mrs. Ames to leave, holding the gavel in his hand, looking at it as though he was saying goodbye. After she left, Bertozzi said, "I've been impressed by one of us who has never been a candidate for chair. My time as acting chair is over and we need to bring the parole board to a better time. I nominate and will vote for and support Jake Fournier."

And then, to Jake's amazement, Mia, her eyes wide and beginning a smile, nodded at Jake affirmatively and seconded the nomination.

For Jake, the situation was unimaginable. A chair known to be a target in a homicide investigation? A chair who had broken rules and precedent? A chair whose resignation was in his jacket's pocket? A chair who might well be publicly connected to a gangland shootout?

Okay, better he than McNally.

Prebys, apoplectic, jumped to his feet. He swung at the air in anger, his face florid, his stream of words barely understandable in his shouting. "He can't be chair. He's only been here four months, he's all over the place in his votes, doesn't have the confidence of two members and," he sputtered with what breath he had left, "to vote for Underwood's parole shows he doesn't have the backbone needed as a chair. We should stop the foolishness now and elect Major McNally!"

At the mention of his name, McNally appeared unruffled. Jake wondered if he was contemplating how long it would be before he replaced Jake. "The vote is obviously three in favor of Jake Fournier," said Bertozzi. "That's how it will read in the minutes."

Bertozzi tapped his gavel, "Jake, in all fairness, we'll make the vote effective the beginning of the next meeting. I'll take the heat for Underwood's decision and what is likely to be a lot of commotion."

Jake could already hear the angry words spouted to the media by Prebys and McNally, the governor's office, the Town of Greenwick, Buddy Callahan, from all the anti-Aaron forces. That thought confirmed his decision; while he would be a short-timer—until Prebys and McNally gained an ally upon Bertozzi's resignation, or the expiration of his term and the governor's replacement—maybe he could do some good, make up for some sins of the past. He would turn to Mia for some ideas as to what a short-timer might accomplish, and to Bertozzi for advice on precedent and procedure. He would put down Prebys and McNally anytime they got out of line. He liked that.

Jake voted yes.

CHAPTER EIGHTY-ONE

AN ASSISTANT WARDEN delivered a brown envelope, the kind that was closed by a red string that wrapped around a clasp, to Aaron who was waiting in the lawyer's room with his sister. Accompanying the assistant warden was a staff psychologist and two COs. Aaron's fingers fumbled it and it was his sister who opened it and pulled out the two-page form and gave it to him. The messengers remained silent, almost respectful.

Aaron's good eye went close to the form. It took him a minute to get to the second page and the blank that said *Granted*.

He sat back, took a deep breath and gave the form to his sister. While she searched the form for an answer, Aaron's scarred face gave no clue to the decision. Even when she erupted in joy, he remained silent. No one in that room could tell from his scarred face if he had a reaction; Aaron was as rigid as a statue. His sister went around the table and kissed Aaron's head. He didn't return the moment of affection.

|||||||||||||||||||||||||||||||||||||||||||||||||||||

"Jake, what happened?" Livia asked, her eyes wide open in surprise.

Jake dropped the keys to her Camry on her desk and said, "Underwood got parole."

"Your face, I mean. What happened?"

Jake hadn't made up an excuse that would make sense to her, and he didn't want to be again untruthful. "I had a tip on Hope's killer, and I decided to check it out. It got ugly. Didn't work out as I expected."

"At midnight, out towards Cranston and Johnston?" she said.

Jake was startled. "How would you know?"

Livia's face flushed with embarrassment. "Jake, you've been acting so strangely, I didn't quite buy into your use of my car. I put a GPS on it, I had one from the days my ex was out all night. And I tracked you. The car was out near the Cranston-Johnston line. I thought you might be a Lone Ranger, without some backup, something to do with Hope and that guy that was killed. I thought of calling Dermott and Garo, but around two, the car moved and was soon in Pawtucket. I apologize, Jake, but it's been so difficult the last few weeks."

Jake was speechless. Would Livia make the connection when she learned of the shoot-out at Rhode Island Scrap? By now, cops should be swarming all over the scrapyard, the story would hit the media, vying for coverage with Aaron Underwood's parole. He promised himself that when it hit the fan, and he was questioned by the staties, he'd give them his complicated but coherent story of the carnage and self-defense, a story of bad guys shooting up bad guys. He was determined to call it factually, even if Dermott attempted to quiet him. But, if no one else knew he was there and the staties didn't put him on the spot, and his risk of discovery might only be with Livia, he could live with that.

He hugged Livia, telling her that her action was understandable, much to her obvious relief, and hoped that he'd never have to explain further, and said he had been elected to chair the Rhode Island Parole Board.

"Jake, you'll do good. And without the Speaker's push."

"Yeah. Wonder what he'll think." Jake responded. Another irony, he thought.

|||||||||||||||||||||||||||||||||||||||||||||||||||||||

At one minute to twelve, the bartender turned on the flat-screen television over the tiers of booze bottles in the taproom. Underwood's parole, leaked to the media, was the lead story on all three local stations, with interviews and shots of jubilation of the Free Aaron partisans in their vigil outside the prison. Jake could imagine the self-congratulations on the Free Aaron website and from advocates and social media celebrities pledging to continue to foster prison reform. He wondered how long that would last after Underwood was no longer their focus.

Chief Bain, suited up for the cameras, shook his head in astonishment that Aaron Underwood would soon reside in his town. When asked if he was going to provide additional protection for Greenwick residents, he acknowledged that he had no such present plans because he never expected Underwood's parole. His actions, he said, would depend upon the terms and conditions of parole, which he understood included a leg locator intended to keep Underwood on the farm. "But," he said ominously, "would it?"

As the day went on, more voices were heard. Despite his intention to shower again and sleep, Jake followed streaming news on his laptop. McNally and Prebys had a press conference in front of the AG's office proclaiming that they had voted against Aaron Underwood's parole and vehemently objected to the "soft-headed" board decision. The governor's office refused comment, but promised to review the parole board's statutory criteria to emphasize community safety as its prime objective. Bertozzi somehow ducked the media, while Mia was a quick counterpoint to McNally and Prebys, explaining her vote in a manner that gave her own advocacy for reform an appropriate spin. The media was unable to reach Jake, who had thus far managed to keep his cell phone number private. His election as chair would likely come to its attention when Bertozzi relinquished the office at the next meeting.

Jake finally got some restless sleep. When he woke, he was hungry and made an omelet. Later, Garo and Dermott called Jake from the taproom at Livia's. They obviously had been celebrating.

Jake immediately brought up Garo's suspension. The detective was nonplussed. "I don't regret it for a minute. I'm not going to speak to the

SIU, which means that I'm going back to being a PI. The board did the right thing today."

Jake didn't ask Garo about *Aaron's Anguish,* but knew that the former PI had the opportunity and technical ability to produce and air the video. He thought for a moment of the reward money for information about Hope's killer that now would never be claimed: maybe there would be a way that it could support Garo's new start as a PI, perhaps to take on other cold cases. Something of a grand gesture, he knew, but worth it to Jake for Garo's loyalty, doggedness, and patience.

He told them under strict confidentiality of his election as parole board chair. Garo was astonished and offered congratulations. Dermott, however, quickly added a dose of reality.

"The parole board's chair is a suspect in Baldolucca's murder? And a guy who voted to release Underwood and gives the finger to Jackson McNally and Frank Harrigan? You better be ready, boy-o."

"I have you as my counsel, right? Then, I'm ready."

After the call, Jake imagined a front-page story of blood and guts in tomorrow's *Journal* in its juicy detail. Until the shootout was revealed, he knew he would wake up every day with the premonition that a statie would be at his door. He went to his computer, composed a detailed account of what happened at Rhode Island Scrap. He printed it out, made a copy for the safe, and another that he would send to himself certified mail. More irony, he thought as he finished; the Chair-elect of Rhode Island Parole Board's reputation rested on the Mob's ability to take care of its own business on the quiet, if that was happening.

HAEC FABULA DOCET
("For Those Who Go Alone")

Moral
The moral is, it hardly need be shown,
All those who try to go it sole alone,
Too proud to be beholden for relief,
Are absolutely sure to come to grief.
—Robert Frost

CHAPTER EIGHTY-TWO

EXCEPT FOR THE MANDATORY pre-release counseling, nothing much changed for Aaron Underwood in the remaining weeks of his prison life. He listened to the shrinks and the social workers, worked on special projects for the librarian, and spent time on the librarian's computer, finishing a project before his release that was to be his revenge on a system he hated.

A few things changed, however. He no longer had revolving-door cellmates; he was asked to train a new library assistant, and Hickman didn't contact him except in a brief exchange when he said that he owed Aaron for the tip that he would get his parole and wouldn't renege. And a few inmates actually tried to engage him in conversation which, for the most part, he tried to avoid without being insulting.

The prison's medical staff seemed to have renewed interest in his wounded face and examined him three separate times in the prison's medical unit along with an eminent plastic surgeon and nurses from City Hospital. Eventually, the surgeon determined a face graft would not be successful because of a lot of biology bullshit Aaron didn't understand that came down to "too late": scars were too ingrained and replacement tissue wouldn't hold. While his sister Millie argued that he should get other medical opinions, it was over as far as Aaron was concerned. He was going home with his face as is and he began to relish the scene of his first outing in Greenwick.

<hr>

While Fat Frankie waited out his ninety days to freedom, he became known to all the staff as a real asshole. He ate and ate, hoping that by the time his parole began, he'd be *Fat Frankie* again, looking as though he had never left Broadway Pawn. He had heard that the Hill action was in the doldrums, that Sal Gianmalvo had been sent on vacation for some infraction, that Donnie DelFusco was now running the scrapyard, that the Dragos were no longer working with the Brow—in fact, people talked of a war. But sooner or later, he figured things would calm down, and a fence with contacts was always in demand.

To record his remaining days in prison, he had a smuggled-in drawing of a voluptuous female figure that provided him the exquisite pleasure of filling in a section of anatomy each day, with his release date represented by her most intimate parts. "Gettin' to my honey," he said often and kissed it most nights.

Hot dogs and beans were Saturday night staples in Medium Security. Fat Frankie loaded up on beans, despite suffering through a week of stomach aches and constipation, obsessed as he was with regaining his playing weight. The hot dogs were skinless and steamed and not exactly high quality Saugies, Rhode Island's favorites. Still, he managed to get down four, with buns, relish, mustard, ketchup and onions, with two servings of beans.

As he gorged himself, Fat Frankie had been thinking about what kind of a deal he would work out with Lucky and the Brow for the extra twenty g's. His cousin Chris could kiss goodbye his ten g's for the parole, choking on the shit stones he already had while building him a new fuckin' garage.

He finished his meal and had placed his tray, plate and cup at the conveyor belt to the dishwashing crew when he felt a stab of pain in his gut, as though a goon had knocked his fist right through to his backbone. He doubled over, holding his belly.

A CO challenged, "Gilletto, what the fuck is going on?"

"I—" He gasped in another spasm of pain, then fell to the tile floor like a sack of potatoes.

"Get up!" yelled the CO.

Fat Frankie, pain coursing through his body, could not answer.

He was taken by ambulance to City Hospital. "Severe bowel distress" was the emergency room intake note, not a triage priority. He was eventually admitted, all the while complaining of stomach pain. Six hours later, he was prepped for surgery for bowel obstruction. Although given medication to reduce his higher-than-normal blood pressure, he blew his aorta on the operating table.

Chris Gilletto was watching TV in Fat Frankie's empty hospital room—the family had been called by the hospital and his mother and aunt were in the hospital chapel—when he was informed that his cousin had died.

"Shit!" he bellowed when the doctor left. He, not Fat Frankie, now owed the Brow as well as the rest of Walter Kramer's fees. Knowing Lucky wouldn't wait, not even until after his cousin was waked, Chris set to work digging up Fat Frankie's basement where he figured Fat Frankie would hide a stash. In private, he screamed, "*Afunggo*," sweaty and filthy with dust and dirt. "Where is it?" His aunt followed him to the basement and watched his every move, chastised him continually. Somehow, she managed to keep him away from the bricks covered with dirt and soot behind the oil burner.

That stash was her son's bequest to her and nobody else was going to get it!

Chris was on his own. Could he somehow convince Lucky to wait for a payment? He'd have to hit the union funds.

CHAPTER EIGHTY-THREE

ON A PRE-ARRANGED JUNE NIGHT, without notice to the media, in ill-fitting clothes brought by Millie, with a duffel bag of his books, his music, ChapSticks and a thumb drive, Aaron Underwood was placed in a state police van for the trip to Greenwick. The powers that be decided against the usual halfway house upon a release of a long-term prisoner in light of the uproar it would cause in any community in which he was placed. Greenwick could have him.

Also aboard the van was Millie, who carried prescription tranquilizers from the medical unit of the prison in case Aaron had a bad reaction to his new surroundings, and the minister of the Greenwick Congregational Church, who attempted to engage Aaron in conversation. He assured Aaron that there were folks in Greenwick who had supported his parole, that there were services available to him, and outreach from sympathetic neighbors.

"Your face," the minister said, even as he gulped, "does not mean you have to be a hermit. In my church, you'd be welcome. That is, when you are permitted to do so."

Aaron's recollection of Pastor Ellsbridge dissuaded him from a response, and besides, he was glued to the sights to be seen outside the van's window.

Once settled at the farmhouse, Aaron initially confined himself to his second-floor bedroom and shared bathroom, and a television room off the kitchen. He found it difficult to get used to not asking for permission to move around the house, or not be on a tightly managed schedule.

It was unnerving for Aaron to spend time outside, even to walk around the house, or as far as the barn.

Only occasionally did he summon enough courage, as the weather warmed, to venture further and sit beneath a gnarled apple tree not far from the house to read his Frost or take in the trails of aircraft landing at T.F. Green Airport, or to walk to a small pond behind the barn where cattails shook in the wind and dragonflies buzzed fleetingly. Noise from ATV engines from a neighbor's field annoyed him, as did the two boys who called to him, clamoring to see his face. They reminded him of lines from Frost:

> *But becoming aware of some boys from school*
> *Who had stopped outside the fence to spy,*
> *I stopped my song and almost heart,*
> *For any eye is an evil eye*
> *That looks onto a mood apart.*

His daytime hours were filled with chores like making his bed, vacuuming, which he enjoyed, doing laundry, washing dishes and the like; most of his time was at the computer and huge monitor purchased with funds donated to the Free Aaron website. He spent hours searching the web for subjects that came into his head, like dreams, what were they and how did they develop. He found that dreams are sort of a memory processor—some are literal resolutions of recent experiences stored in an area of the brain with the ridiculous name *hippocampus*. Memories, some fantastic and some emotional, get mixed there and can combine with recent enhanced experiences so that they become confused with reality.

Millie tried to interest him in live television programs and cable news and newspapers, to which she seemed addicted. Aaron simply couldn't be bothered except that he watched the morning *Journal*'s headlines for any story related to the parole board. He could rely on his sister to pepper him with conversation about anything that she thought might interest him, which it rarely did. It wasn't long before the days dragged by and he became bored. He missed his library.

Other than his bi-weekly visits from a parole officer, he had no visitors. He also rebuffed reporters and magazine writers, and dismissed a freelancer who claimed to want to write about the murder of Lucretia Gist and his imprisonment, like Truman Capote's *In Cold Blood*, of which Aaron had no familiarity and refused to read. Despite Millie's pleas, Aaron also refused to see any of the buzzing lawyers offering to sue the state on his behalf, describing the prospect of millions in compensation. He was resolute. They wanted riches from his face, his tragedy, and he would not prostitute himself for them. He hated prison and his decades of ill-treatment, but he wasn't willing to expose to ridicule his face again.

For reasons he didn't explain, he stayed away from the front parlor.

During his second month of freedom, Millie showed him the *Journal* story that Aaron had been waiting for.

An envelope marked "Personal" to Garo Hagopian had languished for weeks at the public defender's office. The envelope, mailed by Millie to Garo—she thought it was a thank-you from her brother—contained a thumb drive describing a pattern of deference given by parole counselors to clients of attorney Walter Kramer, and that Kramer seemed to have a claim on the recommendation of unnamed parole counselors, including Nelson Lansing, his own counselor, and votes of Floyd Prebys. Hagopian delivered the thumb drive to the state police, and within a week the police had subpoenaed parole board records which pertained to any parole petition in which Floyd Prebys favored an inmate lawyered by Walter Kramer, especially those petitions that had been vetted by unnamed parole counselors.

Prebys, protesting his innocence and alleging a frame-up by progressive bleeding hearts from Aaron's Army, took a leave of absence from the parole board now chaired by Jake Fournier. Aaron put Millie on alert to inform him of further developments.

One topic of particular interest to Aaron was the murder of Old Lady Gist. He searched online and found contemporary reports of the murder, reading about himself as a murderer, and confirmed Greenwick's reaction to the murder and to him.

Could he have done it? His mind rebelled at the thought, and that led to an online investigation of the anomaly of recovered memories, of techniques to be used to recollect—like identifying clothing, smells, being in similar places, touching, using all senses instead of only a specific and possible damaged section of his brain—to regain what had been experienced and lost. Hungry for the truth, he began a journey of recovery as patches of memory were sewn together in a quilt of recollection. He eventually came to the conclusion that thirty years of his life had been spent in prison as the result of lies, or mistake, or televisions screens but failed, as though the portrayals were weak.

Bainsy and Tingle? No. What about the janitor, Mr. Cesar? It took Aaron several days of online searches to find that Mr. Cesar had died in an automobile accident in Florida three years after the Gist murder. There were no other known possibilities.

<hr />

The week of July 4th, Aaron steeled himself for a walk between his home and the fenced-in, abandoned Gist farm, through fields dotted by clumps of bittersweet, cane, briars, and scrub pines, then as far as Slocum Road, and the drainage ditches that still paralleled it. By then, he felt he was gaining control of his past life, and had become fixated on a need to see Gist Castle.

That week, he also found the courage to enter the farmhouse's front parlor one mid-afternoon while Millie left him for the village's Stop & Shop. Grandma's recliner had long since been replaced by a La-Z-Boy in which Millie sometimes napped.

Boldly he sat in the recliner, his hands on its arms, his fingers pressing buttons that extended and retracted the seat and footrest. Without warning, he became dizzy, panic-stricken, his hands froze at the controls, his stomach churned until he choked back bile. As he slid off the recliner, his balance gave way, the room tilted and quaked, and he heard television voices from a long-ago soap opera. He turned to the recliner and faced Grandma Underwood.

She was as horrific as when he retrieved her pills thirty years earlier. She spoke to him clearly through her gaping mouth. *"Do you think you'd been punished enough for killing me? For killing Lucretia Gist? You did it!"*

He fled the room. He took a handful of his prescription tranquilizers and crawled into his bed.

Millie soon noticed Aaron's increased agitation, that Aaron didn't sleep unless medicated. As days went by, his distress increased. She heard him cry out in nightmares, and witnessed a deterioration in his mental stability. He began to lose weight, rarely left his room, had trouble keeping time, had to be reminded of meals, was often forgetful as to where he was, and had memories that became confused with the present. There were episodes when he wasn't sure who Millie was, or why he wore a bracelet on his shin, or what prevented him from leaving the farm. Some mornings, he stood in the hallway outside his bedroom for the morning count.

By the end of August, Millie was considering asking for permission from his parole officer to put Aaron in a convalescent home. His forgetfulness and confusion had become more pronounced and he was becoming more difficult, refusing to wash himself, shouting angrily at her when she insisted on changing sheets or raising window shades. After a particularly difficult week, a year after his parole, at an early supper, she showed him a full color photograph of a red moon on the *Journal's* front page with the state capital in the foreground.

"It's one of them blood red moons tonight. Lunar eclipse. Early, on the moon's rise, sometime before seven. I want to see it. Says here it is a 'super red moon,' closest the moon will come to the earth for two more years, will look almost twenty-five percent larger on the horizon. And very red!"

"A blood red moon?" Aaron mumbled. "A blood red moon?" he repeated and left his sister at the kitchen table.

Later, as he crossed the fields, fractured memories flooded back to him—Pastor Ellsbridge's dire predictions posed by a blood red moon, the need to repent a grievous sin, his planned prank at Gist Castle, and the prizes that would be his, the end of his loneliness, and the tongue-kiss and feel from Brenda O'Malley, the prettiest, most developed, girl in the class.

Where was Brenda O'Malley these days? A farmer's wife? A fat grandma?

As before, screeches of barn owls were heard or remembered as he stomped on loose strands of barbed wire trampled by trespassers, and he set off across long-abandoned fields. The night was crisp, the fields gray in the meager light from a cloud-shrouded moon. His locator sounded, he touched it, but he had no recollection of its purpose. It was all dreamlike, familiar but unfocused, a movie, where present and past rushed at him simultaneously, and he couldn't discern which was which.

His prank had to be something that caused the old biddy to complain noisily in the village, but that wouldn't be traced to him. Only he and Bainsy and Tingle would know. Best would be something he could take and secretly return.

Her Chevy Nova was a perfect target. The whole town knew her car. Prying off its hubcaps wouldn't take long; he'd hide them in the drainage ditch along Slocum Road until he could show them off to Bainsy and Tingle. A day or so later, after the old lady raised her voice in the village as to the hooligans and do-nothing sheriff, he'd sneak back and leave them by the car. Somebody would find them and the whole town would be satisfied that it wouldn't even be stealing, just a prank nobody cared about.

The battered storm fencing that encircled the bungalow had fallen in several places, allowing him easy access to the house. As he came closer, he saw himself pressed against the peeling clapboards of the ell off the kitchen, next to a window, without curtain or shade, that showed an interior light. Inside, a wingback chair and a television with its volume on high, faced a chair at an angle to the window. *Just as before?* He remembered thinking that Lucretia Gist had fallen asleep. *Phew!* He had crouched low for a run to the Nova when Grandma's shriek froze him in place. "Stupid! She's dying! Save her! You can't leave her like you did me!"

Grandma had followed him from the farmhouse? In the chill of a damp wind, tree limbs above him creaked; in the distance came the cries of the feral cats. He looked up. Above the barn, the moon was huge and blood red, just as Pastor Ellsbridge predicted, a reflection of the fires of Hell, portending God's punishment for the evil men do.

Then, he recalled his saving idea. He would ring the front doorbell, hide in the bushes that faced the porch, watch, and wait. If she came to the door, that would mean she was only asleep, not dead, and he'd sneak off, unseen; if she didn't, he'd run home, tell his parents what he saw through the window, take the strapping he would get from his father. But if she was in a fit like Grandma, and Old Lady Gist survived because of his action, he'd be a hero. God would know he saved her, forgive him for his inability to help Grandma. *Pretty smart, pretty brave,* he thought, and nervously he challenged his grandmother's rants that still coursed through his brain. *What do you think of that, Grandma!*

She was silenced by his brilliance and bravery.

Aaron furtively gained the porch only to trip, in his awkwardness, and fall against the front door; it shuddered at his impact and squeaked open. He barely managed to keep upright as he stumbled into blackness inside.

Grandma returned, filling his mind with her rants—he felt the poke of her cane, or had he banged into a piece of furniture? There was nothing for it but to shout, "Hello! Miss Gist? Miss Gist, your front door was open. Miss Gist?"

No response.

The wind followed him inside. The house groaned with every gust. He heard several floorboard creaks. From upstairs? The staircase to the second floor faced him. Maybe she was up there now, would come down and see him! He froze and listened but other than the *tick-tock* of a clock somewhere in the room, he heard only faint music coming from the television. A crack of light sliced the darkness from a doorway to an adjoining room.

He went toward it and saw it led through a kitchen and into the ell where he heard and recognized music from *The Lawrence Welk Show*, a program his parents faithfully watched. He shouted over the music, "Miss Gist? Are you okay?"

No response.

Reluctantly, his heart beating its rhythm in his heaving chest, he took three forward steps around the wingback chair. In seeming response, Lucretia Gist slowly raised her head from her chest, craned it into a strange angle as though it was twisted off kilter, and showed him a withered face, a boney nose, a hanging jaw baring yellowish teeth, whiskers sprouting on a narrow chin. Was there something red and purple at her hair line? Was it blood?

Her fingers buried in the folds of her skirt groped at something, short tubes of some sort, that protruded between her knees. As her rheumy eyes blinked and focused on him, Aaron's hands in surprise and revulsion went to his face, jostling a pry bar from his belt, sending it rattling to the floor. He stooped to retrieve it, his face inches from the old lady's lap. When he looked up, Lucretia Gist's cruel face had been replaced by the specter of Grandma Underwood. Wide-eyed, his throat tight, Aaron screeched, "Grandma!"

The muzzle flash of her shot blinded him momentarily, flung him backwards to the floor. He lay in a state of pain and near oblivion, blood on his face from the mangled fingers of his right hand, the smell of a fired gun in his nostrils. Slowly, painfully, he managed to get to his knees, saw Grandma's face twisted in hatred, and gun barrels, one exhausting wisps of smoke, pointed at his face. Grandma was trying to kill him!

He had no voice to stop her. He swung the pry bar at the gun barrels with all the weight he could muster, falling forward with the swing, missing the gun barrels, and striking Grandma's forehead as a second blast erupted from her lap. His swing must have struck her head but seemed to go right through her.

Grandma's cackle rang in his ears. "Aaron, you clumsy! You murdered both of us. You forgot us but we are still here. Together, every night and every day, we'll come for you again. Murderer!"

|||||||||||||||||||||||||||||||||||||||||||||||||||||||||||||

Suddenly, his mind cleared. Aaron stepped back. Grandma was on the floor at his feet. But where was the pry bar? Feeling sponginess in the rotted floor, he tripped and fell forward, smacking his scarred face into something hard. He staggered to his feet and uncorked the bottle of naphtha he had brought from the barn, smelling its acrid odor as he sprayed the room. He got some on his jacket and trousers and shoes as it wet the walls and floor. He had brought matches and struck one.

In its flame, he foresaw Gist Castle consumed by the fires of hell. He would be free.

As flames spread on the floor and up plaster walls, his first step toward the door cracked through rotted floorboards. He sank knee high. He struggled to pull his leg out, heard his jeans tear as it caught on the splintered edges, his boot snagging on something within the hole. Despite frantic efforts, his foot wouldn't come loose, as though someone clutched it tightly from inside the floor boards. Had to be Grandma. Orange and blue flames snapped at him, smoke filled his lungs, the walls blazed around him.

"Grandma!" he wailed. "Grandma!"

CHAPTER EIGHTY-FOUR

LIVIA AND JAKE HAD A LONG delayed talk in their office on the day after Labor Day when she opened the restaurant's addition. Their relationship had continued to struggle during the summer, and this time, the distances originated more with Livia.

She held his gaze as they sat in their office chairs after the ribbon-cutting and staff party.

"Jake," she said with a long sigh, reaching over to his chair and taking his hand in hers, "we ought to end it while we are still good friends. Partners. It's never going to get better than it was, so let's stop and have great memories. When you need me or I need you, we can always rendezvous. You've got the parole board to run, your migraines are less frequent, you're on an even keel. It's a good time to make our break."

Jake recognized they had been circling one another emotionally for weeks. He owed her, honored her, was her partner, but that wasn't enough to make them the lovers they once were. He noticed her ex-husband at the restaurant and that raised its own questions for him. He rationalized that they could be adults as to where they found themselves, grateful for what they had, and fortunate to have found each other when they did. It would be another emotional zig-zag for Jake, from Pawtucket to Iraq, from Iraq to Hope, through doping and rehab, to Livia and through to the end of what had been, for so long, a hopeless search. Mia was a growing distraction as they spent hours together at the parole board sessions. He no longer thought of himself as a guilty, unfaithful lover.

Jake hugged Livia tightly and left the office. He got into the Camaro, drove to Pawtucket, changed his clothes, and forty-five minutes later was basking in sunshine on the bench by the Brown University boathouse where he had stopped months earlier to consider that night's confrontation with Ricky Squillante. He was winded, soaked with perspiration, having failed to keep up with his exercise routine with his added hours at the parole board.

The staties were taking their time in their investigation of Prebys, Kramer and the parole counselor, and that slowed up the parole process. Once again, the board needed three members out of four to vote for a felon's parole, the sessions were longer and McNally was negative but often outvoted.

He reflected on a recent call from Garo Hagopian who had picked up a rumor from a Providence police buddy that flagged Ricky Squillante for the garrote murder of Aldo Baldolucca. A Mob snitch fingered Squillante as a wannabe who fucked up bad, and that got the staties looking through their evidence bag of junk and debris from Victor's parking lot and nearby street. A latex glove was found, and a DNA check matched that of Squillante. Where was Squillante? Got sent on a permanent vacation months ago, according to the snitch. Baldolucca's case quickly became very cold.

Jake was attentive for other reasons. It was almost six months since Baldolucca's death and the shootout at Rhode Island Scrap, and no staties at his door? *Will it last?* He shrugged; he had made his bed of silence and he would live through.

He heard the calls of a coxswains as Brown University crews of eight skimmed the surface of the Seekonk like waterbugs. He felt a sense of renewed purpose, his migraines had been fewer and less debilitating, and Livia and he had reached an understanding. For now, Mia was there for him.

Jake hadn't quite realized it yet, but he had moved on. Again.

ACKNOWLEDGMENTS

THANKS TO CHRIS LANDI, my IT guy extraordinaire and to Donna Beals, once again so helpful with the text. Editor Dana Isaacson was in top form and trimmed what had to be trimmed, and to Joe Coccaro at Koehler for his assistance and patience. And to all who let me ask questions about parole and incarceration and PTSD as well and to my draft readers Jack Manning, Norah Christianson, and the late Jim Taricani, for their helpful suggestions as to characters, plot, and text. I particularly want to thank the thoughtful administrators, particularly, Warden Sergio Desousarosa and his staff of the Rhode Island Department of Corrections who were always courteous and helpful to me in my research and visits.

The selection of poems of Robert Frost come from *The Poetry of Robert Frost* edited by Edward Connery Lathem.

CPSIA information can be obtained
at www.ICGtesting.com
Printed in the USA
LVHW091952070321
680820LV00004B/130

9 781646 632511